NOT MY OWN

NOT MY OWN

Written By
Yovette B Brooks

authorHOUSE®

AuthorHouse™
1663 Liberty Drive
Bloomington, IN 47403
www.authorhouse.com
Phone: 1-800-839-8640

Published by AuthorHouse   03/20/2012

ISBN: 978-1-4685-7181-3 (sc)
ISBN: 978-1-4685-7180-6 (hc)
ISBN: 978-1-4685-7179-0 (e)

Library of Congress Control Number: 2012905273

Any people depicted in stock imagery provided by Thinkstock are models, and such images are being used for illustrative purposes only.
Certain stock imagery © Thinkstock.

This book is printed on acid-free paper.

Because of the dynamic nature of the Internet, any web addresses or links contained in this book may have changed since publication and may no longer be valid. The views expressed in this work are solely those of the author and do not necessarily reflect the views of the publisher, and the publisher hereby disclaims any responsibility for them.

CONTENTS

In seeking out the meaning of our lives, we must seek out the Savior of our lives, but in doing so we must understand even the Savior's life was *Not His Own,* but that of His Father's.

Anyone who does not love me will not obey my teaching. These words you hear are *Not My Own;* they belong to the Father who sent me. John 14:24

PROLOGUE

IT HAD BEEN one crazy year. She sat thinking in front of her computer. She had been out in the field before, but this time had been different. She was getting older now and really couldn't play the part of a child anymore. She had been put into a military group. It was definitely more challenging; she didn't particularly care for having to watch out for others, she was more the loner type. But still nothing was more rewarding than seeing justice served. Now that she was back in her little white room doing Intel gathering she was quite bored. She saw the small icon in the corner of her screen change color, which meant he was on his computer and needed to talk to her. It was going to be good to talk to her friend, Cloak. Well, she didn't know if 'friend' was the right word, but he was the closest thing to a friend she had ever had. She opened a small black box on the right lower part of the screen so the camera over her left shoulder couldn't see it.

"Where have you been?" He asked. "I have needed help."

"South America. I will never understand why people think they have the right to sell and trade other humans. So, what can I help you with?"

"I have been listening to chatter coming out of the Netherlands, and if I am deciphering it correctly, they need to take some immediate action. But if I am wrong . . ."

"You always do a great job; have some confidence in yourself. It is like I always tell you: think about what you would do yourself if you were in charge."

"Thanks, but you seem to forget I have never been out in the field like you. I just gather and report the Intel; I don't really act on it."

"I know that, but what do you think that last paragraph is for? It clearly says to write in your opinion what actions need to be taken."

"But what if I am wrong and someone gets hurt?"

"They are going to do what they think is right, no matter what you write. They just want to know how we think and if we are ready for the field."

"I don't think I will ever be ready."

"Listen to me, Cloak. You are good; you can decipher all this information as well as I can, maybe even better. You just need to think a little out of the box. Think about the goal, the task at hand. What is the best way to get it accomplished with the least amount of conflict?"

"I would still feel better if you would look it over before I sent it in."

"Send me your file; I'll take a look and let you know what I think."

"Thanks, Dagger; you're the best!"

"Not yet, but I will be."

CHAPTER 1
Rest and Recovery

"**Y**OU HAVE A year for rest and recovery. You will, however, be under constant monitoring, do you understand?" he asked her as they walked up the dimly lit hallway.

"Yes." Her life was always under constant supervision. The two stopped at a doorway.

"This is The Keeper. He will see to it that you have everything you need," with that, the man in the dark suit turned, and left her standing in the doorway.

"Come on in. Call me Keeps, it sounds better than 'The Keeper,'" the young man said. The girl walked in and sat down in a chair beside the man at the desk. He didn't look any older than her. Well, not that she even knew how old she was, but she didn't think he looked older than her.

"So, let's see," the guy said as he typed, "what is your number?" She looked up, "23."

He looked at her with surprise, "Oh, I didn't realize you were … I thought you were a guy, and you would be a lot older, not … well, not …. I just thought you would be older," he smiled at her.

Keeper had received the file on The Maker, or 23 for everyone else, just last week. The file hadn't said The Maker was a woman, and for good reason; she was the best agent in the field. But it did make a lot of the missions make more sense. He smiled to himself; he was now going to officially be her Keeper. He was quite excited.

1

"So, do you know who I am, then?"

He was typing fast now.

"Yes, you're The Maker."

He typed some more. "Now then, you have a year to recover; where would you like to go?" He looked up, and stopped typing.

This was the first time they had given her time off after a mission. Usually, she just spent time in Intel until she was called again. So she really wasn't sure what she could and couldn't do. But she really needed to unwind; this mission had taken up the last four years of her life.

"Limits?" she asked.

"Basically, the same as any mission, but you just don't have an objective. I suggest you find something to do; if you don't, you will get bored after a day or two. Make some friends, get a job, do the normal life thing for a while."

"I would like some time to unwind from the last four years."

"Ok. Do want city, country, desert, jungle . . . . what?"

She smiled.

"I want wilderness; somewhere that I don't have to deal with too many people, though."

He thought for a moment. "Wilderness . . . how about a Forest Ranger? Lots of wilderness." Keeps started typing again. "Ok, you will need a service record that will assure that you will get the job; then all the medical training. I can write that up. You'll need a birth certificate, ID's, drivers license, bank account. All the normal stuff, too." She smiled, as he said, "Now, we just need a name."

She was going to like this Keeps guy. Most of the people, the whole three or four she actually knew, were all business.

"So who do I look like?" she asked.

"Hmm," he looked at her, "Maybe a Lindsey."

She repeated it. "Lindsey . . . I think I could get used to that."

He smiled. "Lindsey it is. How about Lindsey Lorain Jacobs? It has a nice ring that says I can do anything I want and be successful at it."

She laughed, "If you say so!"

"Be back here in the morning, and I will have everything you need."

He stood up as she did.

"Nice to meet you, Keeps," she told him.

"You, too, . . . Lindsey. Now, go down the hall to the last door on the left; it will take you back to the main office."

'Lindsey', she liked the name. After having been in the Middle East for the last four years, a normal name was good, but the clothes were even better. She had been given a pair of jeans and a black T-shirt; man, they were comfortable. Not having to be covered from head to toe was great. Lindsey followed the hall to the last door. When she opened it, the man who escorted her down when she first came in was there.

"I was just coming to get you. I will show you to your room for the night." Lindsey followed the man. "I took the liberty of getting you a few personal items to hold you till you leave, I hope that was ok. Here you are," he said as they came to room 256.

"That's fine, thanks."

"I will see you at 0600; have a good night."

She turned and opened the door. It was a nice room. There were two outfits lying on the bed. She walked over to examine them: shorts, a tank top, jeans, a blue button-down shirt, two pairs of underwear, and a couple sports bras. Toothbrush and toothpaste, shampoo, hair bands, and a brush, were also lying there. He hadn't done too badly.

A hot shower would feel great. She let the water pour over her; let it wash away the last four years of her life. Let it all slide down the drain, she didn't want to remember all the suffering she had seen, all the death that man had caused to those people. She was glad he was dead, even gladder still to be the one that got to end the suffering. She was happy to see the man's blood on her hands, to feel him take his last breath. *Let it go,* she told herself, *job well done; now it's time to rest before you're called again.*

She pulled the towel around her and stepped back into the bedroom. Music, she would love to hear some good music. All those wailing prayers that went on all the time about drove her crazy. She looked around; no radio or anything. She slid on the shorts and tank top, and went out the door. No one seemed to be around, so she headed back to the Keeper; she remembered where to find him. She hoped he was still there. He was typing away at his computer, when she got to his office door.

"I need music," she told him as she entered his office.

He looked up from his desk, "You're not supposed to be out roaming around!"

She strolled over and sat down. "I need to find a radio, CD player, iPod, anything that will play music."

He pulled open a drawer, "Here, you can use this, but I want it back tomorrow." He handed her an iPod.

"So what's on it, anything good?" What she really wanted was Beethoven or Bach.

"There are all kinds on there. I like a wide variety; that way I always have something for whatever mood I am in. Now you better get back before they find you are out of your room."

She got up and gave him her best smile, "Thanks."

She put the ear buds in as she walked, and scrolled through the music titles. Man, he did like everything; he had rap, punk, disco, blues, metal, Contemporary Christian and, oh yeah, classical. She hit the playlist marked classical as soon as she got back to her room, and lay down on her bed for the night.

She loved playing the piano. She had been trained in all kinds of music so she could play most instruments and read music well. But, there was something about playing classical piano ballads that she really loved. She drifted off to sleep listening to Bach.

Keeps was quite surprised when Lindsey had shown up back at his office door asking for music. It wasn't good for her to be out of her room. The King had been so careful to keep the Maker's identity well concealed. There had only been two people who actually knew who she was. Most people like him, thought the Maker was an older guy, even after reading the file on her, he still thought she was older. Every record and note in the file was gender free. Now that he would be the one making the notes, he would have to keep it that way for her protection. The Handler and himself had brought the total that knew her up to four, and he was going to make sure it remained that way.

Up until last week he took care of several agents, but when King had handed him her file, he had told him, "This is now your main objective, keep it safe and well protected." Giving her a number like all the other agents had also helped keep her safe. He still had a few other assignments, but she was now his main concern. Keeps turned on the camera in her room to check on her. She was sound asleep with his iPod lying beside her. As Keeps watched her sleep, he was sure he remembered her when she was younger, when they both were younger.

Lindsey woke long before six. She did a few crunches, pushups, jumping jacks, lunges, just anything she could do in the confines of her room. She then showered, and got dressed in blue jeans and a tank top. She opened the door just before he knocked.

"Morning," she told him.

"I will be taking you back to Keeps, then seeing you off today," he said as they walked.

"So what do I call you?" she asked.

"I am your handler, so Handler will be fine." He talked all *so* formal. They walked back down the long corridor. He was only the fourth person she had seen since she got back. She was debriefed by two men, then given clothes and taken to Keeps. The other two were actually the two that drove her here from the airport. She had Keeps' iPod in her pocket. He was waiting for them when they arrived at his office.

"Well, I think I have you all lined up," he handed her an envelope. "In there is all you'll need. You were born in Florida to an older couple who have since passed on. They were quite wealthy, though, so you won't have any issues with money—like you would, anyway," he smiled. "Just don't go stupid, and you'll be fine."

"You mean I can't buy a yacht?" she laughed.

He smiled. "There are two tickets in there; one will get you to Chicago, and the other will take you all the way to Washington. When you arrive, a Ranger Clearwater will be waiting for you." She nodded. "He will take you to Mt. Rainer and your new home. I included your full history in there so you can read it on the way, and then burn it. Your birth certificate and a few other things are in there that you'll want to put away for safe keeping. Well, you're smart enough to know what to do with all of it. Just a warning, this is your first off grid R&R; don't screw it up. I will be monitoring you constantly. Oh, yeah, and have some fun," he added.

She pulled out his iPod, "Thanks."

He dropped it back in the drawer. "You will also need these." He pulled out a phone and a brand new iPod out of the same drawer. "I didn't load any music, you can do that," he motioned her toward his computer.

She opened it, and sat down. She had it full in minutes.

"I'm impressed," he said as she unplugged it. "You like diversity."

"No more than you." They both laughed.

"Make sure you keep your phone on you at all times in case you're needed or you need anything. Just text me if you do; I am saved as 'Home'. Have a good vacation; see you next round," he smiled and shook her hand.

"Till next time, Keeps," she said as she followed Handler out of the office.

Handler escorted her to a black Hummer in a parking garage. They then drove out into the city. In front of Eastland Mall was where he stopped. "I will leave you here, I am sure you don't want to show up with nothing but what I got you. Your bus doesn't leave till two p.m.; make sure you keep your phone with you at all times."

She opened the door and got out. He reached over the seat and pulled up her backpack. "I will call you when you're needed. I am going to only warn you once: don't do anything stupid and remember you are only here for a while."

She nodded, then closed the door, and he drove off. She opened the manila envelope, pulled out her bank card, and entered the mall.

She picked up some tank tops and a few pairs of jeans at Old Navy. She didn't want to buy too much that would just be more stuff to carry. She could shop more when she got to the park. By two, she was settled in a bus seat with her iPod on. When she arrived in Chicago she had a four hour wait before her flight. She put in her ear buds and waited in the airport. She watched as people came and went. The people here had no idea what kind of battle really raged just out of their sight.

CHAPTER 2

Ranger

WHEN HER FLIGHT landed in Spokane, it was late. She saw the Ranger as soon as she came out into the terminal; his uniform really stood out. "You Clearwater?" she asked as she approached him.

"Yes. You Jacobs?"

"Yes, sir, that's me." They shook hands.

"Let's get your bags, and get out of here."

"This is all I have," she told him as she swung her backpack up on her back. "I didn't bring a lot; didn't know what I would or wouldn't need, so I left everything else in storage."

He smiled. He was very dark-skinned; he must be Indian from the local reservation. He looked to be in his mid 20's. His hair was just below his collar.

"I hope you don't mind, but we are going to stay with my folks tonight on the reservation before heading to the park tomorrow," he said as he led her to a green Ranger's truck.

"I don't want to be a problem; I can just get a room at a hotel."

"No problem at all, they love company."

Lindsey looked over at him as he sped up the highway. "Are you sure?"

He gave her a big grin. "I don't get up to see them as much as I should, so I am sort of using you as an excuse."

"Well, in that case, we better go then," she smiled back.

8

"We're here," he announced, bringing her out of her slumber. The ride wasn't but an hour, but she had jetlag, and fell asleep not long after they left the airport.

"Sorry I fell asleep, it has been a long day."

"That's ok, I didn't mind a bit," he grabbed their bags out of the back of the truck. "By the way, I'm Jacob."

She laughed. They hadn't really introduced themselves. "Lindsey."

He led her up the walk and into the house. A couple got off the couch as they entered. "Jacob," they both greeted him with a hug.

"Mom, Dad, this is Lindsey Jacobs, the new Ranger."

"Glad to meet you," they both gave her a hug. A young guy emerged from the hallway.

"Jacob!"

"Hey, bro!"

The two were on the floor wrestling in seconds.

"Come on you two, we have company and you are acting like five year olds," Jacobs's mom said. Jacob already had his brother in a headlock.

"Alright," Jacob released his brother and got up, "Lindsey, this is Brandon." Brandon was tall; Lindsey only came up to his armpit. His long hair hit the middle of his back.

"Nice to meet you, Lindsey." He gave her a bear hug.

Jacob punched his brother. "Brandon!"

Brandon had a big smile. "Any friend of yours is a friend of mine."

Lindsey smiled.

"Yeah, I know, especially if they're pretty," Jacob said and everybody laughed.

"You can call me Mary," said Jacob's mom. "Now, you have to make yourself at home here, ok? If you need anything, ask or just look for it."

Lindsey smiled at her, "I would really just like to shower and go to bed; it has been a long day."

"Of course." She turned to Brandon, "take her stuff to your room." Then she turned back to Lindsey, "The bathroom is down the hall on the left, the door just past Brandon's room. You will be sleeping in his room tonight." She walked Lindsey to the hall. "Make yourself at home, sweetie."

"Thanks for your hospitality," Lindsey told her.

"Think nothing of it!"

Lindsey walked down the short hall; Brandon was getting clothes out of his closet when Lindsey stepped into the room behind him.

"Sorry about kicking you out of your room."

He turned to her. "No biggie."

She looked around the room, it was small. A chest, bed and a guitar was all that were in it, but nothing else would have fit.

"You play?" she asked.

"Yeah, me, and a few guys have a band." He pulled a shirt and jeans from some hangers, and started out of the room.

"You any good?" She asked.

"Yes." He looked at her.

"Can I come listen to you play sometime?"

He stopped at the door and looked back at her. "Sure."

Lindsey looked through her clothes and picked out a pair of shorts and tank to sleep in, and headed for a shower.

Laughter was coming from the living room as she went into the bathroom. It was tiny; from what she had seen of the house, it was all small. It seemed nice, just small. From what she knew about most reservations, they were poor, so she figured this one was no different. The laughter was still going on when she came out and headed to Brandon's room. She closed the door and crawled up on the bed. Someone knocked on the door.

"It's open."

The door opened and Brandon stuck his head in.

"Mom sent me to see if there was anything you might need."

Lindsey smiled, "I'm good, thanks. But do you happen to know what time Jacob and I are leaving in the morning?"

Brandon came in and sat down on the edge of the bed.

"Well, I figure it will be nine or so. Jacob will want to go see Michelle while he is here."

"Is Michelle his girlfriend?"

Brandon nodded his head, "Yeah, I guess."

"Sounds like you don't like her," Lindsey said.

"She's ok; I just think he could do better."

"So what about you, you got a girl?"

Brandon laughed. "I was seeing a girl right before we graduated, but she went off to college and found someone else."

Lindsey smiled. "What could be better than a guy with copper skin, long hair, and dark eyes?"

"Thanks."

She smiled, got in the covers and snuggled down.

He got up and went to the door. "Goodnight, Lindsey," he said as he shut the door.

Lindsey closed her eyes. She almost laughed when she saw him in her thoughts. It was going to be hard not to dream about him; his scent was all around her.

Brandon closed his bedroom door behind him. Lindsey seemed really nice, not to mention she was gorgeous. He was now glad that he had chosen to go back to the Park this year.

The sun was up when Lindsey awoke. It was seven a.m., the latest she had slept in a long time. She stretched and climbed out of the bed. The house was quiet when she opened the door. She tiptoed into the bathroom, then back to her room. The smell of coffee was coming from the kitchen, so she got dressed, made the bed, and headed for the kitchen. Brandon was sitting on the couch in the living room as she passed through.

"Morning," he said.

"Morning. Is everybody still asleep?"

He laughed. "Everybody's already gone," he got up and followed her into the kitchen. "So what would you like for breakfast?" he asked her.

"I'm fine, don't worry about me."

He smiled. "Mom told me I couldn't fix myself anything until you were up, that way you could have some breakfast, too." He stood behind her as she got a cup of coffee.

"How about you fix whatever you want, and I will help you eat it," she said as she added some milk to her coffee.

"I love BLT's for breakfast; that ok with you?"

"Sounds great, can I do anything to help?" she asked before she sat down at the table.

He turned to look at her. "No, I've got it." He opened the fridge and got out a package of bacon. "I don't know if Jacob told you or not, but I will be going back with you guys today. I have spent the last three summers helping out as a Ranger. This year, since I am not in school, I can help out during tourist season. Jacob says it is always so wild."

"No, he hadn't told me that, but really we hadn't talked much. I think I slept all the way here from the airport."

He laughed. "Yeah, Jacob said you were out cold. Do you mind if I ask how old you are?"

"No; I'll be twenty-three next July. What about you?"

He flipped the bacon in the skillet. "I'll be twenty in January."

"So, I guess you graduated this year?"

"Yes," he answered.

"No college plans?"

He set a few pieces of bacon out on a plate and added a few more pieces to the skillet. "I didn't really like school; can't imagine going to college. Well, not yet, anyway."

She laughed. "Yeah, I hear you, I hated school. Not that I did badly at it, but I just hated it."

He turned and smiled at her. "So what made you become a Ranger?"

"It's the perfect job. You get to camp out, play in the woods; most of the time you're by yourself, so you're your own boss. See? The perfect job."

He laughed. "That's true unless you're a people person, then you'd be so lonesome you'd go insane. I hope you're not wanting alone time now, tourist season is starting so you won't hardly ever be alone." He pulled the rest of the bacon from the skillet and had two sandwiches made in no time. "Here you go," he handed her the plate with a smile.

"Wow, what service!" They both laughed and ate.

"Jacob said he would be home around ten so we've got a few hours to kill before he gets back. "He took their plates and put them in the sink. "Which is good, because I need to get my clothes packed; I haven't even started. Mom was washing them last night." He headed towards his room and left her sitting at the table. She watched Brandon go into his room, then go into another room and come back with an armful of clothes.

"Can I help?" She now stood in his doorway.

"Sure, come in and join the pile," he patted the bed beside him and the laundry pile. Lindsey stepped over Brandon's legs and sat on the other side of the laundry.

"Does everything go?" She asked.

"Most of it." He was stuffing clothes into the bag left and right.

"Ok, stop right there. You're not going to get half of that in if you don't at least fold it." She stood up and dumped it back on the bed. He just looked at her.

"You really don't fold clothes, you roll them." She took a shirt, folded it long ways in half, then rolled it up and put it into the bag. "They only take up a little space like that, so you can get twice as much in." He was still eyeing her. She was rolling a pair of jeans when she caught his look. "Sorry," she dropped the jeans back on the bed.

He laughed. "You must travel a lot to be that picky."

"No, well, I have done my share and I want to get as much in one suitcase as I can; I don't want to have to lug around two or three."

"I guess that makes sense; you came in with only one bag last night." He took a shirt and rolled it up. "How's that?"

She smiled and picked the jeans back up and finished rolling them.

"Great!" She gave him a smile and picked up another shirt to roll.

"That really does work well," he said, as he laid the bag by hers on the floor next to the door. He had gotten everything he needed in the one bag.

Lindsey walked up the hall looking at all the pictures hanging on the wall. There were several pictures of them in full Indian outfits. The one that caught her attention was one of Brandon; he was dressed only in only bottoms. There were painted handprints and other symbols on his chest. He was younger, maybe 12 or 13. His hair had a single feather in it, but was hanging free around his face. There was a similar one of Jacob.

"Hey, Brandon, what's going on in these pictures?"

He came out of his room and looked. "Well, it's sort of like a coming of age ceremony." He looked over the pictures. "See this one? This is Jacob on his first hunting trip, and this one's mine." He had pointed out several pictures.

"So who is this?" She pointed at a picture of a young girl.

"That was my sister."

"Was?" Lindsey questioned.

"She died several years back. She got herself pregnant, then ended up dying with complications at childbirth."

"I'm sorry," she touched his arm.

Brandon looked down at her, Lindsey was touching him. She had an *Oh, I am so sorry* look on her face.

"It's ok, but just don't mention it around mom. She still falls apart when you mention it." Her hand was still on his arm.

Lindsey felt sorry for this loss, to have brothers and sisters would be great, but to lose one would be horrible. She found that she was sort of grateful not to have family. Well, she didn't think she did. She couldn't remember any, anyway.

"She was pretty."

"Pretty stupid," he said. She looked up at him in surprise. "I loved Beth, don't get me wrong; you couldn't ask for a better sister, but she was stupid."

Lindsey could see the anger in his eyes, but yet they were laced with pain, too. He didn't hide his feelings; they were plainly written on his face.

"Mom tried hard to raise us right, but Beth was . . . well, she was determined to fight mom at every turn. She basically became the resident whore. It was bad." Brandon dropped his head and shook it.

Lindsey slid her arm around his waist, she couldn't reach his shoulders. He looked like he needed comfort. She had definitely hit on a sensitive issue.

"We weren't surprised when she got pregnant. Mom was hoping it would change her. Maybe she would settle down after she had the baby." He took a deep breath; a shudder went through his whole body.

Lindsey put her other arm around him and slid in to hug him tightly. His eyes were glassed over, and she thought he was going to completely break down and cry.

"Anyway, something went wrong, and we lost her and Seth both."

Brandon hadn't realized how bad it still hurt to think about her. He looked down to find Lindsey wrapped around his waist.

"I'm sorry, Brandon."

He leaned over and set his chin on her head. She smelled wonderful, and felt good in his arms.

"Thanks, I didn't mean to lose it. I just hadn't thought of it in so long; I guess I am not over it, either." He laughed. "I guess I am like mom."

"Yep, sensitive and loving." Lindsey gave him a little squeeze, then stepped out of his arms and looked up at him and smiled.

He smiled. "So what about your family?"

"What about it?" Lindsey turned and walked up the hallway. He raised an eyebrow. "Not a good family life?" She walked into the living room and sat down. He followed.

"Well, to begin with," she raised her voice to an aggravated tone, "I was an only child. Why they ever had a kid I will never know. They were old when I was born, so they never took care of me; I always had a Nanny." Lindsey had read Keepers report several times, and had it well memorized. "I spent most of the time in boarding schools. Dad wanted to make sure I knew what discipline was, so I was in ROTC every year. So, I was basically raised in the military, with summers in the Orient learning martial arts. I think he must have wanted a boy. I don't know. Anyway, I bet there isn't a martial art I don't know, not to mention the language lessons, music lessons, dance lessons—you name it, I think I probably had a class in it."

He was looking at her. "No wonder you hated school."

Lindsey took a deep breath. "I did more than just hate it, I hated it with a passion. I had classes of some kind year round till I was 19. My parents died in a plane crash that summer, and I finally got to quit."

"So what have you been doing since then?" He asked her.

"Well, I spent the first six months at home. I never had stayed there for more than two weeks before, and so it was nice for a while. I learned all kinds of things about my parents I never knew, just from looking through their stuff. Then, I did a little of this and a little of that, not really knowing what to do with myself."

"So what made you become a Ranger?" He asked.

She laughed, and gave a big sigh. "I know this is going to sound crazy, but for a while, I just drove around the U.S. But one day, as I passed through Illinois, I went by a Park, and I stopped. I camped three days and that did it. I was hooked. Just to sit out in the wilderness with no one telling you what to do is heavenly." They both laughed.

"So how long have you been a Ranger?"

"This will be my first post," she told him.

"You guys ready to go?" Jacob came though the kitchen into the living room.

"Ready and waiting," Brandon told him.

"Well, let's get moving; we need to be checked in and ready by two p.m. I have a Jr. Ranger class at 2:30." Brandon went to his room and grabbed their bags and headed for the truck.

"That's all you're taking?" Jacob asked. Lindsey and Brandon looked at each other and laughed.

"Lindsey helped me pack; I think my whole closet is in here."

Jacob looked at the two of them. "Sure, ok."

Brandon opened the truck door and Lindsey slid to the middle. Jacob and Brandon got in, and off they went. Lindsey sat and listened to Brandon and Jacob as they pointed out all kinds of things as they went. They told about the sites as they passed them on the reservation, then the ones in the park as they drove on.

Lindsey noticed how much the two brothers looked alike. Brandon's hair was quite a bit longer than his brother's, and he was about six inches taller than Jacob. He also was a little broader across the shoulders. But Jacob seemed to be a little more muscular. Jacob had on a T-shirt and jeans today, and you could see his muscles through the shirt. He most likely wore it to impress Michelle. Brandon had on a tank top and cut off shorts, but he was impressive all on his own. His muscles weren't quite as pronounced as his brother's, but he had plenty of them. They were both good looking guys.

"What?" Brandon asked her.

She blinked and found that she was staring right at him.

"What is the big smile for?"

She hadn't realized she was smiling so big.

"I was just thinking I had to be the luckiest girl in the world to be riding between the two best looking guys around." They both laughed.

Had she actually been thinking that? Brandon thought to himself. The small red tint to her face said she had been. Brandon liked the idea that she thought he was good looking.

They drove through the main gate and around the Paradise Inn down to a small area with several rows of tiny little cabins. Lindsey thought they looked more like storage buildings.

"Your cabin is the third one; the door is unlocked, and the keys should be on the table," Jacob told her.

"Thanks, Jacob," she said as she got out of the truck. He smiled and got two bags out of the back.

"Mom sent you a few things since you're new. She figured you wouldn't know all the things you would need, so she gathered up a few things and sent them."

"How sweet of her! Make sure you tell her I said thanks," Lindsey said as she reached over the side of the truck to get her bag. Brandon grabbed it before she had a chance to get it.

"I can get my own stuff, thanks." Lindsey put her hands on her hips. "We are no longer at your house." He handed her the bag. Jacob also handed her the one from his Mom.

She took them and turned toward the cabins. They all had small porches on the fronts with four chairs on each, and a small grill. She opened the door; it was tiny. You stepped in, and you were at the side of the bed; to your right was a small table with two chairs.

At the back of the cabin, which wasn't 20 feet from the front door, was a small stove and fridge; and on the left was the bathroom and closet. It was smaller than any of the rooms she had ever been in, except maybe one. But she didn't want to think about that now; it wasn't a pleasant thought, so she pushed it away and started unpacking. All the clothes went into the closet, of course. She didn't have much, but that was good since what she did have took up most of the space.

The kitchen had a two burner stove, a small cabinet, a half fridge and sink. Some things were not furnished, like pots and pans, but the kitchen wouldn't hold many, anyway. This brought her thoughts to the bag Mrs. Clearwater had sent. She grabbed it from the bed where she had laid it and opened it to find one pan, a spatula, a large spoon, two plastic cups, two plates, and a couple of forks. The only thing she really needed now was some bed linens. Someone knocked on the door as she was putting the plates in the cabinet. She opened the door to find Brandon standing there.

"Hey, Jacob sent me; wants me to take you up to the Inn. You need to check in and go order your uniforms. I'll show you where it is."

He was already in his green uniform. She grinned as she looked him over.

"Just wait till you get yours. You'll look just as bad."

She laughed, "They are hideous, aren't they?"

He turned and headed toward a trail running beside the woods. "Come on, let's get yours ordered so you can be styling, too."

They both laughed as she pulled her door closed. "They will probably give you a couple of park T-shirts till your uniforms come in. That's what they did to me the first summer I came. You can just wear jeans with them." Lindsey walked along beside Brandon as he told her where the laundry was. "Oh, yeah, Jacob told me to tell you that you could use his other set of sheets if you didn't have any."

Another Ranger approached as they got close to the Inn.

"Hey, Brandon."

"Lindsey, this is John Waters; he lives in the second cabin."

"Nice to meet you, Lindsey." He stuck out his hand.

"You, too," she said as she took it.

"Let me know if you need anything. I know what it's like to be the new guy," he smiled.

"Thanks," she told him.

"I am glad you came back this year," he told Brandon. "We have three camping tours, and need all the help we can get. My nephew Todd will be here this weekend to lend a hand." He turned towards Lindsey. "It was nice to meet you. Got to get moving, got a tour to lead in ...," he looked down at his watch. "Crap, I've got less than ten minutes. See you around." He sprinted off down the trail.

"Yep, it sounds like tourist season is going to be crazy," Brandon said as they headed up to the Inn.

"How many Rangers are there?"

Brandon held the door as Lindsey went in.

"There are ninety full time employees here, but during tourist season it doubles, and then some, like Todd and me." Brandon led Lindsey down a flight of stairs to a door that read 'Rangers only'. "This is the common area for the Rangers. That room over there, that's the laundry I was telling you about. Since the cabins are not very big, we have this room for TV, games and that kind of stuff." He took her to the door that read Office across it. He opened the door for her again.

"Brandon!" A young red headed girl perked up at the sight of him.

"Hey, Wendy, this is Lindsey."

She looked at Lindsey. "Oh, the new Ranger." She smiled and pulled out a paper and handed it to Lindsey. "You will need five sets of everything on this paper; so, all I really need from you now is your size." She smiled up at Brandon. "I'm glad you came back this year, I thought you might not." Then she turned back to Lindsey, "Size?"

Lindsey smiled. "Three." Wendy took the paper and put it on the fax machine, dialed a number and turned back around.

"They will be here by Friday. Let me get you some shirts to wear till then." She went out of the room.

Lindsey looked over at Brandon. "Summer girlfriend?"

He sighed. "She wishes."

They were laughing as she came back in the room.

"Here are three T-shirts, your radio, and charger. Keep your radio on channel five. I will be here to get you anything you might need. Now you'll need to go up to the main floor and see Ranger Malcolm. He will fill you in on everything else you'll need, and give you your schedule for the week."

"Thanks," Lindsey said.

"You're welcome. See you around, Brandon." She gave him a big smile.

"See you, Wendy."

They left the office and headed up the stairs again.

"Not interested in Wendy, eh?" Lindsey asked Brandon.

"No, I am not that desperate."

"Oh, one of those," she said.

"Here we are." She reached for the handle, his hand clamped over hers and the handle. He smiled.

"I can open my own doors."

"I know," he laughed, "sorry, it's nothing personal, just in Ranger mode," he told her, and she laughed.

A chubby man stood up from behind the desk as the door opened.

"Come in, Brandon, glad you're back. Is this the new Ranger?"

"Glad to be back, sir. Yes, this is Lindsey Jacobs."

"Glad you're here. We need all the help we can get, especially in September. I see you've been down to see Wendy." He motioned to the stuff she held in her hands. "This is your map of the park; you can pick up a compass, canteen, anything like that you will need in the ready room. Or Wendy can order you new ones whichever you prefer, but you will have to buy the new ones. The others you can use as long as you want; you just have to return them when you leave the park." He handed her a paper. "This will be your schedule for the week; it is mainly checking trails and stuff till you get a grip on the park. Since it's the beginning of tourist season, I don't have any spare Rangers to show you around, so you're sort of on your own. Are you going to be ok with that?"

"I would have it no other way." She smiled at Brandon.

"You're required to carry a rifle while out on the trail; you can check them out from Wendy on a daily basis" He picked up a file, "This says you're an expert shot so I am sure you will have no troubles. Of course, we carry tranquilizer rifles, but they are basically the same. Here is a packet you need to familiarize yourself with on the darts." He handed her a large bunch of paper. "There are some other rules and regulations in there you need to go over, and some information on the Park. Sorry, I am giving you the quick go through, but the tourist season has begun. And from the looks of your file most of the stuff you know, anyway." He went over and opened the door for them to leave. "I am glad you're here; feel free to come here with any questions you may have." He shut the door behind them. Lindsey noticed the sign on the door read Ranger Malcolm. He hadn't even introduced himself. Strange little man, she thought.

"Wow," Brandon said. "That was weird."

"What was weird?" Lindsey asked

"He didn't even swear you in. Didn't give you the speech about the Rangers being an honorable duty; he didn't give you any of it. It was just weird."

Lindsey had to wonder if he had known who she was. But she didn't think so.

"It must be going to be really wild this season for him to skip all that stuff," Brandon said, as they walked back to the Inn door.

"I have to head down to the lower loop trail and check it out; let me see your schedule." She handed it to him. "You're checking out the upper loop, so go drop your stuff off and head down to the ready room. It's just off the common room. Pick up a canteen, fill it and head for your trail; it's right near the Inn. You don't need a rifle unless you're on a camping trail, so don't worry about that. I've got to get going; I have several things to do and places to be. I'll see you later."

"Thanks, Brandon." She gave him a smile. He smiled back and headed out and down the trail in a different direction. Lindsey went back to the cabin, changed and headed back to the Inn for her canteen. The radio felt bulky on her hip. Finding her trail wasn't hard; everything was well marked. The afternoon passed by quickly. The last trail she checked on was number five; it was pretty large, but she made it back at 9 p.m. All the trails closed at that time except the ones to the Inn and the camping trails. She was scheduled to be on a trail at 7 a.m. in the morning. A shower and a bed was what she wanted now. When she got to the cabin a sack was hanging on the door. In it was a set of sheets. After showering and making her bed, she went through the papers Malcolm had given her. Mostly she just skimmed through, but she carefully read the ones about the park. They were quite interesting.

Lindsey's alarm went off at 4 a.m. She dressed in a pair of shorts, a T-shirt, and sneakers. Running was one thing she liked; getting up early, feeling the coolness of the day on her skin. Simple pleasures, yes, that's what it was. Her life was not simple at all, all the missions, and all the things you had to do on those missions. Yep, running was a little simple pleasure she was going to take and after all, wasn't she on vacation? She almost laughed at the thought of working on vacation, but after what she had been through the last four years, anything was a vacation.

She ran till 4:40, then got a shower and was on the trail head at seven. Trail seven was peaceful, just what she had hoped for. She enjoyed looking around the trail as she walked, the trees, the flowers, all of nature. She loved it all, and the alone time gave her time to forget things from her last missions. She made her first rounds and was back by eight, then headed down to the Inn for breakfast.

Jacob and Brandon were sitting at a table in the corner. Brandon invited her to sit with them. "Jacob and I have a camping trip next week, taking a bunch of girl scouts," he was telling her as they ate.

Jacob took a deep breath, "Girl scouts. This ought to be fun, 15 girls and two leaders; all 12 and 13 year old girls who will think Brandon is dreamy." They all three laughed.

"I get the girls, you get the moms. That's the way it usually works," Brandon said.

Lindsey was still laughing. "Why do they send you guys? Why don't they send a couple of female Rangers?"

"It makes them feel safer," Jacob answered her question.

Brandon pulled up his arms and flexed. "They want the strong men."

"But I thought you guys were going?" Lindsey gave Brandon a questioning look. Jacob laughed and Brandon punched her lightly on the arm.

"I've got a tour to lead; I'll see you guys later," Jacob told them, as he got up and left.

"Where're you at today?" Brandon asked.

"Down on seven, how about you?"

"I have campground duty today, not the most fun, but it's always interesting." Brandon told her. "Last year I had an older couple that had just taken a whim to go camping, but didn't have a clue what they were doing," he laughed. "I spent half the day at their site, helping them with one thing or another."

He looked down at his watch, "So when do you have lunch?"

She smiled. "I have 1-2 today, and 12-1 on Wednesday."

"Well, lunch is out," he told her, "our times are different, but maybe I can catch you at dinner sometime." He got up and started to leave. "See you around." He turned to leave.

"Wait," she got up, "I'll walk with you." Trail seven started at the lower parking lot, just past the campground. "If that's ok?"

"Sure."

Lindsey left Brandon at the campground and headed down to trail seven. She liked Brandon; he was nice and always was looking for the humor in life. Her life needed humor; if anything, her life was always serious—life and death. Take a life or have yours taken. Humor, yep, she needed it, and Brandon was always full of it. Lindsey headed down the trail with her thoughts.

Brandon watched as Lindsey walked down the trail. He smiled to himself. This fall was going to be great.

Lindsey hadn't been on the trail twenty minutes when she came up on a little girl crying and all alone. She couldn't have been very old, maybe six. "Hey, sweetie, where's your Mommy?" The little girl pointed at the woods. "Can you show me?"

Sobbing, the little girl took her hand and led her back into the woods. She stopped not far in and pointed to a bluff. "Is she at the rocks, sweetie?" The little girl's cries got even worse. Lindsey scooped the girl up in her arms and hugged her as she pulled her radio from her hip. "Wendy, I have a little girl here that is quite upset; she keeps telling me her parents are at the bluffs off trail seven. Can you send someone to get her while I go take a look?"

"Brandon's the closest; I'll send him your way."

Lindsey headed back up to the trail. "What's your name, sweetie?"

"Ashley," she managed between sobs.

"Well, Ashley, I am going to go look for your mom. Can you stay right here till my friend Brandon comes? He is an Indian. He will take good care of you." The little girl nodded her head. She could hear a four-wheeler coming up the trail. "That should be him, so you wait right here for him, ok?" she sat the little girl down and headed back down in the woods.

When she reached the bluffs she yelled, "Hello!" She climbed up to the top of a large rock. She could see a man at the bottom, leaning over someone lying on the ground. "Hello down there!" she yelled, "Is someone hurt?"

The man stood and turned to her. He had blood on him and the woman on the ground was covered in it. Lindsey jumped off the rock and hit the trail at a dead run, jumping over rocks and over cracks. The man was in shock; he had sat back down and was just looking at the woman. She reached over and touched the woman. She was alive, but badly hurt. From the looks of her, she had fallen.

"Wendy, I have a woman here that has fallen from the bluffs. She's badly hurt; she looks to be in her mid 20's. Give me a minute to check on the man."

"I will send a team immediately; give me status updates as you assess them."

"Will do." Lindsey turned to the man. He backed away from her as she approached him. She stopped and looked back at the woman. "Sir, I need your help." The best way to assess him would be to have him help. He just looked at her. "Sir, is that your wife? You need to help me with her. She's bleeding badly, and I need you to help me stop the bleeding."

Lindsey turned back to the woman and put her hand on a bad cut that was bleeding profusely. The man came around her and knelt on the other side. Terror was still in his eyes.

"My name is Lindsey, what is your name? Put your hand here, hold it tightly to stop the bleeding." She put his hand on a cut on the woman's forehead as she looked over the woman more closely.

"Mike .... Mike Felker," he finally managed to get out.

Lindsey picked up the radio.

"Is this your wife?" The woman was very weak; she had lost a lot of blood.

"Carol, yes, Carol is my wife."

"Wendy, I have a Mike and Carol Felker here. Mike seems to be ok, just in shock. Carol has a couple broken ribs, a broken leg and several bad cuts and bruises. She has lost quite a bit of blood." Mike suddenly looked around franticly. "Ashley is fine, she is with a Ranger; and you know she was the one who told me where you were. You have a brave little girl." Tears ran down his cheeks.

"I have a helicopter en route, and the medical team should be about to reach you," reported Wendy.

"Ranger Jacobs!" Someone yelled.

"Down here!" Lindsey yelled back. A man appeared on the top. Four men came around the trail with first-aid gear. Lindsey stood as soon as they got to them.

"Mike, let's move out of their way, and let them do their job."

"Take him up to the trail; we will get her," one of the men told Lindsey.

"I can't leave her."

"It's going to be fine, we need to get you up to your little girl. She is very upset." The man looked over at Lindsey. He let her lead him up the trail.

"Brandon, you still have Ashley?"

"Yes, we are at the campground."

"Alright, I am bringing her Dad your way." Lindsey fastened the radio back on her belt. "We need to clean you up a bit. You will make her panic." The man looked down at himself; he was covered in blood.

"Wendy, I need a large T-shirt and some water and towels at the trailhead, please."

"No problem."

27

The two made their way up the trail and out to the parking lot. A truck pulled in as they came up onto it. The chubby man from the office got out, Head Ranger Malcolm. He had a towel and a T-shirt.

"Here, you need to clean up; you can't let your daughter see you looking like that."

The man took off his shirt, and then cleaned up using the towel and Lindsey's canteen water. Lindsey opened the package with the shirt and handed it to him.

"We are coming out," a voice came across the radio.

"This is Ranger Malcolm; he will take you to your daughter, then he will see you to the hospital to see your wife." She laid her hand on his arm, "she's going to be fine, Mike. Now go take care of your little hero."

He put the shirt on, then gave Lindsey a big hug. "Thank you."

She smiled. "You're welcome."

Mike and Malcolm got in the truck and sped off up the road. The helicopter was coming over the trees as the truck left. It landed on the parking lot. The team came out of the woods and Lindsey went over to help them load the woman in the helicopter.

"How is she doing?" She asked one of the four men.

"She lost a lot of blood, but I think she's going to be fine." Lindsey waved as the helicopter lifted off.

Lindsey grabbed her radio, "Ranger Malcolm, would you please tell Mr. Felker I just talked to one of the medics and they said his wife was going to be fine."

"Will do," came back.

Lindsey looked down; she was pretty messy herself, but not that bad. She headed back to finish the rest of trail seven. Thankfully, it was peaceful. After that she headed back to the cabin to clean up a bit before heading on the next trail. The rest of her day passed without any more incidents.

Lindsey walked up to the Inn around 9:30 p.m. after coming off trail nine again. She had been on three, seven, and nine all day, and had missed supper, because of talking to a couple on nine. Maybe they would have some leftovers in the kitchen. She hadn't had time to buy anything for her cabin, yet. Lindsey headed up to the desk at the Inn.

"You think they've got anything left in the kitchen? I missed supper."

Misty smiled at her. "You must be Ranger Jacobs. I'm Misty."

"Lindsey, please," she told her.

"There are always some kinds of leftovers, but they take them down to the common room. So just check the fridge down there. Bob, the cook, is good at putting a date on them so you won't get anything old."

"Thanks," Lindsey told her. It had been a long day. "Hey, Misty is there a piano in the Inn?"

"Yes, there is one in the club room."

Lindsey smiled; she loved to play piano at the end of the day to relax.

"Is the door locked?"

"No, it stays open. Do you play?"

"A little, it always helps me to unwind to play a tune or two."

"I guess today was quite stressful. I heard you had a couple down this morning."

Lindsey smiled at her. "Yes, do you think it will bother anyone if I play awhile?"

"No, it's at the end of the hall all by itself. Go ahead."

Lindsey's stomach growled. "Better eat first."

They smiled and Lindsey headed down to the common room. Lindsey heated a plate of casserole. The container didn't say what kind, just said casserole and had today's date. It smelled pretty good. She could see some chicken and veggies in it.

After putting her plate in the trash, she headed up to the club room. Misty smiled as she went by the desk. The room was at the end of the hall. The room was dark. She really didn't need the lights to play, but she did need to see where the piano was and anything else that was in the room. She flipped on the light switch. The room was filled with couches, which made it look like a big lounge. The piano was over in the corner at the front. It was an old upright; she sat down on the bench and ran her finger across the keys. She loved music; it was one thing she had been taught that she loved. Piano was her favorite, and she could play just about anything. She pecked a couple of keys to see if it was in tune. It was a little off, but not much. Most people wouldn't notice it. She closed her eyes and played. The ballad consumed her. Her fingers slid effortlessly over the keys.

The door cracked open, Misty stuck her head in to listen. A smile came to her lips; Misty left the door cracked open so the music floated up the hall. She could hear it at the desk if it remained quiet. An hour later, Lindsey shut the light off, closed the door, and headed up the hall.

"You play beautifully, Lindsey."

Lindsey smiled at her. "Thanks."

Lindsey knew she had closed the door when she went in, but it was open a little when she came out. Now she knew who opened it. She headed for the cabins; it was going on 11 p.m. She showered, and crawled into bed. She enjoyed helping other people. It was not all that different to what she normally did; well, yeah it was, she didn't have to kill any of these people to help. The best part about helping here, was she wasn't being told what to do, she was doing it all on her own and she loved it. She fell asleep with a smile.

Lindsey's run was great. Her eight miles was nothing to what she could run in forty minutes, but why push it if she didn't have to. She showered and headed to breakfast. She couldn't keep from smiling;

she was enjoying the feeling of helping all on her own. She sat down with Jacob and John.

"Morning," she told them.

"Hey, Lindsey," John told her.

"Hey," was all Jacob said.

"What's with the big smile? Ok, what have you been doing?" Brandon came up and sat down beside her.

Lindsey laughed. "It's just going to be a great day, I feel it."

Brandon sighed, "Man, I thought you were up to something sneaky and I want in." They both laughed.

John shook his head. "Don't encourage him, Lindsey; he's always up to something."

Jacob nodded his head in agreement.

Lindsey smiled at Brandon. "Sounds like you're the one that has all the fun."

Brandon gave a huge grin.

They ordered breakfast and ate. Jacob talked about getting things ready for his and Brandon's trip with the Girl Scout trip that was leaving Sunday morning. John had a group leaving on a two-day tomorrow, just four people. Lindsey just listened as they talked.

Brandon caught himself looking at Lindsey. She was so pretty, and was a lot of fun to have around. He found himself smiling. Yeah, it was going to be a good day, maybe even a good season.

They all left at the same time. Lindsey had the campground duty today. Brandon had the trails she had yesterday, so he walked with her down to the campground.

"I didn't see you come in last night. You have a long one?" Brandon asked her.

"Yeah, I got to talking to a couple from Oregon; I didn't get back to the cabin till around 11."

He laughed. "You better watch it or you'll find yourself with no sleep. Have a good one, Lindsey." He headed on to the lower parking lot and trail seven.

Lindsey headed to the camp shack. Ranger Johnson was checking in a couple when she came in.

"Hey, can you go check out these three sites; I have a feeling they could use some help." He gave her a site map, and out the door she went.

Site thirteen was the first site. It was an older couple; he was trying to set up a huge tent as the lady was reading the directions.

"Let me help you with that." She walked up and started putting the poles together. Before long they had it up. They both thanked her and she headed on up to site 57. Four young girls from about ages four to seven were running around the site. The parents were trying to put up their tent, but were also trying to keep the girls from running off and into the road. Lindsey smiled at the couple who looked at wit's end.

"Do you girls know how to play Duck, Duck Goose?"

The couple looked up at her. The small girls ran up and sat down in a circle. She spent the next 20 minutes playing games with the girls so their parents could get the camp set up. She got a few hugs and kisses as she left the site.

She waved at the girls and headed up to number 62. A young couple sat looking at instructions for their tent; all the parts lay on the ground in front of them. She was pregnant.

"Can I help you guys?"

The guy looked up with relief in his eyes.

"We have camped with Mom and Dad the last few years, and I know how to put up their tent. But I can't make heads or tails out of these instructions," the young girl told her. Lindsey took the instructions from her and gave it a brief look.

"Wow, those are confusing. Let's just wing it. You assemble the poles; they look color-coded, so that should be easy. The hard part will be trying to find which hole they go to." They all laughed and began to work.

"Lindsey, can you go check on site 89?" A voice came over the radio on her side.

"No problem," she replied. The tent was almost done; they had changed poles around several times and were down to the last one.

"I think I've got it, thanks a lot."

"If you have any problems, make sure you go to the camp gate." She smiled and left their site. She hoped they had a mattress or something for her to sleep on; the ground would be horrible for her in her condition. She decided she would drop by later and check on them.

Site 89 was a camper site. A man was struggling with some folded up . . . well, she didn't know what it was.

"Let me help you," she said as she took hold of a set of the handles. He turned to meet her smile.

"I have always had my wife to help me with this but . . ." Tears rolled down his cheeks.

"Dad, you about done? It's getting hot in here," a voice came from the window.

Lindsey took a look at the camper; it was different. It was made for wheelchair access. Lindsey smiled at the man. What he had was a wheelchair ramp that folded up.

"Just a minute, Kyle, I'll have you out in a minute."

She helped the man get it stretched out and hooked up to the bottom of the door facing. A young man she thought to be no more than 22 rolled out and down to the ground.

"Man, it's pretty here, Dad. Mom would have loved it."

The man was trying hard not to break down; you could see it on his face and hear it in his voice.

"I know, son."

Lindsey smiled at the two. The older man went into the camper.

"Thanks for helping dad," the man in the wheelchair told her, "I guess I shouldn't have insisted we come, but we both could use some time away from home."

"It was my pleasure to help. How long ago did you lose your mom?"

"It's been three months; she had cancer."

"I am real sorry for your loss. It sounds like you could use a little away time. If you guys need anything, make sure you let us know."

The young man smiled. "My name is Kyle."

"Nice to meet you, Kyle, I'm Lindsey."

Her radio crackled, "Lindsey; I need you up here as soon as you can."

Kyle smiled at her.

"Duty calls. Make sure if you need anything let us know, ok?"

"Thanks, we will."

She waved and headed back to the shack. There were at least ten cars in line waiting to be checked in. Lindsey grabbed a clipboard and headed for the next car in line.

The traffic coming in was pretty steady, so lunch was a sandwich between check-ins. About five, the traffic slowed a bit and Ranger Malcolm brought out supper from the dining hall.

"So, how are you liking being a Ranger?" John asked as they ate.

"It's great; I like helping people."

A car honked.

"I've got it; go on and eat." Lindsey opened the door and went out. Kyle and his father were sitting in a car waiting on her.

"Is anything wrong?" She asked.

Kyle smiled. "No, we were just heading up to the Inn to get something to eat, wanted to know if we could get you anything?"

She smiled, "Thanks for the offer, but . . . well, I hear the cook makes a great cobbler."

Kyle smiled, "One piece of cobbler coming up!"

She waved as they pulled off.

"Everything ok?" John asked as she went back in.

"It was the father and son from 89. We may want to check on them often, the boy is in a wheelchair, and this is their first trip without the mom; she died a few months ago. I think it is going to be a hard trip for them. They just wanted to know if I wanted anything from the Inn."

He smiled at her. "Made a good impression on them, did you?"

She smiled and picked up her tray and finished eating her supper. Forty-five minutes later Kyle and his father pulled back up. Lindsey went out and took the cobbler from them.

"Dessert," she said as she opened the lid. There were two forks; they had seen John through the window.

They closed up at nine, and headed out. Lindsey headed for one last walk through the campground. Campfires were going; people were coming back from the shower houses. It had been a good day.

Back in her cabin, Lindsey stood in the shower for a while. She lay down for a bit, but couldn't sleep. She put on some flip-flops and headed for the Inn. She peeked in the door, nobody seemed to be stirring. Since she was in her shorts and tank top, she really didn't want to be seen. She gave Misty a wave as she went past the desk. Lindsey left the door cracked for her. She left the lights off this time, and made her way to the piano. She played a soft ballad. Lindsey again lost herself in the music.

CHAPTER 3
Insane or Hero

L INDSEY OPENED HER door to rain Thursday morning. She smiled as she set off on her run.

Brandon got up to use the restroom at 3:55 a.m. He could hear the rain on the roof as he headed back to the bed. He looked out the window as he sat down on the edge. It was still dark, but something was moving. He looked through the sheets of rain. Lindsey was running up the trail. He lay down on the bed beside Jacob. He looked forward to seeing her every day. He smiled as he drifted off; she was just crazy enough to run in the rain.

"You're insane, you know that, right?" Brandon told Lindsey as he sat down beside her at breakfast. "I saw you out running in the rain this morning."

She looked up and laughed. "Why didn't you join me?"

"I said you were insane, not me."

"Where are you today?" Lindsey asked.

"Campground."

"Would you do me a favor and check on site 89? There is a guy and his son there. The son is in a wheelchair; first time they have been out since the wife died."

Brandon looked over at Lindsey; she had a heart for people. "I'll do it first thing."

"And the couple in 63; she is pregnant."

Brandon smiled. "Ok."

She gave him a big smile. "Thanks Brandon, I owe you one."

"It's not wise to owe him anything," Jacob said as he sat down at the table with them.

Lindsey laughed. Brandon gave his *What? Me?* look.

"Have you given any more thought to the trip for Mom and Dad?" Jacob asked Brandon.

"I don't know if I have enough to go in half with you. How much do you think it will cost?"

"If we do one week it will be around $1500, I think. Not real sure, yet."

"What are you two talking about?" Lindsey asked.

"Mom and Dad's 50th wedding anniversary is coming up in November; Jacob wants to send them on a cruise."

"Can I help? I have the best travel agent, and I bet he could get you a great deal."

Jacob looked up at her. "Well, I guess it wouldn't hurt for you to ask about it."

Lindsey pulled the phone from her pocket and started typing. "Alright, give me some details."

Brandon looked surprised. "Is that a Blackberry?"

Lindsey smiled at Brandon in answer to his question as she typed.

"I would love for them to go on a cruise that made lots of stops in exotic ports. Two weeks would be great, but I figure one is all we can afford." Jacob smiled.

Lindsey typed away as he talked. "Does this need to include airfare and transportation? Do they have their Passports?"

Jacob looked at her, he hadn't thought of all that. "Yes and no; they have never been anywhere."

Lindsey sent a message to Keeps. "Hey, I need a favor: can you check on something for me?" Her phone beeped when he answered.

"How do you get service here? There are no towers anywhere around here," Brandon asked when her phone beeped.

"You can get satellite service anywhere. What weeks?" She asked Jacob.

"Their anniversary is on the 25th. I would like to have them leave that night, if possible."

She smiled and typed.

"Anything," was the reply on her phone.

She typed back, "I need a trip for two. Leaving on the night of November 25th; I need airfare, transportation, the works. I want a two week cruise with exotic ports of call. First class all the way." She pushed send.

Her phone beeped again. "Give me two days."

She smiled. "He said to give him a couple of days. If anyone can find a good price, he can. And since it's still a couple of months away, it will be cheaper, too."

Jacob smiled at her. "Thanks, Lindsey."

"No problem. Are you having a party for them?"

"That would be a great idea. We could give it to them there," Brandon piped in.

"That's more money, Brandon."

"Maybe not," Lindsey added. "Is there not a community center or something on the reservation?"

"Yeah," Jacob answered.

"Then you can talk to all their friends; have everyone bring a finger food of some kind. You'll have a great party in no time."

Brandon smiled, and shook his head. "Oh yeah, you know everyone will want to come, and they will all bring something."

"The only other thing I can think of is checking with both their employers to see if they can have off before you actually book the trip," Lindsey added.

"Yeah, that would be wise, but I don't think we will have a problem with either of them."

"Crap," Brandon said, "it's getting late. I've got to go if I am to check on sites 89 and 62. See you guys later." He headed out the door quickly.

"You really think your friend can get a good deal? We really don't have a lot of money to spend."

"Don't worry," Lindsey said as she got up from the table. "He is the best. Have a good one, Jacob." She left him sitting at the table.

Lindsey smiled as she left. Keeps would get it all planned and paid for and she would give Jacob a price quote that she knew they could afford. Like she was going to really let them pay for it, anyway; she would slip the money back in their accounts.

Trail two was right off the side of the Inn and was very short. Trail four branched off trail three so she had to walk part of three to get to it. She came up on the man and woman from site 62 as she came around a corner. They were sitting on a bench.

"Good morning," she gave them a cheerful greeting. The young woman wasn't looking very good. "Are you ok?" she dropped to her knees in front of the lady. Her breath was hard and shallow, and she was holding her back.

"I just need to sit a while." She looked up at Lindsey.

"She didn't sleep well last night."

The woman had all the signs of labor, her breathing was hard, but shallow, her eyes were dilated, and her hand was on her lower back.

"How far along are you?" Lindsey asked her.

"Seven and a half months."

Lindsey picked up her radio. "Wendy, this is Lindsey, could you tell me if the nurse is in today?"

"She won't be in till 10 this morning. Anything wrong?"

Lindsey smiled at the couple. "Not at the moment, but I will let you know if that . . . ."

The lady in front of her let out a large gasp. Blood and water poured down the bench.

"Is there a mule close to trail four?" The lady let out a loud scream of pain.

"No, they are out on the camping trails today. What's up?"

"I have a lady going into labor here. I need water, towels, blankets and a way to get her back to the Inn."

The man had fear in his eyes.

"What is your name, ma'am?"

"Mendi," she got out before another pain wracked her body. That was the second pain in less than a minute. "No moving her; Wendy, I need a blanket, water and towels, now!"

"They're on their way."

"Sir, we need to . . ."

"Jack, my name is Jack," he looked at Lindsey; panic was written on his face.

"We need to get her more comfortable. We need something clean to for her to sit on." Lindsey stood up and took her T-shirt off. She took her knife and split the shirt down the middle so it was bigger. Luckily, she always wore a tank top underneath. Lindsey spread the shirt out on the ground. "We need to get her down on the ground." The lady let out another scream.

"Jack, I need you to talk to her, it will get her mind off the pain."

Jacob came around the bend on a four-wheeler. He cut the engine, and jumped off.

"I need the blanket, Jacob."

Jacob opened a yellow emergency blanket and handed it to Lindsey. Mendi was screaming in pain. Lindsey threw the blanket over the lower part of Mendi, then pulled off Mendi's underclothes.

"She's almost fully dilated," Lindsey told Jacob. "Mendi, you need to calm down. Try to keep your breaths short. 'He He Ho Ho' is the best. All the screaming is just going to frighten anyone in the park and not help, so please try, ok?"

Jack coached his wife in breathing.

"Give me a towel and bring some water here."

Jacob never questioned anything, but just followed orders.

"An ambulance is on the way," Wendy's voice came over the radio.

"She's fully dilated now. Mendi, I need you to bear down and push with everything you have at the next contraction." Mendi shook her head as the pain hit her. Lindsey pushed Mendi's bent knees towards her head. "That's it, you're doing it." The pain subsided for a few seconds then came right back. "One more big push and you'll be through. Come on Mendi, you can do this."

The baby slipped into Lindsey's hands. Lindsey turned it facedown to let all the water and blood drain from it's mouth, then ran her finger through it's mouth to make sure it was all out. A loud cry broke through the woods. Jacob handed her another towel.

"You have a very handsome little man here," Lindsey said, as she wiped him down and wrapped him tightly in the clean towel. She placed him in his mother's arm.

"Baby and Mom are doing fine," Jacob announced over the radio. Two paramedics came around the bend in the trail. Lindsey stood up and got out of the of the paramedics' way.

Jack stood up and went to Lindsey and put his arms around her. "Thank you!"

She smiled and looked over at Mendi and the baby. "It was an honor."

Tears slid down Jack's face. He hugged her once more then went back to his wife. Lindsey noticed Jacob staring at her. "I'm glad I didn't have to do that."

"You would have done fine," she told him.

"I don't know about that," he said.

Lindsey and Jacob followed as they took Mendi to the ambulance. Mendi gave Lindsey a wave as the doors shut. Jacob handed Lindsey the towel that held her shirt.

"You might want to get your name badge off this."

She took the towel.

"Tourist season started three days ago and there have already been two rescues. It is going to be a heck of a fall."

Lindsey smiled and headed for the cabins. She took her name badge off her shirt and put the shirt in the trash. A shower was in order, to get all the mess off her. She jumped in and out as quickly as she could; she dressed and headed back up to trail four. She hadn't made it very far the first time. She went through the dining hall at lunch and grabbed a sandwich. She was now way behind, so she ate as she walked. The rest of the day passed with only small happenings. She had come upon the couple with the four small girls and had to stop and play a game of Duck, Duck Goose. She had given a band-aid to a man that had cut his finger.

As she walked back to her cabin for the night, she made a quick trip through the camp sites. 62 was still set up; Jack most likely had stayed at the hospital with Mendi.

There was still a fire burning brightly at 89.

Kyle saw her. "Lindsey!"

She smiled as she walked up close to the fire.

"Are you guys enjoying yourselves?"

Kyle's Dad stood up. "Thank you for sending Brandon to check on us this morning." She smiled. "He was here when you delivered the baby."

"Well, I hope I never have to do that again," she smiled and Kyle laughed. She sat down on the edge of the picnic table.

"Can I ask you something?"

"Sure, Kyle, what is it?" She looked over at him; she hoped he wasn't going to ask about details of the delivery.

"Why is it you don't wear a uniform like Brandon?" She laughed, what a relief.

"Mine haven't come in, yet. I am new here this year. But I should get them tomorrow."

"You'll have to come by and show us."

42

Lindsey stood up. "I need to head back. You guys have a good night." She gave Kyle a big smile. "I'll try." Then she left.

She made her way back to the cabin. She would really like to go play, but she couldn't do this every night, maybe every other. She pulled out her Blackberry and typed. *I need an acoustic guitar, with excellent sound.* Then she hit send. She had barely got it laid down when it beeped.

"You'll have it by Saturday; still working on the other request."

She smiled and slid off to sleep.

Brandon set an alarm and got up early. He was sitting on Lindsey's porch when she opened the door at four. "I thought you weren't insane?"

He smiled at her. "I'm not. It's not raining."

She stretched out her legs and headed out.

"So, how far you do run?"

She grinned. "About eight miles. You think you can survive that?"

"Lord, I hope so."

She laughed at the concern in his eyes.

"Why in the world do you run? We walk all day," he asked her.

"It makes the walking easier."

After running up and past the Inn, Lindsey slowed the pace. He wasn't going to make even five miles.

"You said back at the house that you were sent to boarding school and China and places. Does that mean your family was loaded?"

She laughed. "Was and still are."

"So, why in the world are you Rangering? I mean I know you camped once and was hooked, but you just could have bought a piece of mountain land and built a house or something."

"So, you're saying you wish I hadn't come here?"

"No, no, I am glad you're here, but you're loaded; you could be anywhere."

She stopped and looked at him. He was panting pretty hard. "I like helping people. Setting alone in some cabin doesn't sound like the least bit fun."

"But you wouldn't have to sit there. You've got money; you could do anything."

"Having money does not guarantee happiness, Brandon."

"Ok, now you sound like Mom."

Lindsey took off at a slow jog. "My uniforms are supposed to be in today. So, I guess I get to look as snazzy as you guys, now." She put as much sarcasm in the word snazzy as she could.

He laughed at her. "I don't think anyone could look good in those things."

They laughed together. "Man, that wasn't too bad," Brandon said as they got back to the cabins.

"That was barely three miles," Lindsey looked at him.

"Oh!" he said and dropped his head and walked back to Jacob's. She laughed at him.

Lindsey made a swing by the office to see if Wendy knew what time her uniforms would be in. "Usually he brings them around ten a.m. I'll give you a call when they're here."

Lindsey then went to the dining hall for breakfast. Brandon had his head down and Jacob was eating. She heard a small snore as she got close to the table.

"You're going to kill him getting him up that early," Jacob said as she sat down beside Brandon.

"I didn't ask him to get up. I didn't even know he was going to join me this morning," she told Jacob in her defense. Brandon's head was lying on his arms which were crossed on the table. She took her finger and ran it down the side of his face. He had high cheek bones and a strong jaw line. He opened his eyes.

She smiled at him. "Wake up, sleepyhead," she told him. He stretched his arms and yawned. "Are you going to make it today?"

"I'm good, just needed a power nap."

Brandon stood up. "I am helping with tours today, so I've got to go. See you later."

Jacob waited till he was out the door.

"Man, he has got it bad."

Lindsey looked up at him, he was looking at her. "Sorry, not intentional," she dropped her head.

"Yeah, right," was all he said.

Lindsey didn't wait for breakfast; she grabbed a muffin and headed out the door. She and Brandon hadn't spent that much time together; their schedule made sure of that. But she did have to admit she did like him. She would never want to hurt him, though.

She headed down to trail seven; she passed though the campground to see if Jack might be there. He was there and was pulling the tent down. She went to give him a hand.

"Lindsey." he gave her a big hug as she came on the site.

"Hey, Jack, how's the family?"

"They are great, thanks to you!"

"Let me help you get loaded up." She helped him get the tent down and everything back in the car.

"Thanks again, Lindsey!" He yelled as he pulled out.

Lindsey headed on toward the trail. She made the loop and headed over toward trail five. It was a four mile round trip, so she swung by the Inn and picked up some water. She hadn't been out long when her radio crackled.

"Uniforms are in, Lindsey."

"Thanks, I'll swing by at lunch," she replied to Wendy. The rest of the morning passed by peacefully. She dropped by the Inn and picked up her uniforms and headed to the cabin to change before lunch. The uniform fit right, but it was stiff and rough. She put her new name badge on and looked in the mirror; it was fine. She slid the cover on, or hat, or whatever they called them, she didn't really care, and went out the door.

John, Brandon, and Samantha sat at a table in the corner. The pictures of all the Rangers were hanging on the wall in the lobby; that was how she knew it was Samantha. Lindsey headed toward them; Brandon's back was to her, so she put her hands on his neck and gave him a quick shoulder rub. He smiled as she came around to sit beside him.

"Wow, I didn't think anyone could look good in these uniforms," John said, and Brandon agreed.

"Thanks, guys," Lindsey said.

Samantha looked at both of them.

"Hey, I'm Lindsey," Lindsey stuck out her hand to Samantha.

"Sam." She shook her hand.

John smiled at Sam. "You still look good in yours, too."

She just laughed. "I am so ready to sleep in a bed tonight. Four days on the ground is way too long." She had just returned from a camping tour. The only camping tours they gave were to Troops, Girl Scouts, Boy Scouts, Brownies, and 4H kid groups. She had just spent four days with some Boy Scouts. "They were all about ten and drove me crazy. I had to actually tell the leaders to keep all of them together in a circle just so I could go pee without one of them following me." They all laughed.

"Jacob and I have the Girl Scouts next week," Brandon told her. "And I know it sounds hilarious, but I know it's true. I had this one last year that even slept outside my tent door." Laughter erupted again. "Jacob always has the moms. Of course, most of them are married, but they can't seem to help fantasize about a tall dark Indian, that's what a lady told me one year."

The stories kept coming one right after another. John had a woman come in his tent late at night, once. Sam told about the one year that a 15 year old proposed to her. The absurdities just kept coming, and Lindsey laughed till her side hurt.

"Well, I have to go. Brandon, I bet I can beat you at a game of pool tonight," Sam said as she got up.

"You're on!" He replied.

"I play winner," John threw in.

"9:30?"

"See you, then."

She left, and John followed.

"So, are they dating or does he just have a thing for her?"

Brandon smiled. "If it's that obvious, why doesn't she have a clue?"

"Who said she didn't?"

"Well, she sure doesn't act like it."

Lindsey laughed. "Some girls like to make the guy work for it. They don't just give it away."

He smiled at her. "If that was the case, I would understand. But she is not one of those, she puts out."

Lindsey raised her eyebrow at him. "I guess you would know?"

He glared at her. "Not from personal account, I assure you."

Lindsey smiled. Brandon didn't.

"You know the story of my sister; I was 13 when that happened. I made up my mind then and there not to be like that. So, I have strong views about sex and marriage."

"I'm sorry, I didn't mean to offend you. But that does tell me why she is flirting with you so hard. You're the ultimate prize." He smiled at her. "Handsome, and you have honor and morals. Not something you find these days."

Brandon finished his last bite and got up. "So what about you?"

She smiled at him. "Virgin! Waiting for mister right."

"And you say I'm rare," he smiled and left.

Lindsey sat there thinking. In her job she was trained to stay pure, but with all the diseases these days how could someone not make that choice. Today, sex was a comparison game, why not save yourself for the one you marry, then there is no comparison. You can discover all the fun games together. Lindsey smiled and left the table.

She had ten minutes before lunch was officially over, so she headed down to the campground to see if Kyle and his Dad were around. Their car wasn't there so she headed toward the trails. Lindsey had her first trail done quickly and headed for the next one. The day sped by, and it was soon nine, time for all the trails to close. Lindsey headed for the campground. Kyle and his Dad were roasting marshmallows over the fire.

"Are we making s'mores?" Lindsey asked as she approached the two.

"Sure are, will you join us for one?" Kyle's Dad asked.

"I would love to. So, what do you think?" Lindsey gave a twirl.

"Looks good on you," Kyle said. His Dad agreed.

Lindsey sat for an hour talking with the two. They were pulling out tomorrow. Lindsey said goodnight and goodbye and headed for the common room to see how the pool game had gone.

Jacob, Samantha, John, Brandon and two others were all in the common room. John and Samantha were playing pairs with Jacob and Mike Walker, another Ranger. Lindsey sat down on one of the couches. Brandon and Todd, John's nephew, were playing Halo on an X-Box. Lindsey sat and watched for a while before heading to the cabin to get a shower. She put on a pair of shorts and a T-shirt and went back to the commons. Samantha and John were gone, along with Mike. Jacob was talking to Brandon when she sat down.

"You better be figuring it out. You can't work here for the fall then have nothing when you get back."

"Me and the band . . ."

Jacob cut Brandon off, "You and the band? You didn't even bring your guitar to practice, and you're talking band. You need to have something stable, Brandon."

"Hey, we are good, and you know it."

Lindsey looked up at Brandon. "How good are you?"

Jacob turned to her. "They are pretty good when they practice, but ... "

"But, what you think is, I can't make it as a musician?" Brandon was getting pretty mad.

"I am just saying you need to have a backup plan or a job to do while you all practice. You just can't live on Mom and Dad till you hit it big. Haven't Brett and Todd signed up for college this fall?"

"Yeah," Brandon said as he dropped his head.

"You know music is a serious business; if you're not going to take it seriously, you won't make it," Lindsey looked at Brandon, who now seemed kind of shocked.

"You haven't even heard me play, and you're on Jacob's side."

Lindsey shook her head. "No, I'm just saying if you're really serious maybe you should take a few music classes, like theory and writing."

Brandon got even madder. "You don't know anything about my music. I know how to play and write, and I am not bad at it, either."

Lindsey shook her head and got up and left. She sure hated to see someone take a musical gift and throw it away because they weren't willing to learn. Lindsey walked up the stairs, she pointed down the hall. Misty gave her the thumbs up.

Lindsey sat down at the piano and ran her fingers down the keys. The melody she played was soft and gentle; it grew louder as the piece got intense, then back down. She smiled to herself. Music was so much more than just notes; it was in the soul.

Brandon headed out of the commons and towards the cabins. He had not been very nice to Lindsey. Or so Jacob said, but Lindsey was the one who said he wasn't serious about his music. Brandon didn't want Lindsey mad at him either way. He really liked her being around. When he arrived at her cabin the lights were off. He knocked, but she didn't answer. He checked the handle; it was unlocked so he peeked in. She wasn't there. He turned and headed back up to the Inn.

"Do you know where Lindsey went when she came up awhile ago?" He asked Misty.

Misty smiled. "Follow the music." Brandon got still and listened. Somewhere there was a piano playing softly.

"Who's playing?" He asked her.

"Lindsey. She likes to play at the end of the day. She leaves the door cracked so I can hear her. She plays like a concert pianist."

Brandon followed the music up the hall to the club room, the door was standing ajar. There was no light inside, so he slid in and stood listening. Lindsey could really play. The ballad she played was beautiful. She had said she took music lessons when she was younger, but she didn't say she was good. Brandon listened as she played one piece after another.

"Come here, Brandon," Lindsey said, as one piece got really soft. He walked up and sat down beside her on the bench. "I didn't mean to make you mad; I just don't understand if you have a gift why you wouldn't want to develop it as much as possible. Taking a few classes would give you every possible advantage. It could teach you so much." Brandon sat there listening for a few minutes.

"You play beautifully," he said when the piece was finished. "I don't have the money for college, and if I help Jacob with this trip, well, that will take what little I have saved."

She turned on the bench to face him. "I'll tell you what, you help Jacob with the trip and I'll help you with college."

He just looked at her. "I can't take your money."

She laughed. "Remember, I'm loaded. You can just borrow what you need and pay me back later."

He took a deep breath. "What if I am not really good enough?"

"I don't think there is anyone that is really good at it, but what you learn will amaze you and you can use it in the way your music needs it. I'll help you if you want."

He smiled at her. "I'll think about it."

Lindsey sighed, and got up. "Good night, Brandon."

"May I walk you down?"

"If you want to." Lindsey was still a little aggravated at Brandon. An 'I'll think about it' usually means I'll think of fifty thousand excuses not to.

"You don't want me to?"

Lindsey looked over at him as they exited the club room.

"I don't care either way."

"Did I say something to upset you, Lindsay? I didn't mean to," he asked as they passed by Misty. "I just don't know what my future holds and I guess I am a little scared about it."

Lindsey laughed as she thought to herself. *Don't know what his future holds; at least he has one. I have no clue where I'll be.* "Your future will be great, I know it; don't be scared about it. Just embrace it! If music is what you love, then play music; don't settle for some job at the local Wal-Mart. Too many people settle because they get comfortable. Make your life the best! Take some music classes, learn all you can about it, every chance you can. Then you will find yourself one day living the dream you had today."

He smiled at her. "You sound so passionate about it. What about you, what do you really want to do?"

Lindsey stepped onto her cabin porch and turned to face him. "My life . . ." Lindsey just wanted to tell him the truth. "Well, it's different."

"So, what you're saying is, you can dish out the advice, but you won't take it yourself."

Lindsey took a deep breath. "No, that's not it. My life is not my own, and that is all I will say; so don't ask any more about it, because

I cannot tell you anymore. But if I had a choice I would be following you down that music trail."

They stopped in front of her cabin. "Thanks for walking me home, goodnight." She turned and went in; she didn't want to give him any time to ask questions.

Lindsey crawled up on her bed. Her phone beeped.

'*Crap,*' she thought, '*I said too much and they are going to pull me out tonight.*'

She looked at the message. "Guitar is on the way, should be there tomorrow. As for the trip, the departure date is the 28th. Can't get anything closer to the 25th. They could spend a night in a destination half way, like Branson, or Pigeon Forge. Just let me know."

She gave a sigh of relief, then typed back. "I'll let you know tomorrow. Thanks Keeps; you're the best." She hit send. It beeped again.

"I am supposed to take care of anything you need. No thanks are necessary."

She laughed and typed back, "Don't care if it's your job or not, get used to them. Thanks, again."

She laid the phone on the table beside the bed and curled up and thought of Brandon. This life was so easy and he was scared. He had no idea what scared was. A few memories of times that she was beaten or almost raped passed through her mind. Her life was all about getting into and out of those scary situations so others didn't have to go through them. And he was scared about whether to take a few music classes . . .

She took a deep breath and went to sleep.

Brandon lay in bed thinking. What had she meant her life wasn't her own? Did it have to do with her parents? But they were dead. Maybe they had left her with a business to run or something. College, he thought, he really didn't like school. But maybe if it was for something he really loved, maybe it wouldn't be too bad. Money was one thing he didn't have; he knew she had offered to help him, but should he accept it? Maybe, if Jacob didn't know, it would be ok. She said she would help him, how much did she know? What schools had she been to? Was she as good at other instruments as she was the piano? Man, she was amazing. Misty was right about the concert pianist. Brandon tossed and turned, thinking. He finally fell to sleep thinking "College . . ."

Lindsey sat beside Brandon at the breakfast table.

"I think I need two or three power naps," he said as he lifted his head.

"You said not to go easy on you, so it's not my fault. I still didn't do my usual."

He dropped his head back to the table. Jacob laughed at him.

"Tomorrow starts our trip with Girl Scout troop 54."

"Which trail are you taking?" Lindsey asked.

"We will be on C6."

"I am scheduled to take a four-wheeler on C2 Sunday."

"That's cheating, you know; you can make the whole trail by nightfall if you move pretty quickly," Brandon said through his crossed arms.

She smiled. "Oh, darn, I won't have to camp."

"I would take stuff just in case," Jacob told her.

"I was planning on it. I would rather be prepared than not." Brandon let out a small snore. "Brandon, it's almost eight, you better wake up." Lindsey reached over and gave him a little nudge. He lifted his head.

"Five minutes, is that too much to ask for?"

Lindsey smiled at him. "I talked to my travel agent last night; he said the cruise leaving the closest to the time was on the 28th. He suggested that they spend a day in Branson, Missouri or Pigeon Forge, Tennessee, on the way to Florida so they could still leave on the 25th."

Jacob looked at her. "Did he say how much, yet?"

"No, he needs to know if you still want them to leave on the 25th, or wait till the 28th."

"Have him price it both ways and we will go from there."

"Alright, have you asked about them getting off work, yet?"

"I have asked Ms. James. She's good with mom, and she even wants to help with the party. But I haven't reached anyone for dad yet, but I'm working on it."

Brandon stretched and got up. Lindsey got up with him.

"See you later." Brandon told Jacob as he and Lindsey headed out of the dining hall.

"I've been thinking about what you said last night about the music classes," Brandon talked as they went through the front door. "Would you help me look for some schools?"

Lindsey lit up. "I would love to!"

Brandon smiled. He loved to see her happy. He really wanted to ask about the other comment she made, but didn't want to spoil her happiness. So he kept quiet.

They parted at the parking lot. Lindsey headed for the campground. She liked working there; she always met lots of people. John was the other Ranger working there today. He gave her a list of sites to check on as she walked in; she turned and walked back out. The morning had been cool, but it was already getting pretty warm. She headed down to the first site on the list; 18 wasn't far at all. She could hear a dog barking before she got there. A man was trying to get a tent up and a woman was barking orders at him. She and the dog seemed to be competing on who could be the loudest.

"Can I help you with that?" Lindsey asked the man.

"He can do it fine by himself!" The woman smarted off.

Lindsey smiled at the man who had a plea for help in his eyes. Several people walked by and glared at the lady who was still barking orders. Lindsey walked over and started helping the man, anyway. The woman glared at her.

"I said he could do it himself; he doesn't need you to help him."

The man looked at her.

"What kind of dog is that? Man, it's very cute."

"It's a Pomeranian; she is a pure bred that has won more dog shows than most dogs her age."

The man and Lindsey managed to get the tent up as the woman went on and on about her beloved dog. How well trained it was, and how she kept it groomed, and all the time she spent keeping it cleaned, and so on and so forth.

"Well, it looks like she was right. You didn't need my help after all," she told the man as he put the last pole in. He gave her a smile of thanks.

"I told you he didn't," the woman said.

Lindsey turned to the woman. "I am sure glad your dog is so well groomed and trained. The kids love dogs, maybe you could put on a show for some of the kids."

The woman smirked. "I don't know, I will have to think about it."

Lindsey waved to the man, "You all have a great stay." Lindsey felt sorry for the people in the site next to them as she heard the woman and dog both start back up.

Twenty-two was the next on the list. Two teenagers sat on the picnic table watching as an older couple fought with a tent. Lindsey dropped down on the picnic table beside the boy, who was dressed in all black. He looked up at her and pulled out one of his ear buds.

"You would think they would know how to do that," the boy said.

"So, what are you listening to?" She asked.

He looked up at her, "Paramore," was all he said.

"Hey, they're good; I like Decode."

The guy gave her a half smile.

"I really like Fireflight and Flyleaf," Lindsey added.

"Flyleaf, I like; never heard of Fireflight."

She smiled at the boy. "I'll tell you what," she pulled her iPod out of her pocket. "You help me help them get the tent up, and I will let you listen to them and some of the other great music I have on here."

He looked at her.

"Blackmail," he said.

"Whatever works." She smiled back at him.

"Alright," he said and got up. "Let's do this."

The younger girl that sat there with him got up, also. "Can I help, too?"

Lindsey smiled at her. "Sure." With everyone helping, the tent went right up.

"I have all kinds of music on there. But check out the playlist that says girls; I think you will like most of them." He took it and put the buds in his ears and started scrolling down the list.

The older lady thanked her and she left.

She went by three more sites; most of them were doing well, and didn't really need help.

"Lindsey?" Her radio crackled.

"You have a couple of packages at the front desk when you make it back to the Inn." Her guitar must be in.

"Thanks," she replied.

John was checking in a car when she made it back to the shack. She waited for him to finish.

"You're going to get a bunch of complaints today. Site 18 has a dog, and I don't know which was barking louder, the woman or the dog." They both laughed. The rest of the morning went by pretty smoothly, except for the line of complaints mounting against site 18.

Brandon brought them lunch today.

"Hey, would you do me a favor?" She asked him.

"Sure."

"I have a couple of packages at the front desk. Would you get them and take them to my cabin?"

He smiled. "Packages? Anything good?"

She just smiled. "I'll let you know once I see for myself."

"I'll need your key."

"It's unlocked; there isn't anything in there good enough to steal, so I never lock it."

"What about after I put the packages in?"

"Just leave it unlocked."

Brandon took the empty trays and headed back to the Inn. Lindsey went back to helping check in cars and John went and checked out a few sites.

"Lindsey, this is Paige at the front desk. Brandon says he is to pick up your packages, is this correct?"

"Sorry, Paige, I should have called you. Yes, please let him have them."

"Ok, will do."

Lindsey checked 30 cars in over two hours. Most of the campsites were full by five p.m., and by 8:30, she was turning people away. She had a list of other campgrounds in the area, and was telling people to try them.

When the gates closed at nine o'clock, she found herself sort of wound up, instead of tired. She wanted to get to the cabin and check out the guitar. Lindsey ordered a sandwich at the coffee shop at the Inn, and headed to the cabin. The two packages were on her bed. One was big, and one was small. She opened the guitar; it was in a hard case. She laid back the lid; it had great black sides trimmed in silver, with a mingled red and black front. She opened the smaller package and found a tuner, picks, a strap, extra strings, a cloth and oil. She grabbed her phone and sent Keeps a "Thanks, it's perfect." She had it tuned in just a few minutes; it had a large body, and the sound was full and deep. She sat it on the bed and ate and showered quickly. Lindsey sat at the table and played. She closed her eyes and sang as she played.

"Play with your feelings; music isn't all about notes, it's a feeling," she could hear the man she called Mike, that taught her guitar, saying in her head. She had had a different teacher for each instrument she had learned, five in all: piano, guitar, cello, violin, and drums. Each teacher was passionate about their music. It had made learning difficult because taught differently and felt differently about music. She was also given voice lessons; she had thought they were even harder than the music she learned to play. She never did please that teacher. His music wasn't in her vocal range, and he did eventually give in some, but was never really happy with her.

Brandon wondered why Lindsey had not come to dinner. He had even checked to see if she was playing the piano, but she wasn't there, either. He then remembered the packages he had taken to her cabin earlier and figured she must have liked what she had received. His curiosity got the better of him as he got to the cabins and so he walked down to hers. As he reached the porch he could hear music. He figured she had the radio on till he glanced in the window as he got to the door. She was sitting and playing. He didn't knock, he just slowly turned the knob and opened the door and listened. He stood staring at her. Lindsey looked up to find him standing with the door open staring at her.

"Wow, you can play guitar and sing, too. What else can you do?"

She smiled at him. "Shut the door; I really don't want bugs in here."

He closed it behind him. He pulled out the other chair and sat down. She played softly. He watched in amazement. Brandon sat looking at her, his head filling with thoughts. Why was she here? She had talent. The Ranger story was starting not to fit. The last thing she said the other night came back to his head. "My life is not my own." It echoed in his head. Who was she? Maybe she was in some kind of witness protection or something. She played and sang better than anyone he had ever heard. It seemed so natural to her. No wonder she thought of music the way she did.

"Music is so much more than just notes. It's a feeling you get while you play, the calmness of a day or the craziness of it," she continued to play as she talked, "Music can turn a bad day into a good one. Or it can make a night passionate." As she talked about each feeling, the music changed and matched what she talked about. "It tells a story, what it is, is up to you. It can tell the story of anger, confusion, excitement, love; it can turn an ordinary night into one of passion." She stopped and opened her eyes and looked at him. He was staring at her. She got up and handed him the guitar. "Tell me a story, Brandon."

"I don't think . . ."

She stopped him.

"Don't think, just play."

He took the guitar and sat there a minute.

"I don't know what to play."

"What is your favorite thing to play?"

"I play lead and its hard music, not soft."

She smiled at him. "Ok, play your favorite riff, but slow it down, make it smooth. Play it note by note, feel each note."

Brandon played a few notes slowly.

"Feel what you play, make your own beat."

"Maybe I'm not cut out for music." He struggled to play it slowly.

She laughed. "You have just played garage music; you haven't been taught to feel it, yet. That's what the classes are for. They will show you how to take what you know and harness it into so much more than just fast beats and lead riffs."

He handed the guitar back to her. "Looks like I have a lot of learning to do."

"But are you willing?" She asked.

He smiled at her. "I think so."

"Good." She took the guitar from his hands.

"Are you good at everything?" He asked.

"Only the things I was taught. Failure wasn't an option."

He looked up her. "What else do you know?"

"About what?" She asked as she put the guitar in its case.

"You said you spent summers in the Orient learning the martial arts."

She put the case in her closet. "I did. I have four black belts, and a master rank in two others that don't use belts, if that was what you were asking."

He smiled. "Wow! What else?"

"Like what?" She sat down on the edge of her bed.

"You said you took dance."

"Yes, I took dance."

"And you're good at that, too?"

She smiled. "Take me dancing sometime, and you'll find out."

He turned a little red in the face. "Maybe I will."

She got up and walked over to where he was still sitting. Lindsey stopped in front of him so he had to look up at her. "I don't like talking about me. I am nothing special. I had a rough childhood. Well, really, no childhood, just work and classes. So, I would rather forget about that for now, ok?"

Lindsey had thought how true that was. She didn't ever remember playing; she was always in some learning environment. Or, whatever they wanted to call it.

Brandon looked up at Lindsey as she stood in front of him. Her eyes were so beautiful. He wanted nothing more than to pull her into his arms. As he stood up in front of her, his heart raced.

"I better get going."

She smiled at him, he was so handsome. Those dark eyes and that long hair. Lindsey didn't move from in front of him, so he had to side step her to get to the door. He opened the door and looked back at her.

"Have a good week. Jacob and I will be heading out about nine in the morning and won't be back till Friday afternoon."

Lindsey walked over, took his arm and pulled him down enough to kiss him on the cheek. "Be safe, Brandon." He smiled at her, then left.

Lindsey leaned on the door and watched him walk up to Jacobs's cabin and go in. Her heart was pumping pretty hard. She closed the door and climbed into the bed. Her thoughts were all of Brandon. This was insane; her heart was pounding as if she had run a mile. She finally did a few breathing exercises to calm down and go to sleep.

CHAPTER 4

New Ideas

LINDSEY WOKE AT three a.m., all hot and sweaty. The dream she had been having about Brandon was quite intense. Her heart was still racing. She got up and went to the shower. She tried to get her thoughts elsewhere, but she just kept seeing the two of them kissing.

Liquid Gold came to her thoughts. It was a game she had been through in one of her many classes. This one just happens to be in sex education. She smiled to herself; maybe she could teach him how to play. She laughed out loud, then lay back down on the bed; it was only 3:30 a.m.

After ten minutes she got up and got dressed. There was no sleeping anymore. She went outside in the dark; sat on the porch. A noise to her right caught her attention. Brandon emerged from Jacobs's cabin. Lindsey slid off the porch and into the dark shadows beside her cabin. She went around the cabin and up between John's and Jacob's. She stopped just inside the darkest shadow. Brandon sat on the edge of the porch and looked at the row of cabins.

"It's going to be a long day," he said out loud to himself.

Lindsey stood in the shadow watching him.

Brandon sat on the porch step of the cabin. He had awakened with images of Lindsey, and had to get up. If he would have been sleeping alone it would have been fine, but since he was sharing a bed with Jacob it was just best to get out of there. He also needed to calm himself down before he and Lindsey ran. So he had taken a shower and now sat in the cool air. As he sat there he could swear he was being watched, every hair on the back of his neck stood on end. He looked around, but saw no one; he even listened closely, but heard nothing. He couldn't shake the feeling and looked back between the cabins once more, but saw nothing.

She smiled; he must feel her watching him.

"Am I freaking you out?" Lindsey suddenly said. Brandon jumped. Lindsey stepped out into the light.

"I knew there had to be someone there; I could just feel it," he said as she sat down beside him.

"What are you doing up this early?" she asked him.

"Couldn't sleep. You?"

"Me, either." They both laughed. Lindsey had sat close enough that their legs barely touched.

"So what kept you awake?" He asked.

She smiled. "Honestly . . . you did."

He looked over at her. "Feeling's mutual," he said. His heart began to race when she said he had kept her up.

Lindsey looked up at him, why did he affect her so? Her heart had started to race when he admitted that she was the reason he now sat outside.

"It's going to be a long week?" He said as he shook his head.

"Yeah." She smiled at him, she hadn't noticed until then his hair was wet like hers. She laughed.

"What?" he asked her.

"Get a shower?"

His face turned red. "Had to. You?" He touched her wet hair.

"Yeah," she leaned over and bumped him. Her mind raced; she didn't want to give him the wrong impression. She may have liked him, but that was where it was going to stop. There was not going to be any sex. She had strong obligations and feelings on the subject of sex.

They sat there in silence as the sky started to lighten up. "I need to say something here," Lindsey finally spoke. He looked at her. "When I told you I was waiting for mister right, I wanted you to know that I meant I was waiting for marriage. And regardless of how I feel, that vow stands."

He smiled at her. "My turn. I told you I had strong views on sex and marriage; well, I guess you and I have vows in common."

Lindsey laughed and laid her head on his shoulder. "Doesn't that just beat all, we are probably the only two virgins in a hundred miles." They both burst out in laughter.

"Sure takes the stress out of a relationship though, doesn't it?" He asked.

"You mean you actually have had one? If you aren't going to put out, most men don't want you. Well, unless they want to be the one that makes you break your vow."

"Yeah, there are those. Dated a girl for about six months before; I won, she lost."

Lindsey got up. "Let's go run off some of these hormones; I think my heart rate is a steady 110 already."

He laughed and got up. "Let me grab my shoes." He went in the cabin for a few seconds and came back with shoes and socks in hand. Lindsey got up and started stretching.

Brandon found himself watching her instead of putting on his shoes. She looked up to find him watching her.

"Put your shoes on."

He smiled.

They took off up the hill as soon as his shoes were tied. They ran six miles today. Brandon was getting better at running, but he wasn't ready for running the eight miles, yet.

Jacob was coming out of the cabin as they came back down the hill. "I can't believe it. We are going to be hiking all day today, and you're out running," he told Brandon as he passed.

Brandon just smiled at him. "I'll be fine, running makes the walking easier."

Brandon headed into Jacob's cabin and Lindsey headed toward her cabin. She paused as she opened her door. She looked over at Jacob's cabin. Brandon was standing there staring at her. Lindsey took a deep breath when he walked off his porch and toward her. He stopped just inches in front of her.

"How do you feel about kissing before marriage?" he asked.

She answered with her lips on his. Her hands slid around his neck. His held her waist. Lindsey did not want the kiss to end, but knew it had to, and pulled away. Brandon was breathing just as hard as she was.

"Shower," was all he said as he turned and left.

Lindsey watched him as he went back up to Jacobs's cabin. Lindsey headed in as soon as he did. Oh crap! What had she just done? She was leaning on the door; why in the world had she just kissed him? This was not supposed to happen. Her first real off-grid rest, and she was going to ruin it by getting into a relationship. *We're just friend's*, she told herself. *Yes, I can do this, I can control this situation, I am an expert on controlling the situation., I have just made some friends and that's it, we are just friends.* She stripped and climbed in the shower. He was sitting on the porch when she came out.

"What time are you guys leaving?" She asked.

"We are meeting them at the Inn at nine a.m. So I have a couple of hours. You want to get some breakfast?"

They headed up to the Inn. John, Sam, Todd, and Jacob were eating at the corner table.

"Lindsey, I need to see you before you head out this morning," came over her radio.

"Sure thing, Wendy. Can it wait till after breakfast?"

"Yeah, that's fine," She and Brandon sat down at the table next to the others.

"You ready for Troop 54?" Sam asked Brandon as he sat down.

"Ready as I will ever be."

"Good," Sam said, "cause I think they're already here." She pointed out the window as a bus stopped and a bunch of girls started getting off. The group came into the dining hall and sat down for breakfast. There was already pointing and giggling going on.

"Looks like you're going to have a great time," Lindsey laughed.

"Any advice?" Brandon asked.

"Girls at that age are into two things: music and boys. Take an iPod and talk music with them; you have the hot boy thing already covered."

Brandon smiled and laughed. Sam laughed behind him.

"They don't need music, they are here to earn their wilderness badges," Jacob said.

Brandon rolled his eyes then went back to eating.

"Maybe we can get an early start," Jacob said as he got up and left the table.

"Jacob doesn't sound like he is going to be much fun." Lindsey looked at Brandon.

"He never is," he finished his eggs. "I better go get my gear together," Brandon said as he got up from the table.

Lindsey got up and put her napkin on her plate, "I'm done." The two of them left the room together. Lindsey helped Brandon gather all his stuff and walked him back to the top of the stairs.

"Have a good week," he told her.

"You, too," she touched his arm. He smiled down at her, and then walked away. Lindsey took a deep breath and headed over to talk to Wendy.

"I just wanted to remind you, you need to check out a rifle since you're going out on camping trails today," Wendy said as she entered the office.

"Thanks," Lindsey told her.

"Make sure you have your radio turned to the battery saving setting, too."

Lindsey always kept in on that, anyway.

"Anything else?" Lindsey asked.

"The four-wheeler isn't going to be back till noon, so you're going to have to stay one night out."

"No problem."

She left the office and headed for the campground. She would like to have her iPod back before she went out. She passed John at the shack. Site 22 was peaceful, the boy was sitting at the picnic table and the girl and her grandmother were cooking breakfast. Lindsey waved at the girl as she came up behind the boy. He turned and pulled out his ear buds.

"You have some awesome music on here," he said as she sat down beside him.

"Well, good, I am glad you found some you liked."

He handed her back her iPod. "I had to make a list of bands so I could look them up when I get home."

Lindsey smiled at the young man. "So are you guys doing some hiking today?"

The boy sighed. "I guess."

"You don't sound excited about it. You know nature is the best for inspiring music."

"How is that?" The boy asked.

"Are you serious? Ok, let's see, the bees and all the bugs furiously work to get hives built. Think of it as a fast hard guitar solo. Then you have the birds flying over head; they are the rhythm playing to match the bees' fury. The bass is the bear foraging. The drums are the beats of their hearts urgent to get it all done by winter. There is so much music in nature."

"I never thought of it that way."

Lindsey smiled. "When you're out today, at some point stop for a few minutes and listen to nature. See what she has to say, then find a song and listen to it real low so you can still hear the nature, find something that matches each beat. You will see that music and nature are partners."

He smiled at her. "Ok, I will."

Lindsey got up to leave. "You all have a good day; I'll come back in a couple of days to check on your nature experience."

The grandmother came up and walked with her as she left the site. "Thanks so much. Taylor didn't want to come, but I think he is starting to like it, thanks to you."

"You're more than welcome; you guys be safe today." With that, Lindsey and the lady parted ways.

Back at the Inn she went to the ready room for supplies; it had everything. She got a backpack, tent, first aid kit, compass, bedroll and map. She also checked out her rifle and darts, and picked up some food. The food was all vacuum-packed and sealed to keep from smelling. From there she headed to get her clothes packed up.

"Lindsey?" Her radio crackled on her side as she was rolling her clothes.

"We have a change of plans, the four-wheeler has a messed up boot and they won't let you take it, so you'll have to go on foot."

Lindsey smiled. "No problem." She could handle two nights of solitude; maybe it would help her get her head clear on a few issues. She put her iPod on charge and finished packing, then went back up to the Inn to pick up a few more packs of food. She would need to get going if she was on foot. After getting back to the cabin and finishing getting the pack all situated, she took her iPod off charge and headed out. The camping trails were about two miles from the Inn. Malcolm picked her up and took her to the trail head. She waved as he drove off.

Her map and compass were in the pocket on her pants, so as she walked she looked over the map. All the camping trails started out on the same trail, but parted after about three miles in. She could see a bunch of small footprints on the trail as she walked. Troop 54, she was sure.

Lindsey walked at a pretty good pace for several hours, wanting to get as far as she could the first afternoon. She snacked as she walked. Her mind was a series of thoughts, mainly on Brandon. What had ever possessed her to kiss him? So she was attracted to him, that didn't mean she had to kiss him. He was attracted to her, too, but what made it worse, they seemed to be like a couple of magnets pulling together. Lindsey didn't want to hurt him, so she needed to back off and not be kissing him; that would just complicate things. The fact that he was dedicated to no sex before marriage was going to work great. Now, if she could keep herself from kissing him, which she really wanted to do, things might work out ok. If . . . If was a big word. With all the training she had gone through over the years, she thought she was prepared for anything and everything. She was finding out she was wrong. She was not prepared at all for Brandon.

The day flew by as she walked. She watched birds and bees and all the things in nature that were going on around her. The sun started sliding down when she found a place for the night. She would have to hurry to get camp set up before it was dark. She cleared a place for the tent and got it set up. She really didn't need a fire so she got her bedroll and put it in the tent, then hung her backpack from a tree and lay down for the night. Her mind was still on Brandon. She would have to look on the internet and see if she couldn't find some good music schools nearby. Maybe one not so close; that way there would be some distance between them. Maybe down in L.A. or San Diego. She fell asleep thinking of classes he should take.

She woke before the sun was up. She could barely see, but she didn't mind and got up and rolled up her bedroll. She also got her pack from the tree and started taking down the tent. By the time the sun was up she was on the trail again. She ate as she walked.

About eight, her radio was crackling. "Wendy, I have a problem. Jacob is sick and I don't mean just a little, he is burning up with fever, and is throwing up." It was Brandon.

"Where are you, Brandon?" Wendy came back.

"We are out on mile 12 on C5."

Lindsey got her map and found where they were. If she cut across country, they were about six miles from her. Lindsey picked up her radio.

"Can I help? I am six miles away."

"Brandon, can you get him to Bull Rock? I can get a helicopter to meet you there, if you can. Lindsey, take off in their direction."

"I will have him there as soon as I can," Brandon answered Wendy.

Lindsey looked at the map; they would come up on Coyote Valley in two miles. Lindsey was already moving toward them at a good pace, wasting no time.

"Brandon, Coyote Valley is two miles up the trail; have the Troop meet me there."

"Ok," he answered.

Lindsey picked up the pace to a jog; she didn't like leaving the Troop alone. She could do a mile a minute at a full run for almost a full ten miles, but this was rough ground with lots of rocks and trees.

"Are you going to be ok to go the rest of the week with the troop, Lindsey?" Wendy asked.

She paused only long enough to answer. "Sure, no problem." She had already covered a half mile. If she pushed herself, she could cover a mile in eight to ten minutes, if the terrain wasn't bad. She was running a good pace, watching carefully as she took each step. She had to slow down when she came to a rocky area, but soon was able to pick the pace back up.

She came out on trail C5 at mile marker eleven. It had taken her over forty minutes. At mile twelve she found Jacob and Brandon's packs. She hooked Brandon's to hers and got the food out of Jacob's, then hung it in a tree.

"Wendy, I am hanging Jacob's pack in the tree at mile twelve."

"Ok, are you already there?" Wendy asked.

Lindsey smiled. "Yes."

"Did you run or what?"

Lindsey laughed. "No, not all the way." Lindsey was putting the food packs in hers when she noticed one of them. It didn't look right. It was a thing of trail mix that had been opened. She slid the slider over and looked down in the bag. It smelled like dried fruit, but there was another smell, too. She closed the bag.

"Wendy, I found a bag of trail mix in Jacob's pack. It is opened, so he must have eaten some of it, but I think it's rancid. He may have food poisoning."

"Roger that."

Lindsey dumped the mix out and pushed the bag back in Jacob's pack then lifted it into the tree. She took off down the trail to the meadow. Lindsey had heard the helicopter about twenty minutes ago, but had not seen it come back, yet.

"Jacob's on his way; I'm heading back towards the troop," the radio crackled as Lindsey came into the meadow. There were fifteen girls and two adults waiting there for her. The two adults stood up and came her way.

"Hey, I'm Lindsey," she stuck out her hand.

"This is my wife, Jessica, and I am Mike. Do you know how Jacob is?" The helicopter flew over them.

"There he goes now. We know he is on his way to the hospital. But that's all we know for now."

"He was really sick," Jessica said.

"He'll be ok, he's tough." Lindsey gave them a reassuring smile. "We better get moving, or we are not going to make it by Friday." Lindsey turned to all the girls, "Let's get moving, gals." They didn't look too enthusiastic.

"Where's Brandon?" One of the girls asked.

"He'll catch up, he's Indian you know; he will track us down in no time." The girl smiled and picked up her pack.

"You two are our caboose, we don't want to lose anyone," Lindsey told Mike and Jessica. "Brandon, we are heading up the trail." Lindsey headed toward the trail on the other side of the meadow. "Well, come on, we have some catching up to do."

The girls all dropped their heads. They didn't look like they were having too much fun. "So, what had Jacob been showing you guys?" Lindsey asked as they walked. No one really answered. "If I know Jacob, he has been showing you something. So what has it been? Plants, animals, what?"

One girl finally spoke up. "He showed us a few kinds of Poison Ivy and fungus." Lindsey noticed the resemblance between this girl and Mike; she had to be his daughter.

"So if you guys are not really into this, what are you into? Music? Guys?" A few heads came up. "So who is the hottest guy in Hollywood?"

"Rob Pattinson." One of the girls piped in.

"No, Matthew McConaughey," said another. They were all adding their favorite star to the list of names. Lindsey would add a, "Oh, he's cute" or "Yeah, I agree," to the names as they said them. Lindsey pointed out a plant as they passed.

"You see that plant? It's Poison Ivy, you better know that cause you sure wouldn't want to bring Rob Pattinson up here and give him Poison Ivy while you were trying to kiss him." The girls all giggled.

"It has three leaves?" One of the girls asked.

"Yep," Lindsey answered. "Although, you see this plant? Most people call it Touch Me Not; you can always tell it by its little orange flowers. If you make a paste out of its leaves, it's supposed to help soothe Poison Ivy so if he does get it, you can rub this all over him." All the girls stopped and looked at the plant. Mike and Jessica smiled at Lindsey. Lindsey just grinned back at them and winked.

The troop moved on up the trail as Lindsey pointed out several kinds of trees and things, all with some kind of reference to one of the guys the girls had named. Lindsey kept the pace pretty fast most of the time. As they went along, the girls talked movies and guys and Lindsey added her little remarks and tree lessons and plant lessons along the way.

About two, they stopped for lunch and a break. The girls all sat around Lindsey and they talked music; about their favorite singers and bands. Brandon came into their talk soon. All the girls thought he was hot. Lindsey joined in and agreed with them. Lindsey only took a fifteen minute break and had them up and getting ready to leave when Brandon came up the trail from behind them. He was shirtless. Lindsey turned her back to him and gave the girls an "Oh, my gosh, he is so hot!" look. All the girls burst out in laughter. Lindsey could smell him before he got to her. His shirt was wrapped up on a ball in his pants pocket; he had evidently washed it out in a stream because his pants were soaked, but he still smelled like vomit.

Lindsey wrinkled up her nose at him. "You stink!"

He laughed, "I know, sorry."

Lindsey handed him her canteen and the rest of her jerky. He reached for his pack.

"You don't want to touch this; you will have it stinking, too. Let me carry it till we set up camp, then you can wash off in a stream or something."

Brandon smiled.

"At least let me get a shirt."

Lindsey smiled at the girls.

"You better wait till you wash off," she winked towards the girls. They all smiled at her. He looked at her, then at the girls. He chuckled.

"We better get going then."

The girls all popped up and followed Brandon as he headed for the trail. A couple of the girls pointed out a few things to Brandon as they went. He smiled back at Lindsey, and praised them for learning what the plants were. Lindsey fell to the back with Mike and Jessica.

"Sneaky, aren't we?" Jessica said.

"Anything to get them to learn." All three of them laughed as they watched all the girls following Brandon's every word.

They set up camp about five beside a stream. Lindsey got Brandon a set of clothes and some biodegradable soap and made him head to the stream first thing, while the girls set up camp. He came back in 30 minutes and hung his wet uniform on some low branches to dry. His hair was wet and dripping so he had left his shirt off so it wouldn't get soaked.

He walked up to Lindsey as she was helping the girls get the fire going. "Can I talk to you a moment?"

Lindsey stood up and followed him over to the side of the camp. "You realize Jacob was carrying our tent?"

Lindsey smiled. "You can sleep with me, I don't care."

"I knew that, but I wondered if it sent the girls the wrong message?"

Lindsey looked over at them. She hadn't thought of that. "I'll see if Jessica will swap you places." He smiled at her as Lindsey stepped close to him.

"You smell better."

He laughed and picked up his radio.

"Hey, Wendy, how's Jacob?"

"Lindsey was right about the food poisoning. He's going to be fine, but it is going to take him a couple of weeks to recover."

"Thanks. What food poisoning?" Brandon asked Lindsey.

Lindsey told him about the rancid trail mix she found in his bag. Then Lindsey went to talk to Jessica, as Brandon went and sat down by the fire with the girls. Jessica agreed to switch tents with

Brandon for the rest of the trip. Brandon's shirt finally dried, and he put it on.

Brandon told old Indian legends to the girls as they sat around the fire. Lindsey sat and listened with the girls. Soon most of them were about half asleep so Lindsey sent them to bed. A few were still talking to Brandon when she got her stuff and headed downstream. She didn't have enough clothes to change, but she did want to get herself clean even if her clothes weren't. She stopped just around the bend in the stream and stripped. The water was cool and felt wonderful. She washed her hair and her undergarments; she would wash them every night if she had to. She sat down on a rock to drip dry a few minutes. She was suddenly aware she wasn't alone. She looked around and didn't see anyone, but it was obvious to her that someone was there. She had been trained well, and she could always feel when things were out of place. She scanned the tree line around her. They were across the stream from her. She sat still and waited. "You might as well come out here instead of lurking in the shadows," she finally said.

Brandon stepped out of the tree line. "Sorry, I wasn't trying to find you; I was looking for a place to use the restroom."

Lindsey smiled and stood up. She didn't hide anything. His eyes raced down her as she walked across the stream to where he was. Lindsey stood a foot from him now. She smiled at him. "Looks like you need a cold shower."

She reached over to her clothes that were sitting on the rock close to him and started getting dressed.

"Thanks to you I do," he told her.

"Serves you right for hiding in the trees and watching me."

"I wasn't hiding in the trees watching."

She was nearly dressed now. "Are you sure?"

"I was looking for a place to use the restroom; I didn't mean to come up on you taking a bath."

"So why didn't you just go on then?" She smiled at him.

"I . . . well . . . ok, point taken," he said, "but you didn't have to come over here like that."

She laughed. "This is where my clothes were."

He reached out and touched her check. His hand was trembling as it touched her face. Lindsey stepped close to him. Her head turned till her cheek was in the palm of his hand. She heard his breathing speed up. Her heart was already racing. His lips found hers. She suddenly found herself pushed up against a tree; his hands were holding her there. Her hands were in his hair. Lindsey loved the way it felt. His kiss was full of need and want, and she met it with her own need and want. His shirt was on, but still open in the front. She slid her hands over his smooth chest. Lindsey's head was spinning; never had she wanted anyone so badly. Brandon molded their bodies together against the tree. He kissed down her throat. He lifted his head, his eyes met hers.

"What are you doing to me, woman?" He said, all ragged-voiced.

"I am the one pinned, not you."

He pulled back from her.

"You didn't stop me."

"No . . . no, I didn't." She looked down; this was going to be harder than she thought.

He sighed and backed away from her. "We are going to have to do better, or we are both going to break our vows before the summer's over."

Lindsey moved away from the tree, and picked up her shoes and socks. "You're right." They walked back towards the camp. "I shouldn't have taunted you like that; I'm sorry."

He laughed, "I should have not stuck around long enough for you to taunt me." They stopped before the camp came into sight.

"I can't go back, quite yet," he said.

He smiled at her, then leaned over and kissed her hair. "I'll be back in a bit." With that, he turned and vanished into the darkness.

Her phone vibrated in her pocket. She pulled it out slowly and looked at the message. "Watch it," was all it said.

Keeps couldn't believe that Lindsey was letting herself get so close to this Brandon. She knew better than that. Maybe she was just playing with him. Yes, that had to be it. He convinced himself she was just playing him, she would never compromise herself. She would never put herself in jeopardy like that. He laughed. What was he thinking? She was the Maker. Man, she was good!

The camp was quiet; Jessica was asleep when Lindsey crawled into the tent beside her. Lindsey's head and heart were both racing. Why had she let this get so far? She had never come across anyone like him. She wanted to feel him, touch him, give every inch of herself to him. What was wrong with her? She knew better, this was impossible. She would be leaving in a year; earlier if she didn't watch herself. She was going to have to keep her distance from him from now on. Keep her head clear.

The Troop was up and off early. They still needed to make up a little time. The morning came and went quickly. Lindsey kept the girls talking about movies and what scenes had a certain tree or area of the park in it. Stuff that would keep their attention now that Brandon was fully dressed. Brandon added things as they went along. Lunch came as they came to a set of bluffs. So they stopped and had lunch there. Lindsey sat out on the edge watching off in the distance.

Brandon sat down beside her.

"Where are you?"

She turned to look at him; all the girls were sitting close by and were watching them.

"Enjoying the view. I love most everything about nature, the views, the smells, and the quietness of it all."

"So, what don't you like about it?" He asked.

"I hate the fact that we don't take care of it as well as we should. I mean we don't need to go crazy and all, but we do need to take care of what we have left, or there won't be any for the next generation."

Brandon knew she was talking for the girls. He let their legs touch as he sat there. She moved her leg to part them again. Lindsey glanced at him, then looked away. In those few seconds, her eyes spoke volumes without a word being said.

But what he saw was not what he expected to see. He saw regret and worry. What was she worried about, breaking her vow? He was not going to let that happen. He was going to keep his vow if it killed him, which he might have to do, if he couldn't control himself better. He looked back at her. What was the regret for? Why would she regret anything? Nothing happened.

The girls started talking about what they could do to help take care of the wildlife and nature where they lived. Mike and Jessica helped them with ideas on what they could do. By the time the lunch was over, they had big plans on cleaning up the neighborhood park. Brandon led the conversation, but Mike and Jessica were now talking with the girls on things they could do and how they could help out. The girls had lots of ideas.

The rest of the afternoon passed quickly as they discussed their plans. By eight they had made up the time lost when Jacob was sick and had their campsite set. Lindsey sat listening to Brandon as he talked to the girls about some conservation ideas, and how to get their community involved.

Marcy, one of the girls, came over and sat down beside her. "So what's up with Brandon today?" She said very quietly so only Lindsey could hear. Lindsey looked at the girl. "Surely you have noticed he has watched you all day."

Lindsey leaned over. "I have noticed. I was wondering if I was wearing something wrong. I have only been a Ranger for two weeks. I thought I might be wearing the uniform wrong or something."

The girl laughed. "Yeah, right!" She bumped Lindsey with her shoulder. Lindsey smiled at her and giggled.

Bedtime came and everyone turned in. Lindsey made a wide track around the campsite just to make sure everything had been taken care of properly, and then went out for a pit stop. When she got back Brandon was sitting at the fire by himself. Lindsey tried to walk by him, but he caught her by the arm.

"Everything ok?" He asked; she had avoided him all day.

"Yeah, fine." She smiled at him.

"You don't lie very well," he told her as he got up and stood in front of her.

Lindsey looked up at him. She was going to have to end this before it got any farther, before . . . Brandon gently kissed her on the lips. She almost came unglued.

"Goodnight, Lindsey," he told her. She stepped in close to him and locked her arms around his waist. He unlocked her arms and took her by the hand and led her away from the camp. When they were far enough out, he turned her around to face him.

"What is it? I can see it in your eyes." He could see the tears threatening to fall from her eyes; they looked so glassy.

"What is it?" He pulled her into his arms and held her tight.

"I wish this could work, but it can't. I wish that I wouldn't have to leave, but I will. And I really wish I didn't care for you, but I do. So this makes this that much harder."

Brandon pulled her away from him so he could look her in the eyes.

"It's ok, Lindsey, I am scared, too. I have never come across feelings like these before, either."

Lindsey stepped away from him.

"That's not it, Brandon; this really can go no farther. Haven't you been listening? I'll be leaving in a year and I don't want to hurt you."

Brandon just looked at her. "Where are you going?" He said it so calmly.

"I don't know, but I know it won't be here. And every second we get closer, the harder it will be for me to leave and it's something I have no control over." Lindsey turned to leave.

"I love you, Lindsey Jacobs."

She stopped in her tracks. She turned to face him; the moon glistened off the tears that now fell from her eyes.

"Oh, don't say that." He stepped close to her again and reached up to wipe the tears from her face, but she pulled back away from his touch. "Don't ever say that!"

"Why not? I would have never believed I could fall in love with someone in a week, but I had never met anyone like you before, either." He walked up and tried to put his arms around her; she stepped back away from him once again. "Why are you so sad about that, is there someone else?"

"No, Brandon there is no one else. But this is not going to happen."

"I think it already has."

"You have no clue what you're saying; you have no clue what danger you're putting yourself in."

"Danger?" He looked at her, "What danger is there in loving someone? Well, besides losing themselves." He smiled, but she didn't.

She looked up at him. "You really have no clue." How could he?

"Clue about what? I know that I am in love with you."

"My life is not my own, Brandon; I'm sorry." She turned to leave again.

He grabbed her arm. This was the second time she had said her life wasn't her own. "I just want to love you, Lindsey; please let me just love you."

"Love is not love without the hope of a future, and there is no future for us, none whatsoever." He pulled her back and looked into her eyes. She really believed they had no future. That was clear, you could see it in her eyes, hear it in her voice. She was very serious. Who controlled her life, if not her? Was she in trouble with the law and on the run? Maybe she was in witness protection. All kinds of things flew through Brandon's head.

Lindsey could see he was really thinking about what she said. Did it sound as crazy to him as it did to her? How could you love someone without the hope of a future? Isn't that what it was all about? The hope that one day you could get married and have kids and a life. She had no hope of that; she was a tool used in a game of war.

He looked at her; she was staring off into space just over his shoulder.

"Tell me one thing? Do you love me?"

Her heart was screaming, Yes! Her head was saying, No!

Say no, Lindsey. Keeps was listening for her next words.

"Your eyes say, yes, but you're having a problem with that. Why?"

"You could never understand."

"Try me."

Keeps started typing; he had to do something. She evidently did have feelings for this guy. But he could not let her jeopardize herself.

Her phone beeped in her back pocket. She pulled the phone out and read the text. "You're treading on thin ice." She held the phone for him to read.

"Who is that?"

The phone beeped again.

"Keep it up, and I will have to pull you out. End it now!"

She let him read it once more.

"Pull you out?"

Crap! She had crossed a line and he was going to cross it right along with her. Keeps started typing again.

"Lindsey, you have crossed a line here. What are your intentions? Be honest, or I will pull you out within the hour." Lindsey read the message, then let Brandon read it.

"I don't know," she said as she looked at Brandon. "I . . ." tears resurfaced and slid down her cheeks.

Keeps had to make a decision here. Should he pull her out? His job was to keep her safe. Did it mean breaking her heart? He began to type again.

Her phone beeped again. Brandon looked up at her as she read the message. Who was she? Who was on the other end of the phone? Could loving him really put her in danger?

The message read, "What some people don't know won't hurt them, but some things have to remain hidden and be said without words. But your vow must remain intact. Choose now, Lindsey!"

Lindsey read the message and then let Brandon read it. Could he love her without knowing what was truly going on? Lindsey slowly reached out for Brandon and pulled him close to her; she wasn't sure what he was thinking.

He looked down at her. Who was this woman? Did it matter to him? Lindsey was looking at him. His heart raced. Her lips touched his. Brandon wanted her, but at what cost to her? Should he kiss her or not? Lindsey pulled back and let him go. The hurt in her eyes was unbearable. He pulled her back to him and held her. He could feel her tears soaking into his shirt. He lifted her head with his hand. His eyes locked with hers.

"I don't understand," he told her.

"And you never will," she told him, "but can you live with it or not."

He rubbed the tears from her eyes. The only thing he knew at this point was that he loved her. What difference did any of the rest matter?

"Stay," he told her.

Her phone beeped in response to his answer. "You now hold three lives in your hand, Lindsey. Never speak of it again."

Lindsey looked at Brandon, then to her phone. She had never thought of the danger she had put Keeps in as well. She looked up at Brandon. Had she made the right choice?

"We better get back to camp," she told him.

He looked at her. "Ok."

They walked back to camp without a word.

"Goodnight," she told him then she turned to her tent. She crawled in beside Jessica. She pulled out her phone and began typing. "I owe you."

A message came back, "My job is to keep you safe. But I cannot guarantee his safety or ours if they find out."

Brandon lay awake in the tent beside Mike thinking about Lindsey, and about the person on the phone. What had really happened? Were they really in danger? Did he really want her that badly that he was willing to, what? Keep a secret, put her in danger, and love her with all he had. His heart won out over the questions that plagued him. Exhaustion took over, and he fell asleep.

A sound woke Lindsey. It was still dark. The first thought was for Brandon, had they found out? Were they here? What had she done? She very quietly made a small hole in the zipper. The moon was bright. There was something large over by one of the tents. Lindsey let out a small sigh of relief when she realized it was a bear. She smiled to herself how bad it was that she was more afraid of what they would do than the huge bear that was right outside. Lindsey reached over and pulled a bottle of spray from her bag. She gently held it out the tent and gave it a small spray. The immediate smell of skunk filled the area, but it wasn't strong. The bear only needed to catch the scent. She got her rifle and darts ready just in case; she hoped none of the girls woke and screamed and frightened the bear. She loaded a dart and took aim. She waited. If the girls remained asleep, maybe he would leave. A noise brought her attention to another tent. A cub was playing with the string on the tent. Crap, a mother bear and cub; nothing more dangerous. The bear sniffed at the air, she turned, made a couple of grumps and walked toward the edge of the camp. The cub followed and they walked back into the woods. Lindsey crawled out of her tent. She slowly followed after the bear to make sure she left the area. The bear wasn't too far ahead of her, so she checked the wind; it was calm. She hoped she was staying back far enough that the bear would not catch her scent. The bear and cub headed up toward High Rock. She followed them about two miles then turned around and headed back to camp.

The sun was coming up as she came back into the camp. Most everyone was up. Lindsey quickly deposited her rifle by a tree; safety on, since it was loaded. No one seemed to notice as she talked to the girls. No one, until she saw Brandon looking at her. Had he seen her or did he still want questions answered from last night? Lindsey walked to her tent and started rolling up and packing her stuff.

"Where were you?" Brandon said quietly behind her.

She turned to him. "Bear and cub."

He glanced around the campsite. "Here?"

"Yeah, about an hour ago; we were lucky no one woke."

"Where are they now?"

"Heading towards High Rock."

Brandon looked at her, his mood changed before her eyes. Lindsey saw worry and fear in his eyes.

"I can take care of myself."

"It was the girls I was worried about," he told her, then walked off.

84

Lindsey just stood there for a moment. She hadn't expected that. Was he mad at her, had he changed his mind? Should she leave?

Lindsey gathered her rifle as they headed out of camp. She hung behind a second to unload it, and then caught right back up with the group. Today the girls got to learn to identify animal tracks, starting with a bear. Brandon said it looked like it had been through a couple of days ago to keep the girls calm since it was right outside the camp. The morning went by with raccoon, possum, squirrel, deer, wolf, and skunk tracks. They discussed their habits and why they would ever enter a human camp.

"Say, for instance someone didn't dispose of their food correctly or had some in their tents," Brandon was sure to add on the bear subject.

Today they would have to cross the river on a suspension bridge. Brandon was hoping to reach it about time to camp so they could catch fish tonight for supper. It would be a good lesson for them.

Before noon, Lindsey heard a couple of far-off gunshots. The one thing she knew was a gunshot when she heard one. The girls were all chattering and no one else seemed to notice. Lindsey caught up with Brandon long enough to shut his radio off without anyone noticing. Then she fell to the back, and then behind a bit.

"Wendy, I heard gunshots. Has anyone fired?"

"No one has reported any firing."

"All right, thanks. I think I might go check it out. We came across some bear tracks this morning, and that's the direction of the shots."

"OK, stay safe."

Lindsey caught back up with the group and turned Brandon's radio back on. They were stopped, looking at some tracks. The girls were trying to figure out what kind they were. Lindsey pulled Brandon aside.

"I am heading up toward High Rock; I'll be back by camp time."

He looked at her. "What's up? I saw you shut my radio off."

"I heard a couple of gunshots toward there. Just want to check to make sure no one is hurt."

"Are you sure they were gunshots?"

She just looked at him a second. "Yes, I know a gunshot when I hear one; you were busy talking with the girls."

She seemed irritated to him, he took hold of her arm. "Be safe, call if you need me."

"I can handle myself."

Lindsey turned and headed into the woods. Brandon went back to the girls who had now decided they were raccoon tracks. He looked at where she had entered the woods. Did the gunshots have to do with the person on the phone?

Lindsey moved along at a quick pace, picking up more speed as she went. She was soon running toward High Rock; it was about eight miles from where they camped, and they had come several miles since they left camp. Lindsey had a bad feeling and the closer she got the worse it got. Her pack was heavy. She stopped and lifted it into a tree. She took her knife and gun and took off at a dead run. She came out at High Rock 30 minutes later. She had stopped only twice. It was quiet; she walked around the edge of the tree line. She watched the ground carefully; if anyone or anything was hurt they would be bleeding.

She came across blood on the upper side. It was the bear; it was hurt. She found tracks and followed the blood. She saw no sign of the cub. The bear was heading higher into the mountains. She followed; the bear was bleeding worse now. She stopped in her tracks as she came up on a sickening sight. She slid behind a tree to hide. She turned her radio off; that's all she would need for it to give her away. She peeked around the tree. Four men stood over the bear carcass, they were skinning it. The cub was tied to a tree not far away. She was furious. Lindsey backed away from the area very quietly till she was out of earshot and flipped on her radio.

"Wendy, I am just north of High Rock. There are four poachers skinning a bear a mile from me. They also have a cub."

"I'll call in a chopper."

"How long?"

"At least thirty minutes."

"They are about done now; they will be long gone by then. I'll follow them at a distance and keep you up on their location."

"Don't put yourself in danger," it was Brandon this time.

"I won't. Lindsey out." She shut her radio back off. She quickly headed back to where the men were. They were already packed up and heading out, the cub in tow.

"We need to get out of here. With you shooting at this one, I am sure the shots have been reported by now." The older looking of the four was talking to the youngest looking guy.

"I didn't know she had a cub, and she went nuts. There was nothing I could do unless you wanted me to die."

"You'll need stitches in that; we better head out pretty quickly," one of the other men said.

Lindsey noticed the bloody sleeve on the young man. One of the other men came up and patted the man on the shoulder.

"Survived a bear attack, and can't tell a soul about it," he laughed.

They were moving at a quick pace. The oldest man was carrying two pelts; they looked like wolf. One of the others had the bear skin, and one carried a couple of rifles. The youngest guy who was bleeding and had his arm wrapped, was pulling along the cub which was now whining and crying.

"Come on!" He was jerking it along.

Lindsey took her knife and sent it sailing. It sliced through the rope holding the cub. It hit the tree with a hard thump and stuck out.

The cub ran. "Someone's out there." The young man reached over and pulled the knife from the tree.

"Not a wise move, friend," the older guy said loudly. He handed two of the guys a rifle. They put their skins down. "Find them," he said to two of them. "You go get the cub." The young guy headed off for the cub. The others headed in her direction. She took off as quietly as possible. She headed around and back toward where the cub had run. She could hear the young man as she got closer to a large group of rocks.

"I've got you now, there is nowhere you can run."

She came out behind him; he had the cub cornered in the rocks. The cub was crying loudly and trying to climb up the rocks. Lindsey came up behind him and had him down before he was even aware she was there. She tied his hands and gagged him with a piece of her shirt. His eyes got wide when she rolled him over and looked at him.

"You are in the wrong park." She pulled him over to the rocks and tied his feet. "I'll be back, don't go anywhere." She smiled and looked at the cub. She placed the man so the cub would feel trapped and stay put. He would need to be helped. He was very small, and wouldn't survive on his own.

She headed back toward the woods and the other men. Lindsey was cautious as she approached the older man still standing by the skins. He stood looking in the other direction, but he was well aware of his surroundings and turned toward her direction before she could get close to him. She was still hidden, but he knew she was there.

"Come on out, I know you're there." He still held a rifle; she lifted hers and carefully slid it up on the tree. A shot rang out, Lindsey hit the ground. He knew exactly where she was. She belly crawled along till she heard him running towards her. Then she jumped up and ran. She could hear him loading as he ran; she turned and fired. He fell. She didn't know if he avoided the shot or she hit him. She dropped to the ground when she heard the two men coming toward them.

"It's a freaking Ranger; he got Jake with a tranq dart," one of them yelled.

"Come on, Ranger," the other one yelled; he wasn't far from her.

She slid on her belly slowly toward him.

"Jake was running this way, so come on," the one closest to her yelled to the other. He started walking towards her. There was a big group of ferns between them. She lay still just on the other side. He stepped right beside her. She grabbed his foot, turned and twisted it till he fell. She hit him square in the jaw, knocking him out. The other guy was running towards her now. She stood up to face him.

"Well, well, it's not just any Ranger; it's a girl."

Lindsey smiled. He cocked his rifle. She was still smiling at him.

"You seem awful confident for someone who has a gun pointed at them." He smiled at her. Lindsey laughed; he was about 20 feet from her, she needed to close the distance. She took a few steps toward him. "That's right, girly, come on."

Lindsey got about five feet from him and stopped.

"You seem to be under the impression I'm alone." She looked over the man's shoulder and nodded. He glanced behind him and that was all she needed.

Lindsey tied all of them up and pulled them beside their friend and the cub. She turned on her radio, "Wendy, how close to the helicopter?"

"It's lifting off now. Where are you?"

"Still at High Rock. I'll flag them in."

"Roger, that."

Lindsey had gathered all the pelts and had them beside the men; all but the bear's and she set it over for the cub that now was curled up against it. Lindsey climbed up on the rocks and watched for the helicopter. It came over the ridge in a matter of minutes. Lindsey waved at them as they flew over.

Her radio crackled. "Is that all of them?" The pilot asked Lindsey.

"Yes, all four."

"We will have to land up the way a little bit and make our way back to you."

"If you have smelling salts, you might want to bring some; three of them are unconscious."

"Roger, that," the pilot said.

Lindsey climbed down. She pulled the gag out of the young guy's mouth; he was the only conscious one.

"Jake will kill you for this," the young guy told her.

"Let him try," Lindsey said as she walked over and sat down beside the cub. He didn't seem to be scared of her. She reached over and rubbed his head. He climbed up into her lap as she rubbed on him. It wasn't long before three Sheriffs came around the rocks.

"Nice job," one of them said.

Lindsey stood up, the cub in her arms. "He's too small to survive on his own."

One sheriff woke the three men. Jake began cursing her. Lindsey smiled at him.

"Looks like you and your buddies have been busy; I bet we find some more if we search."

"They were heading north east as they were leaving."

The sheriff smiled. "Well, I know exactly where they were heading then, there is an old saw mill that way. Of course, it hasn't been used in 70 years, but it might be a good base camp." The younger man's eyes got big. "Yep, I would say that's the place."

Jake dropped his head and swore at the young man. Lindsey followed the men up to the helicopter and handed off the cub.

"Thanks for the help; we have been trying to find this bunch for a while."

"Glad to help."

"You need a ride back?" one of them asked.

Lindsey smiled. "No, I have a Girl Scout troop waiting on me." She closed the door and waved as they lifted off.

"Lifting off, all four poachers and cub secure," her radio crackled.

Lindsey picked up her radio, "Heading back to Troop 54."

"Roger, that," Wendy said.

Lindsey headed back towards her backpack. She set a good pace, but wasn't running this time. Once back to her pack, she changed shirts. She had used most of her other one for ropes.

Lindsey got to the suspension bridge just as the Troop finished setting up camp. Brandon saw her as she came out of the trees. He had her in his arms within seconds of seeing her. Lindsey didn't resist his arms or his kiss. A lot of "OOOO's" brought them apart. They both laughed and walked towards the girls.

Marcy met them half way. "I knew it." She gave Lindsey a big smile.

"We heard you on the radio," Kayla said.

"How did they catch them?" Marta asked.

"Tell you what. You guys fix me supper, and I will tell you all about it."

"Who's up for fresh fish?" Brandon asked. All the girls raised their hands. "Well, let's go catch some." All the girls followed Brandon as he headed for the stream. He had a knife on the end of a long stick.

Lindsey was filthy except for her clean shirt. Mike and Jessica were getting the fire going.

"I'm going to clean up. Be back in a bit," she told them. She grabbed her stuff and headed towards the stream. She found a deep spot not too far down. She stripped and jumped in. After washing her hair and body, she also washed out her pants. Then she dressed and headed back. She spread her clothes to dry over some low branches and sat down by the fire.

"You look tired," Mike told her.

"Didn't get a lot of sleep last night," she told them.

"Not to mention the poacher wrestling you did today," Mike added.

Lindsey laughed.

"What will they do with the cub?" Jessica asked.

"He is so young that they will have to feed him, so most likely he will end up in a zoo somewhere."

Brandon and the girls came back down the stream with six large fish. Brandon cleaned the fish in the stream down from camp. Lindsey pulled the griddle out of Brandon's bag and set it across the fire to get hot. The fish sizzled when Brandon put them on. Soon the smell of cooking fish filled the air. Lindsey leaned up against a rock and closed her eyes for a moment.

Brandon touched her cheek and asked, "You hungry?"

She had fallen asleep. She took the fish he offered her and sat up. The girls were all gathered around to listen to her tale about the poachers. She told a great story about tracking the blood and finding them with the skins; she left out the part about seeing them skin the bear. She told the girls the sheriffs had rounded them up; it was a little tense for a while, but once the cub had gotten loose, they rounded them up fairly easy. Lindsey led the girls to believe the Sheriffs did it all and she just mainly watched. She did not want them to get any heroic ideas. After her story they all turned in. Lindsey was the first one in the tent and was out long before Jessica.

Lindsey woke with a kiss from Brandon. He was lying beside her in the tent. Lindsey looked at him, "Where is Jessica?"

"She got up to use the restroom."

It was still pretty dark, but the sky was just beginning to lighten up.

"Why didn't you tell the girls the truth about the poachers?"

Lindsey smiled, "Who said I didn't?"

"I talked to Wendy last night. I wanted to check on Jacob. But she had talked to one of the Sheriffs. They said you had them rounded up by the time they got there."

Lindsey closed her eyes and smiled. "Didn't want the girls getting any foolish ideas in their heads. I knew what I was doing, Brandon. One thing I know well is how to wage war and win."

Brandon didn't say anything. Lindsey rolled onto her side and up on her elbow. She leaned over and kissed him on the cheek. "You don't have to worry about me ... ever. I don't do stupid."

They could hear Jessica talking to Mike outside. Brandon crawled out of the tent and Lindsey followed. Mike and Jessica were sitting by the coals of the fire. None of the girls were up, yet. Brandon sat down and Lindsey sat down and leaned over on him.

"One more night," Mike said.

"You guys have been great. No offense, Brandon, but I don't think they were warming up to Jacob."

Brandon laughed. "None taken, and I think you're right. Jacob would never have done any of the things Lindsey did. Especially let me run around without a shirt." They all laughed.

"But it worked, didn't it?" Lindsey said.

"Yeah, I think they are all in love with him," Mike added. More laughter erupted as some of the girls started coming out of the tents. Brandon got up and pulled Lindsey up, too.

"Let's get the party started."

Mike and Jessica got up, too, and started waking the rest of the girls.

"Rise and shine!" Jessica told them. "Last full day, let's make it the best yet."

The girls cleaned up in the stream and got their tents packed up and ready to go. Jessica made them all get in front of the bridge so she could take a picture. Jessica's one picture started a picture frenzy. Every girl had to have a picture with Brandon. Marcy wanted one with Brandon and Lindsey together. Then so did everyone else.

They finally got across the bridge and on up the trail. They made a little side trip up to Gobblers Knob. It was a great high spot from where you could see a big part of the park. The girls loved it. Lindsey sat down on a rock and marveled at the beauty. Lindsey took off her Ranger hat and was letting the breeze blow through her hair. Jessica took a picture of her. Brandon looked over Jessica's shoulder at it.

"I want a copy of that," he told her.

"Go sit with her, I'll take one of you two together." Brandon threw off his hat and shook out his hair and sat down with Lindsey. Lindsey looked off at the bluff and Brandon looked at Lindsey and Jessica took a picture. Then they both looked at Jessica for a picture. Jessica looked at the pictures she had taken.

Brandon got up and looked at them. The one with Lindsey looking off and him looking at her was amazing. "Wow, I want that one, too!"

She looked at Brandon. "How long have you guys been together?"

Brandon smiled. "We're not together, just the best of friends."

Jessica smiled, "If you say so. Make sure you give me your address before we leave tomorrow, and I will send them to you."

"Thanks."

Lindsey got up and was talking with the girls. Brandon sat down on the ground off to the side of where they were; then got up and joined the conversation.

"We better get back on the trail or we won't find a good camping spot for tonight," Lindsey told the girls.

"Hey, Lindsey!" Brandon called Lindsey over to where he had sat earlier. The girls started back down the trail. Brandon looked down at something then walked off. Lindsey walked over and looked. Brandon had taken a bunch of small rocks and formed three words, "I love you." Lindsey smiled and picked up one of the small stones. She handed it to Brandon as she walked by him. He smiled and laughed. She glanced back with a big smile. Brandon slid the rock in his pocket.

The day was full of lessons and laughter. Brandon told some legends from his tribe as they walked: the story of Father Sun and Mother Earth. The girls loved the stories. A few of the girls shared funny family stories. Mike and Jessica shared the story of their honeymoon; well, the mix up that left them without a room and how they had slept on the beach and got hauled to jail.

The day passed quickly and soon they were sitting around the campfire talking about the moon and stars. They all laid on their backs in the meadow behind the tents looking at the constellations and trying to name them. Lindsey was lying between Marcy and Marta, Brandon was on the other end of the line next to Kayla.

Lindsey closed her eyes and listened to the conversations around her. Her mind wandered. Until now her life had been one constant mission after another. Maybe a summer in Intel, but mainly out doing what she had been taught to do: kill people. Not that it wasn't the right thing to do, but no one should have to live like those people, or even worse, those kids. Why could life not be as simple as it was now? Why was she the one chosen for this life? She could never remember having a choice. Her life had never been her own. Why did she have to be The Maker? She looked at the stars, why her? She would love never to have to go back, but she was theirs to command, to control, to let live or let die. Keeps came to her mind, did he have a choice or was he like her: born and bred for one single purpose?

They were never alone; always someone looking over their shoulder making sure they were in line. Yet, Keeps had gone against his objective: he had let her have a secret and had joined her in keeping it. She smiled; if he could do it, then she could, too. She would have to be careful, but wasn't that what she was trained to be? She was the best agent in the field, they had taught her how to avoid being detected and how to hide. She smiled to herself;

she could use it against them. She made up her mind right then and there. If there was a way, she would break free of them. She was going to beat them at their own game. Her mind wandered to Brandon. She would find a way for them to be together someday.

Brandon saw Lindsey sit up, so he looked her way. She had a crazy kind of smile on her face. He smiled back at her. Her smile got even bigger. She was up to something, you could see it. But what, he wondered; from what he knew of her, which was basically nothing, was that anything could happen.

Lindsey got up and headed back to the fire. Jessica followed suit, and soon most of the girls were there. Brandon and Mike were the last to come back. It was getting late, but no one wanted to go to bed. Finally the yawns took their tolls and they headed to bed one by one. Lindsey glanced back at Brandon as she crawled into her tent. He smiled at her.

Slowly it got quiet. Lindsey lay there plotting in her head. She needed a laptop; one she could do some hacking with. If she was going to get away, she needed to set up some false records and stuff. She would need a life to silently move into. She would start a business online; of course, encrypted and untraceable. She was the best at unbreakable and untraceable hacks, so who better to make one? She closed her eyes when Jessica crawled in beside her.

Lindsey awoke with something in her hand. She looked down to find the rock she had given to Brandon in her hand. She smiled and crawled out of the tent. The sun was just coming up. Brandon was the only one awake. Brandon walked toward the trees, Lindsey followed. She found him not far, waiting. He never said a word, but pulled her into his arms. Brandon held her tightly; she loved the feel of his arms around her. He finally turned her around to face him. He kissed her on the forehead. Lindsey laid her face on his chest and hugged him and then kissed him on the cheek. They both smiled and then headed back to camp, hand in hand. They broke apart as camp came into sight.

"Good morning," he said as they came into the camp.

"Did you sleep well?" She asked him.

"I am ready for a soft bed tonight."

Lindsey laughed. "Me, too."

Mike came dragging out. "You two get up way too early."

"It's her fault; when we're at the Inn she has us up running at four a.m."

Mike rolled his eyes. "Wow!" Mike looked at Lindsey.

Lindsey smiled at both of them, "Don't let him fool you, he has only run with me three days. Then he slept through breakfast." Mike laughed and Brandon smiled.

"I'm working on it."

Jessica stuck her head out. "You guys are awfully loud."

"Sorry," Lindsey said.

"How far are we from being back?" Mike asked.

"About five miles, we should be back before lunch," Brandon told him.

"I am going to need a lot of coffee to stay awake on the drive home," Mike said.

"How far do you have to go?" Lindsey asked.

"It took us five hours to get here."

Lindsey smiled. "You were here by eight that morning."

Mike smiled. "I got everyone up at three a.m."

Lindsey laughed. "And you think I'm crazy for getting up at four! You had to get 16 girls up at three a.m. You were living dangerously!" They laughed.

Jessica crawled out. "No use in trying to sleep, because you guys won't be quiet."

"Sorry, babe," Mike told her. Some of the girls were moving around, but none came out. Brandon poured water on the coals of the fire to make sure it was completely out. Lindsey took down her tent and Mike took down his. Jessica and Lindsey went to wash up at the nearby stream.

"You and Mike are really super for doing this for your daughter."

Jessica smiled. "I loved the scouts when I was younger, I don't think Marcy is as excited about it like I was, but I think she likes it a lot more after this week, thanks to you guys."

Lindsey smiled at her. "It's all in the way you approach things; getting on their level, so to speak."

Jessica laughed. "Yeah, I think you're right, with you talking guys, then Brandon shirtless . . . ." They both laughed.

"It was crazy, but it got their attention." They walked back up to camp. Most of the girls were putting up their tents and loading their backpacks.

"Morning," Lindsey said to Marcy and Kayla as she passed them.

Marcy yawned a "Morning" back. Kayla looked up and gave a tired smile.

Brandon woke the rest of the girls by giving a loud wolf howl. A couple of the girls howled back. Everyone laughed.

The hike started out slow, but picked up as they went. Brandon quizzed them a little on stuff they had learned. Lindsey talked about projects they said they were going to do when they got home. Soon they were walking up the road towards the Inn.

Lindsey invited them all to lunch with Brandon and her. The girls were thrilled, and Mike and Jessica agreed to leave right after they all ate.

The troop dropped off their gear at their bus and met Lindsey and Brandon in the dining room. Lindsey had it set for 20 when they arrived. Lunch was full of fun, laughter, and pictures.

Lindsey paid for the meal, but not without protests from Mike. She and Brandon followed the girls to the parking lot to see them off. Lots of hugs ensued. Brandon gave Jessica the park address so she could send him some pictures.

Finally the girls loaded up and Lindsey handed Mike a cup of coffee. "You guys be safe."

"Thanks." Mike took the coffee. Then they drove off, all the girls waving out the windows. Brandon and Lindsey waved back till the girls were out of sight. They then returned to the Inn and retrieved their packs and went and turned in their rifles and gear they had checked out.

Brandon went to check on Jacob as soon as they got to the cabins. Lindsey followed; she wanted to know, too. Michelle answered the door when Brandon knocked.

"Hey, how is he?"

Michelle stepped out on the porch and pulled the door closed behind her.

"He is still running a low fever and is throwing up some. But not near as much as he was. So he is better; the doc said it would be at least two weeks."

"You staying?" Brandon asked her.

"Yeah, if that's ok."

"That's great! I sure don't want to have to baby him." He gave her a smile.

"Hi, I'm Lindsey."

"Sorry," Brandon said.

"Figured as much; I'm Michelle."

"I'll need my stuff," Brandon told her.

"You can bunk with me," Lindsey told Brandon.

"You sure?" He looked down at her.

"I don't mind."

Michelle turned to Brandon. "Get it quietly; try not to wake him." Brandon opened the door and went in, leaving Michelle and Lindsey standing on the porch.

"Staying with you ought to make Brandon happy."

Lindsey looked at Michelle.

"Jacob says Brandon has a thing for you."

Lindsey smiled. "Yeah, I know." Brandon handed some uniforms out the door to Lindsey and disappeared back inside.

"Looks like the feeling is mutual," Michelle smiled at Lindsey.

"I don't know; he is mighty cute though." Lindsey told Michelle with a wink. They both giggled quietly. Brandon came out with his duffle bag in hand. Lindsey handed him back his uniforms and picked up their camping stuff and they headed to her cabin. Brandon hung his uniforms in the closet.

"You sure this is, ok?" He looked at her intently.

Lindsey smiled at him. "Well, I guess if you would rather stay somewhere else, you can."

He smiled at her. "I'm good if you're good."

"Well, I am most definitely good." She smiled. "I am heading to the shower; I feel nasty."

Lindsey walked past Brandon and into the bathroom. The water felt so good and warm. Lindsey stepped out of the shower and realized she hadn't brought any clothes with her to put back on. That was something she hadn't had to do until now. She wrapped a towel around her and stepped out of the bathroom. Brandon was sitting at the table, but looked up when she stepped into the room.

"Your turn," she said trying to take the focus off herself in her towel. Brandon got up and came to stand in front of her.

"Nice and squeaky clean are we?" He asked.

Lindsey turned and faced the closet. He tried to slide beside her to go in the bathroom, but the buttons on his shirt caught the edge of the towel. It came loose and fell to the floor.

Lindsey laughed. "You know paybacks are usually rough, and you already owe me one." She turned to face him.

"I really didn't mean to, I promise." His eyes locked with hers. He was trying very hard not to look down.

Lindsey turned back to the closet and Bandon darted into the bathroom. Lindsey laughed; he hadn't taken anything in there either, and she had the only towel out with her.

Lindsey pulled on a pair of jeans and a T-shirt; then pulled her guitar out of the closet. She turned her chair facing the bathroom and sat down and waited. Lindsey heard the water quit, then an "Oh, crap!" She just laughed, got up and picked up the towel, cracked the bathroom door, and stuck it inside. His wet hand took it from hers. She went back to her chair and continued playing.

"Do I have to?"

She laughed. "Come on out."

He stepped out with the towel around his waist. She laid the guitar on the bed and walked up to him and put her hand on the towel. He closed his eyes. Lindsey removed her hand and left the towel in place.

"You were willing, that's all that mattered." He opened his eyes to look at her. She went and picked up the guitar, sat down and started playing again.

"You're going to let me off that easy?"

"For now; well, unless you just want to show off."

He grabbed the towel as if he were going to rip it off. Lindsey never blinked, but just sat and played.

"It about unnerved me to see you, and you don't care one way or the other."

Lindsey smiled at him. "You have to know how to play the game. Remain calm at all cost."

"Now where is the fun in that?" He asked her.

She stood up; laid the guitar back down on the bed. Lindsey walked up to him forcefully enough to back him into the wall. She grabbed the towel and removed it from him, but she never lost eye contact with him. "You can't be affected by your surroundings, no matter what." She dropped the towel to the floor and put one hand on one side of his face, and the other on the other. "Never lose focus." His eyes were big. "Never let what you want interfere with what has to be done." Lindsey spoke steadily.

"And what's that?" He asked. You could hear the unsteadiness in Brandon's voice. Lindsey pulled back from him.

"Payback!!" Her eyes starting gliding down his chest. She heard his breath catch in his throat. He was staring at her; her eyes never went farther than his chest.

"Get dressed, Brandon." She turned and went back to the chair. Brandon just stood there for a minute, and then reached for his bag at the bottom of the closet. He grabbed some clothes and stood up; he glanced at her. She was looking directly at him and smiling. "Nice." Brandon's face turned four shades of red. Lindsey laughed so hard she almost fell out of the chair. Brandon dropped the clothes and closed the distance between them in two seconds. He had her off the chair and on the bed in another second. Lindsey was still laughing.

"Don't tease me, woman!"

Lindsey flipped him on the bed. "I never tease." She smiled down at him. Lindsey got off of him and off the bed.

"Maybe I better find somewhere else to stay."

Lindsey smiled. "Only if you can't control yourself."

"You are not going to make this easy, are you?"

"I told you paybacks were rough." She picked up the guitar and started playing again. Brandon put some shorts and a T-shirt on.

Brandon pulled out the other chair and sat down. "How can you be so dang calm?"

"Just close your eyes and relax. Let the music fill you up."

Brandon took a deep breath and closed his eyes. Lindsey played, then started singing a soft song. Lindsey watched Brandon as she sang; he started relaxing. His breathing calmed and got steady and slow. When she stopped he opened his eyes. Lindsey reached over on the little table beside the door and picked up the rock from earlier and handed it to him. He smiled at her. She took the guitar and handed it to him.

"You work on it some. I have to go up to the campground and check on a site."

"I don't know if . . . ."

"Just think of the most peaceful place you have ever been and play how it makes you fee." Lindsey got up, slid on her flip-flops and went out the door.

Lindsey knew him being here was going to be hard. The fact that she had just about lost it in there was proof. But she was never going to let him know that.

When she reached the campground, she found Taylor's sister and grandmother cleaning up some pans at the campsite, but she didn't see Taylor.

"Hey, guys," Lindsey said as she walked up into the site.

"I almost didn't recognize you out of uniform," the girl told her.

"Taylor's out hiking," the older lady looked up, "he even went without his music thingy."

"It's an MP3, grandma."

Lindsey smiled. "I told him I would stop by in a few days; didn't know it would be a whole week, though. I got called out on a different trail and had to stay a few days. So when are you guys leaving?"

"Probably tomorrow, but I am not real sure; we may stay a few more days," the older lady said.

"Well, maybe I'll see you again, then. Tell Taylor I stopped by."

"I will," the young girl said.

"You guys have a good evening." Lindsey waved and headed back towards the cabin.

"Hey," Taylor's sister caught up to her.

"Will you take a picture with me?" She had her camera in hand.

"Sure." Lindsey put her arm around the girl and the girl held out the camera and took the picture; she flipped the camera to look at it.

"He will be sad he missed you out of uniform. You sure are pretty."

Lindsey smiled. "Thanks."

The girl ran back toward her campsite. Lindsey waved.

Back at the cabin Lindsey stepped on the porch quietly; she leaned up against the door to listen. Brandon was playing; he was doing better. She opened the door as silently as possible and stepped in. He was sitting with his eyes closed gently strumming the stings. Lindsey sat down and listened. He was playing the same four chords over and over, but he was feeling what he played.

"Try picking the chords apart," Lindsey said very quietly. He never opened his eyes, but gently picked the notes in the chords. It flowed smoothly and softly. He went through them several times before opening his eyes to look at her. "That was great. See, it really doesn't matter what notes you play, it's the feeling you play with."

"I think I sort of understand; it's like how you greet someone. You can say the same word, but it's the way you say it that sets the mood."

Lindsey smiled. "Exactly! That's how music is, you can be angry and raw like a lot of bands, and they are good, but most of them don't really know music, they know how to be angry. Music is so much more; you have to play all the emotions."

Brandon got up and put the guitar in its case. "I'm sorry about earlier. You have the strangest affect on me, and I just lose it."

Lindsey smiled. "You're not so easy on me, either; I'm just better at not showing it."

"Maybe you could show me how to not show it."

Lindsey laughed. "I have never had a problem not showing it till you came along, and now it's a constant fight."

Brandon smiled. "You sure didn't show it earlier; you were cold as ice."

"Maybe on the outside." She smiled and winked.

Lindsey pulled the chair out in the middle of the floor. "Come here and sit down." He walked over and sat in front of her. "Lesson one," she said, "you have to be in control of yourself before you can control the other person."

He laughed. "That's the problem; I can't control me."

"Yes, you can; when it's important, you can do anything. That's the key, make it important. Get serious!" His smile dropped. "Now when you feel like you're going to lose it, find the calmest spot, whether it's a place you love to go, or just a tune, but it has to be a gentle relaxing place. Ready?"

Lindsey pulled her shirt over her head. His breath caught. "Focus, Brandon, find your spot." His breath smoothed back out. He focused on her eyes. She undid her jeans and let them fall to the floor. Now she stood there in her underwear. He was trying hard to keep his breathing even.

"This is torture," he said to her.

"Focus on being calm."

"I really don't want to be calm, I want . . ."

Lindsey put her finger to his lips, "Shhhh!" He about came unglued when her finger touched his lips. He shook visibly.

"Sorry." Lindsey removed her finger. "Vision first, and then touch."

Brandon was taking large, deep breaths. "I don't know if I can do this."

"You can do anything you put your mind to." His breathing was getting calmer and smoother. He closed his eyes for a moment, then opened them.

"Very good." Lindsey bent over and picked up her clothes and laid them on the bed. Brandon watched her every move. He started breathing hard again.

"Find your calm spot, Brandon." She looked down at him.

He reached out, but Lindsey stepped out of reach. He was almost panting now. He was about to lose it big time, and she could see it. Lindsey reached for her clothes, but he grabbed them before she could reach them. He threw them across the room. Crap, she was going to have to get drastic. He had her up against the wall in seconds, his lips crushed down on hers. She reached up and took hold of a pressure point on his shoulder. He fell back, out cold. She pulled her clothes on, then pulled him up on the bed. He would be out for a while; she had to use quite a bit of pressure. She slid his shirt up and ran her fingers over his chest. Then leaned over and kissed him. Her heart raced, control was definitely hard. She traced his face with her finger and kissed him on the lips. Her breathing was not as steady as it should be. She took a few deep breaths, then got up and started to leave.

The rock sat on the table; she placed it in his hand and left the cabin. It was getting close to supper time; not that she was hungry, but just needed to get out of the cabin. So she headed to the Inn. Not being hungry, she headed down to the club room; the doors were open. Two older men sat playing chess. One she recognized as Taylor's grandfather.

"Would you gentlemen care if I played the piano?" She asked them.

"Not at all, sweetie."

Lindsey sat down and closed her eyes. The music flowed through her; she had so many feelings going on right now. Her heart was with Brandon; her mind was trying to find a way for them to be together. All the things she needed to figure out. Most of her missions were set up and she just had to go in and clean house so to speak. The one thing that was really in her favor is that she always knew of ways the job could have been done better and more efficiently. So, this time the planning was hers, and she was going to slide right under their noses. Her mind worked hard as her fingers played.

Bach, Beethoven, her fingers played fast and furiously as her mind raced. She needed a laptop; she would have Keeps get her one, and then she would use it. She would start compiling all she needed. Suddenly she was aware of someone standing behind her.

Taylor was standing beside her, to the right, staring at her. Lindsey smiled at him as she played.

"Have a seat." She slid over on the bench as the piece calmed. He sat down beside her.

"Wow, you're good!"

"Thanks." Lindsey moved to an even slower ballad.

He smiled.

"I hear you've been enjoying nature?"

"It's really cool when you look for the music side of it."

Lindsey laughed. "Ever seen the movie August Rush?"

"No."

"Well, you need to watch it; it's about a boy who hears music in everything around him."

"Cool."

Lindsey finished her song and closed the piano top. Clapping turned Lindsey around; there were about 20 people in the room now. Lindsey smiled, got up and took a bow, then laughed. "Thanks."

Brandon was standing in the doorway. He had never heard her play like that. It got to be really intense there for a while. He smiled to himself; maybe he had affected her more than she was letting on.

"You want to come eat dinner with us?" Taylor asked her.

Lindsey smiled. "That would have been great, but I already have plans."

"Come on, Taylor, we better not keep the girls waiting," his grandfather said.

"Maybe next time," she told him, as Taylor followed his grandfather to the door.

"So, who are you having dinner with?" Brandon asked as she walked up to him.

"I thought you, but if you're mad at me, I guess I would understand."

Brandon laughed. "What did you do to me? I can't remember anything; well, a few things, then nothing."

Lindsey smiled but didn't answer as they walked down to the dining hall and found a table.

"What were you thinking back there? I have never heard you play so intensely." He grinned at her.

She shook her head. "That is not what I was thinking of."

Lindsey pulled her phone from her pocket and sent a message: "I need a laptop." Then she waited for a reply, which took all of five seconds. "Give me a couple of days," it read. Lindsey slid the phone back into her pocket.

"I need a laptop. We need to begin looking for some music classes for you this fall."

"Oh," was all Brandon said.

"You know they have some good schools in San Diego," Lindsey told him.

"That's not very close to home. I would have to find a place to live."

Lindsey smiled. "Oh, don't worry about that, not yet, anyway. Do you know how to play the piano?"

"No."

"Maybe I can teach you a little; it will help you with classes. Do you read music?"

"Well, not really. I know some chords from charts, but not really; I just listen and find the same sound."

"Maybe, I can teach you some basic music reading, too."

"Maybe, we should forget the music thing."

Lindsey looked at Brandon.

"Just kidding."

Lindsey finished her last bite and got up. "How about your first piano lesson?"

"Seems like a day for firsts, so why not?"

The two of them went back to the club room. The doors were still open, but there was no one in it. Lindsey sat down on the bench and Brandon sat beside her.

"First thing are the notes. It's basically like a guitar in that aspect: a, b, c, d, e, f, g." She played up the notes. "You also need to know about the main placing of the fingers. Both thumbs are for middle C." She laid her fingers on the notes. "Anything on the right hand will be on the treble clef and anything for the left hand will be played on the bass clef. Get up; let me see if there is some sheet music in the bench." She pulled out an old song book. She flipped it open. "Here's the top scale which is the treble clef so it is for your . . . ."

"Right hand," he finished her sentence.

"And this, the bass clef, it's for . . ."

"Your left hand; ok, I've got that."

"Now, just like a guitar, a chord is made up of several notes put together."

Lindsey and Brandon sat in the room working on chords and notes for an hour. She would show him the chord and he would tell her the notes of it and play it back to her.

"I am beat. You think we can call it quits for now?" Lindsey asked; she had already started yawning.

"Sure, you're the one doing the teaching."

They got up and headed out. When they got to the cabins the light was on in Jacob's cabin so Brandon went to check in on him; Lindsey went on home. She brushed her teeth and changed into her sleeping attire, sports bra and boxers. Then, laid down on the bed and put her ear buds in and turned on her iPod. When Brandon came in she took them out.

"How is he?"

"He was awake, but looks like death warmed over. Michelle said he actually was looking better." He looked around on the floor. "So, where do you want me to sleep?" Lindsey shook her head.

"Here," she patted the other side of the bed.

"You're asking for trouble."

Lindsey smiled. "No, but you will be if you don't behave."

He took a deep breath. "Are you sure?"

"I would not have told you that you could stay here if I was going to make you sleep on the floor."

"What should I sleep in?"

"What you normally sleep in. See, I am."

"I usually just sleep in my boxers."

"That's fine."

"All right, then."

He went into the bathroom and brushed his teeth. Then he came out, stripped to his boxers, and crawled in bed beside Lindsey. She laid her iPod on the table and shut the light off. Lindsey listened to Brandon breathing.

"I don't know if I can sleep beside you; my mind keeps wandering."

"Fine, roll over on your stomach."

"What for?"

"Just do it."

Brandon flipped to his stomach.

"How do you normally sleep?"

"What?"

"I mean how do you lay, on your side, what?"

"Usually on my side, why?"

"Cause, once you fall asleep, I will need to make you move if you don't sleep this way."

"What?"

"Just lay still and relax," Lindsey got up on her knees and straddled him and started rubbing down his back.

"This is not helping."

"It will."

She touched pressure points down both sides of his neck and back. The more she touched and rubbed little spots, the more relaxed his body got. Finally she heard his little snore, the one he always did in the morning when he fell asleep on the breakfast table. She got off him and gave his arm a little shove and he turned to his side. Lindsey, however, couldn't sleep now. Feeling him beneath her was quite exciting. She took long slow breaths for a while, just to get her heart rate back to normal. Then, finally she had to play music in her head—her counting sheep, so to speak.

Lindsey woke at 3:30 with her alarm. Brandon's arm was lying across her stomach. After she reached over and shut it off, he pulled her towards him. He molded her back into him. Her back was to his stomach. He kissed her neck. "Morning."

"Sleep well?"

"As well as I could; all I can smell is you, so you're all I dreamed about all night."

Lindsey laughed. "I had that same problem the night I stayed at your house. I may not have known you, but you were all I could smell and dream about."

He chuckled. "So, how did you sleep?"

"Better than I have in the last five nights. I really missed my bed." Lindsey pulled away from Brandon and got up.

She pulled her shorts and tank top out of the closet and went in the bathroom to change. Brandon already had his shorts and tennis shoes on when she came out. She sat down and put her shoes on while he used the restroom. They left the cabin and only stopped long enough to stretch, then took off. Lindsey went the full eight today. She ran her normal run. Brandon did his best to keep up, but fell behind several times. Lindsey made it back long before Brandon.

"You're going to kill me." He was breathing hard.

"No. Maybe get you in shape, though."

"Even if it kills me?"

"Stop whining and go get your shower."

Brandon walked straight to the bathroom without his clean clothes again. He will learn, Lindsey thought to herself. Brandon came out in his towel. Lindsey smiled at him. His hair was even blacker when wet; he was totally sexy looking standing there in just the towel. A picture of him without it flashed through her head. She grabbed her towel and clothes and headed into the bathroom. She gathered up all the dirty clothes and stepped back in the hall to put them in the laundry basket. He evidently was not expecting her to come back out and was standing drying his hair with his towel. Lindsey stopped in her tracks for a second, and then quickly returned to the bathroom without a word. Lindsey almost needed a cold shower. When she came out dressed, he smiled.

"I think we're even."

Lindsey laughed. "I guess."

Neither one of them had picked up their schedule for the week, so they had to make a stop by to see Wendy before heading to breakfast. Once breakfast was over they headed out for the day. Lindsey had several trails to walk today; Brandon had the campground. Clouds moved in around lunch and the rain followed suit. The whole afternoon was wet and soggy. Most people retreated to the Inn, but a few braved the weather and still hiked around. Lindsey was half way around trail two when Wendy came on the radio.

"Looks like we have a bad one getting ready to move in; everybody check your trails, make sure everyone is off them."

Lindsey picked up the pace. She only saw one couple she had to tell to head back. She had two trails so she headed for the other one quickly. Trail five was back down past the campground. She took off at a run to get to it before the storm. She had just gotten to it when the rain started coming down in sheets. She had to slow down because she couldn't see.

"Lindsey, you got five?" It was Brandon.

"Yeah, what's up?" She hovered under a tree for a few minutes to answer him.

"Got a young girl here says her brother was on trail five and hasn't made it back, yet."

She could hear the girl in the background, "Tell her it's Taylor."

"Says to tell you it's Taylor."

"I'll find him, but call me if he gets back."

"Will do."

Lindsey had a good idea where he might be: the bluff where she found the hikers her first day. It was the perfect spot to sit and listen to nature. She wasn't far. She took off as fast as she could without slipping in the mud.

"Taylor!" She yelled as she got close to the bluffs. The rain was coming down so hard she could barely hear herself yell. She slid as she went around the side of the rocks. These little side trails were just mud now. She caught herself on a low hanging branch before she went all the way down.

"Taylor!" She yelled again. The water was pouring down the path and her feet could not stay up in the onslaught of water. She rode the water as she bounced off rocks and bounced into trees, she was covered in mud when she spilled out at the bottom. A hand reached out and touched her. Taylor was crouched at the bottom of a large rock. He had a large cut on his forehead. Lindsey stood up and looked around; there was really no place to get out of the rain, and there was no going back up till it stopped raining. Lindsey bent over him to get the rain off of him.

"You ok?" She asked him.

"Yeah, I tried to make it up."

Lindsey reached for her radio. "I have Taylor, but we are going to have to stay put till the rain lets up."

"Roger, that."

Lindsey looked over his cut; it wasn't that deep, but just like all head cuts, it was bleeding like crazy. Lindsey stuck her hand out to let the rain wash it off then applied pressure to stop it. "It's not bad," she told him, "head wounds just bleed a lot."

She pulled off her hat and placed it on his head to keep the rain from the wound. Lindsey picked up her radio again.

"Hey, is there anywhere at the bottom of the bluffs on five that we might get out of the weather?"

"Only of you go down about a half mile there are some overhangs," Brandon replied.

"I would go for it; this isn't going to let up for a while," it was Wendy this time.

"Ok, thanks."

She looked down at Taylor. "You up for it?"

He looked up at her. "My ankle hurts really bad."

She leaned over; she couldn't do anything while holding his head.

"Put your hand here."

She took her knife and cut the bottom off of her shirt and tied it around his head. Then she removed his shoe. His ankle was already swollen and turning black. She looked around for something to brace the ankle with. Branches and twigs were rushing by in the water. She finally grabbed two branches. She ripped more of her shirt off and wrapped his ankle with the branches on either side.

"Come on," she pulled him up to stand on his one good foot. "Get on my back; we can't take a chance you putting that foot down." She bent over and let him climb on, piggyback style.

Carefully, and very slowly, she made her way through the rocks, not getting out where the water was rushing. She slipped several times, but caught herself. The rocks were almost as slick as the watery mud running beside her. What should have taken ten minutes took almost forty. But finally, she stepped through the sheet of water coming off the overhang to the protection of it.

Lindsey and Taylor weren't the only ones taking refuge there. Several small animals were hiding in the back against the wall. Lindsey sat Taylor carefully down on a rock.

"How's your ankle?"

"I think it would hurt less if we just cut it off."

She smiled at him. "I think you broke it." She removed the wrap and sticks and slid her finger very gently down the side feeling for the bones. Taylor gritted his teeth and rolled his eyes back.

"Sorry, it's definitely broken." She put the splints back on and wrapped it back, being very careful this time.

"When is this going to let up?" She called to Wendy on her radio.

"It looks like it may be here for the night."

"Great," Lindsey said, not on the radio, though.

"Can you make it out?" Wendy came back.

"Don't chance it, Lindsey, that area is treacherous in the rain," this time it was Brandon.

"We are not going anywhere."

Lindsey stood up and looked around. There really wasn't much in there. There were a few twigs and things, but not really anything to burn. "Looks like we are going to be here for the night. Let's get you moved over against the wall so you can lean up against it."

Lindsey pulled him up again. He dropped his foot once and screamed out in pain. Lindsey picked him up and carried him to the wall. Tears were running down his face. Lindsey put him down, then sat down beside him and put her arm around him. Lindsey took hold of his shoulder and knocked him out the same way she had Brandon. There was no need for him to lay there and hurt. She leaned back against the wall and closed her eyes.

"You guys, ok?" Her radio crackled.

"We're fine, Brandon, Taylor is already out."

"Alright, then, see you in the morning."

Lindsey closed her eyes again.

Taylor woke up once and Lindsey knocked him back out as fast as she could, not being able to see him. Sometime in the night a movement woke her. Taylor was shivering. She pulled him between her legs and wrapped both arms around him and put her legs against his. She touched his shoulder one more time to keep him from waking.

"Lindsey."

Lindsey opened her eyes, it was light and Brandon was standing in front of her. Taylor woke with a scream of pain.

"His ankle is broken, and he is going to need a few stitches in his head."

"Why didn't you say he was hurt?"

Lindsey touched his shoulder, and he fell back in her arms. "Let's get him out of here before he comes to again."

Brandon lifted Taylor up from between Lindsey's legs.

Lindsey got up; Brandon leaned over and kissed her.

"Are you ok?"

Lindsey looked down at herself. She was covered in mud and dried blood and the whole bottom of her shirt was gone. Lindsey laughed. "I'm fine. I may not look it, but I am."

Lindsey called out on her radio. "We need a truck at trail head five; got a kid with a broken ankle and a cut that needs a few stitches."

"On my way," it was Malcolm.

"He is from Site 22. You might want to stop and get his grandparents; it's going to take us a little while to get up to the trail."

"Roger, that."

Brandon had mud up to his knees from coming down.

"It is slick, so be careful."

"You be careful, you're the one carrying someone."

They slowly made their way up around the side of the overhangs. It was a lot easier than the way she came down. Thirty minutes later they came out on trail five, but were not at the entrance yet.

Taylor woke up and grabbed at his ankle. "It hurts." Tears ran down his face.

"We are almost back; they'll be waiting to take you to the hospital," Brandon told him.

"When did you get here?" Taylor looked around, "Where are we?"

Lindsey came around the side of Bandon so Taylor could see her. "Hey."

Taylor looked at her. "I don't remember anything after you sat me down by the wall."

Lindsey smiled. "Sorry, but I knocked you out. You were in so much pain, and I couldn't bear to see you hurt."

"You knocked me out?" He reached up and touched his jaw.

Lindsey laughed. "I used pressure points; it's fast and painless."

"I can feel my heart in my ankle, it hurts so badly."

"I can knock you out again if you like."

"No, my grandparents might freak."

"You're probably right about that." Lindsey took Taylor's hand as she walked beside Brandon. He held tight to it as they came out into the opening where his grandparents sat waiting with the truck.

"You, ok, sweetie?" His grandmother rushed to his side.

"My ankle. Lindsey said she thought it was broken."

"What happened?" she asked him.

"It got muddy fast when the rain started and when I tried to go up the trail, I slipped and fell all the way down. I think I passed out for a while because I don't remember anything till I heard my name being yelled. Then I saw Lindsey slide out of the mud in front of me." Brandon sat Taylor in the backseat of his grandparent's truck.

"Will you go with me?" Taylor looked at Lindsey.

"Sorry, sweetie, but I have to clean up and get back to work. But I will come and check on you when you get back. Just tell the Ranger at the camp shack to let me know, ok?" Lindsey waved at Taylor as they drove away.

"You ok, Jacobs?" Malcolm asked her.

"I'm fine; all the blood is his from the cut on his head."

"All right then, you want a ride up?"

Lindsey opened the tailgate and sat down, Brandon sat beside her. Malcolm stopped at the parking lot for the cabins and she and Brandon got off and shut the tailgate.

Lindsey went straight to the shower. She knew she was going to have bruises from sliding down, and she was already somewhat sore. But when she removed her pants, she was black and blue from her right hip all the way to her knee. She also had a few minor scrapes on her arms, but nothing major. She stepped out of the bathroom in her towel and grabbed some clothes. Brandon dropped to his knees and looked at her leg.

"I thought you said you weren't hurt. He slid the towel up to see where the bruise stopped. "It's just a bruise. I'm fine."

He looked up at her. "Crap, what happened?"

"I slid down in the mud." He started looking her over for other injuries. He took her towel from her to see if she had anything hidden beneath it.

"Brandon!"

He turned her around. The only other bruise he found was on her side. He touched the bruise on her side to check for broken ribs.

"They're not broken, just bruised. Don't you think I checked it out myself?"

He pulled her close to him. "Are you sure you're ok?"

"I'm fine, I promise. Can I get dressed now?"

He bent down and kissed her gently on the lips. He reached in his pocket and pulled the little rock out and handed it to her. She smiled up at him.

"Me, too."

Brandon had been so worried about her being hurt and checking her for injuries that it wasn't until that very moment that he fully realized she stood before him completely naked. Lindsey noticed the minute he realized it. He backed away from her slowly.

"You owe me again," she said as she put her clothes on.

"Crap!" He said from across the room. Lindsey turned to look at him; he had already changed out of his muddy clothes and was in uniform and ready for the day. Lindsey took her clothes and threw them in the laundry basket along with his.

"How about some breakfast? I'm starved, I missed supper last night. Oh, by the way, good control."

He smiled, and shook his head.

They headed for the Inn for breakfast. They sat down by themselves in the corner.

"Is that what you did to me the other night?"

Lindsey smiled. "Yep."

"Where did you learn that?"

She had to think for a minute. "Well, you could say it was part of my martial arts training." He didn't ask anything more about it.

"Wow, that looks good," Lindsey said when Sarah brought their food. Until she smelled breakfast, she hadn't realized just how hungry she was. They ate in silence for once.

"Hey, you ok?" John and Todd came up and sat down with them as they were finishing.

"Yeah, I'm fine."

"Have you heard how the kid is yet?" John asked.

"No not yet. Where are you at today?" Lindsey asked him.

"I'm on five and seven."

"I have the campground," Todd said.

"Would you want to trade?" She asked Todd, "I have three and six. But I would really like to be at the campground so I can see Taylor when he gets back."

"Sure, I don't care."

"Thanks, Todd, I owe you!" She smiled at him.

Brandon and Lindsey finished just as Sarah brought John and Todd's food.

"Lindsey," the radio crackled, "there is a call for you at the front desk."

"Be right there," Lindsey headed out to the lobby. Carla pointed to the receiver off the hook. "This is Lindsey."

"Lindsey, this is Mrs. Newman, Taylor's grandmother."

"Yes?"

"Taylor asked me to call you."

"Yes, ma'am, how is he?"

"Well, he has twelve stitches in his head. They think they may have to go in and put some pins in his ankle, but not till the swelling goes down."

"Oh, wow, how's he holding up?"

"They gave him pain pills and put a brace on his ankle. Said it will take a few days for the swelling to go down so we are going to come back, pack up and head for home. He wanted me to call and let you know."

"I'm glad you did; I switched shifts with a friend so I have the campground. I will see you when you come in."

"Alright, it will be a while yet; we have to fill out paperwork and get him checked out."

"Alright, then, I'll see you in a bit." Lindsey hung up the phone and turned to leave.

"Was that about the boy?" Carla asked.

"Yeah, he's ok, got twelve stitches, and is going to have to have pins put in his ankle, but he is fine."

"Glad to hear he's going to be fine; when you said he was hurt this morning and Misty told me you were out there all night ... well, I'm glad he's going to be ok."

"Me, too," Lindsey told her. She walked toward the door.

"Hey, wait up!" Brandon came out of the dining room.

"That was Taylor's grandmother. He has twelve stitches in his head and they are going to have to put pins in his ankle."

Brandon looked at her, "I'm glad it wasn't you."

She stopped and looked at him. "I would rather it have been me than him." Lindsey walked out the door. She was mad; how in the world could he be that cold?

"Lindsey," he grabbed her by the arm. She turned on him, and had his arm pulled behind him before he had time to think.

"Ouch, that hurts!"

She let go. "Sorry."

"I wasn't saying I was glad he got hurt; I was just saying I was glad you weren't." Brandon was rubbing his wrist. "You're fast."

"You have no idea. I'll see you later." Lindsey turned and walked toward the campground.

The day went by slowly, people checking in and checking out. Lindsey stayed in the shack and Sam did the running round on the campground. Malcolm brought down food trays at lunch for her and Sam. The Newmans pulled in while Malcolm was still there.

"Go ahead, I'll stick around here and help out for a while."

"Thanks." Lindsey walked down to site 22. Taylor was sitting on top of the picnic table with his foot on a pillow.

"Hey, Taylor!" She said as she came up behind him. "How's the ankle?"

"They gave me some good drugs, I don't feel it. Matter a fact, I don't feel much of anything." He smiled. "Look at my stitches!" He lifted his hair.

"Hey, the scar will go with the whole Goth thing you've got going." He laughed. The other three were pulling the camp apart.

"Can I help you guys?" Lindsay asked Mr. Newman.

"Just keep an eye on him; I think they gave him so much medication he is about high."

Lindsey laughed. "OK." Lindsey sat down beside Taylor on the tabletop.

"You sure are pretty." He leaned over and laid his head on her shoulder.

Lindsey laughed. "I see what you mean about the medication," she said loudly to his grandfather.

"I lost my MP3 somewhere in the mud."

Lindsey pulled her iPod out of her pocket; she always kept it with her.

"You can have mine."

"Really?" He took it from her.

"I don't use it much; I'm always too busy."

"Thanks!" He said.

"You're welcome."

"Hey, Mary," Taylor called to his sister.

"What?" She said as she loaded stuff into the back of the truck.

"Where's your camera?" Mary went to the door of the truck and retrieved the camera. "Take a picture of Lindsey and me." Mary looked at the screen. Lindsey leaned over and gave Taylor a kiss on the cheek. Mary took the picture. Lindsey winked at Mary. Mary laughed.

"Look, she gave me her iPod," he told Mary.

Mary smiled at Lindsey. "You shouldn't have done that; he can get a new one when we get home."

"But what's he going to listen to on the way home?" Lindsey asked her.

Mary sat the camera down on the edge of the table and went back to helping her grandparents. Lindsey picked up the camera and took a couple of pictures of them loading the truck. Then she held it out and took one of Taylor, then one of them together. She turned and smiled at him; he leaned over and tried to kiss her. Lindsey laughed at him.

"You're way too young and drugged up."

"No, I'm not!" He said. "On which account?"

"Either. So how old are you?" She asked.

"I'll be 18 in December."

"And I'll be 23 in July."

"That's just four years."

Lindsey looked into his eyes. "You're really great, but I have someone, and he's only 19. So age really isn't the issue." He leaned close to her again.

"Just one for the road?"

She smiled and took off her hat, held up the camera and touched his lips with hers and snapped the picture. The second the picture took, the kiss ended. "Something to remember me by." She looked up to his grandmother looking at her. Lindsey smiled and winked at her and put her hat back on. "I have to get back to work." Lindsey stood up.

"You guys have a safe trip home."

"Hey, can I call you?"

Lindsey saw Ms. Newman stop to listen.

"Sorry, Taylor, but no."

"Why not?"

"I have already told you I have someone else. But I am quite flattered that you would want to call me." Lindsey turned to the rest of the Newmans and waved. She looked back at Taylor. He was watching her. She turned and gave him a big smile. He raised his hand and waved. Lindsey waved back to him, then turned and left. She headed back to the camp shack. Malcolm headed out as soon as he saw her coming.

"He's not much for work is he?" Lindsey asked Sam.

"The only work he does is sitting at his desk making out the schedules and driving lunch down here on occasion." They both laughed. "So how was the boy?"

"Love struck."

Sam laughed. "Oh, no, one of those?"

Lindsey laughed. "Yeah, he asked for my number." They both laughed.

"I hope you let him down gently."

"Of course, I did. He's a sweet kid." The Newmans honked as they drove by the shack. Lindsey went to the door and waved.

"I usually tell them I'm seeing someone," Sam said from behind her.

"Yeah, that's what I did," Lindsey said as she shut the door.

Three cars pulled up and they went back to work; the rest of the afternoon slid by. Lindsey thought of Brandon and felt bad about how she had acted towards him.

The line of cars got really long about suppertime. Lindsey was working with a clipboard checking people out as Sam checked people in. Lindsey saw Brandon with the supper tray coming from the Inn around six. There was no time to stop and talk. He left the tray and went back to the Inn without a word to her. He had every right to be mad at her; she had twisted his arm and acted ugly to him. The campground was completely full by seven and she put the 'full' site sign up on the shack along with the names of three other local campground names. Lindsey and Sam sat down to eat about 7:30.

"It has been a long day," Lindsey told Sam.

"I imagine you're still tired from last night. Since we're not checking people in and out, I can handle this place by myself. Why don't you go back and turn in early."

"Are you sure?"

"I wouldn't have offered, if I wasn't."

Lindsey smiled. "That would be so great, thanks!"

Sam smiled at her. "You look really tired, go on."

Lindsey got up and headed out the door. "Thanks again," she told Sam.

Lindsey headed straight to the cabin; she was sore and really tired. She showered and was in bed before 8:30.

The alarm going off woke her. She reached over and shut it off; pain shot through her side. Brandon was lying beside her. His eyes were still closed. She gritted her teeth and let the pain subside, then took her finger and pushed some hair from his face. He caught her hand and opened his eyes.

"I'm sorry about yesterday; I think I was just tired," Lindsey told him.

He still held her arm. "I saw the Newmans as they left yesterday. Taylor showed me his pictures."

Lindsey grinned and laughed, but not hard. Her side was beginning to pulse. He had shown him the picture of them kissing. He smiled, and let go of her.

"Why in the world would you lead him on like that?"

Lindsey tried not to let the pain show. "He didn't have much confidence in himself, so I gave him just a little."

"A little what?"

She giggled.

He started to pull her close to him, but his arm brushed her side and she flinched.

"Sorry."

He pulled back the covers and flipped the light on. Her side looked horrible and her hip and leg looked even worse. He looked at her sympathetically.

"They always look worse before they look better. I'll be fine."

His looked changed. "So do you get lots of these?"

She shook her head.

"No, I'm talking bruises in general, silly."

"Oh, ok."

"What time did you make it in last night?" She asked him.

"About nine. You were out cold. You didn't even budge when I flipped on the light. I didn't know you were here."

"I got in bed about 8:30. The campground got full so Sam let me come on back."

Lindsey went to move her leg. "Oh, crap, that's sore. I don't think I can run today, the jarring would kill me."

Brandon smiled. "And I was so looking forward to going."

He reached over and flipped the light back off and slung the cover back over them. He rolled up on his side to face her. Lindsey still lay on her back staring at the ceiling.

"You're really beautiful, you know that?"

Lindsey turned her head to face him. "You sound like Taylor." She smiled.

"Are you going to give me a little kiss like Taylor?"

She laughed. "No! No kisses for you."

"Oh, why not? Do I have to be hurt?"

"Yep, that's it."

Brandon took an imaginary knife and stabbed himself with it and fell backward on his back. Lindsey pulled herself up on her side; the pain was horrible. He was laying there with his eyes closed and his tongue hanging out. He opened his eyes and smiled. He pulled her up on top of him. She moaned at the touch of her side and leg.

"Sorry, I didn't ..."

She didn't let him finish the sentence. Her lips touched his. The kiss got hot quick, and Lindsey had to put out the flame. She pulled back; he pulled her back to him.

"Oh!"

He had grabbed her by the side.

"Crap," he said and let her go.

She slid off him and the bed. Her leg hurt so bad she fell to the floor. Brandon jumped up and was at her side immediately.

"You ok?"

"Yeah, I just wasn't expecting it to be that sore. Help me up, I have to get some of this soreness and stiffness out of my leg."

Brandon picked her up and set her on her feet. He held her so she couldn't fall. She slowly walked around the room.

"Maybe some hot water would help." He helped her to the shower, then left. She slid her shorts down, but lost her balance and fell into the side of the shower. Brandon was there in an instant.

"You ok?"

She had hit her side on the handle, and tears ran down her face.

"Let me help you." He took her shorts and bra off. Then he turned the water on for her. He stood beside her as the water ran down both of them. He stood there in his boxers, holding her up. Her bare back was against his chest. She leaned her head back against him. Brandon found himself looking down at the water running over her. She suddenly was aware of just how much this was affecting him so she stepped away from him.

"Are you going to be ok?" He asked in a ragged voice. His arms were still around her, and she could see the muscles tighten up in them.

"Go on, I'll be ok."

Brandon took a deep breath and stepped from the shower. Lindsey held the shower door to keep herself steady. She could see him through the door. He stripped his wet boxers off and wrapped in a towel.

"Brandon." He looked up. "You're getting better."

He laughed. "You have no idea how hard that was. How hard it still is." Lindsey stretched her leg and bent to the side to stretch it. She was sore, but it was feeling better.

"Hey, Lindsey?"

"Yeah?"

"Your phone beeped."

"See what he wants."

Brandon picked up her phone from the table; so it was a he on the other end. He read the message as he walked back to the bathroom.

"Take pictures of her bruises, I need to see them."

Brandon came back into the bathroom. "He wants pictures of your bruises."

Lindsey shut the water off and opened the door and stepped out in front of him.

"Can you find the camera on there?"

Brandon scrolled down the menu till he found it. "Got it."

Lindsey stood there while Brandon took two photos: one of her side and one of her hip to her knee. Lindsey took the phone and sent the pictures.

It beeped back. "I'll send you something that will help with the soreness and bruising; you should get it this afternoon." Lindsey typed back, "Thanks."

"What's up?" Brandon asked.

"He is going to send me some medicine."

"I guess that was your doctor?"

Lindsey smiled. "Yep."

Brandon handed her the towel hanging on the rack. "Cover yourself."

Keeps looked at the pictures of Lindsey. He had a hard time focusing on her bruises. He wasn't expecting her to be naked in the pictures. She was beautiful; well, she would be without all the black and purple. No wonder this Brandon guy had fallen for her in a couple of weeks. He sure wished he could switch places him.

Lindsey took the towel and wrapped it around her, then went to get her clothes from the closet. Brandon went to the table and sat down a minute. He picked up a pencil and looked around for something to write on. In the nightstand table he found a small tablet that looked like it had been there for years. He wrote something, then handed it to Lindsey.

"Who is that on the phone?"

Lindsey took the pencil from him.

"It's best if you don't know." She handed it back.

"Who are you?"

Lindsey thought for a moment. "You don't want to know."

He flipped the paper. "Yes, I do."

"I can't tell you, it could get you killed," she wrote back. Lindsey handed him the paper and pulled her pants on.

"Would you hand me my shirt?" Lindsey said aloud.

"Sure," he said as he wrote.

"What are you, a spy or something?" He looked up and handed her the note. "Here you go," he said out loud.

"Something," she wrote, then paused. How could she explain to him what she did without explaining what she did? All kinds of things flooded her head. It stopped on movies. "Jason Bourne without the torture," she wrote then handed it back. Surely he had seen those movies. Brandon looked at it, then at her. She took the paper from him and burned it in the sink.

"You ready?" She asked.

"Almost," he said, but he never took his eyes from her.

"Have you checked on Jacob lately?"

He broke the eye contact and put his shoes and socks on. "I stopped by yesterday for a second. Michelle said he was doing lots better. She thinks she will probably be able to leave Tuesday."

"Glad he's feeling better."

"Yeah, me, too," he said as he got up and grabbed his shirt. He walked over and opened the door. Lindsey stopped in front of him and looked up at him. She wasn't sure what was in his eyes, they were sort of blank. She reached out and touched his arm; he just looked at her. They walked to the Inn in silence.

Brandon walked beside Lindsey to the Inn in silence, but his head was not silent at all. Jason Bourne was all he could think. He loved those movies, but now he was having a hard time grasping that the person walking beside him could actually be something like him. He knew there were real spies and things like that, but still. Did she actually kill people? Could he be walking next to a killer?

"You want to work on the piano a little before breakfast?" Lindsey asked. "I can write some scales out for you." Brandon didn't say anything, he just stood there in the lobby and waited for her. "I'll get some paper from Carla."

"Hey Carla, can I get some copy paper and a pencil?"

"Sure." She handed it to Lindsey.

"Thanks."

Lindsey walked toward the clubs room as Brandon followed in silence. He sat down and played some chords while Lindsey got a book and sat down to write out scales. She put a piece of paper in front of him.

"I told you, you didn't want to know. So now what, you going to pull away from me every time I get near you?" He looked at the paper, then took her pencil.

"I don't know. How can you kill for a living?"

She looked at it. "It's not a living Brandon; it's what I was born into, why I was even conceived. I am what they raised me to be."

He looked at her. Fear and disgust was in his eyes.

"Why are you here?"

"To rest and take a break."

"So what am I?"

Lindsey took the paper and wrote, "Someone that has stolen my heart."

"Do you even have one of those?"

Lindsey read the paper, looked up at him, a tear slid down her check. She put the rest of the paper down and the pencil, took the one sheet and left. Lindsey headed out of the Inn and back toward the cabin. When she saw John on the way up she changed her mind and headed for her first trail of the day. Luckily number seven was down past the campground, so she was already heading in the right direction. Lindsey walked the trail slowly. Why had he even wanted her to stay if he was going to be like this? She had told him he couldn't know what she did and she had sort of told him and now what? Maybe she should ask Keeps to move her. Her heart felt heavy as she walked.

She was way ahead of schedule, so she didn't need to rush. She finished seven and headed back up towards two, which was up by the Inn. Hopefully, Brandon would be gone by now, it was going on eight a.m. Lindsey saw Brandon as she passed the campground.

Brandon couldn't believe it. Lindsey killed people. That was what she did. How could she? How could he love someone like that? What if she got tired of him, would she kill him? He walked to the camp shack after Lindsey left. He saw the tears in her eyes. *How could she kill people?* was all he could think. Brandon was checking a car in when he saw Lindsey walk by. She seemed to be going slow. He wanted to just forget the last week, the last two weeks. Forget her. He finished with the car and went back into the shack. How was he going to face her again? What about sleeping arrangements? He would either go in early, or sleep late, or leave when she went for her run. Michelle would be leaving in a couple of days then he could go back to Jacobs's cabin. A killer, how could she be a killer? Although, it did explain why she was always saying she could take care of herself and why she had no trouble apprehending those poachers. He had even noticed how fast she was when she twisted his arm when he grabbed her. His mind wandered over the last two weeks to every little thing she had said or done. Some of what she said made sense now. Her life was not her own. He had always wondered about that statement. Now he knew why, and he wasn't so sure he wanted to know.

Lindsey spent her day on the trails, not really talking to anyone unless she had to. At lunch she picked up a package from the front desk. In it were four things: a laptop, medication, iPod, and the trip tickets and arrangements for Brandon's parents. Lindsey gave herself a shot, then placed the rest in the fridge. The laptop she put on the table along with the tickets. The iPod, which was loaded just like her other one, she stuffed in her pocket and went back to work. She sent Keeps a quick "thanks" on her way back to seven. Brandon was talking to a lady in a car when she went by. A tear slid down her check. She took out her iPod, put in the ear buds and walked on.

The next few days were the same; she would come in and go to sleep. Brandon would come in later, then would be gone by the time she came back from her run. He never spoke to her. The tickets still lay on the table where she had left them. He never looked at them. He never looked at her. Tuesday he went back to Jacob's. Lindsey saw Jacob at supper that evening.

"I have the tickets for your parents. You hadn't given me an answer, but the reservation had to be made so I went on and made them."

"So how much do we owe you?"

"Well, the whole thing was $1,800; I know you said not over $1,500, so just consider three hundred my gift."

"You shouldn't have done that."

"Maybe not, but I wanted to."

Lindsey turned to leave.

"Hey, Lindsey?"

She turned back. "Yeah?"

"What happened with you and Brandon? And don't tell me "nothing" like he does. I know something's wrong."

Lindsey sat down at the table. "I really don't know what to tell you. My life is not really here; this is just a break from my real business. I think he didn't like that fact."

"So what do you do?"

Lindsey looked at him and took a breath, and got up from the table. "Don't worry about it, he's better off now, anyway." Lindsey smiled at him and walked away. Her phone beeped. She pulled it out of her pocket.

"You told him, didn't you?"

Lindsey didn't answer.

"Are you trying to get us all killed?"

Lindsey still didn't answer.

Lindsey put the phone back in her pocket and walked back to the cabin. It was early enough to make another round, but she didn't. She sat down at the laptop and worked on things for Brandon's school. She wasn't sure he would even go now, but maybe.

What in the world had possessed her to tell him what she did? Keeps was about half frantic. She was lucky he was doing her fulltime monitoring now. Luckily he knew when King monitored, he had set up the whole network and had everything running through his computer so he could see it when it kicked on. He was going to have to take strong measures to make sure things didn't get out of hand. Who was he kidding? They already were out of hand.

Her phone went off, this time it rang.

"Yes?" She was expecting Keeps.

"You're needed."

It was the Handler's voice.

"Will I be returning?" Her heart raced not wanting to hear the word 'no'.

"In a few weeks. Arrangements have already been made with Malcolm. A chopper will pick you up in the morning at 0400."

"I'll be ready."

CHAPTER 5

Surprise

L INDSEY WORKED ON the laptop most of the night to finish what she had been doing. A few weeks could mean anything, so she needed to set things in motion now. Lindsey pushed the power button and shut the computer off. She left it open and lay down on the bed. She needed to be sharp, but sleep wasn't coming. Her mind was stuck on Brandon. At 3:30 a.m., she got dressed and turned the alarm off. She shut off the lights and went up to the parking lot to wait for the chopper. Just before four it landed. She got in, and only then looked at Jacobs's cabin. Brandon was standing on the porch watching.

Brandon couldn't sleep past 3:30, after staying with Lindsey. But he wasn't going to run and take a chance running into her, so he just lay in the bed. A helicopter landing nearby brought him out of the bed. He could see it in the parking lot. He opened the door and went out to see what was up. Lindsey was climbing into it. He watched from the porch. He walked down to her cabin, the door was unlocked like always. He flipped on the light. Everything was still there; her laptop, her clothes, her guitar, her phone. Her phone? She never went anywhere without it. What was going on? He walked over and picked up the phone, then sat it back down. He would like to know who the guy on the other end was. Why should he care where she was? She was a killer. She was nothing to him. He laid his hand on the bed. His heart felt like it was being ripped from his chest. Tears slid down his face. He turned and left. Back at Jacob's cabin, he put his shoes and socks on and ran. He ran harder and faster than he ever had. He ran till his side hurt, till his whole body hurt, till he couldn't run anymore.

"So what's up?" Lindsey asked Handler as they flew over the park.

"The government is in an uproar. Four Special Ops Marines have been killed in 48 hours."

"So why am I here?"

"Clean up. We need you to go in and kill the guy responsible for this mess. Here is the logistics and the man's picture. This one is your call. One other thing, you have to talk to the generals in charge of the Ops missions. Your voice will be altered."

"Why am I talking to them?"

"Not sure, but the meeting's started; you will be patched in from here."

"Do they matter or have anything to do with me? I am not in a good mood."

Handler smiled. "No, this is your call."

"Alright, patch me through." Lindsey could hear several men talking.

"Are you there?"

Lindsey answered. "I'm here."

"We have had four Marines killed in the last 48 hours; we have been told you can take care of the problem."

"That's why I am here."

"All right then, we have two Marines waiting for you at the rendezvous point; they will take you in."

Lindsey laughed. "Sorry, gentlemen, but I need no escort. I will find my own way in and out. If you have men being killed, I don't want anywhere near you."

"You will need men; do you know who you're up against?"

"Yes, I have the file right here. I will let you know when the job's done."

"I don't know who you think you are . . ." came an angry voice.

Lindsey cut him off. "I'm someone who is cleaning up your mess. Goodnight, gentlemen." The call ended. "Connect me to The Keeper; I need a few things."

"Keeper here."

"I need a few things."

"What do you need?"

"I need dye for my eyes, skin; I also need an ethnic outfit and a knife."

Keeps laughed "Done. Anything else?"

"Four pin charges, two trackers, and a nine millimeter and a sniper rifle."

"You got it. It will be waiting for you at your next flight."

Lindsey went over and over the maps and charts in the file. She read all they had on the man; he was trafficking in guns and girls. He was ex-military and had a good knowledge of procedure.

Her next flight was a jet; all her things were waiting for her in a bag. She gave herself the retina and skin shots, and then changed into a black jumpsuit. The outfit was in her bag; she would change once she was on the ground. She switched back to a helicopter and jumped ten miles out.

When Brandon got back to the cabin after his run, there was a manila envelope lying on the bed addressed to him. He picked it up and sat down at the table. Brandon looked down into the envelope. He reached in and pulled out a picture. It was from Jessica, the pictures of Lindsey and him. He got up and took the envelope and went to Lindsey's cabin. He poured everything out on her bed. There were letters from the girls, some addressed to him, some to Lindsey. There were eight pictures, four for him and four for Lindsey.

He separated hers and his. He took hers and sat them on the table beside her laptop. His, he put back into the envelope, except for two pictures; the one of her looking off and him looking at her, and the one of just her. Tears streamed down his cheeks. Why did he have to love her? He curled up on the bed and cried like a little baby.

A noise from Lindsey's phone brought Keeps to his computer. Who was in her cabin? He kicked on her computer camera to see who was in the room. Brandon lay curled up on her bed crying.

"Brandon," a voice said. It had an electronic sound to it. He sat up quickly and looked around.

"Pull yourself together." The laptop on the table had an avatar figure standing on the screen.

"Who are you?" Brandon's tears dried up quickly.

"I am the guy on Lindsey's phone."

Brandon got off the bed and walked over in front of the computer.

"What do you want?" Brandon asked.

"I want to know why you're here."

Brandon looked down at the pictures he still had in his hands. Then up to the screen. "Who are you?" Brandon asked again.

"Who am I or who I am to Lindsey?"

"Both," Brandon said.

"I am Lindsey's keeper."

"Her what?"

"Keeper, I take care of her and of all her needs; wherever she may be."

"So you provide her with the means to kill?" You could hear the anger in his voice.

"If that's what she needs, then yes. So she did tell you what she does."

"She told me enough."

"But she didn't tell you everything, did she?"

"What are you talking about? She kills people, and I don't want to know any more." His anger was getting the best of him.

"Let me show you something. Sit down, Brandon." The computer screen blinked and news stories started playing.

"The oil tycoon found dead in his house had been linked to several arms dealers." "Linked to human trafficking found dead in a bar it . . ." "Remains were found today of that notorious human trafficker . . ." Little pieces of newsreels telling of people being killed.

The avatar appeared again.

"She may take life, but she saves lives, too."

"All those were her?"

"Yes, and that was just a few."

Brandon pulled out a chair and sat down. "Why are you telling me this? I thought I wasn't supposed to know."

"I'm not telling you anything!"

Brandon looked down at Lindsey's picture. "Where is she?"

A news story with yesterday's date appeared on the screen. "The bodies of the four Marines gunned down on a recon mission were returned home today."

"Cleaning up a mess."

"Is she safe?"

"She takes no unnecessary risks. But I have no idea what she is doing; I only provide her with what she asks for."

"Will she be coming back?"

"As far as I know, yes, but she could change her mind. She will be the one who decides whether to come back or not." Brandon put his head in his hands. "Do you want her back?"

Brandon looked up at the screen, tears streamed down his face. Brandon nodded his head.

"One thing you need to remember. This conversation never took place."

With that, the screen went black. Brandon got up. It was going on nine and he hadn't even showered. He left his pictures on Lindsey's bed and left.

Three weeks later ...

"A letter arrived for you today," Carla handed Brandon the envelope. The return address read San Diego School of Music. Brandon opened the envelope and took out the letter. His eyes got big, he ran to the dining hall where Jacob sat. He handed the letter to Jacob.

"Wow, I didn't know you even applied for a school! And this says you have been awarded a full scholarship, The Jacobs Music Scholarship." Brandon had spent the last three weeks in Lindsey's cabin waiting for her to return. "It also says here your classes start in three weeks, that's not long to get ready." Brandon took the letter back from Jacob. "There's a number on there it says to call; you better do it quickly. Don't make them wait."

"I'll do it now." Brandon headed for the office to use the phone.

"Administration office, this is Kelly; how can I help you?" The voice on the phone said.

"Yes, this is Brandon Clearwater; I received a letter."

"Yes, Mr. Clearwater I have been expecting your call. Classes start in three weeks, you need to come down at least a week early and familiarize yourself with the area. Your apartment and equipment are set and waiting for you."

"Did you say apartment?"

"Oh, yes sir, this scholarship is a full one: it includes an apartment, four years of schooling and all the equipment, guitars, piano, computer, and all software needed to complete each class."

Brandon was speechless.

"When you arrive, come by the office and I will give you your apartment key and schedule."

"Thanks," Brandon said.

"You're welcome. We'll see you in a couple of weeks."

Brandon walked back to the dining hall in shock.

"I have an apartment and everything."

"This is great! Mom and Dad will be so thrilled."

Brandon took the letter and went back to the cabin. He knew she had gotten him the scholarship. But why hadn't she come back? Maybe she had decided not to. He wasn't going to think like that. She was coming back. But he would be leaving for school soon. It was October now; when was she coming back?

Lindsey ran to the helicopter and climbed in.

"Were you successful?"

"I wouldn't have called you to pick me up if I weren't."

"The generals have been in a panic for weeks."

"I always finish what I start, and running in is what got those Marines killed."

He smiled at her. "I know."

Lindsey had been gone for over five weeks. It was November the 20th; her mind wandered to Brandon, his parents' party was in five days.

"You will be debriefed, then, you can get back to your R&R."

"It's not rest, if you call me up."

Lindsey was jetted back to Keeps. Her hair was black and she was very dark skinned.

"You ready?"

"For what?"

"To get back to your vacation."

Lindsey laughed. "I think I am."

"I left the stuff for your hair and skin in your room, also a pair of jeans, shirt, jacket and shoes. The weather is cooler than when you left. You need to be in room 4C in an hour to give your report, then we will see about getting you back on schedule."

Lindsey gave her report as always, behind a glass so she could not be seen. Very few people knew who she was, and they tried hard to keep it that way. After that she gave herself the retina and skin shot. Lindsey wandered back down to see Keeps. She pulled her iPod from her pocket. "Can I use your computer to put some music on here?"

"Sure." He slid to the side and worked on some paperwork. He reached over and pushed a couple of buttons; a video loaded on her iPod.

"Sorry about that, it gets a glitch sometimes."

"No problem," she said, she didn't acknowledge the download. She piddled around on Keeps' computer for a while, then unhooked.

"Thanks, I think I have run this music into the ground."

"I'll have your arrangements for your departure in the morning; you should be back on vacation by nightfall."

"Thanks, Keeps, you're the best."

She went back up to her room. It was late, so she turned in. She put her ear buds in and turned on her side. She put the small screen under the edge of the pillow beside her head. She watched the video of Brandon coming into her cabin curling up on her bed and crying. She saw and heard the whole conversation. Her heart about leaped out of her chest at his answer to wanting her back. She slept soundly with dreams of Brandon all night.

She went in to see Keeps in the morning to get her stuff. She handed him her iPod. "I think your glitch got on my iPod."

"Let me see." He plugged it up and deleted the video.

"That should do it."

"You'll be dropped off just like you left this time. You should be there by nine."

Lindsey got up and walked around and gave Keeps a kiss on the cheek.

"Thanks for taking care of me."

He smiled. "It's my job, you know that."

"Yeah, well, you're good at it."

The Handler came into the room. "You ready?"

"Yep, let's get out of here."

Handler dropped her off about 8:45 pm in the parking lot. Jacob came out of his cabin.

"You're back. Brandon is going to be mad that he missed you."

"How is Brandon?" She asked.

"He is at music school, got a full scholarship."

Lindsey smiled. "I'm glad to hear that; I knew he could do it."

"He will be in for Mom and Dad's party. You're going, right?"

"I wouldn't miss it."

"Matter of fact, that reminds me, I still haven't paid you for it."

"Whenever is fine, I am not hurting for it."

He laughed. "That's what Brandon said. He says you're loaded."

"He's right."

"See you in the morning." Jacob went back in.

Lindsey opened her door. It was mainly just as she left it. There was a stack of letters and some pictures on the table. She would look at them tomorrow, she was beat. She showered and headed for bed. On her pillow lay their rock. She smiled, laid it beside her on the table and went to sleep.

Things basically picked up where they left off. She went back to walking the trails. She talked to Malcolm about going to the Clearwater's party Friday. Now that the tourist rush was over, he had no problem with it. The week passed like all the rest had before she left, except there was no Brandon.

She ate with Jacob most nights. He asked about her being in the reserves and why she had been gone for three months instead of the normal weekend once a month. She told him that there was a bunch of Intel coming in and they needed a few extra people to get it all sorted out.

"I haven't talked to Brandon since you got back so it will be a surprise when you show up at the party Friday night," he told her. "And after the party, after mom and dad leave, we are going to go swimming. The pool is inside and we are going to let all the little kids go home first."

"Problem, I don't have a swimsuit."

"Michelle probably has an extra you can borrow. We'll leave at nine in the morning. Pack a bag, we are staying tomorrow night and will be back early Saturday."

Lindsey's stomach immediately started doing flips; she was nervous about seeing Brandon. What if he had meet someone at school? What if he was still mad at her? She knew what he had said on the video. He wanted her to come back, but that had been over three months ago. He might have given up on her.

Lindsey didn't sleep well, but she did finally fall asleep around two. She was wide awake again by three thirty.

The ride to the Clearwater's seemed to take forever. Finally, they pulled into the driveway. Jacob's parents met them at the door.

"It's good to see you, Lindsey. Thanks so much for the trip. Jacob and Brandon said you got it all together for them." Mary put her arms around her and gave her a hug.

"Brandon made it in, yet?" Jacob asked.

"No, he didn't want to miss a class so he will be here later."

Michelle came in the door. "Jacob said you needed a suit. I hope you don't mind a bikini; I think it is the only thing I might have that would fit you, you're so tiny." Michelle handed her a bag.

Lindsey looked down in it. It was a string bikini. "It will be fine; thanks for the loaner."

"No time to waste; we need to get down to the hall and get things set up." Michelle ushered Jacob and her out the door.

"Your limo will be here at four, so be packed and ready, you two," Michelle told the Clearwaters as she went out the door.

The community hall wasn't far and they went in and started setting up tables and chairs, people seemed to be coming from everywhere to help set up. Michelle had gone all out for the party. She had tablecloths, flowers, and a cake; the whole nine yards. Lindsey helped put on the tablecloths and set up the flowers. They hung streamers and balloons everywhere. By three the place looked like a wedding hall. By four the place was packed. The Clearwaters arrived at 4:05 and the party got underway. The toasts had just started when Brandon came through the door. Lindsey stayed in the very back as the toast went up. There was a small ceremony, then they ate. Brandon was sitting with his parents, and Jacob and Michelle.

"Where did Lindsey go? She should be sitting with us," Mary asked Jacob.

Brandon stood up so hard and fast, his seat fell over backwards. "She's here?"

Jacob smiled. "She's here somewhere."

Lindsey stepped outside when they started serving the food. Her heart was racing so hard she could barely breathe. He was here.

Brandon scanned the room, but didn't see her.

Lindsey opened the door and stepped back inside. Brandon almost ran across the floor when he saw her. He stopped just inches from her.

"I'm sorry," he blurted out. Every table around them looked up.

Lindsey stepped back and opened the door behind her and pulled him outside. Jacob smiled. Lindsey slid her arms around him and pulled him close. She pulled something from her pocket and put it in his hand closing his fingers around it. A single tear rolled down his cheek. He was holding their rock. His lips found hers.

"We better go back inside and spend time with your parents before they leave," she told him.

"Alright, but I am not leaving your side tonight."

She smiled, "Good."

He took her hand and led the way back inside and back to the table where he sat her down beside him. Jacob had a big grin on his face.

"It's good to see you two talking again."

Lindsey smiled at Brandon who was staring at her.

The food was finished and the cake was cut, then the happy couple got into the limo and left for the airport. Clean up took longer than the set up, but once it was over and most of the guests were gone, the party in the pool started. Several of Brandon's friends stayed.

Lindsey put on the bikini. It barely covered anything.

"So, is it ok?" Michelle asked.

Lindsey stepped out of the stall.

"You look great."

Brandon had seen her in nothing, but no one else had seen her in so little. Not that it really should bother her she really wasn't modest. She couldn't be in her job.

"If you really think so."

"All Brandon's friends are going to be so jealous of him tonight!"

Lindsey smiled. The two of them exited the bathroom and headed for the pool. Brandon and his buddies were already in the pool when they walked in. Lindsey felt every guy in the room look at her, all at once. She walked to the pool and slid in beside Brandon.

"Wow, you look hot!" the guy to the left said.

"Lindsey, these are the guys from the band. This is Brett, Todd, and Jordan."

Lindsey smiled at each of them.

"How in the world did you end up with him?" Todd asked.

"Just lucky, I guess," she answered.

Brett elbowed Brandon and smiled. Brandon shook his head. Michelle pulled out the stereo from the dining hall and plugged in her iPod.

"Anyone for dancing?" she yelled, a couple of girls got out of the pool.

"Honey, you have to have better music than that if we are going to dance," one of them told her. The other one went to her bag and pulled out her iPod and switched it.

Lindsey smiled. "Now that's dance music."

Brandon looked at Lindsey. "I guess you like to dance, too?"

"There is nothing like sex on the dance floor."

Brandon and his buddies all looked at her as she climbed out of the pool. The two girls were now dancing and some more were joining in.

"Do you have any Missy Elliot?" Lindsey asked one of the girls.

The girl smiled. "Something tells me you know how to dance, girl."

Lindsey smiled at her. The girl scrolled through the music then smiled. "Do you know how to do the booty shake?"

Brandon watched.

"Where did you find her?" Todd asked him.

"She's a Ranger."

"She's a hot Ranger," Brett added.

"Yeah," Brandon agreed. The next song started and Lindsey swayed sexily to the music.

"Wow, it wouldn't take much to imagine her without that little suit on," Jordan said.

Brandon punched Jordan in the shoulder.

"Ouch! You know you're doing it!"

Brandon smiled. "I don't have to imagine."

Brett slapped Brandon on the back. "Finally, some girl broke you in!"

Brandon laughed. "Nope, still waiting."

146

"Alright, let's hear it then," Brett said.

"Jacob got sick a while back and I stayed with her for several days."

"So you slept on her couch? Big deal."

"No, I slept in her bed with her." They all looked at him.

"How do you sleep beside that and remain a virgin?"

"Is she gay?" Jordan asked.

"No," Brandon said, "she is waiting, too."

They all looked at Lindsey dancing.

"That can't be waiting," Jordan said.

"Oh, she is, though."

"But, how did you see her in the raw?" Brett asked.

"Which time?" Brandon asked.

Lindsey walked around the pool and slid back into the water. Jordan watched her intently as she got in.

"Ok, something is so wrong with both of you," Jordan said.

"What?" Lindsey asked.

Brett and Todd laughed.

"Spill it," Lindsey said.

"Jordon doesn't see how you can be a virgin."

Lindsey smiled. "Easy. I don't have sex."

"Why the heck not?" Jordan asked.

"That's easy. I want it to be me and my husband and no one else. I want us to learn together. I don't want to compare or be compared."

Todd looked at her. "So, if that's true, how come you're letting him see you without your clothes?"

Lindsey turned and looked at Brandon. "Accidents happen. Although they seem to happen an awful lot when he's around." Brandon and Lindsey both laughed. "But paybacks are quite rewarding."

Brett looked at Brandon. "Paybacks, eh, so what were the paybacks?"

Lindsey smiled at Brandon.

"No comment," Brandon said.

Lindsey winked at Brett, "Torture can be so fun." Lindsey put her arm around Brandon and pulled him close to her. "So much fun." Her eyes met Brandon's.

Brett laughed. "I don't see how you do it," Jordan said.

Lindsey wrapped her legs around Brandon. Their eyes never left each other's. His arms were on her hips.

"They aren't going to make it too much longer," Brett said.

Lindsey looked at him. "You guys have no control."

She let Brandon go. He smiled at her.

"You're getting better," she told him. "So when am I going to get to hear you guys play?"

"We are practicing this weekend," Todd said.

"I don't have to be back till Monday," Brandon told her.

"I wonder if Malcolm would be mad if I didn't come back this weekend?" Lindsey asked Brandon.

"Ask and find out."

"Can I stay with you?" She asked Brandon.

"You know you can."

Lindsey climbed out of the pool. "I'll be back."

She walked over to her bag and pulled out her phone and called Malcolm. She made a deal with him. She would work the weeks before and after Christmas so everyone could go home and see their family, if she could have off this weekend and one week in December. Lindsey walked over and talked to Jacob, then went back to Brandon.

"Done deal," she told Brandon as she slid back into the pool.

"So who sings?" She asked.

"That would be me," Todd said.

"Bass," said Brett.

"Drums," said Jordan.

"I can't wait to hear you."

"Don't expect too much," Brandon told her.

Brett looked at him. "We're pretty good."

"Yeah," added Jordan and Todd.

"No offense guys, but she can play us all in the ground."

They all looked at Lindsey.

Lindsey looked at Brandon. "I don't know about that."

"So, what do you play?" Brett asked her.

"Yeah." She said.

"Everything we do plus more."

Lindsey thought it best not to say anything to that.

"So what do you like to play the best?" Jordan asked.

"I love to play the piano best of all."

"We could have a keyboard player," Todd piped in.

Lindsey laughed.

The party went till late. After cleaning up again, it was close to three a.m. when Jacob dropped off Brandon and Lindsey.

"See you Monday, Lindsey. I'm staying at Michelle's. See you later, bro," Jacob told them as he left.

"Sweet," Brandon said, "we have the whole house to ourselves."

"Dibs on the first shower," Lindsey said as Brandon opened the door.

Lindsey took her bag to Brandon's room and went straight to the bathroom. When she came out Bandon was asleep. He had sat down on the edge of the bed and laid back and fell asleep. Lindsey stood in her towel in front of him. She put her shorts and bra on, then took the straps back off and put the towel back around her so you couldn't tell she had anything on. Then she climbed up and straddled him. She leaned over and woke him with a kiss.

"You need to shower, you smell like chlorine."

He opened his eyes. Lindsey sat there in her towel.

Brandon smiled, "What are you doing?"

"I've been thinking about this all night and I've decided . . ." She reached up and yanked her towel off, "to torture you!"

He laughed then flipped her on the bed so he was astride her. He pulled off his shirt, kicked off his shoes and unfastened his pants.

"You can't get those off sitting on me."

He got up and went to the shower. Lindsey laughed. She slid her straps on and climbed into the bed. It wasn't long before he was back in only a towel.

She reached up and grabbed it from him. "You still owed me."

He turned and faced her with a smile.

"You know you are going to make some girl very happy someday."

He blushed and turned to his chest and got a pair of boxers out and put them on. "You mean make you happy someday."

"You already make me happy, just not like that."

He climbed in the bed beside her. She snuggled up against him.

"I'm glad you're back. I was afraid you might not want to," he told her. She squeezed his arms around her.

"I'm glad you're not mad," she told him.

"How could I stay mad at you?" He asked her.

She wasn't going to tell him she almost hadn't come back. He kissed the back of her neck. Lindsey sat up and reached over the bed and grabbed a pen that was sitting on Brandon's beside table. She flipped over to his bare chest. She drew a heart on his chest. In it she wrote L.L.J.

"That's mine and you own it."

He smiled and kissed her.

"My turn," he took the pen from her. He scribbled a little heart with initials in it on her stomach. Lindsey took the pen from him. He lowered his lips to hers, then he lay down beside her and pulled her into his arms. She snuggled back against him and fell asleep. Brandon looked at her snuggled up in his arms. He loved this woman more than anything. What was he going to do when she left one time and never came back? He pulled her more tightly to him and kissed her gently on the neck.

Lindsey woke with three pairs of eyes watching her. Brandon's arms were still around her, and she could hear his gentle snoring in her ear. Brett, Jordan and Todd stood at the foot of the bed.

"What time is it?" he asked.

"Going on eleven," Brett said.

"Long night?" Jordan asked.

"Yeah, we had to stay and clean up." That was not what Jordan meant and she knew it.

Brandon cracked his lids, "Crap, guys, what are you doing in here?"

"I thought we were practicing today, but if you're going to stay in bed all day . . ."

Lindsey climbed out of the bed and walked past them to the restroom.

Brandon sat up.

"Nice art work."

Brandon laughed; he had forgotten about the heart Lindsey had drawn on him. Lindsey came back into the room; all three guys were still standing there.

"I would like to get dressed, do you mind?"

"Not at all," Jordan said and sat down on the edge of the bed.

"Out!" Lindsey pointed at the door.

They all went out of the room. Brandon started to follow, but she shut the door before he could leave. "Give them something to talk about," she said as she grabbed her bag and got her clothes out. Brandon grabbed a pair of jeans and shirt from his closet. Lindsey got dressed and they both left the room. All three guys had big grins on when Lindsey and Brandon got to the garage.

"No, we didn't, so get your heads out of the gutter," she said as she sat down on a chair to watch them get hooked up and ready to play.

Brandon turned on his amp and tuned his guitar. Todd turned on the mic, and plugged in his guitar. Brett was already playing along with Jordan. Soon they were working on a Linkin Park song. Lindsey just sat and listened. They played a few songs by Metallica and some by Seether.

"Know any Flyleaf?" Lindsey asked. Brett started playing the bass part to Fully Alive. Jordan and Brandon joined in.

"I can't sing it, so I guess you have to," he told Lindsey as he joined in playing rhythm.

Lindsey stood up and smiled, "Do you know All Around Me?"

Jordan started with a drumbeat and counted them off. Lindsey walked up to the mic. Lindsey blew them away.

Todd told them all, "I need to be replaced as singer. Crap, girl you can sing!"

"You know, you guys aren't half bad, but you need to work on your own music if you're ever going to make it. Covers will only get you so far."

Todd sort of got offended at her remark. He put his guitar on his stand and walked into the house.

"Don't worry about it, I'll go talk to him." Brandon took off his guitar and walked into the house after him.

"I didn't mean to come off harsh; I just think if you have talent you shouldn't waste it playing covers. Cover bands are a dime a dozen."

Jordan looked at her. "He knows that."

Brett put down his bass. "Maybe this is a good time to break for lunch."

"I'm with you." Jordan put his sticks down.

"Wonder if the Clearwaters have anything?"

"I doubt it, they are supposed to be gone for two weeks," Brett told him as they went into the house.

Lindsey picked up Todd's guitar and strummed a song. Brandon came out the door as Lindsey looked up at him and started singing a Goo Goo Doll's song, Iris. Brandon sat down and listened; she had changed a few words to fit Bandon and her. When she finished, she put the guitar down. He stood up and pulled her in his arms and kissed her.

Brett opened the door to find them kissing. "I would tell you to get a room, but all you two would do in it is sleep. We are ordering pizza. What kind do you like, Lindsey?"

"I like anything, so whatever you get will be fine." She smiled at him.

"Is Todd still mad at me?" Lindsey asked Brandon.

"No, he's not mad; he just knows it's true and figures we are about to split up. It's not like we have time to do anything together anymore, anyway."

"Sorry," Lindsey told him, "I've been meaning to ask. How are you liking school?"

"I feel like an idiot in most of the classes, most of the people are way ahead of me."

"Sorry about that, I was going to try to give you a few more basics, but ..."

He cut her off, "Don't get me wrong, I love the classes. The ones that know things, they don't pay much attention to them, so I get a lot of one-on-one help." He opened the door to the house, as they talked.

The rest of the guys were on the couch watching TV. Brandon sat down in the only other chair and Lindsey sat in his lap. Brett and Todd left to pick up the pizzas, and Brandon and Lindsey got out plates and drinks.

Lindsey's phone beeped in her pocket. Brandon looked up, then went back to pouring drinks. Lindsey read her phone. "Nice singing earlier" was all it said. Lindsey smiled, and wrote back, "Thanks." She put it back in her pocket.

"Everything, ok?" Brandon asked.

"Yeah, just fine."

Lunch came and went and the band played a few more songs before sitting down to talk about school. Brett was majoring in science, Jordan was in an automotive mechanics school, and Todd was taking a few music classes at the local community school. Lindsey listened to them talk about playing at their high school one year and about other birthday parties and things they had played at over the years. They had been playing together since Jr. High. They mainly just ended up watching a football game on TV.

Lindsey cleaned up and went back to the garage and played on the guitar. Brett was the one who noticed her missing when he went to get another drink from the fridge. He could see the light on in the garage. He walked over and stood at the door listening to Lindsey play and sing.

He walked back in the living room. "Come here and listen to this."

"Listen to what?" Jordan asked.

"Listen to Lindsey; she is out there playing and singing." Brandon looked around. Crap, he hadn't even noticed her being gone. They all stood around the door and listened.

"You should hear her on the piano."

"She is so good. Why isn't she doing music?" Todd asked.

Brandon had to think a second. "She would love to, but it's just not possible right now."

They all walked back to the game, but none of them seem to be interested in it, anymore. "I think I will call it a night," Todd was first, then the others followed suit.

"Yeah," Brett said, "I better visit with my folks for a while before I have to head back to school."

"Me too," added Jordan.

"Tell Lindsey 'Bye' for me," Todd said.

"Us, too," Jordan and Brett added. They all headed for the door.

Jordan was the last one to the door, "Hang on to her Brandon; I think you've got something good there."

Brandon smiled. "Thanks, I do, too." Brandon shut the TV off as he walked towards the garage. Lindsey was coming in as he came into the kitchen.

"Who left?" She asked.

"All of them." He gathered Lindsey up in his arms and carried her to his bed.

"I need to add something."

"Alright." She lay back on the bed and lifted the bottom of her shirt to expose the little heart. She looked down at him as he wrote around the edge of the heart. He sat up and smiled. She looked at her stomach and read, *I love you! You're the blood that runs through my veins.*

She smiled up at him. She sat up and pulled off his shirt. "My turn." He lay down and she straddled him. He watched her as she wrote around his heart. *I may come and go, but my love for you will never leave.* She leaned forward and kissed him on the chest. He responded with his own kisses on her head.

Lindsey rolled off him and onto the bed smiling. She was going to find a way. They were going to be together if it killed her.

Lindsey woke with light coming through the window. Her head was laying on Brandon's chest, her arm thrown over him. She put her chin on his chest and looked at him. She rubbed her hand across his smooth dark chest.

"You better stop," he said without opening his eyes.

Lindsey got still. "I thought you were still asleep."

He smiled. "How about we just stay like this all day?"

"I love the way you feel against me." He opened his eyes and looked down at her. She smiled at him. Lindsey could feel every inch of her body against him. "Probably not wise." He rubbed his hand down the back of her arm in a soft gentle caress.

Brandon did his best not to wash the heart off his chest. He looked at it in the mirror. The picture of her that Jessica took came to his mind. That was the picture that needed to be in the heart. He smiled in the mirror; he had always wanted a tattoo.

"I am so hungry," he told her as he came back into the bedroom.

She laughed. "Me, too."

"Mom didn't leave anything."

Lindsey looked at the clock on the wall, it was 9:30 a.m. "Does anywhere deliver?" She asked.

"Not this early. But we could walk down to the mini mart and pick up something."

"Sure, sounds good."

They dressed and walked down to the gas station, it was just off the reserve. There were three guys in the store, all standing talking at the counter, when they went in. Brandon walked to the aisle that had some food.

Lindsey got an eerie feeling. The same feeling she got when something wasn't right. She walked over by the chips; she could see the big round mirror up in the corner. As she looked in the mirror, she could see one of the guys had a gun on the guy behind the counter. She picked up some chips and Brandon grabbed some bread and lunch meat. They walked to the counter and paid for their stuff. Lindsey eyed the second guy, looking for a gun or any weapon. She and Brandon were standing right between the two guys, so Lindsey waited till Brandon was out the door.

"I'll be right back, I forgot something," she stepped back in the door. The three guys looked up as she walked up to the counter. "Can I ask you something?" She stood between the guy with the gun and his buddy.

"Sure," the guy smiled.

Lindsey reached up and grabbed his shoulder, rendering him out cold instantly. His friend made a bee-line for the door, but Lindsey had him on the floor and put out of his misery in seconds.

Brandon stood in the doorway looking at Lindsey.

The store clerk grabbed the phone and dialed 911. "How did you know I was being robbed?" he asked her.

"Saw them in the mirror holding a gun on you."

Brandon was still staring.

"Man, you're fast," the clerk said.

"You ready?" She asked Brandon.

"You can't leave, you have to wait on the police," The clerk told her.

"Just tell them you got a little help from a Good Samaritan." She smiled at him.

"Come on." She pulled on Brandon's arm. He followed her out of the store.

"I was standing right there and didn't notice."

Lindsey smiled. "It's ok, most people don't notice what's going on around them."

He looked at her. "You are really fast."

"Not really," She said, "they just weren't expecting it." Lindsey walked at a pretty fast pace to get back to Brandon's. "What time is your flight?" she asked him as they walked.

"Two o'clock," he answered. "I've been meaning to ask you about Christmas. Are you going to be around?" He opened the door for her.

"I'll be at the Park as far as I know; I had to agree to work the weeks before and after Christmas to get this weekend and one week in December off. The week before the week of Christmas, I have off. When do you have Christmas break?"

He laughed. "We get the week before and after Christmas off."

"Figures," she laughed, "maybe I could stay with you the week I'm off, then the week after Christmas you could come stay with me. That will give you the week of Christmas with your folks."

"That sounds great."

"Maybe I could sit in on a few of your classes the week I'm there."

He smiled. "Sure." He put the sandwich meat on the table and got out some plates. "Sandwich?"

"You fix the sandwiches, and I'll pick out a movie," Lindsey told him.

Her phone vibrated in her pocket, "Can't you do anything without drawing attention to yourself?" She read. "You know I can't just stand by and let innocent people suffer," she wrote back.

She went in the living room and looked at the bookshelf. There weren't a lot of movies, but the range was wide. Evidently their mom loved to watch movies more than the guys, or at least she was the one who must have bought most of them; over half were chick flicks. Lindsey picked out two as Brandon came in the living room with the plates.

"Which one, 'First Knight' or 'Pride and Prejudice'?" She asked.

He smiled at her. "I don't care, they're both ok."

Lindsey looked at them again. "First Knight has more action in it."

She put the other one back on the shelf. Brandon turned on the TV. Lindsey put the DVD in, then sat down on the couch. Brandon went back to the kitchen and grabbed them a couple of drinks, then returned to sit down beside her.

Lindsey curled up in his arms after she finished eating. She could get used to this, she thought to herself.

"I'm going to miss you," he suddenly said.

She looked him in the eyes. "This," she pointed at where she had drawn the heart, "goes with you, and I won't be whole without it." He kissed her and held her close.

As soon as the movie ended, they headed back to Brandon's room to get their clothes packed back up and ready to go.

Lindsey looked in the mirror at the heart Brandon had drawn. How could she keep it? She headed back to his room and found a piece of paper.

"Trace it, it's the only way I can keep it." She held up the paper and pen to him. He took the paper and carefully traced the little heart and the writing for her.

"Thanks." She looked at his chest.

"Darken mine up." He handed her the pen then took off his shirt. She carefully retraced her heart and words around it.

"There you go."

He smiled and looked in the mirror.

"How are you getting back to the park?" He asked.

Lindsey laughed. "You know, I hadn't really thought of that." Her phone vibrated and she smiled at Brandon. She pulled her phone out and looked, "Helicopter to pick you up at 2:15 p.m." She smiled and typed, "Thanks, what would I do without you?" Keeps typed back, "Stay in trouble."

Lindsey and Brandon finished packing and took their stuff to the living room. Brandon's ride would be there in 15 minutes.

"Let me give you my number." She got a pen and paper and wrote down her cell phone number in a heart. Then wrote, "mind what you say" underneath it. He took it from her. He pulled her in his arms and held her tight. He grabbed a piece of paper and pen and wrote.

"I love you, Lindsey Jacobs, or whoever you are."

She wrote back, "I don't have a name like you, I have a call."

He gave her a puzzled look.

"007 is James Bond's call. Get the picture?"

They sat down at the table and passed the paper back and forth writing.

"Can you tell me your call?"

"I really shouldn't. There are very few people that actually know it, but if you really want to know, I will tell you."

"Why do so few know it?"

"Safety for me. Most people think that I am a guy twice my age, or at least they think the person with my call is."

"So you really don't have a name?"

"No, no name, no birth certificate, no social, no fingerprints, no anything."

He picked up her hand and looked at her fingers. She smiled.

"That's crazy."

"Yep, I am a nobody," she wrote.

He wrote back, "Yes, you are the person I love."

A car honked outside. Lindsey took the paper and shoved it in her pocket.

He picked up his bag and went and opened the door. "Lock up when you leave."

She put her arms around him, hugged him and gave him a kiss. When she pulled back, a single tear slid down his cheek. She kissed it away.

"See you in December, call me sometime."

"I will," he said.

She walked him to the car and watched him get in and then watched the car drive away.

Her phone vibrated in her pocket, "There is a car on its way to pick you up to take you to the helicopter."

Lindsey went back in and picked up her bag and looked around then closed the door behind her making sure it was locked. A black car pulled up in front of the house. She walked out and got in. She rode for 10 minutes before coming to the helicopter; from there it only took 15 minutes to get back to the park.

Lindsey went in the cabin and pulled her clothes out, she would need to do some laundry. She burned the note in her pocket. The paper with the heart she got out and sat on the table. She walked by it several times, then got an idea. She pulled her guitar out of the closet and etched it in the front lower corner, then rubbed some oil over it to darken it. She smiled when she finished. It looked good. Lindsey sat down at her computer and worked on things for their future the rest of the night.

CHAPTER 6

School

ONDAY MORNING CAME and went; work went by as usual. Things weren't busy anymore, so the days dragged by. Lindsey spent most nights on the computer and her days on trails. Brandon would call about once a week and talk about school, how he loved this class or wasn't very good at that. But it was always hard to say goodbye, so he didn't call often.

Lindsey had managed in two months to accumulate several million dollars, and to start a business with no trace. The company was called New Life; it was a business where they restored homes. She had managed to hire a woman and man to run the business in the States since she was out of the States, or so they were told. She put everything under Brandon's name, that way if anything ever happened to her he would get it.

The man, Joe Felker and his wife, Jill, were already restoring houses, but were working for a less than reputable man that had stiffed them on the last job. The two of them, however, came highly recommended. Lindsey put them on a salary and put them to work. They got their own jobs, but the business would front the money for the jobs. Then they would get a cut when it was complete. They already had a few jobs in the works.

Lindsey hacked into banks all over the world and had taken 1 cent from millions of accounts. It was so small and only one per bank that most never noticed it. It had worked for the scholarship, and was now working for her.

Her being on the internet left a trail, but she had it so well hidden that she wasn't sure if even she saw it she could find it. Lindsey was very pleased with all she had accomplished in so little a time. Lindsey had even worked on her Christmas present for Brandon. She had sent their rock off to a mason to be chiseled into two smaller pieces. Then they were going to a jeweler so a red ruby heart and silver waves coming from the heart in the center could be placed in both pieces. Then the two pieces were to be made into two necklaces, one for him and one for her. The mason and jeweler were in San Diego so she could pick them up when she went to visit Brandon.

December came in with several snowstorms. The Inn was basically empty and the trails were closed, so most of the days were spent in the Inn. Jacob, John, Sam and she played lots of Halo and pool. Lindsey was decent at pool, but sucked at Halo which she thought was funny.

Jacob was looking forward to going home for Christmas. He was planning on proposing to Michelle on Christmas Eve. Sam had plans to visit a cousin for Christmas. Her folks were both dead, but she was still close to her cousins. John was planning on going home and seeing how Todd was doing in school. Lindsey was the only one staying over Christmas, but that was what she had worked out, so she was fine with it. It wasn't like she had family, anyway. What Lindsey was looking forward to was next week. She was going to stay with Brandon. So, of course, the days crept by. She stayed as busy as possible, but there were just so many things you could do in the Inn, so she would find herself sitting playing piano or guitar for hours.

"Brandon tells me you're going to stay with him next week." Jacob came up behind Lindsey one night as she played.

"Yeah."

"I'm glad things seem to be working out for you two."

Lindsey smiled back at Jacob.

"So you're proposing to Michelle," she wanted to change the subject, "on Christmas Eve. Are you doing it at your house . . . her house . . . where?"

"Well, we are spending Christmas Eve at her house."

"Do her folks know?"

"Well, her dad does."

"Did you ask him for her hand?"

Jacob smiled. "Yes."

Lindsey smiled at him. "There is a little old fashioned in there somewhere."

"Maybe a little."

"How about your folks, do they know?"

"Yeah."

"You make sure someone takes pictures, I'll want to see them."

"I'm sure her mom will be all over that," he answered.

Lindsey finished playing her song and headed back to the cabin. Tomorrow was Saturday. She was catching a helicopter to the airport, then a flight to San Diego. She should be there somewhere around midnight to one a.m. Her clothes were all clean and packed. Lindsey got a shower and sat down with her guitar.

"Hey, Lindsey." It was Keeps on her computer. He had activated it and there was an avatar standing on the screen.

"What's up?" She answered him.

"I need to tell you about some modifications I have made."

"Alright, let's hear it."

"I did a little hacking. Now if King or anyone besides me tries to monitor your phone, the blue charge light will come on. That way you know."

"Does King monitor me a lot? I thought only you did that."

"Why else would I always be on you to watch what you're saying? And, yes, he does occasionally. Anyway, you can talk and have a little privacy now, well, except for me. But I already know what's going on by the nice work on the scholarship. I have no clue where you got the money, but you're a better hacker than me."

Lindsey laughed. "Are they still in the dark on that?"

"Yeah."

"So, how did you come across it?"

"I heard Brandon talking about it when you were gone, so I did some checking. Makes me wonder what else you have been up to."

Lindsey smiled. "Love your avatar, he looks nothing like you."

Keeps laughed. "Don't you like my ripped abs and sword?"

"Yes, you're so handsome."

"Get a load of this." A girl avatar walked out on the screen with him and kissed him.

"She almost looks familiar."

"She should; she looks like you."

Lindsey laughed.

"Got to go, someone's coming." The screen went black. Lindsey put her guitar up and went to bed.

Lindsey sat the next day in the Inn waiting for the time to pass. The snow was coming down pretty hard outside and no one was checking in or out, but just staying put. Lindsey played a couple of games of chess with some older gentleman and took a couple of kids down to the commons to play Halo.

She also talked to a lady about piano; the lady used to teach it. She and Lindsey played a duet together. Then they played Christmas songs and everyone gathered around and sang. Late in the afternoon the snow let up. She and the boys that played Halo earlier went out and made a large snowman, then had a snowball fight.

Lindsey headed to her cabin about 8:30; her ride was supposed to be there at 9:15 and she needed to shower and change. By nine she was ready and waiting. The helicopter was there by 9:10, and they were off to the airport. By quarter till 10 she was on a plane. She had butterflies in her stomach as her plane landed. She caught a cab to Brandon's. Her coat was now hung over her arm.

Brandon was standing in the hall when the elevator opened. He had on a pair of khaki shorts and a T-shirt. He took her bag and ushered her into his apartment. Lindsey looked around; she was pleased with what the scholarship had been used to get. But she had been quite specific in what she had told them to use it on, too.

Brandon wrapped his arms around her, and he put his lips on hers. "Man, I have missed you," he told her.

She smiled and kissed him again. "I've missed you, too."

She looked around again. "Your apartment's great!"

He smiled. "Yeah, I agree. It's better than our house."

Lindsey walked over and looked out the window. "Not a bad view, either." Brandon walked up behind her and put his arms around her. She leaned back against him.

"How are your classes going?"

"Ok, I guess. I am not very good at the history, but not bad otherwise. Mr. Brokofsky teaches strings class and he is a little over the top sometimes. He also likes the girls in his classes."

"There is always one that seems interested in them a little more than they should be. Does he grade fairly, though?"

"Close, I guess. They always make a little higher, but not much. I guess I am just lucky, my class is mostly guys. Only a few girls, 7 girls out of 20." Lindsey turned in his arms. "You look tired," he told her.

"I worked today, then flew, so I am."

"You better get some sleep, then." Brandon walked over and picked up her bag and took it and laid it on the bed for her. "I have something to show you." He pulled off his shirt. Her heart was still there, but a little bigger and in it was a picture, not her initials. She reached up and ran her finger over it. "Now, you're with me forever."

She leaned in and kissed the heart. "It's really great, but you shouldn't have done that. Tat's aren't cheap, and to find one that could do the picture really cost, I'm sure."

He looked at her. "It was worth it."

She kissed him. Then she took out her phone and laid it on the nightstand, glancing to check for the blue light. It wasn't on. But she could see it if it did kick on.

"Why don't you go change for bed, I need to finish a little work I was doing," he told her.

"Sounds good." Lindsey went in the bathroom, washed her face and changed.

Brandon was sitting at the keyboard when she came out. He was playing a simple tune, but using chords so it sounded more elaborate than it really was.

She walked up behind him. "That's real good; you should try mixing the chords and note structures."

He turned and got up. He walked over and flipped off all the lights, but the one by the bed. Then he went to the bed and patted the spot beside him. "Come on, sleepyhead." She crawled into bed. He shut the light off and pulled her to him. Lindsey closed her eyes; she wished this was the way it could be forever.

Lindsey woke to the smell of eggs cooking. Since the apartment was a studio, she could see the whole place and Brandon was standing in front of the stove.

Lindsey sat up and took a good look at the apartment. It was a nice size, and decorated very nicely, as well. All his school stuff sat close to the window. A keyboard, his electric and acoustic guitars, and a cello sat next to a small table, which held a laptop.

Lindsey climbed out of the bed, went to the kitchen and sat down at the bar.

Brandon turned to find her smiling at him. "How long have you been sitting there?"

"Not long, just a couple of seconds."

"You hungry?" He asked.

"Yes."

"Hope you like eggs with mushrooms and cheese."

"Sounds good to me." He got out two plates and split the contents of the skillet.

"Milk or juice?"

"Juice, please."

He grabbed a couple of glasses and poured them both a glass full.

"So what are we doing today?" Lindsey asked as she ate.

"I was going to leave that up to you. The day is yours, what do you want to do?"

Lindsey smiled, "Hum . . . let me think on it a bit. I would like to go for a run, the weather has been bad at the park and I haven't been able to run in almost two weeks."

He laughed. "How horrible," he said sarcastically. Brandon sat down on the stool next to her and ate. "You really want to run?"

"How about we skip today, but run the rest of the week?"

"That I can handle; so, what else would you like to do?"

"No clue, never been here. What is there to do?"

"Well, if we can't find anything else, some of the guys are getting together this afternoon at the Y to swim."

"I had to borrow a suit last time, and I don't have one."

"There are lots of stores that carry those, you know."

Lindsey laughed. "As long as it is not a string bikini like last time."

He chuckled. "But you were so hot-looking in it."

She looked over at him. "Ok, why do you really want to go?" She lifted her eyebrow.

He smiled. "Well, to tell the truth, there is going to be this girl there that I would love to introduce you to. She has been annoying me since school started, and no matter what I tell her, she is determined that we should be dating. I have told her a million times there is someone else, but she doesn't listen." Lindsey laughed. "It's not funny."

"Yeah, it is."

"You wouldn't think that if it was you she was following everywhere. She drops by here at least 3 times a week; I just lock the deadbolt and pretend not to be home. I had to tell the super not to let her in. She had told him I forgot to leave her the key and he tried to let her in, but I had it dead bolted. Then, I had a talk with him about her when she left."

"Ok, maybe it's not that funny if she is stalking you." Lindsey finished her breakfast and put her plate in the sink. "Can I borrow your computer a minute?"

"Sure."

Lindsey sat down at the little table. "What is her name?"

"Mary Chesterfield."

Lindsey started typing. "She's from money, looks like an only child. Probably used to getting whatever she wants."

Brandon put his plate in the sink and came over to stand behind her. The page had a picture of The Chesterfield family including Mary. A little black box popped open on the side of the screen.

"Let me handle that for you," it said. Keeps was always on top of everything.

"Nothing bad, just get her out of his hair."

"Consider it done." The boxed disappeared.

Lindsey looked up at Brandon and smiled. "I wouldn't worry about her. I'm sure she will find someone else to bother before long."

Brandon looked at her. "How can you do that, be so nonchalant about everything."

"Sorry, just the way I'm wired, I guess."

"I still wouldn't mind seeing you in a skimpy little swimsuit."

Lindsey stood up. "Well, let's go then."

They got dressed and headed out on the street. Brandon hailed a cab and they went down to the Get Wet store.

Lindsey had never seen so many suits. "You pick them out and I will try them on," she told him.

"What size?"

"Three."

Brandon started going through the racks and picking out suits. "Try these."

She changed and modeled each one. Not one of them was right. He looked till he came back with only one. It was almost like the one Michelle had let her borrow.

She changed into it. This one fit a lot better and it was sort of cute. It was a tie-dyed blue and green color.

"Well?" She did a spin in front of him.

"Oh, yeah, that's the one."

"It's not half bad."

She changed back into her jeans and T-shirt, then looked around and picked out a couple of shirts and shorts and then they left.

"How about a tour?"

"Quarter tour or nickel tour?" He asked.

"Whatever, just as long as we're back by pool party time."

"Sea Port Village," he told the cab driver.

Brandon and Lindsey spent most of the afternoon just wandering around. Around four they headed back to his apartment to change.

"Are you ready for this?" He asked as he opened the door to the YMCA.

"Well, who is this?" A girl came walking up before Brandon had even let go of the door. Lindsey recognized the girl as Mary.

"Hey. Mary, this is Lindsey, my girlfriend that I have been telling you about."

"Oh," was all she said. Mary turned and marched off.

"I don't think she likes me," Lindsey said, then laughed. They headed on in to the pool area. Several people were there.

"Hey, James!" Brandon yelled at a guy on the other side of the pool. He came running around the pool. "This is Lindsey. Lindsey, this is James."

"Hey, James."

"Wow, you said she was beautiful, but I didn't think she could be this gorgeous."

Lindsey laughed. "Alright, that's enough." Brandon pulled off his shirt.

"You know, the tat doesn't do her justice," James said. "But it does look like her."

Lindsey took off her shirt and shorts.

"Holy crap!" James said as he looked at her. "You better keep her close, or someone might try to steal her."

Lindsey noticed the pool had gotten quiet. She looked up to find most every guy in the place staring at her. She smiled and turned a little red in the face.

"I would like to see them try," Brandon told him.

James scooped Lindsey up in his arms and threw her in the pool. Brandon laughed and shoved James in, then dove in after them. Lindsey came up to find Brandon right beside her.

"I owe him for that," she told Brandon.

Several guys swam up to be introduced to her. Most of the guys were quite small and looked like orchestra material, but there were a few that looked pretty tough, James being one of them.

Lindsey noticed Mary watching her several times. No one seemed to be paying her any mind.

James and Brandon had a diving contest to see who could make the biggest splash. Mary jumped at the chance to talk to Lindsey, "So, you're Brandon's girlfriend; I hope you don't mind, but he has sort of been talking to me."

Lindsey just smiled. "He can talk to whomever he wishes."

"So, you wouldn't mind if we went to the movies sometime?"

Lindsey laughed at her. "Good luck with that."

Mary looked at her. "Before the year is out he will be mine, so you might as well say goodbye now."

Lindsey laughed even harder. "I hope you did notice the tattoo; that's me, not you."

"What's so funny?" Brandon came up behind her and put his arms around her.

"Mary seems to think you are going to leave me for her; by the end of the school year according to her."

Mary looked up at Brandon. "Well, I don't know what she's talking about, she must be jealous that we are friends or something, because I didn't say anything like that; just that we talked a lot," Mary looked at Brandon.

Brandon laughed. "You have no shot, Mary; I am all hers."

Mary turned and swam off. James came up in front of Lindsey. He looked back at Mary.

"She is a real pain, but I hear she's loaded and has her daddy wrapped around her finger. So if she says anything bad about you, she can get you kicked out of school."

Lindsey looked at Mary. "She doesn't want to tangle with me."

Brandon smiled.

James looked at Lindsey. "It takes money to make these people listen."

"Well, I have plenty of that, so that is no problem."

Brandon looked at James. "You know of my full scholarship, The Jacobs Music Scholarship?"

"Yeah," James said.

"Meet Lindsey Jacobs," Brandon said. James smiled. Lindsey hadn't been sure Brandon had caught the scholarship thing, but now she knew he had.

"I hear the Jacobs donated a couple of million to the school to get the scholarship."

"2.5," Lindsey said.

Brandon looked at her. "Really?"

"You're worth every penny and more."

Brandon was speechless.

Lindsey had given 2.5 million dollars to get him a full scholarship. The thought of that just blew his mind.

Brandon was still staring at Lindsey. "I don't know what to say. I didn't know you did that."

"Drop it; I don't want to hear another word about it. OK?" He looked at her for a second, then put his lips on hers. James laughed and swam away from them. Brandon had Lindsey against the side of the pool.

Lindsey pushed him away. "Alright."

"Sorry, got a little carried away. I still can't believe you gave that much."

Lindsey put her finger to his lips. "No more talk on that subject, ok?"

"Ok, you ready to leave?"

"Sure."

He and Lindsey climbed out of the pool and dried off. They waved at James as they left. "James is cool."

"Yeah, he is about the only really down to earth one that I've met. Don't get me wrong, there are some great guys here. James and I just seem to click."

"Well, I'm glad you found a friend."

They walked part of the way, then caught a cab the rest of the way home. Lindsey hit the shower as soon as they were back to the apartment. Brandon got one as soon as she was out.

Lindsey took the opportunity of being alone and sat down at the computer. She checked on Joe and Jill and the business, then checked on a few details of her money. The money was growing at a good rate; she would soon be in the billions. It was amazing how a few keystrokes could send a glitch that could divert millions of dollars with no one knowing. She added a few more security features and bounced the signal all over the world and did a few more encryptions. She logged out when she heard the shower shut off.

Lindsey's phone beeped. She went and picked it up off the table. "What are you up to? I see you log on, then you go to the library. What are you really up to?"

Lindsey smiled. "Who says I am not looking up stuff at the library?"

"Anything I can help with?" He typed back.

"Just get Mary off Brandon's back and we are good."

"In the works as we text. I also have a little Intel to pass along. There is a job coming up that they have been working on for the last two years. In the last three months things have started coming together quickly, so you may get a call in the next few weeks. There are a few more pieces that have to fall into place, but it's getting close."

"Thanks for the heads up."

"You're welcome. Hey. Can I ask you something?"

"Sure."

"Oh, never mind, I have to go."

Lindsey smiled at him. "Hey Keeps, I need to have a little heart-to-heart with Brandon. Would you warn me if they start monitoring? Do something with the computer, you've got mail or something. I don't want to have to be watching my phone."

"Sure."

"Thanks." Lindsey put her phone down. Lindsey turned the computer toward the bed, then went and sat down.

"Come here."

Brandon sat down beside her.

"What?"

She smiled at him. "We have a few minutes we can talk. Keeps is watching for monitoring and will let us know if they tune in, so for right now we can talk freely. Anything you want to ask me or know?"

He smiled. "Really, I can ask you anything?"

"Yep."

"Did you really give the school 2.5 million for me?"

"Yes, that was what I donated to the school. The scholarship was what they created for me and that was another 100 thousand. Is that all you want to know about?"

He thought for a minute. "Do you enjoy killing people?"

"No . . . and yes."

Brandon looked at her.

"When you have seen what I have seen, you would have been glad to have killed them, too."

"You once said you were bred into this, what did you mean?"

Lindsey sat there a second then took a deep breath.

"I have no idea how old I am and I don't remember parents or siblings. What I do remember is combat, bomb making, guns, computer classes. I remember this lady talking in German to me, another man talking to me in Russian. All I ever remember throughout growing up is classes. I could kill a man with my bare hands and I knew all different kinds of hand-to-hand combat before I hit puberty. And by the time I had gone through puberty I had already had several successful missions. I was taught music, art, dance, cooking and other skills to blend into any surrounding. I know well over 30 languages, fluently. Now do you understand why I say that?"

"Why you?"

"I don't know."

"I can answer some of that," Keep's avatar popped up on the computer screen. "There are ten of us that started out together. We were all trained, but some of us showed more potential in one area or another and then finished training in that one skill. That's why I am here; I wasn't good at hand-to-hand or anything really physical, but a computer, now that's my field."

Lindsey looked at Keeps. "I didn't know that, where are all the others?"

"Handler's one," he told her, "most of them work here as specialists in their fields. There are only three that go to the field, but none of them do what you do. They have limits set for them."

"How do you know all this?"

"I am the computer geek, remember? I hack anything and anybody."

"Keeps?" Lindsey said.

"Yeah," he answered.

"Why are you risking your neck for me?"

He didn't say anything for a minute. "You remember spending a summer in Intel?"

"Yes, I spent it in a room all by myself; the only person I got to talk to was Cloak . . . Were you Cloak?"

"Yes, I was Cloak and you were Dagger."

Lindsey smiled.

Brandon laughed. "You called yourselves Cloak and Dagger?"

"I was good, but you were better and you taught me so much that summer. You were the only one who ever treated me like more than just a resource. You made me feel like I actually had a friend."

Lindsey smiled. "You are my friend, Keeps."

"Brandon?" Keeps said.

"Yeah."

"Knowing what you know is very dangerous, especially for Lindsey. After today don't ever speak of it again."

Brandon looked at Lindsey, who was looking at him. "I won't, thank you for trusting me."

"Lindsey?"

"Yeah, Keeps."

"One other question, how in the world did you get your hands on 2.5 million?"

"I thought you could hack anything and anybody." She laughed.

"You are definitely the best hacker in the world, girl. I have to go, someone's coming. Can't keep an eye out, you're on your own." The screen went black.

Lindsey looked at Bandon. "I love you, Brandon Clearwater."

He smiled. "I love you, too." He pulled her into his arms.

Keeps screen went black as Handler walked into the room. "I need you to pick up Intel from 25," Keeps handed Handler an envelope, "and give her this."

Handler turned and walked out of the room. Keeps moved his mouse over a file on his desktop. He began to type on his report on the Makers events of the day. He always made it very general and somewhat less informing. These files were for the King's eyes only and he made sure that the files made sense, so if King did listen in he would only hear what he had read. Keeps typed, but let his mind wander to the latest files he had been able to hack into. He had told Lindsey about there being ten of them, but he had left out lots of details. Like the fact they all had been genetically altered, the girls more than the guys. It really wasn't hard to understand about some of it. Each of them could change skin tone and eye color with a simple injection, but the file talked about the girl subjects accepting the alterations better than the boys. One in particular had excelled and had been given several more alterations. The Maker was indeed special.

"Morning." Lindsey kissed Brandon on the cheek. "You promised we would go running before school."

Brandon stretched. "Let's do it then."

They got up and dressed and headed out on the street. Three miles later they were back. Brandon was worn out.

"Why did you stop running when you started school?"

Brandon shrugged his shoulders. "Lazy, I guess."

They hit the shower then headed for school. Brandon's first class was music theory. Lindsey sat at the desk with Brandon as the teacher talked. The class was two hours long, but Lindsey thought it flew by; she liked the class. Strings was the next class, James was in this class. He normally sat with Brandon, but let Lindsey have the seat.

"Sorry, Mr. Brokofsky is sick today, you will have to manage without him." A tall thin man came into the class.

Brandon leaned over, "That's the Dean."

Lindsey smiled. "Dean Hollingsworth?"

"Yeah." He looked at her, she giggled.

"He sure looks a lot different than he sounds like on the phone."

"You can work on things from last week and I will be back to check in on you in a bit." The Dean left the room. All the kids started talking. Lindsey got up and walked up to one of the cellos. She picked up the bow and sat down. She slid it across the strings and adjusted the tuning a little. Brandon and James came and stood in front of her.

"Grab a guitar," Lindsey told Brandon. "You grab another cello," she told James. They pulled up chairs and sat by her. She grabbed a pencil and wrote a series of notes on the paper then handed both of them one.

"Play yours in 4/4," she told James. "Brandon, yours is a picking pattern, follow his lead." James started playing. Brandon joined in. Lindsey listened for a minute. Then she picked up the bow and played a heavy fast pattern. It sounded great; soon the whole class was standing around them.

"We could use a few more cellos and a violin or two." Soon Lindsey had everyone playing something she had written down. Lindsey's part was a lead; it made the whole piece pull together. When they finished the piece, they heard clapping. The Dean had come back in and was now listening.

"Very good," he said, "I don't think I have ever heard Mr. Brokofsky play that, though. Is it something new?" He walked up and looked at the notes written down.

"She wrote it," one of the guys pointed at Lindsey.

"And you are?"

Lindsey stood up and put her cello down. "Lindsey," she smiled at him, "I am visiting, Mr. Clearwater."

"Ah, yes, our scholarship winner. Did you graduate from here?" The Dean asked.

"No," she answered.

"What school then?"

She smiled at him. "No school, sir, I was home tutored."

"Well, you are quite amazing."

"Thank you."

The Dean turned. "Mr. Brokofsky will be out all week, he is in the hospital," he paused, then turned back to Lindsey. "How long are you going to be here Miss ... what was your last name?"

Lindsey hesitated. "Jacobs."

His eyes got big. "Are you Lorain's daughter?"

"Lorain was my mother's name, but it is also is my middle name. She died several years back."

He smiled. "So was it you I talked to on the phone?" he asked.

"Yes."

"You are younger than I thought."

"Yes, most people tell me that."

"So, how long are you visiting Mr. Clearwater?"

"All week."

"Well, feel free to visit any class you want, and if there is anything we can do for you, please don't hesitate to come by my office."

Lindsey smiled at him, "Thank you." Everyone was staring at her when she turned around. "That's what happens when you ..." James was talking and Brandon elbowed him real hard.

"Ouch." James looked at Brandon.

"Shut it," Brandon warned him. James looked at Lindsey who also had a 'keep your trap shut' look on her face.

"What?" James said when class ended.

"Just keep what you know about Lindsey to yourself," Brandon told him, as they walked out the door.

"Why?" He wanted to know.

"She doesn't want to stand out or have people acting weird around her," Brandon told him.

Brandon and Lindsey ate at the coffee shop. Several of the students seemed to be in there. A lot of staring seemed to be taking place.

"Ok, the staring is starting to annoy me," Lindsey finally said.

"They just want to know who the hot girl is with me." He smiled at her.

Lindsey laughed. "Oh, if that's all," she let the sarcasm ride the sentence.

"I forgot we have a Christmas party Friday night. It is a school event and everyone is required to go. And it is black tie."

Lindsey smiled, "I bet you'll look great in a crisp white shirt and tie."

"You can let me know Friday if I do or not. You'll go with me, won't you?"

"I'll tell you what, I have to run and pick something up tomorrow, so I'll go pick out a dress and surprise you with it on Friday."

"What kind of errand?"

"You'll see."

"You're not going to tell me?"

"No, I should be back before lunch unless I have trouble finding a dress."

"Do I get to see the dress?"

"No. If you see it, you won't be surprised Friday."

"Alright." He looked at the clock on the wall. "We better get going; we don't want to be late to Ms. Yuri's class. I really like her. She makes learning fun."

Piano I was Bandon's next class. James was in that one, too.

"Hey, you'll never guess what I just heard." James came up and sat down by Lindsey and Brandon, "Mary's dad pulled her out of school."

"What for?" Lindsey asked.

"Her dad is some kind of financial advisor and a couple of deals fell through and he got some death threats made against him and his family."

"Well, that's never good," Lindsey said.

"Unless you're the one she's chasing, then it's great news," Brandon chimed in.

Class started and Lindsey just sat and enjoyed listening to Mrs. Yuri as she taught basic piano skills. "Don't forget that Friday is the Christmas party and I will be picking one student from each class to play so you better all practice, because it may be you." She walked by Brandon and stopped in front of Lindsey. "You must be visiting Brandon?"

"Yes ma'am," Lindsey said.

"I'm Ms. Yuri." She stuck out her hand.

"Lindsey." She didn't add her last name.

"Do you play, sweetie? I noticed you paying more attention than most of the people in the class."

Lindsey smiled. "A little."

"She plays more than a little, she's very good," Brandon said.

"Did you come here to school?"

"No, I had tutors."

"Well, come on up, let's see what you can play."

Lindsey glared at Brandon. "That's ok."

"Oh, come on, sweetie, you can't be any worse than anyone else in here."

Lindsey stood up and walked with Ms. Yuri to a piano.

Lindsey sat down. "What would you like to hear?" Lindsey asked. Ms. Yuri looked surprised at the question.

"Play the lullaby you're so fond of," Brandon said from behind Ms. Yuri.

Lindsey closed her eyes and began to play. The music rolled off her fingers gently.

"Oh, my!" Ms. Yuri said, "That is beautiful. Is she why you're learning music, Brandon?"

He smiled at her. "Yes, ma'am, she is."

Lindsey finished the piece.

"That was beautiful, dear."

"Thank you," Lindsey told her.

Ms. Yuri looked at Brandon. "She's quite the inspiration."

"Yes, ma'am, I know."

She walked off and went to talking to some of the other students before class ended.

Music History with Mr. Walker was the next class. He was an older gentleman that looked quite full of himself; Lindsey sat and listened as he talked Beethoven, Bach and Chopin. He did know his music, but he wasn't very merciful when someone got an answer wrong. He was quite harsh on them. Lindsey noticed Dean Hollingsworth walking up and down the hall; he passed by the door at least twice. Lindsey was happy when the class was over, she didn't care for Walker at all. Brandon didn't care for him much, either. Brandon said no one did.

James caught up with them right outside the school. "Do you care if I come work on some music tonight, or is it not a good week for company?" he looked at Lindsey.

"No, man, come on over," Brandon told him.

"I'll see you later, then." He waved and walked on.

Brandon looked at Lindsey. "He doesn't have one of the computer programs I have, so I let him use mine."

Lindsey smiled. "That's nice."

"What would you like for supper?" Brandon asked her.

"I have been feeling like Italian lately, any good restaurants around?"

"They all cost an arm and a leg."

She laughed. "So when has money ever been an issue for me?"

"It's not the fact that you can or can't pay for it. It's the fact that I haven't paid for anything yet. I thought I could at least buy you supper."

"Oh good grief Brandon, I am paying and that's final"

He shook his head in defeat, "The best is downtown." He held out his hand and hailed a taxi. The line was long when they went in, but Lindsey persuaded the Maître D with a couple hundred bucks, and they were seated right away. The restaurant was very nice and the food was great. Lindsey even ordered some extra and took it back to the apartment.

James was sitting outside when they arrived. "Have you been waiting long?" Brandon asked him as they walked in the doors of the building.

"No, just got here. What smells so good?" he asked.

Lindsey held out a box. "Italian."

James worked on the computer and Lindsey and Brandon sat and talked. "So, are you excited about Jacob asking Michelle to marry him?"

He looked at her. Evidently he hadn't been let in on the secret yet. "Oops, I figured you knew! Don't let him know I let the cat out of the bag."

"I figured he was going to do it sooner or later."

"Well, crap!" James said.

"What's wrong?" Brandon asked.

"Your computer doesn't seem to like me tonight."

"What's it doing?" Lindsey asked.

"It keeps freezing every time I try to save something." Lindsey got up and walked over to where James was sitting. "See, it just did it again." The computer screen was flashing a blue color and had gone blank.

"Crap, you've got a virus. Move over. Let me see if I can catch it before it wipes out everything." James got up and Lindsey sat down. She hit a few keys and brought up a line of code. She worked for ten minutes blocking the virus, then spent another ten sending it back to the server it came from, plus a few extra bonus bugs. She smiled when she hit send. "Serves the person right for sending it."

"I think most of your stuff is still here, but it may have got all you did tonight." She got up from the computer. "Remind me before I leave to update your virus protection," she told Brandon.

"I just updated it a couple of days ago."

"It is evidently not a good enough program; I'll put a good one on it."

James smiled as he sat down at the computer again. "You're handy to have around."

Lindsey laughed. "There are a couple of things I know: one being computers, the other is music."

Brandon looked at her as if to add several more things to the list, but he didn't say them out loud. Lindsey sat back down on the couch beside Brandon. "So where are we meeting for lunch tomorrow? I think I should be back by then."

"I usually just eat there at the coffee shop like we did today."

"Alright, then, I think I am going to head for the shower." She got up.

"I need to do some work on the keyboard, anyway." Brandon went and sat down and put the headphones on.

Lindsey got her clothes and went to the bathroom; she took her sweet time. She wanted to let him practice. When she came out, he and James were both still working, so she quietly sat down on the bed and pulled out her phone.

"What are you doing?" She typed in.

"Working, how about you?" Came back.

"Any other developments?" She asked.

"Yes, but I am glad to report they are good ones in your favor, so you still have plenty of time." Lindsey smiled.

"Did you know they monitored you today?"

"No, what was I doing?"

"You were at school playing the cello. Quite well, I might add. But they didn't stay on long enough to learn anything. They thought you had the radio on."

"Good," Lindsey typed back.

"Enjoy the rest of your week. Tell Brandon I said 'Hi'."

"Getting all friendly now, are we?"

"Whatever I have to do to keep you happy," he wrote back.

"So you're just superficial."

"Aren't we all?"

Lindsey laughed. "No, not unless I have to be. You said there were ten of us, why ten?"

"I have no clue; it just mentions ten subjects."

"What all did they do to us?" She asked.

"Lots of stuff," he answered. He wondered how much he should tell her.

"Genetically?" She asked.

"Yes," he answered. He knew she would have figured out some of it.

"Are we all the same?"

"No, not all of us accepted the genetics. I have to go."

Keeps closed Lindsey's window. How was he going to tell her she was the only one that had accepted all their genetic coding? From all his reading, she was the closest thing to a super human there was.

Lindsey put her phone down on the table and went and picked up the acoustic guitar. "Will it bother you if I play?" She asked James.

"No, I am just about done."

Lindsey sat down on the couch and tuned the guitar, then began to play. The music was soft and soothing, very gentle.

James smiled as he listened to her play. "Brandon said you were good, then today in class, now this. Why in the world are you not teaching, or professionally playing?"

Lindsey smiled at him, "I have business obligations. I do other things like the Ranger, but I am always being called away. So I don't want to start and then have to quit, so I just play for relaxation."

"What kind of business?" He asked.

"Family stuff, the kind you inherit."

"Well, that tells me a lot," He said.

"I am not going to tell you; it would freak you out to know exactly what I run."

"I think I could handle it."

Lindsey laughed. "Well, you'd be the first. Sorry, still not telling; I have learned my lesson on that subject."

James got up from the computer. He glanced up at Brandon, who was sitting, playing with his eyes closed. "You know he is afraid he will disappoint you."

Lindsey looked up at Brandon. "He could never do that. I don't care if he makes it big or just goes home and plays for his family. I just wanted to give him the opportunity to do something he loved."

"Make sure you tell him that. Anyway, it's getting late, I better go."

Lindsey got up and walked James to the door. He turned and looked back at Brandon and then smiled at Lindsey.

"Goodnight."

Lindsey put the guitar back on the stand and then went and sat back down on the couch. She watched Brandon play.

"You going to sleep there?" Brandon asked her. Lindsey got up; Brandon had already showered and was standing there in his boxers. "When did James leave?"

"About 10:30 I think. What time is it?" She asked.

"11:30," he answered.

Lindsey pulled her tank top off and lay down on the bed. Brandon flipped off the lights and joined her.

"Brandon?"

"Yeah."

"You know that I don't care if you make it big in music or not, don't you?"

"What?"

"I mean, I would love for you to make it big, but if you don't, I am ok with that, too. I didn't send you here to make it big. I sent you here to give you the opportunity to learn and do something you loved. So if you make it big or not, it doesn't matter to me."

Brandon reached over and traced her jaw line with his finger. "Thanks, that takes a little pressure off."

She laughed. "I didn't mean to put you under pressure." She rolled over and glanced at her phone then rolled over and up on her elbow to face him. "You know I love you more than anything, right?"

He looked at her and got up off the bed and pulled her along with him. "Come here."

Lindsey grabbed her phone so she could keep an eye on it. He pulled her over to the couch and sat her down. He dropped down on one knee in front of her.

"I want to make you a promise. I want to promise you that no matter what happens and how far apart we are that you are the one I plan on spending the rest of my life loving. And if we never get to be together then I will die just like I am, a happy virgin."

Tears ran down Lindsey's face.

"Brandon . . ." she looked down at her phone, "I put us all in danger, but this is my promise to you: no matter where I go or how I have to change, I will always come back to you, if possible. Granted, I may look different on occasion or have a different name, but I will come back."

The phone lit up and beeped.

"I promise to keep you two safe as long as I can."

Lindsey and Brandon smiled.

"You're the best friend I have ever had," she typed.

"Correction, we have ever had," Brandon pulled her up and kissed her. "You are in my heart and soul," he said. She smiled.

"And you will remain there forever," she added on.

Keeps listened to Lindsey and Brandon talk. He wished he was Brandon. To love the Maker would be the ultimate prize. He already cared for her more that he should. He often dreamed of her.

Keeps looked over the Intel for the Switzerland mission coming up. Her virginity hinged on this mission. The human trafficker they were watching only dealt in virgins. He was hoping something would change and that they could send her in, in a different way, not as a slave being sold. Not that she hadn't been sold into slavery in the past, but her being older now it would make a difference. Keeps sat at his computer and compiled all the Intel he could. He was going to send it to Lindsey; maybe she could see something they weren't. Maybe she could find a way.

Lindsey got up at five and left Brandon in the bed. He was snoring softly, but hadn't budged since she got out. She dressed and headed to the street for a run.

The morning was great. Vendors were just getting to their businesses and deliveries were being made for the day. It was nice running early.

She went through a coffeehouse on the way back to the apartment and picked up a couple of Cappuccinos and muffins for

Brandon and herself. He was still asleep when she went back in. She showered and crawled back in the bed with him. He was lying on his back, so she climbed up on top of him and spread out on him.

He opened his eyes, "What are you doing with wet hair?"

"I had a shower, duh."

He chuckled. "You already ran, didn't you?"

She smiled. "Yep, saved you the agony."

He kissed her. "Thanks. What smells so good?" he asked.

"Muffins and coffee, I made a pit stop around the corner."

"Sounds good."

Lindsey heated up the coffee and muffins while Brandon showered and then got dressed. She would need to leave early if she was going to make it back by lunch. Finding a dress would be the hard part; she had no idea where to look. Brandon came out of the bathroom and got dressed.

"I am going to head on out after we eat, or I won't get back by lunch."

He walked over to the bar holding his shirt. He was sure sexy without it, Lindsey thought.

"Alright, then."

They sat down and ate. She had picked up banana nut muffins and they were good.

Lindsey kissed him bye and headed out the door. "See you at lunch."

She caught a taxi down on the street to the Custom Jewelers of San Diego galleria.

"Yes, I am here to pick up some jewelry I had made," she told the lady behind the counter.

"That will be Phil, I will be right back." The lady walked back into a hall then returned with a man following her.

"Can I help you?"

"Yes, I am Lindsey Jacobs. I sent you a couple of rocks . . ."

"Oh, yes, the rocks with the rubies in them. Joan will show you into one of the viewing rooms and I will go get them. I think you will be pleased with them." The little short chunky man walked over and down a hall.

"Right this way," Joan said, as Lindsey followed her to a series of rooms. "The room Joan seated her in was small with a desk and two chairs and a magnifying light sitting on the desk.

"I was really wondering how they were going to turn out," Phil handed her a box. "But as you can see, they turned out beautifully."

Lindsey opened the box to find them both lying inside. The two stones were about the size of dimes with red ruby hearts and waves of silver coming out from them in all directions. The stones were held on by silver wrapping the edges and then fastened to silver chokers. Lindsey smiled, they were perfect.

"They did turn out nicely," she told the man. She took both of them out and examined them thoroughly.

"It is all guaranteed; so if you have any problems, bring them back and it will be fixed. No matter what happens to them, they are covered in the warranty you purchased."

Lindsey placed them back in the box, and stood up.

"Thank you." She shook his hand.

"Come back if we can ever do anything for you again, Ms. Jacobs."

"Thank you. I will."

Lindsey slipped the box into her purse and headed out the door.

"I need to find a dress for a black tie event. Can you take me to somewhere I mind find such a dress?" She asked the taxi driver.

"No problem, there is a Macy's not far from here," he told her.

Lindsey tipped the taxi driver and went into the store.

Ladies department was on the second floor. She took the escalator and went up. There was just about every kind of dress you could think of. There were shirts and blouses and just everything. Lindsey wandered through the aisles.

"Can I help you find something?" A middle aged lady asked her.

"I have a black tie party Friday night and need a dress."

She looked at Lindsey. "You look about a size 3."

Lindsey smiled at her. "Yes, ma'am."

"Do you have any preferences on what kind of dress?" She asked.

"Just one that will take his breath away when I walk in the door."

The lady smiled. "Come with me; I have some of those."

She led Lindsey to a selection of dresses beside the dressing rooms. The lady looked through several dresses and then pulled two off the rack. "These will look nice on you." She handed them to Lindsey. One was very short and was black; the other was long and flowing, but a beautiful red. Lindsey went into the dressing room. The black was very nice, but the red one was perfect. She walked out of the dressing room in the red dress.

"I like this one," she told the saleslady.

"You'll need some nice lingerie for under that one." The dress was very low in the back, but had a beautiful neckline in the front.

"I need everything for it. Shoes, jewelry, everything."

"That will not be a problem." The lady smiled at Lindsey. "By the way my name is Kathy."

Lindsey smiled. "Lindsey."

"Well, Lindsey, I will go get you the lingerie you need and you can change into them to see if we have the right look."

Lindsey sat down and waited as Kathy grabbed a few things.

"I think these will do." She handed them to Lindsey.

Lindsey came back out of the dressing room. "Very nice," Kathy said. "We need to find jewelry and shoes, so just leave the dress on and follow me."

Lindsey and Kathy headed for the jewelry department. There they picked out a silver and diamond necklace and earrings, and then they headed to the shoes for some heels. Lindsey had the whole ensemble on when she looked in the mirror.

"Do you do hair and makeup by any chance?" Lindsey asked.

"Oh, yes, what time do you need to be ready?"

"The party starts at five."

"So what time do you need to be done and ready?" she asked.

"Four, I guess."

"Alright, let me call down to the salon and make you an appointment for three."

Kathy walked over to the service desk and called down. Lindsey looked back in the mirror, Brandon was going to flip. She already looked not too bad, but with hair and makeup she should be a knockout.

"You're all set for three p.m. Friday afternoon."

"Can you keep all this here for me until then? I don't want him to see it until I am ready."

"Yes, ma'am; we would be happy to do that for you."

Lindsey went back and changed into her jeans, and then followed Kathy to a register. "Since you're not taking the dress with you, you only need to pay a deposit until Friday, then you can pay your total."

"Can you have the dressed cleaned? It is a little itchy."

"Yes, ma'am, I will send it off this afternoon for you." Lindsey thanked the lady and tipped her for her excellent help and left.

It was going on Eleven. She had done great on time; Brandon's second class was just starting. She had one other errand to take care of.

She went straight to the Dean's office at the school. "May I help you?" The lady at the desk asked her.

"Yes, I need to speak with Dean Hollingsworth."

She picked up the phone.

"Yes, sir, there is a . . ."

"Lindsey Jacobs."

"Lindsey Jacobs here to see you, sir, yes sir, I will. You can go right in."

"Thank you." Lindsey walked around her desk and opened the door and went in.

He stood up when she entered. "How can I help you Ms. Jacobs?" He asked.

Lindsey pulled a card from her purse. "I know this is going to be a little crazy, but I was wondering if when Mr. Clearwater graduates, you could give him this for me? I don't know if I will be here, and I don't want to take the chance on him not getting it.

He took the card from her hand. "I will place it in his file and make sure he gets it at graduation."

"Thank you very much."

"You're welcome. Is there anything else I can do for you?"

"No, I think that is it."

"So, how do you like the school?" He asked her.

"I am very pleased; you have some great teachers here."

He smiled. "Are you going to be here for our party Friday night?"

"Yes, sir; Mr. Clearwater is escorting me."

"How wonderful!" He said.

"Well, I have to meet Mr. Clearwater for lunch. It was nice to see you again; thanks for taking care of that for me."

"It was no problem. If there is anything else, please come see me again."

Lindsey left the Dean's office and headed for the coffee shop; she was going to be a little early, but she didn't mind. She sat down at a table in the corner. The card she had given the Dean she had written out back at the Park one night while it was snowing. She had made it look all official with congratulations and all, but had also put ten thousand dollars in it. She would have liked to make a personal one, but was afraid someone might get their hands on it, so she didn't.

Lindsey pulled her phone out of her pocket, the blue light was on.

"What can I get you?" A waitress came up.

"A French vanilla cappuccino is all for now."

The girl walked away.

Lindsey wondered how long they had been monitoring; she was hoping they weren't on when she was in the Dean's office.

"Here you go." The girl set it down in front of her. "Just let me know if you want anything else."

"I will, thanks."

Lindsey watched as the light remained on. Students started coming in, class was out. Brandon and James walked in the door. The light went out, Lindsey smiled, thank goodness.

"Hey, did you get it all done?" Brandon asked.

"Yep, all done."

James pulled up a chair. "Do you mind?" He asked.

"Nope, not a bit, how was class today?"

"Fine, nothing new since yesterday," Brandon told her.

"Brandon said you were out dress shopping for Friday night."

Lindsey smiled. "Yeah, I think I did well. Well, I hope so, anyway."

"I don't think you could look bad in anything." James said looking at her.

Lindsey laughed. "You going to let him hit on me like that?"

Brandon smiled. "As long as that's as far as it goes."

Lindsey scooted her chair over toward James's. Brandon grabbed it and pulled her back towards him.

She laughed and kissed him. "So, James, you taking a date Friday?" She asked.

"No, going all alone, just by myself."

"He sounds pitiful, dosen't he?" Brandon said as he looked at Lindsey.

"Do you want an invitation to go with us? It's not like we are not all going to be there, anyway."

He smiled.

Lindsey smiled back. "I don't care if you join us, but it's up to Brandon."

"You can arrive with us, but we are leaving without you; that will be Lindsey's last night."

"Alright," he said, "I get the picture."

The waitress came by and took their orders.

"Are you going home for Christmas?" Lindsey asked James.

"Yeah, going home to good ole Montana. I almost dread it."

"What for?" Lindsey asked.

"My sister Julie has five kids and Lacy, my other one, has three. It's like baby fest at my house."

Lindsey laughed. "So how many siblings do you have?"

"Four sisters and one brother, I am the youngest. My brother Frank and his wife have two kids. Two, but they are both teenagers. And Michaela, she has three, but they are about grown, too. It's Julie and Lacy's kids that are so small, and they are into everything."

Lindsey laughed.

"So, when you going to have kids?" James asked.

Lindsey was sort of taken aback. "Not for a long time, yet. I am not even married."

"When did that have to do with anything it? Julie's not married and has three."

"I plan to be married before kids are involved."

Brandon smiled at her. They would have great kids together, he thought. Lindsey could see it on his face. "Don't be getting any ideas," she told him.

He smiled at her. "I can dream, can't I?" She just looked at him.

James laughed at them both. "You better watch Brandon, he may have a few on the side. He is quite popular with the girls."

Lindsey laughed; James evidently didn't know Brandon too well, "I don't think so, I know him better than you do."

"I don't know." He patted Brandon on the back.

"She's right, James, she has you beat on the subject; you might as well drop it."

"Man, you give in way too quickly; here I was trying to help you out."

"I don't need any help when it comes to Lindsey."

"I was just trying to get you some major hot sex and you blow the whole thing."

Lindsey and Brandon just rolled.

"Ok." He wasn't quite sure how to take their sudden outburst of laughter.

"James," Lindsey said, "I am waiting for marriage, so all your efforts were in vain."

He looked at her. "Waiting for marriage?" He looked at Brandon. "And, you're ok with that?"

"She's not the only one waiting, James."

"Where is the fun in that?"

Lindsey smiled. "You'd be surprised." They both laughed again.

"So what's the big deal about Lindsey's last night if you guys aren't doing the wild thing?"

Brandon laughed. "You wouldn't understand."

"Ok, you guys are weird."

"We better get to class." Brandon got up and left a tip on the table.

They all walked to Ms. Yuri's class. "Nice to see you again, dear," Ms. Yuri said as Lindsey and Brandon walked by her.

"I'll be here all week, if that's ok."

"Be glad to have you," she said with a smile.

Lindsey sat and listened as they all worked on some scales and some songs. Ms. Yuri made each person in the class feel good about what they were doing. Some were way ahead of others, but she praised them just as much as she did the others. She was a good teacher. She knew how to get each of them to want to do their very best for her.

Lindsey walked over and sat down at a piano; she closed her eyes and laid her hands on the keys. A smile came to her face.

"You have been sitting smiling for ten minutes, but haven't played a note." She opened her eyes to find Ms. Yuri looking at her.

"I don't have to play it to hear it in my head."

"Class is almost over; play something for us, please."

Lindsey's melody started softly, but it wasn't long before it was a grand and masterful piece.

"Beautiful, my dear. I didn't recognize it though. Who wrote it?"

Lindsey smiled. "I did."

Ms. Yuri smiled, "You are quite accomplished, my dear. Would you want to play that in the program Friday night?"

"I don't think I will remember it that long."

She looked at Lindsey. "You mean you just wrote it right then?"

"Yes ma'am. that's why I was smiling. I had a melody in my head."

Ms. Yuri went and brought back a paper and pencil. "Here, write it down."

Lindsey took the paper and pencil from her and began to write. Class ended and Lindsey was still writing.

"I'll catch up with you in a few; go ahead," she told Brandon. A new group of students came into the room. Lindsey got up and started to leave.

"Are you finished?"

"No."

"Go ahead and finish; you're not going to bother anyone in here."

Lindsey sat back down and wrote out some more notes. Every little bit she would lay down the pencil and play a little, then pick them back up and write some more.

"How's it going?" Ms. Yuri asked her.

"I really don't know about this. I have never really written down any of my pieces."

"You can do it; I know you can."

Lindsey smiled; Ms. Yuri was a great teacher. Lindsey finished writing her notes then put it down and began to play the piece.

Ms. Yuri came back over to her. "Very good, now you need to write it out on proper sheet music and don't forget the timing."

"I will work on it tonight."

"Good, I will expect to see the finished piece tomorrow."

"Thank you."

She smiled at Lindsey. "You're most welcome."

Lindsey took the paper and left the classroom. She went to the history class and sat down outside. She wasn't too upset about missing the class; she didn't like Mr. Walker. The class finished and Brandon came out.

"Hey." She stood up.

"So, did you get it all written down?" He asked.

"Well, it's all scribble, but I am going to try to put it on music sheets tonight." He put his arm around her as they walked up the hall. Lindsey loved being here with him in the school, learning and living.

Brandon heated up leftovers, as Lindsey sat at the keyboard; she had it hooked up to the computer. She would play and it would write the music. Brandon watched her, she was so happy. He wanted to do something special for her for Christmas, but he didn't know what. He had been writing a song, but it wasn't going to be finished. It still had a lot of work that needed to be done, and he wanted it to be perfect. He had considered buying her some jewelry, but she couldn't keep it with her, so he ruled that out. He was at a loss for what to do for her. Lindsey had headphones on and didn't hear her phone beep on the table. Brandon picked it up and looked at it.

"I have some Intel you need to look at when you are back to the park."

Brandon typed back, "Can you talk a second?"

"Lines are clear, what can I do for you?"

"What can I get her for Christmas?"

"Brandon?"

"Yeah."

"Where is Lindsey?"

"She is playing on the keyboard. She has headphones on."

"I don't know. Let me think about it. I will get back to you before she goes back to the park."

"Thanks."

"Welcome. Make sure she gets the message about the Intel. I'll erase the text history for you."

"Thanks, again." Brandon sat the phone down and went to get the food out of the oven and put it on plates.

He tapped Lindsey on the shoulder, "You ready to eat? The food is hot."

She took off the headphones and went and sat down at the bar. "A message came in for you awhile ago; Keeps says you have some Intel waiting for you back at the park you need to look at."

"Alright, anything else?"

"Nope." Brandon sat down beside her as they ate.

"This is just as good as it was yesterday," she told him.

"I agree with you on that," he said.

"Miss the atmosphere, though."

"I don't." He smiled. "We can sit here in our underwear if we want," Brandon grinned.

"I guess that's true."

Brandon stood up and took off his shirt; his hair was hanging half down his back and half down one side of his face.

"I didn't know you were suggesting it, though." She smiled.

He walked over by her and turned her stool to face him. "I thought it was a good idea." He took hold of her shirt.

"You're asking for trouble, mister." She took hold of his hands.

"Promise?" He smiled.

"No."

"I am going to miss you when you're gone." He kissed her gently on the forehead.

Lindsey glanced over at her phone lying on the bar, no blue light. "I'll miss you, too." She pulled him down and kissed him on the lips. Lindsey ran her finger over the tattoo on his chest.

"It was the only way to keep you with me." He smiled at her.

"I put yours on my guitar," she told him, "etched it right in the front. It looks really great."

"I bet it does." He smiled. "Someone will wonder one day what it means."

"I don't think so; I plan on keeping it."

He smiled and leaned over and kissed her. "So what are we going to do tonight?"

"Your house, your rules."

"Oh, my, let's see." He put his hand on his chin. "I can think of a lot of things I would like to do." He grinned. "But I have a vow I plan on sticking to, so they are out of the question."

Lindsey laughed. "I know what you mean. Darn vow!"

They both laughed. "Let's start with the dishes and then we can go from there."

Lindsey got up off the barstool and picked up her plate.

Brandon dried and put away, as she washed. They then cleaned up the apartment and turned in.

Lindsey lay awake for an hour as Brandon lightly snored. She reached over and picked up her phone. "What is the Intel about?"

"The mission I was telling you about that's coming up," Keeps replied. "I want you to look over it, tell me how you would go about taking it down."

"I thought they had it planned out pretty well."

"I don't like what they want to do, and I hope you can figure out something better."

"What do they have in mind?"

"All the information is waiting for you. I am not going to go over this on the phone with you."

"Ok, sorry, didn't mean to aggravate you."

"Sorry, it's not you."

"Maybe I can take a look at some of it on Brandon's laptop, but it needs cleaned and some spyware added. I will let you know when I am ready for it."

"Fine."

Lindsey got out of bed and went to Brandon's laptop. After about an hour cleaning it up and putting extra antivirus and spyware on it, she sent Keeps a text.

"Ready, send me what you have."

Lindsey spent several hours going over the Intel they had. This one was a big ring; there was no way this one guy was running it all. She needed to do some serious hacking and research, but not tonight. She glanced at the clock, it was going on three am. She sent all her stuff to her computer and cleaned it back off Brandon's, then climbed back into bed.

Lindsey woke late. Brandon was on the computer working on schoolwork. He was sitting in his boxers, his hair hanging down his back. She got up and walked over and kissed him on the shoulder.

She whispered in his ear, "I love you." He turned and faced her, she glanced at her phone. Brandon walked over, turned the stereo on and set her phone directly in front of the speaker.

"I love you, too." He pulled her into his arms. "What am I going to do when you leave and don't come back?"

Lindsey looked up at him. She knew that when he left the Park after Christmas, they would have to have a big fight and break things off. It would have to be more than just a little fight; it would have to be a long week or two, hate-you-forever fight. She took a deep breath.

"What?" he asked.

"You know that we have to break this off after Christmas, and make it sound convincing."

"Why?"

"I cannot have anyone using you against me."

"I thought no one knew about you."

"They don't, but there is always a chance that something will go wrong or someone will go bad and get a their hands on a file or something, and I don't want them to use you or your family against me. Because they could, you know; I would do anything for you."

He traced her face with his finger. "I am sorry."

Lindsey smiled. "Don't be, you have made my life worth living." He kissed her gently.

Brandon had put his life in danger to love her, she had also put hers in danger, too, but she had been honest with him. He loved her with every fiber of his being and if breaking up was what it took to keep them safe, then when the time came he would make sure it was one hard and believable break up.

"It's almost time for school, we better get ready," he told her. She smiled at him, then went to get dressed.

Brandon turned the stereo off and pulled on a pair of jeans and a shirt. Lindsey was already ready and waiting on him. She had the music she had printed out in her hands.

Theory class went by slowly, but strings were ok. Still no teacher, so everyone just worked on their own stuff. Lindsey took the opportunity to play her piece on the cello; she liked it just as well on that as the piano. Several of the kids gathered around her and joined in with her as she played. The sound of them all together was beautiful; all it needed was a little piano in it.

James joined them for lunch again at the coffee shop.

"How about you write me a song for my writing class? Then I know I would pass," James was telling her about trying to write a song and not feeling like he was doing very well.

"You can do it; I saw some of the stuff you had written on Brandon's computer. It looked great."

"It doesn't sound great to me," he told her.

"You'll do fine."

"So, I guess that's a no?"

Lindsey shook head and laughed. "Definitely a no."

James dropped his head.

Brandon laughed at him. "So what about tomorrow night, you meeting us here or what?"

James perked up, "I don't know."

"I will be ready by four, and I think I will get a car to pick me up. I will pick up Brandon at his place, you could just go there and get ready, then I can pick you both up," Lindsey told them.

"You're not getting ready at the apartment?" Brandon asked.

She smiled. "Nope, I have plans made for that. I just need to call and get a car."

"I guess that will be fine," James said.

"Alright, then." Lindsey smiled.

"You have a devious smile going there," James said.

"I can't wait to see your reaction to my dress," she said, then laughed.

"I am sure you will look great," Brandon said.

"I don't want to look great, I want to look knockout gorgeous!" Lindsey gave a big smile.

"Lord, help us all," Brandon said.

They finished lunch and headed to Ms. Yuri's class.

"Let's see it," she said to Lindsey as she entered the class. She looked over the work. "Very good, now let's see if when I play it, it sounds like you want it to."

Ms. Yuri got up from her desk, went to a piano, and sat down to play.

Lindsey was quite excited to hear her music being played by someone else.

"Wonderful!" Ms. Yuri said after she played through the piece. "Does it sound right to you; is it all you want it to be?" Lindsey thought for a minute about the strings class.

"I think if there was a cello playing with the piano it would be perfect."

"Then write it out and add it to the piece. Be prepared to play it tomorrow night; maybe Brandon could help you out by playing the cello."

Brandon's eyes got big. "I am not good enough for that!"

Lindsay smiled. "It wouldn't be a hard piece; maybe you and James could help me."

"I am sure James will do it if you agree to help him with his writing."

"I don't care to help him, but I won't do it for him."

Ms. Yuri smiled at Lindsey. "I am sure the Dean will be pleased to hear you play."

Lindsey didn't know she knew who she was until that very moment.

Ms. Yuri called the class to order and began her lesson. Lindsey sat scribbling on her music. She had to keep it simple, but since there would be two people, she could have two simple things going that when played together hard and intense.

Brandon looked over at Lindsey scribbling on her paper. She was smiling. It was really a shame she could not be a professional musician; she was so talented and loved it so much, he thought. He hoped he could live up to her expectations; he knew she said it didn't matter to her, but it mattered to him.

Lindsey stayed in Ms. Yuri's class when he went to history. He didn't mind. As long as she was happy, he didn't care. When he left history, she was waiting with James. She had already made a deal with him to look at his music and help him.

"So what are we eating tonight boys?" She asked, as they walked out of the school.

"I don't care," Brandon said.

"Me, either," added James.

"I feel like Mexican; know any good places?"

"There is one over on 34th."

"Is it cheap or is it good?" Lindsey asked.

"Cheap," Brandon replied.

"I want a good one."

"The best one is El Braceros, but it is always crammed," James told her.

Brandon smiled at James. "That's ok, she talks their language: money."

They caught a cab and headed to El Braceros. Lindsey had them a table in fifteen minutes despite the long line outside.

"It must be nice to have money," James told her.

"Only when you want something, otherwise it is just a pain."

"How in the world can it be a pain?" James asked.

"It's the business part of it that is such a pain. You have to take care of the business 365 days a year to have it."

James looked at Brandon, "What a terrible problem to have," he said sarcastically, "I think I could get used to it."

Brandon just smiled.

The waiter was Mexican and the guys were having a hard time understanding him, but they finally got their orders placed. Lindsey, however, ordered in fluent Spanish; both guys glared at her. The waiter just smiled and went to put the order in.

"I hate to ask, but how many languages do you speak?" James asked.

"Then why are you asking?"

"I guess I am just trying to find something you're not perfect at."

Brandon laughed. "According to Jacob, she sucks at Halo."

Lindsey smiled. "Yeah that is true; I am horrible at it."

"Is that it? You suck at a video game? Is there anything else?" James looked at Lindsey.

"I haven't tried a lot of things, so I have no idea if I am good at everything or not."

James shook his head. "How in the world did you end up with her?" He looked over at Brandon.

"Just lucky, I guess," Brandon remembered her telling the guys at the pool that while they were at his mom and dad's anniversary party.

"So, how many languages?" He repeated.

"Well, 30 fluently, but I know several more. When you do business all over the world you have to speak their language, or you can get taken for a ride and lose millions."

"Yeah, I can see where that might come in handy," James had to admit.

"It's also nice when you're in a different country to know what people are saying about you," she giggled, "they get all messed up when you suddenly talk to them in their own language."

"Sounds like fun to me," James said.

"Oh, you have no idea."

Their food was soon delivered to their table and they ate and were on their way back to Brandon's. They dropped by the school and picked up a second cello as they went.

Lindsey sat down at the computer and finished writing out the cellos' parts. Soon she had them both playing as she played on the keyboard. Their parts she kept very simple, but it sounded really good all together. They practiced for several hours before Lindsey called a break.

"Did you call about a car?" Brandon asked her.

"I forgot." She pulled out her phone.

"All taken care of, just need to know where to pick you up. You can give the driver directions from there."

"Macy's," she typed back.

"Done," came back.

"All taken care of," she said with a smile. Lindsey sat back down at the computer and looked over some of James' music. She added a few notes here and there, then smiled. "I think this piece will get you an A, it just needed a little tweaking."

James smiled at her. "Thanks."

She smiled back. "Thank you for playing." Lindsey got up and headed for the shower. "I am going to shower, then we will go over it another time or two."

Brandon and James sat down and flipped the TV on. Lindsey could hear some ballgame playing just before she turned the water on. She stood under the water for a good 15 minutes.

The week had flown by and she would be leaving Saturday. She would have the Inn to herself since everyone was going home. She was there mainly just to be a security guard. The first week would be slow, but then Brandon was going to be there for the second week. Lindsey decided to give him the necklace before she left, just in case. She didn't want to be called out and not be able to give it to him. She would give it to him tomorrow night after the party. She dried off and put her shorts and bra on with a tank top over it. The guys were still watching the game when she came out.

"That was a bad call," Brandon was saying.

"You can see it clearly on the replay. I can't see how they are going to let the call stand," James said.

"You guys ready?" Lindsey walked up behind the TV.

"Yeah, the game sucks; the refs are making all kinds of bad calls." Brandon flipped off the TV and got up.

James sat down at his cello, Brandon sat at his and Lindsey began to play. Soon the music filled the room. Lindsey was happy with the way it had turned out. They went over it twice more, then decided to call it a night; it was getting late. James left and Brandon headed for the shower. Lindsey got the necklaces out of her purse and looked them over one more time. It was going to look great against Brandon's dark skin; she hoped he liked it. She put them back in her purse as Brandon shut the water off in the shower. Lindsey shut off all the lights but the one beside the bed and climbed in. She took off her tank top and dropped it on the floor beside the bed.

Brandon came out drying his hair with his towel. "Are you happy with the way your song turned out?" He asked her.

"Yeah, I think I am. What do you think about it?" She asked.

"I think it's great. It would probably be better if you had a couple of people that could play the cello better."

Lindsey smiled at him as he hung the towel over the bathroom door. "You two are doing great, I wouldn't want anyone else playing with me."

He climbed in the bed beside her. "You're amazing, you know that?"

"Not really, maybe just a little better than average."

He laughed. "Yeah, right." He rolled his eyes.

Lindsey curled up in his arms and closed her eyes.

Brandon put his face in her hair. "You smell so good."

"Just wait till tomorrow," she told him, "I am going to knock your socks off."

"You already do that," he told her.

Lindsey opened her eyes to find Brandon looking at her.

"What?" she asked.

"Nothing."

"Then, why are you staring at me?"

"No reason, just enjoying you being here." She smiled at him.

Lindsey got up. Now was the time for the necklaces. "Don't move." She told him. She turned on the stereo, placed her phone in front of the speaker and got the box out of her purse.

"I know this is a little early for Christmas, but I don't want to take a chance on anything happening and me not giving it to you." She climbed into the bed and held out the box. He sat up, took the box and opened it. "There is one for you and one for me."

He looked up with tears in his eyes. "Is that our rock?"

"Yep, I had it split. What do you think?" She asked.

Tears were running down his face, "They're perfect." He took out hers and put it on her, then she put his on. "One thing, you know I can't wear it all the time, but Keeps will have it when I don't. If anything should ever happen to me, he will see that you get mine."

Brandon pulled her in his lap. "I love you, Lindsey."

"So, you like it?"

He put his lips to hers and kissed her.

"Yes, thank you. How did I get so lucky?" He looked at her.

"I ask myself that all the time," she told him as she turned to straddle him.

Brandon kissed up her neck; he truly loved this woman with everything in him. How was he ever going to live even for just a little while without her? If he could, he would marry her this very instant.

"Brandon," Lindsey pushed on his chest. She could see he was off in thought, but his lips and hands were telling a story all their own as to where he was.

"Brandon," she had to say it again.

He blinked; his hands were on her breasts. He moved them instantly.

"Sorry."

"Well, I don't have to ask what you were thinking."

"I ..." he stumbled for words, "I was ... never have I ever wanted to break my vow as bad as right now."

"Worse than in the woods ... never mind, I know the answer to that question." She got up off him.

"Sorry," he told her.

He wasn't the only one that was affected by his hands. Her heart was racing and her insides wanted nothing more than to just throw the vow out and give herself to him in every way imaginable.

"Maybe I better sleep on the couch tonight," he told her as he got up off the bed.

"Brandon," she said. She so wanted him so bad that a certain sex game she had been taught came to mind. Well, it was sex without sex, or something like that.

"What?" He turned to look at her.

She decided it wasn't wise, she might not be able to control herself. "Don't go."

"I don't know if I can control myself." He looked at her.

"Yes, you can." She climbed in the covers and held them back for him to climb in.

Brandon took a couple of deep breaths and climbed in beside her. "You are going to kill me, woman."

"If you die, I die." She looked at him.

He closed his eyes and lay back in the bed. '*Breathe*', he kept telling himself. '*You can control this, just breathe*'. He felt Lindsey curl up to his side. Every bit of control that he had gained he started to lose again, when she laid her head on his chest'. He rubbed the little heart around his neck with his fingers. They were going to be together some day. He opened his eyes and looked over at Lindsey. He would need Keeps' help to do it, but it was going to happen or he was going to die trying.

Lindsey lay on his chest listening to Brandon breathe. She was having just as much trouble breathing as he was. She closed her eyes and listened to his heartbeat. It finally slowed and became steady.

When Lindsey woke up, the stereo was still playing. She looked over at Brandon. He was propped up on his side just watching her.

"What are you doing?"

"Well, I was watching you sleep."

"What time is it?" She asked.

"Going on Nine."

"Were you just going to let me sleep through classes?"

"I was thinking about it." He smiled.

"Come on." She pulled back the covers and got up. "We need to get dressed and go."

James noticed the necklaces as soon as they walked in the door. "Nice, where's mine? I thought we were a trio."

Brandon laughed.

"Sorry, but I don't think they could have cut the rock into three pieces," Lindsey told him.

The first class passed quickly, they really didn't work on theory. It was more like cram for performances that night. Strings class was the same way.

Everyone was working on music for the party. School was only a half day so that everything could be ready for the party that night.

James, Brandon, and Lindsey had subs for lunch. Then they took a taxi over and got James's clothes and headed back to the apartment. They went over the music piece a couple of times, then Lindsey left for Macy's.

Kathy was waiting for her when she went in the door. "Lindsey, are you ready for the big night?" She asked with a smile.

"Nope, you haven't transformed me into a knockout, yet!"

Kathy led Lindsey to the salon. "This is Jenny, and she is the best hair and makeup lady in the business." Lindsey smiled. "I have your clothes in the back waiting, and as soon as Jenny's done we will get you dressed."

"Thanks," Lindsey told her. Jenny ushered her to a chair. She walked around and looked at Lindsey a minute or two.

"I think your hair needs to be down in the back, but all this," she pulled back the top of Lindsey's hair, "needs to be up."

"You're the expert."

Jenny washed and dried Lindsey's hair, then started pulling pieces back in place adding curls as she went. Soon Lindsey's hair looked stunning. "Follow me, it's time to put on your face." Jenny led Lindsey into another room and sat her on a chair surrounded by makeup and brushes of every shape and size. She worked for about 30 minutes on her makeup.

"Well, what do you think?" She turned Lindsey around to face the mirror.

"Wow! Is that me?"

Jenny laughed. "Yes, do you like it?"

"Yes," she told her.

"Let's get you dressed," Kathy said from behind.

Lindsey followed Kathy to yet another room where her clothes were all laid. "I will wait out here, but if you need any help just let me know," she told Lindsey.

Lindsey took her clothes off and slid on the new lingerie.

"Hey, Kathy, can you help me get this over my hair without messing it up?" She said at the door.

"Of course." she carefully pulled the dress over Lindsey's head.

"Thanks."

Lindsey sat down and put her heels on, then put on the jewelry. She hated taking off her other necklace, but it didn't quite look fancy enough for the dress. Lindsey stood up and looked in the mirror.

"You look stunning, Lindsey," Kathy told her.

"I need some kind of perfume, something that smells heavenly."

"We have about ten minutes; we should be able to find something."

Kathy gave Lindsey a bag to put all her clothes in, then they walked down to the perfume counter. Everyone stared as Lindsey passed. Lindsey found two she liked. Finally she had Kathy hold them behind her back and mix them up, then Lindsey chose a hand.

Lindsey was ready, all she had left to do was to pay for it all. Lindsey followed Kathy to a register where she had a list of all the items Lindsey had purchased. Lindsey handed her card to Kathy. The total was over five thousand dollars; the jewelry was the biggest cost.

"Thank you for your help, Kathy," Lindsey handed her a tip of three hundred dollars.

"It was my pleasure, ma'am."

Kathy walked Lindsey to the door. A limo sat outside with the driver standing beside it. Lindsey smiled and walked towards the car.

"Ms. Jacobs?" He asked.

"Yes."

He opened the door for her and she got in. She gave the driver Brandon's address.

They were there a few minutes ahead of schedule, which was great; she could take her clothes and put them in the apartment. The car pulled up in front of the apartment and Lindsey got out.

"I will be right back." She carried her bag to the door and hesitated before turning the knob. Brandon was just coming out of the bathroom when she opened the door.

"Holy crap!" James said as she shut the door behind her. Brandon was just staring.

"You guys about ready?" Lindsey said as she put her bag of clothes on the bed. Brandon hadn't moved yet.

"Brandon," Lindsey said.

"Wow!" He managed to say.

"You like?" She did a little twirl.

"I . . . you . . . wow!" He stumbled over his words, which made her smile.

"You look amazing!" James said.

"Yeah," Brandon agreed.

"So, are you guys ready? The car is waiting downstairs."

"We're ready," James said.

"Let's go, then."

Brandon walked over and held out his arm, Lindsey took it and he escorted her out of the apartment.

"I should have known," James said as they walked out on the street to the Limo.

"No other car would have sufficed," Brandon told James.

"You're right about that."

The driver opened the door and they all got in.

Brandon just kept staring; he couldn't seem to take his eyes off of her. "I don't think there is a word that could describe how amazingly stunning you look tonight," Brandon told her. She leaned over and gave him a kiss. "You smell amazing, too." Lindsey smiled; this is what she was hoping for, a way to leave him breathless.

James leaned over and smelled of her. "What is that? It smells great," James asked.

"The bottle is at the apartment, but I don't really remember the name, I looked at so many."

They pulled up to the auditorium and the driver opened the door. Brandon held out one arm and James held out the other. Lindsey slid her hand through both their arms and up the steps they went. Dean Hollingsworth was greeting everyone as they entered.

"Ms. Jacobs," he said. "You're seated up at the front left table. Boys, all students are seated at the tables on the right."

"I would rather sit with them, if you don't mind," she told him.

"Not at all; sit where ever you like."

"Thank you, Dean."

They crossed the floor and almost every eye in the place turned as they went by. Brandon pulled out the chair for Lindsey to sit on. Brandon sat on one side and James the other. Brandon's eye stayed on Lindsey no matter who came by to talk to them.

"I believe we are the best looking group here," James said.

"You mean we escorted the most beautiful one here," Brandon corrected him.

"I think I have the best looking escorts," Lindsey added. She looked at Brandon; then leaned over to him. "I knew you would look great in that. So are you glad I made you wait?" she asked.

He smiled. "Oh, Yeah."

Dean Hollingsworth approached the microphone. "Good evening students, ladies, gentlemen, and honored guests. We hope that each of you will enjoy our Christmas Music Gala. This year we were proud to offer a new scholarship, the Jacobs Music Scholarship Program, with the winner receiving all four years of studies paid in full, along with all the musical and computer requirements and apartment being paid for, by the scholarship. This week we have been honored to have, Ms. Lindsey Lorain Jacobs, visiting and participating in several of our classes. Tonight we are going to start things off with a very special performance by Ms. Jacobs and her scholarship winner, Brandon Clearwater. They will also be joined by James Masterson. Ms. Jacobs, if you will." Lindsey stood up, Brandon and James escorted her to the stage. Lindsey had the boys go set down as she walked to the microphone.

"Thank you, Dean Hollingsworth, I have enjoyed visiting every class this week. I was quite impressed with the school and its teachers. Tonight we are going to play *Inspiration* for you; I hope you enjoy hearing it as much as I enjoyed writing it." Lindsey walked over to the piano and sat down. She smiled at both Brandon and James. "Let's do this," she whispered.

The melody flowed smoothly; it was the best performance either James or Brandon had given. The crowd came to their feet when the piece was finished. Lindsey stood along with the guys as they took their bows.

Ms. Yuri walked up on stage and gave her a hug. "Beautiful, my dear, absolutely beautiful."

Lindsey smiled at her. "Thank you." Lindsey and the guys returned to their seats.

One by one each teacher called a set of students up and they played. Lindsey enjoyed the evening. There was an hour of music, then a meal, then another hour of music.

The evening ended with the Dean going by each table and talking, then saying goodnight, and excusing the table to leave. Of course, he went to all the important tables first so Lindsey and the boys got to leave right away.

"See you in a couple of weeks," Brandon told James as he and Lindsey got into the Limo.

"Hope to see you again," Lindsey told James.

"It was nice to have finally met you, Lindsey, and I will see you after Christmas," James told Brandon. Brandon leaned up and told the driver something.

"Where are we going?" Lindsey asked. Brandon smiled, "I thought we might go out to the pier."

Lindsey smiled. "That sounds great."

The moon was full and the weather nice; cool, but nice. Brandon took his jacket off and put it around Lindsey's shoulders as they walked down the pier.

"You look amazing tonight," Brandon told her as they walked.

She smiled. "Thanks, you look pretty sharp yourself."

They stopped at the end of the pier and stood looking out over the ocean. Lindsey had purposely left her clutch in the Limo with her phone in it. Brandon put his arms around her and held her close.

"Brandon." She turned in his arms to face him.

"Yeah." He looked down at her.

"I have a feeling that I won't be around much longer. I thought I would have till next summer, but I have a feeling I will be leaving before then."

Brandon took a deep breath. "I have been expecting you to tell me you were leaving the whole time you were here, I guess it was just inevitable, but that doesn't make it easier." He kissed her gently.

"I will know more when you come after Christmas, but I just want you to be prepared," she told him.

Some noise from the other end of the pier caught Lindsey's attention, but she only watched casually as if not to pay attention. Five guys had walked out on the pier; they all seemed to be high. Brandon noticed them, but paid no attention to them.

"Come on, it's getting crowded," Brandon took her hand and led her back down the pier. Something shiny flickered in the moonlight as one of the guys turned away from them as they passed. Lindsey picked up the pace.

"What is it?" Brandon asked.

Lindsey glanced over her shoulder; the group wasn't very far from them.

"We need to get out of here, fast." Lindsey could hear the group now getting closer to them.

"Get to the Limo and get out of here, I'll catch up with you." He looked at her. "Don't ask, just do, please."

Brandon's eyes were big. "What's wrong?" he asked.

"Just go. Now!"

Brandon sprinted to the Limo. Lindsey turned to face the five guys that were behind them. The five men were less than ten feet from her. The guy in the middle was holding a gun on her. Lindsey heard some commotion behind her and turned to find Brandon standing there with a gun at his head and the man smiling that held it.

"Well, well," the man holding Brandon said. "Did you think we would not find you, my dear?"

Lindsey knew the man; it was Kalahari Binabi. Lindsey had met him five years ago when she had killed his son.

"Kalahari, how nice to see you. I see you're still mad at me for killing Carlos."

"I knew it had to be you, you were the only one that could have done it. He was my only son; mad is not the right word for what I am."

"Your son was dealing in humans and you knew it."

"You didn't have to kill him."

"Were you going to stop him, then?"

Kalahari just looked at her. "It was his business, not mine."

"Then why are you here?"

"You took my only son from me, now I am going to take something from you." He put the gun to Brandon's head.

"If killing him will make you feel better, go ahead; he's nothing to me, just another job. It will save me the trouble later." Brandon never made a move. He knew she was trying to save his life, whether it sounded that way or not.

Kalahari smiled. "Prove it." He chambered the gun then pulled out the clip and held it out to her. Lindsey smiled and took the gun.

Brandon felt a sharp pain in his neck as he heard the gun fire in Lindsey's hand. Brandon fell to the pier. Kalahari laughed, looked at her for only a moment, before he then fell forward to the pier at the same time the four behind her fell.

Lindsey knelt beside Brandon, he was out cold; she pulled the dart from the back of his neck. Handler came up on the pier; the other four snipes were already climbing into a black hummer.

"You ok?" He asked as he leaned over and checked each of the men lying on the pier. Lindsey smiled at him. She had never been more happy to see him.

"Yes."

"Let's get him loaded into the Limo; the cleaning crew is standing by."

The Handler picked Brandon up and took him to the Limo; the driver got out and opened the door. Lindsey noticed it was now a new driver.

The Handler lay Brandon on one of the seats, then got back out to face Lindsey. "You're expected back Sunday." He glanced at Brandon. "Take care of this, and clean out your cabin. I will be there to pick you up at 0400 Sunday morning."

She looked up at him. "I'll be ready."

He nodded his head as a black van pulled up. "This will bring him around." He handed her a syringe, then he turned and walked away.

Lindsey got in the Limo. Lindsey rolled Brandon over and gave him the shot in his hip. When they arrived back at the apartment building, Brandon was very groggy so she needed the driver's help to get Brandon up to the apartment.

The driver left as soon as they dropped him on the bed. Brandon was talking out of his head. Lindsey knew that the drug they had used was a hallucinogenic. That way it was easy to make the person think that it was a dream.

Brandon's computer kicked on and Keeps' avatar popped up. "We have to talk, but they are monitoring your phone." The words popped up on the screen instead of sound. Lindsey walked over to the computer. "Wow, you look hot!"

Lindsey smiled. She sat down at the computer.

"Thanks, did I get you in deep crap?" She typed.

"Not too bad. I was able to keep Brandon mainly out of it, but you have to break it off in the morning, convincingly, or it's not going to work." With that the screen went black.

Lindsey got up and took her dress off; then pulled all the pins out of her hair and let it fall. Lindsey climbed up on the bed beside Brandon; he was still just mumbling. It would take several more hours before the effects of the drugs would wear completely off. She undressed him and pulled the covers over him. She put her phone beside the bed. The blue light was on.

Brandon was still talking with his eyes closed. "What note was that, I don't think I can find it, mom where are my clean clothes, can we get a dog, not little Seth, can I ride the horse now?" Nothing he said really made sense; it was just rambling. "Don't fall, is Michelle coming? Todd, that's not the right note, marry me, I will love you forever, kill the stinking thing." Lindsey listened to him as he dreamed. She had to smile when he asked someone to marry him. She hoped he was dreaming of her, but hoped he wouldn't say her name.

Lindsey finally got up and went to the shower. With all the hairspray and makeup she had to get off, it took her a while. It was about midnight when she climbed in the bed beside Brandon; he had almost completely stopped talking now. Her phone light was still on. She pulled up next to him and laid her head on his chest. His arm pulled her closer and she looked up to find him looking at her. He blinked a few times, then his eyes closed again. She snuggled up to him and tried to sleep, but she really didn't want to. This was the last night she would have with him and she didn't want it to go by quickly. About three, she got up and sat at the bar with pen and paper and wrote a letter.

> *Brandon, I know last night was strange and you don't remember much from it. It's better that way. But because of last night, today will be the last day for Lindsey Jacobs, so today must end in a major fight. But know this, no*

matter what I say or what I do, know that I love you with all my heart. I don't expect you to wait for me forever. I don't know when I will be back; it could be months or even years. And all that matters to me is that you are happy. So be happy. And if you find happiness with another, that's ok. And if you do, then simply take your necklace off and don't wear it. Then when and if I find you again and see that you're not wearing it I won't disturb you. I will have Keeps keep my necklace and if anything were to ever happen to me he will return my half to you. I am sorry that things have to end this way, but you must understand why it does, especially after last night. It's better that I leave now anyway, I don't want to take any more chances of people finding me. I love you, Lindsey. Burn immediately!!!!!!!!

Lindsey folded the letter and walked back to the bed. Brandon was sleeping on his side; she climbed in and pulled his arm across her waist. She tucked the letter under Brandon's pillow and pulled in close to him. "I love you," she whispered in his ear, then she kissed him on the cheek.

He mumbled, "forever," and pulled her tighter to him. She smiled and closed her tear-filled eyes. A shudder wracked her body as tears fell freely down her cheeks.

A sudden shaking brought Brandon from sleep, he opened his eyes. His eyes took a few minutes to pull the light from the room to focus. Where was he? The last thing he remembered was ... He lay there a minute trying to think, what had happened? He remembered going out on the pier, running to the Limo, a gun being held on him, and then a sharp pain and gunfire. He could feel Lindsey in his arms. He looked at her. She sobbed very quietly beside him; tears were streaming down her face, she shuddered again and took a deep breath. He reached up and felt his chest, no holes.

Lindsey noticed him lift his arm to his chest. She reached for the letter and placed it in his hand. Then she got up and went to the bathroom. Brandon sat up and flipped the light on beside the bed, then unfolded the letter and read it.

He then got out of the bed, went to the sink and burned the letter, as tears streamed down his face. He walked to the bathroom; he could hear the shower running. He turned the knob and opened the door.

Lindsey was just standing in the water, still in her shorts and sports bra, just letting the water hide her tears. Brandon opened the shower door and stepped in beside her. He turned her and pulled her into his arms letting the shower hide his own tears as well.

Lindsey was sure they would be watching her more closely from now on, and she might never get the chance to see him again. The fear and sadness was lighting a hot fire in her. She pulled her shirt and bra over her head and threw it over the shower top.

"Don't," he took hold of her arms, "not like this. Not until it's done the right way."

"But it may never happen," she pleaded with him.

He smiled at her. "Out of all the people in the world, we found each other and I believe that we will find each other again. Something or someone is pulling us together, so I have faith that it will all work out."

Lindsey looked at him. "What if they never let me go again? I give myself freely, no regrets."

Brandon kissed her. "I want you more than life itself, but not like this. I want you as my wife first."

Lindsey fell completely apart, her knees buckled under her and she nearly fell, tears and sobs tore from her chest. Brandon held her up; he pulled her to his chest and rubbed down her back trying to soothe her.

He had meant what he said; he wanted her as his wife and would wait for her no matter how long. The tears that racked her body tore his heart in pieces.

"Lindsey," he rubbed her hair, "they can never keep us apart, no matter how hard they try." He was trying to lift her spirits. "We have Keeps on our side."

She looked up at him with red eyes.

"Now come on," he told her, "we have to break up and I want it to be convincing. We have to get them to take their eyes off me so you can find me again."

She stood up, "I will make you a promise. We will be together again one day if I have to kill every last one of them."

Brandon almost felt scared. He had never seen her so angry, not like this, anyway. She had definitely meant what she said.

"From here on out." She took a deep breath.

"I know your anger will be for them, not me. I love you, Lindsey."

She hugged him. "I love you, too."

He took a deep breath and opened the door.

The light on her phone was still on. She pointed to it and he nodded his head. Lindsey started gathering things up around the apartment and she wasn't being very quiet.

"I am trying to sleep here." Brandon smiled at her. "What are you doing?" He asked.

"Packing, what does it look like?"

"I thought we had till noon before you had to leave."

"You expect me to stay till noon after last night? I don't even know why I stayed last night."

"What are you talking about?"

"Do you remember anything from last night?"

223

"Sure we went to the Christmas party, then went to the pier, then . . ." he paused.

"What did we do after the pier?" Lindsey asked. "That's what I thought. You got smashed and don't remember a thing."

"What?" He asked.

"You got into the bar in the Limo."

"No," he said, "I don't remember it."

"You got quite drunk."

"So, I got a little drunk. What was wrong with that?"

"A little would have been fine, but I bet you don't even remember the hookers, do you?"

"Hookers?"

"Yes, hookers; three of them you invited into the Limo. I had to pay them just to get them to leave. And that is just part of it, I might be able to have even let that slide, but once we got here you were all over me. I thought you were going to rape me. For once I was glad Dad made me take all those martial arts lessons."

"Holy crap!" He said. "I'm sorry; I don't remember any of that."

Lindsey took a deep breath. "I really like you, Brandon, but after last night I have discovered I really don't know you and I think it's time for me to move on."

"What?"

"You heard me. I think I am going to put in my notice at the Park and move on. I've been thinking about visiting Paris, anyway."

"Lindsey, I didn't do it on purpose. I don't even remember doing it at all, but I'm sorry, please don't leave."

"Save it, Brandon, I have made up my mind. I don't want anything to do with a drunk."

"But I don't drink, or I normally don't."

"I went to all kinds of trouble to look my best last night and make it special for you and you just ruined it, you ruined everything. You're not who I thought you were, Brandon, and I think it would be a big mistake to remain friends."

"Lindsey, you're being ridiculous! Come on, give me a chance here. Let me make it up to you."

"I guess what they say is true about when you get drunk. Or maybe you have been lying to me about that, too."

"What . . . what are you talking about?"

"Waiting till you get married, there was no waiting last night. You were all over me."

"I am waiting."

"Sure."

"This is ridiculous. I would know if I had sex with someone or not."

"You don't even remember trying to have sex with me, so what makes you think you would remember it."

"I would just know."

"Yeah, you keep telling yourself that. Your poor wife will end up with all kinds of diseases from her so called virgin husband."

"That's it, get out!"

"What do you think I have been packing for?"

"Don't forget this!" He picked up her dress from last night.

She smiled and closed her bag.

"Maybe you can find someone else to wear it, I don't want it. I don't want anything that reminds me of last night."

She picked up the necklace and earrings that went with it and handed them to him. She walked to the door. Brandon followed her. She threw her arms around his neck and kissed him. She took a deep breath and picked up her bag.

"Have a nice life."

She opened the door, went out and slammed it behind her. Brandon looked out the window as she walked out on the street and caught a cab. He picked up the dress and smelled it, it smelled so wonderful. He hugged it to him and sat down on the couch and rubbed the stone from his necklace between his fingers.

Lindsey took the cab to the airport; there she sat for the next four hours waiting on her flight.

Her phone vibrated in her pocket. "Very convincing."

"Did you have any doubts it would be?"

"Not really."

"I want you to Cloak and Dagger with me on the Switzerland Intel when I get back."

"Of course. You got any ideas?"

"A couple, but I need to know if they are plausible," she typed.

"Ok."

Lindsey noticed Brandon when he entered the waiting area. Keeps had put them on the same flight so they could be together. She exited the line and walked to the counter. Her ticket was coach, maybe if she upgraded, they would not be together.

"Yes, ma'am, can I help you?" The small brown-haired lady behind the counter asked.

"Is there any seat left in first class? Could upgrade to first class?"

The lady smiled. "Let me check and see." She typed on her computer a moment. "Yes, ma'am, there are several available."

Lindsey got her card out and handed it to the lady. She took it from Lindsey and swiped, then wrote on the ticket and boarding pass. "You're all ready; they are getting ready to board so go on and give it to the attendant, and you will be first on."

Lindsey thanked her and walked over to the attendant by the boarding desk. "I was getting ready to call, go right ahead." The lady looked at her boarding pass.

Lindsey heard her announce boarding as she walked into the plane

"Right this way." An attendant showed her to her seat.

Lindsey sat down; leaned her seat back and closed her eyes; she was tired, she hadn't slept much last night. Lindsey was just about asleep when the attendant came over the speaker and went through the safety procedures. Lindsey just blocked the sounds and slipped off into welcome slumber. She barely noticed when the plane's engines roared and they took off. Her dreams were filled with Brandon.

Lindsey woke when the plane touched down. She sat her chair up and waited for the plane to unload. She only had one bag and she just carried it on so she didn't have to go through baggage claim.

First Class was unloaded first, so she was off and waiting on her helicopter when she saw Brandon get off. He glanced her way; she turned as if she hadn't seen him.

"We're ready." The pilot came up to her.

"Good," she followed him and climbed in.

She was back in her cabin within an hour. She cleaned the cabin, washed all her clothes and packed them. When everything was cleaned and packed, she set down at her computer to look at the Intel from Keeps again.

Why did it always have to be a human traffic ring? What was wrong with these people? The man was American, his wife was Swedish. John and Maria Madison; they had two kids, Hans, age five, and Marta, age twelve. From the Intel, the wife was oblivious to the dealings of her husband.

John's targets were usually young, anywhere from age 13 to 22. Mainly girls were taken, but the demands for boys were growing. John's specialty was virgins. Lindsey cringed at the thought that they might have brainwashed her into thinking she had to stay pure until marriage for this job. No, she thought, Brandon thought the same way. She had been caught and sold into these rings before, but she was younger and her virginity hadn't really played a role because she was so young. Until now. She was going to explore all the options of how to get close to this man and his business without being sold.

Lindsey spent hours going over John's life, places he had been and things he had done. He had spent a lot of time traveling, Maria and the kids usually went. They also had a full time nanny and tutor that went with them. From all the information Lindsey had, his wife spent hours shopping and being pampered at local spas. The kids were mainly shuttled to museums and historical sites for lessons.

John didn't seem to go anywhere without his family by his side. The nanny or the tutor might be her way in. She was sure he wasn't the head of the ring, so if she could get in and set up some hacks on his computer then she could find out more.

Lindsey spent half the night gathering data on the nanny and tutor. Both were older women, which would work in her favor. She smiled as she wrote a small summary of what she wanted to do and forwarded it to Keeps.

A note returned. "I knew you would find a better way than what they were thinking. We will talk when you get here."

Lindsey flipped off her computer and lay down on the bed, five hours till pick up.

She closed her eyes and Brandon appeared. They walked, talked, danced and loved till her alarm woke her at 3:45. She got up and stripped the bed and left them in the pillow case. Her uniforms, she left hanging in the closet.

She grabbed her bag, laptop and guitar and headed out the door, as the helicopter landed. Malcolm was going to be left in a pinch with no one to stay over the holidays. She hated to do that to him, but it wasn't her choice.

She opened the door and slid her baggage in the back then climbed in and put her headphones on.

The Handler took her directly to Keeps, then left. Lindsey pulled her necklace and a jump drive from her pocket and handed them to Keeps. He smiled and slid them in his desk drawer. She also gave him all her ID's and cards and he put them in a manila envelope.

"I took your proposal to the King, he liked it. You will be leaving in three days. I am going to do some work on your laptop so you will be able take it with you." He looked at her guitar. "I will put that in lockup for you."

She smiled. "Thanks for Kalahari, too. I never saw him coming."

"Well, that is sort of my fault. I found him searching for you on the net. I should have warned you. He was using some face recognition software and found a picture of you that one of the girls from Troop 54 uploaded. He still wasn't sure it was you until you addressed him on the pier. But I think he was going to kill you and Brandon either way, just in case. I set up a team as soon as he entered the country."

"How long had he been on me?" She asked.

"He had one guy following you for a week, but he had just arrived Thursday morning."

"I should have noticed."

Keeps smiled at her. "You were supposed to be on vacation, not watching over your shoulder. That's why I am here."

"But I am supposed to be the best."

Lindsey got up and walked around the desk to him and gave him a kiss on the lips. "I owe you," she winked at him, "for so much." He smiled, then went back to typing on his computer. Lindsey walked back and sat down.

"I have you set up in a hotel. You're visiting Switzerland after graduating from Harvard. Your mom died two years ago from cancer and you never really knew your dad. He left when you were two right after your younger brother was born. Your mother worked hard to put you and your brother through school until she got sick, then she sold the family house and all she had to pay for the rest of your schooling and give you a graduation present, a trip to Switzerland.

CHAPTER 7

Unforgettable

3 1/2 YEARS LATER . . . .
"I am going, Seth," Kally told Keeps.

"You're going to get us both in major trouble if they find out."

"That's why they are not going to. You don't think I asked for a vacation at this time of the year for any other reason, did you?"

"I knew you would want to go. I think I have everything you will need." He opened one of his suitcases and handed her a small bag. "One more thing." He took a small pen-like object and ran it over the back of her neck. "This is you now, so if they turn on your tracker, it will find you here."

"Are we all low jacked?" She asked him.

"Yes, but it uses radio waves and is almost undetectable because it is such a low Tec wave. You must know the exact frequency to find it."

Kally kissed her brother Seth on the cheek. "You're the best."

"You only have 24 hours, be careful." Seth smiled at Kally.

"Aren't I always?" She walked to the door of their L.A. Hotel.

"Tell him I said hi."

Kally smiled. "I will."

"I placed a phone in there, tracker free; I will let you know if something comes up."

Kally opened the door and slid out into early morning darkness.

Seth sat down at the table in front of his laptop. He had a lot of data to go through since the last three years had been so successful. Kally having a younger brother had worked out perfect for him to visit and pick up Intel from her.

He looked at the pictures of them on the table. They had taken several since arriving. Proof of their vacation. They both had sandy blonde hair and green eyes. Looked like brother and sister easily, even their skin coloring was the same. He loved the one of them on the beach.

Kally got a room at a motel; it took her almost two hours to get there. She had given herself a shot on the way and was now a golden color. Her hair would be too noticeable changing so she had waited to give herself the shot for her hair till now. It was already changing into a black shiny color; it almost had a blue tint. Her eyes turned instantly to a very dark brown when she injected herself with the shot. She looked in the mirror. She could pass as Indian, either Native or from India. She quickly changed into her dress and heels.

Kally caught a taxi in front of the hotel. "San Diego School of Music," she told the driver. She got out 20 minutes later right where she had gotten out of a Limo over three years ago. People were all climbing the stairs to the auditorium.

The floor was covered with rows and rows of chairs. As she entered, Kally saw Jacob and Michelle, along with Brandon's parents, were on the third row from the front as she entered. They weren't hard to pick out with their tall statures and long hair. Kally made her way down and sat two rows behind them. Michelle stood up and stretched; she was pregnant, looked to be about eight months. Kally could barely hear them talking due to all the noise around her.

Jacob was concerned about Michelle sitting so long. Michelle was telling him she was just fine. Mrs. Clearwater was on Michelle's side and was trying to convince Jacob she would be ok. Kally smiled as she listened to them.

The lights flickered and it got quiet. Dean Hollingsworth walked out on the stage. "We have had an exciting four years. Everything from new scholarships, flu outbreaks, to the fire in Mill Hall, but we have overcome and are now here to honor the graduating Class of 2010." The crowd clapped. "We will have three special performances from our top graduates, Michael Fox, James Masterson, and Brandon Clearwater." The crowed clapped again. "Without further ado, the class of 2010."

Music started as the students marched in from the left to seats on the stage to the right of the Dean. There were only about 100 students, so it didn't take long. They came in and filled the last row first so Brandon was one of the last to come in.

Kally felt a tear run down her cheek as she watched him stand in front of his seat.

"You may be seated," the Dean said, "Michael Fox will be our first to perform tonight. All three performances are original music written by the performer. Michael, would you please come and take the stage?"

A guy Kally recognized from strings class stood and came to the front of the stage. He sat down in a chair behind a cello and began to play. It was beautiful; the orchestra played softly behind him. The crowd came to their feet with applause when the piece ended.

"Thank you, Michael, we are proud to announce Michael has been accepted into the New York's Philharmonic Orchestra." The crowed burst into applause again. "James Masterson is our next performer."

James got up and picked the guitar that sat next to the cello. Kally recognized the piece; it was one that she had helped him with, but he had added several new things to it. Again the orchestra played in the background. The crowd came to their feet again when the piece ended.

"Our last performance is by Brandon Clearwater. Brandon was the Jacobs Music Scholarship winner. We have watched and been amazed at his growth over the last four years. Brandon has been working in a local studio as studio musician for the last year, and has his own full band for his performance. Brandon?"

Brandon got up, so did James, from the side of the stage. Todd came in along with another two guys Kally didn't recognize. Brandon picked up the acoustic guitar and stood in front of the mic; Todd had keyboard, James lead, and the other two guys got bass and drums.

"I started this song the first three months I was here. I kept hearing this tune over and over in my head and after the third year here, it finally found its way onto paper. I hope you enjoy it."

Kally sat in a trance as he sang.

"Stand on the edge with me, hold back your fear and see nothing is real till it's gone."

Every word in the song was for her and him; tears rolled down her face.

"You're all that I need in my life."

The crowd rose to their feet and clapped when it finished; Kally just stood there with tears flowing down her cheeks.

"Wonderful guys, just wonderful!" the Dean said, "I have a feeling we will be hearing more from this band. Now, the time you have all been waiting for. As your names are called, graduates, please come and get your diploma, then walk down and out to the reception area. We ask everyone to remain seated till our last graduate is out the door, then you are dismissed."

Kally sat and listened as each person's name was called, but her mind was still stuck in the song she had just heard. She played it over and over in her head.

The crowd around her moved before she realized the last name had already been called. Kally walked to the reception area and congratulated every student she walked by. She even found James and congratulated him and told him she enjoyed his song. There

233

were so many people that she managed to talk to him and leave him before he could ask who she was there for.

She slowly made her way toward Brandon. "Congratulations, loved your song." Brandon shook her hand and smiled.

"Thanks." Jacob stood beside him.

"Lindsey would have loved it, bro." he put his arm around him.

Kally looked at Brandon; his eyes got glassy for a second. She quickly turned and left before she fell apart. Kally made a stroll around the room then back toward Brandon to listen and see if there was any chance of getting him alone.

"Brandon." Dean Hollingsworth came up to him. "I have something for you. Ms. Jacobs told me to give this to you."

Brandon looked around. "Is she here?"

"No. She gave this to me the year she came and visited you." He held out an envelope.

"Oh." His head dropped. "Thanks." He took the envelope and opened it. He pulled the card out and read it, then opened the smaller envelope and smiled and put it in his jacket pocket.

"So what's in the small one?" Jacob asked.

"I'll tell you later."

Kally smiled. Ten thousand dollars was what she had put in the small envelope, a little something to help him get started. But really that was just the tip of the iceberg; the business she started for them was booming and they were trillion-aires.

"We're heading back to the hotel, Michelle needs to rest. We will be at your place at eight to get you loaded up to leave," Kally heard Jacob tell Brandon.

"Alright, I am going to stick around and say goodbye to a few friends; I'll see you in the morning."

Kally watched the Clearwaters all leave, then she watched for Brandon to say goodbye to everyone.

"So, who are you here for?" Kally turned to find James standing beside her.

"No one really. I have just always wanted to come to school here, so I sneak in at graduation and listen and dream."

James laughed. "Have you applied for a scholarship?"

"Yes, but I never seem to get one."

"You should apply for the one Brandon got. It pays for everything."

"I will next year; it's already passed the deadline for the coming year."

James smiled at her. "A bunch of us are going out to celebrate, you want to go?"

Kally smiled.

"Hey, James." Brandon came up behind him.

"Yeah?" James turned.

"Sorry, man, I just wanted to say bye, I am heading home. I'll call you in a week, and we'll figure out when we're going."

"Sure thing."

Kally smiled, Brandon smiled back at her then turned and left. James turned back to her.

"Well?"

"I really better get home; but thanks for the offer."

"We are going to have a good time," he tried once more.

"My mom is watching my kids and I can't leave her hanging, but thanks for the offer." That did it, mention kids and James made a fast retreat.

Kally now knew Brandon was going home so she headed out right before he did.

Once at Brandon's apartment, she let herself in. Brandon came in and walked straight to the bathroom; he didn't even turn on a light. He came out 20 minutes later and turned on the bedroom lamp. He had on his boxers and his necklace. Kally stood in a shadow, she watched as he walked over and stood looking out the window. She quietly walked over behind him.

"Don't turn around," she said.

Brandon froze. "Lindsey?" He asked.

"Yes." She held his arm when he tried to turn.

"Not yet, I need to give you a little warning. I don't look like I did."

"That's ok," he said, "I don't care as long as you're here."

"Would you be surprised if I told you I talked to you at graduation earlier?"

"You were there?"

"Yes."

"And I talked to you? Wow, you must look totally different, if I didn't recognize you."

"I do." She let go of his arm and he turned to look at her.

He smiled. "I remember you! You liked my song; well, your song." Kally slid her arms around Brandon. "What is your name?"

"Kally."

He hugged her. "I love you, no matter what your name is or was." He pulled away from her and looked at her, "You make a great looking Indian."

Kally laughed. "You think so?"

"How long are you staying?"

"I have to leave before two."

He was still staring at her. "Are you that color everywhere?" He asked.

Kally laughed. "Yes," she replied.

"You're so beautiful, not that you weren't already, but there is just something about you looking all Indian that I find quite hot."

Lindsey laughed and rubbed her finger over his necklace.

"Where's yours?" He asked.

"I am on assignment, but snuck out for a few hours so it's put up in a safe place till I retrieve it."

He pulled up and looked at her. "That means you're close."

"Just for a few days; I'm on vacation on my job so I am visiting LA for a few days; my brother Seth and me."

He looked at her. "Brother?"

"Oh, by the way, he says to tell you hi," she smiled at him. "It's just Keeps; I left him working on Intel."

He laughed. "Keeps is playing your brother?"

"Yes, I finally managed to get him out of that white, forsaken room he has been stuck in for years."

Brandon pulled her into his arms and kissed her. "I have missed you so much the last three years."

"I love you, Brandon, and I have missed you, too."

"Can I ask what you're doing?"

"It's better if you don't know."

"That's fine, I understand." They walked over and sat down on the edge of the bed.

"You said something to James about calling him to go somewhere, where are you going?"

"That's right, you were talking to James when I left." He laughed. "Was he putting the moves on you?"

Kally smiled., "He was trying. I mentioned something about having a couple of kids and he almost ran away." They both laughed.

"We are supposed to record a couple of songs next week. The band I have been helping in the studio; they got it set up for me."

"Demos, cool."

"Oh, yeah, thanks for the money."

Kally smiled. "I figured it might help you get started, but if it runs out . . ."

Kally got up. "Come here." She walked over to his laptop and opened it. "I have something for you, well, for us, but if you need it, use it . . ."

She clicked on the web, then to the Grand Cayman Island Bank. She went into accounts and typed in an account number and password. 'Welcome, Brandon Clearwater' popped up on the screen along with the total of the account which was over one million dollars. Kally turned to look at Brandon, his mouth was hanging open.

"Is that right?" He finally got out.

Kally laughed. "That is only one of the four accounts we have, so you can use all of this one if you want." She clicked over on to the banking page and clicked that she would like a debit card issued and entered his parents address for it to be sent to.

"One of four," he said.

"This is the one with the least in it." She smiled.

"Can I ask how we are getting this money?"

"We own a business, and it's very successful."

"It must be. Is it legal?"

She laughed. "Yes, it is all perfectly legal and all in your name so you are the sole heir to it all."

Brandon looked at her.

"I have been working on it for years and I did it under your name so if anything happens to me, it's all yours. If something ever does happen and you receive my necklace and a jump drive, it's encrypted and needs a password." She stood up and traced his tattoo. "This is the password. All of it, no spaces."

He pulled her into his arms. "What did I ever do to deserve you?"

Kally smiled. "I feel the same way; I have no clue why you picked me, I must be the luckiest person in the world."

Brandon laughed, Kally sat back down and logged out of the bank. She opened a word document and typed in a number. "This is the account number; I will save it in your documents under our names, which is the password. Never use this password or the other one I gave you for anything else, ok?"

"Ok. What does my business do?"

Kally smiled. "I'm not telling, yet. It takes care of itself, so you don't have to worry about it for now."

"Ok." He took her hand and pulled her up into his arms. "I love you . . ." He kissed her.

Lindsey's heart was racing. She wanted nothing more than to stay with him here forever. Lindsey pulled him back to the bed.

"What are you doing?" He asked.

"Since we can do nothing else, I say we do some serious making out."

Brandon threw back his head and laughed, then pushed her to the bed and began kissing her.

At one thirty they stood in front of his door.

"I love you." She wrapped her arms around him.

"I love you, too." He opened the door. "Any clue when you might be back?"

"No," she answered.

"I'll just show up one day when you least expect it."

"I'll be waiting," he said. She gave him a quick kiss, then left. Brandon watched her walk up the street from his window.

Brandon walked over to the computer and clicked on the web then back to the bank, he typed in the number and password. The page popped open, he just stared; he had over a million dollars. He also had ten thousand in cash in his jacket pocket. He was in shock. What a day he had had. He graduated from music school, Lindsey had come to see him, and now he was a millionaire. He logged back out and went and lay down. The only thing that could have made the day more perfect was if Lindsey would have been able to stay. At least, she had been able to come see him, and that would have to do for now. He laughed at himself for still calling her Lindsey. She was now Kally.

Kally had gone back to the room at the motel, gave herself a couple of shots then headed back to Keeps in LA. She was back in the room by 4:30. Seth was asleep on one of the beds, she crashed on the other. Clicking keys woke her. She looked over at the clock; it was 12 noon.

"How was your night?"

Kally sat up. "Nice."

"Good," he said

"And yours?"

"I spent all mine working on Intel. I think you're going to like what I found."

Kally got up and walked over to Seth at the computer. "Show me."

Seth started opening pages.

"Is that right?" She reached over Seth and hit a few keys, "If we can bring him down, then they all will fall."

Seth smiled up at her. "I know. You were right about there being a bigger fish behind it."

"Have you sent this in?"

"Not yet, I thought you should be here when I did."

Kally gave Seth a quick kiss.

"What was that for?" Seth asked.

"For being the best." She smiled. "Now send it in." Kally flipped open her laptop on the other side of the table and began working on a plan.

The last three years had gone well. She had entered the life of John Madison when the children's tutor had a heart attack and ended up in the hospital. She simply answered an ad in the paper and had been selected to take the tutor's place. Soon, she was intercepting computer messages and breaking encrypted codes from John to potential buyers and sellers. She knew John was not the leader, but the agency didn't agree with her. She had spent the last year and a half looking for the "bigger fish" and now she had her proof. She was going to take the whole thing down; not just John Madison, but Mr. Ziafat, too.

"They said take it down, all the way," Seth told her.

"I was going to. Hey, check something for me. The four kids that seem to have a parent in common, was it Arabic?"

Seth typed fast. "It was, and it's paternal."

Kally smiled. "All the girls John has taken to Ziafat have been older; child-bearing age."

"You think he is selling his own kids?"

"I do. I think he is breeding those girls, and having John selling them for him."

Seth shook his head. "Sick."

"Yep, he is, and he is going down."

Kally looked at Seth. "I only see one way to do this."

"I thought we had gotten it where you wouldn't have to do that."

"Me, too, but it's the only way I can see getting to him."

"So, what do you have in mind?"

Kally smiled. "I need to have a little heart-to-heart with Maria, female issues." She smiled, "that way John is sure to know."

CHAPTER 8

Scars that can't been seen

ONE YEAR LATER . . .

"Nashville is always a good place to visit," Keeps told her. "There is a music festival that goes on there in the summer, usually a lot of new bands."

She sat up in her chair and smiled. "Sounds good, but I want a few things this time."

"Name it," Keeps said.

"I want a car, and not just any car. I want an old muscle car."

"Give me specifics," Keeps told her.

"I want a 1968 Chevy Camaro, with the tail and I want it black, fully loaded."

Keeps smiled. "Anything else?"

"I want tattoos."

"You going grunge?" He asked.

"Yeah, I think it's time to do something different."

"What name?" He asked.

"I don't know. What do you think?" She asked him.

"I don't know; I'm not good at grunge."

"I've got it, Violet Patterson. I'll go by Vi."

"Not bad," he said, "background?"

"Not a good one, this time. I am going to be rough, so I want a rough background."

"All right, I will have it by morning. Anything else you want or need?" He asked.

"I'll think about it, and let you know," she got up and started to leave.

"You may want this," he handed her an iPod. "I loaded it."

"Thanks." She took it and left the room.

Vi went up the hall and to her room for the night. She showered and lay down on the bed, put in her earbuds and closed her eyes. The last few months flashed through her head.

John taking the whole family to visit his friend, Ziafat. Then once Ziafat saw her, she was taken from the family and stripped bare and beaten severely for several weeks. To learn her place, she was told. She was given three weeks to heal in a back room, and then she was given to Ziafat.

She squeezed her eyes shut harder and curled up in a ball and tried to forget. She turned the music louder to drown out the memories. Those poor girls that had endured him for years; she was glad they were free. Each of them had a child every year and were not in good health. One girl she met was only 30 and had been there since she was 20. She had had ten kids and looked like she was 50; it had taken such a toll on her. It was worth any amount of pain she endured and almost being raped to see those girls free. The best part was seeing Ziafat's eyes when she castrated him and left him to die. Her only regret was not getting to kill the man that had beaten her daily for weeks.

Vi got out of the bed; she didn't want to be alone. She walked out of her room and back down to see Keeps. His office was dark, but she knew his room was at the back, so she walked through and tapped on the door.

Keeps opened the door. "What?"

She smiled, "I can't sleep."

He backed up and let her in. Keeps' room was different. It looked more normal; there were posters hanging up and stuff lying everywhere. Keeps was in a pair of shorts and no shirt. He was quite muscular for being so small. He walked back to his bed and lay down. His eyes closed the second his head hit the pillow.

She looked around the room. He had several computers lying in pieces and tracking devices and all kinds of wires and gadgets everywhere. A small picture on the wall by a desk in the corner caught her attention. It was the two of them as Kally and Seth. She remembered taking some pictures while they were in LA to show Hans and Marta when they got back. This one was of them on the beach; her in a bikini and him in a pair of trunks. He had his arm around her; a guy on the beach took it for them. She walked over and looked at Keeps. He was sound asleep. She lay down beside him on the bed and closed her eyes.

An alarm going off woke her. She opened her eyes and looked over to find Keeps staring at her.

"How did you get in here?" He asked her.

"You let me in."

"Are you sure?"

She laughed. "I think you were still asleep because you let me in and walked straight back to the bed."

"Why are you in here?"

"I couldn't sleep."

"Anything wrong?" He asked.

"I can't get that man out of my head. I close my eyes and he is there hitting me." She sat up. "Would you wipe me? Just him. The rest is fine, but I don't think I will get to sleep any if I can't get him out of my head."

Keeps got up out of the bed and pulled a pair of pants on. "What did he do to you?"

"Please, Keeps, this is one thing I want to forget."

"Ok, I'll do it tonight; be here at eleven. For now you need to get back to your room. I will hold up your paperwork and stuff for the day so you'll leave tomorrow."

Vi got up and put her arms around Keeps. "You're the best." She ran her finger down his chest. "So did you enjoy sleeping with me?" She laughed, then turned and walked to the door.

Keeps followed her and when she turned to say bye, he put a hand on either side of her and boxed her in. "Getting you in my bed has always been a dream. Maybe I should take advantage of this."

Vi laughed and slid her arms around his waist and pushed him back towards the bed. "So you've been dreaming about me have you?" She pushed him to the bed and crawled up over top of him. She leaned down as if she was going to kiss him, but touched him gently on the shoulder and knocked him out. She smiled and left.

Vi went back to her room and got dressed and then walked back towards his office. She had been careful to not use much pressure so he wouldn't be out long.

He was sitting at his desk when she walked in. "You have any tattoo designs picked out?" He never looked up at her.

"You mad at me?" she asked.

"No." He looked up at her.

"I haven't looked at any, yet."

"Well, come here and pick some out." He got up from the computer and let her sit down. He had pages of designs open.

"So, what do you like?" She asked.

Keeps flipped through a few pages. "I like the armbands, some of the tribal stuff would be cool, too." He pointed out a few designs.

Vi sat down and looked through the pages. "These will do." She picked out seven, three of which were the ones he had pointed out.

"Fine, I will send them down to Deck."

"I want to get my hair cut, too," she told him.

"Alright, go ahead, drop by and see Deck when you're done."

Vi had her hair cut short, styled and tipped, then went to see Deck.

"Where do you want them?" He asked when she walked in.

"I want that one across my lower back." She pointed at the picture. "And that one I want on my wrist. Those on my arm and shoulder and that one I want right here." She pointed just above her belly button. Vi thought of one more she wanted. "I'll be right back." She ran back up to Keeps' office.

"Where is my guitar?" she asked.

"Still down in lock-up."

"Can you get it and make a copy of the design on the front? I want a tattoo of the design."

He smiled. "I'll bring it down there in a few, go let him get started."

"Thanks." She turned and went back down to Deck.

"Sorry, I have one more. Keeps will bring it down."

"Alright, let's get started." Vi took her shirt off and lay down on the table. The tattoo that went on her back was a butterfly with a series of lines coming off of its wings. Deck went right to work and had the majority of it done in twenty minutes, when Keeps dropped by with the design off of her guitar.

"Nice work," he told Deck, then left.

The tattoos he gave her were just like real ones. He even used a needle to put the ink in her skin.

It took Deck about three hours to do all the ink work.

"If you need them off." He handed her a small bottle and syringe.

Deck looked over his work. "You know if you want to play that kind of part you need accessories." He pointed to a case of shiny metal rings.

"What do you have in mind?" she smiled.

Lindsey stood and looked in the mirror; she now had a lip ring, a stud in her nose, a belly ring and six earrings. All that she needed now was the black eyeliner and lipstick.

"Nice," Keeps told her as he looked over the work, when she returned to his office.

He opened his desk and pulled out her necklace. He had taken it off the silver choker and put it on a black leather strap. "This will go right with it."

She fastened it on her neck. He handed her jump drive to her and she slid it in her pocket.

"I should have everything you need in the morning," he told her. "The car you will have to wait a few weeks for."

She smiled. "Alright."

"You can take your guitar and computer now if you want."

"Thanks, at least I will have something to do now for the rest of the day."

Vi left Keeps' office and went back to her room. She opened her guitar case and smiled at the little heart. She was sort of excited about going to Nashville. Music was going to be back in her life.

She spent all afternoon playing her guitar and writing the chords down she kept hearing in her head. There was a song in there trying to find its way out. She thought of Ms. Yuri as she wrote the notes down.

Vi never noticed the time till there was a knock on her door. She glanced at the clock on the wall as she walked to the door. It read seven p.m.

Handler was standing there with a tray of food when she opened the door.

"Hungry?" He asked.

"Thanks." She took the tray from him.

"Keeper says you're pretty good at that." He pointed to her guitar.

"Not bad. Would you like to hear?" She stepped back from the door so he could enter.

Handler entered the room and shut the door behind him. Vi sat the tray on the desk then picked up the guitar.

Handler just stood tall and silent near the door as she played.

Vi was sort of taken aback that he had talked normal talk to her, he was usually all business.

"Did you not learn music?" Vi asked. Keeps had said he was one of the ten.

"They tried, but I was not good at it."

"So what is your specialty?" She asked.

"Surveillance," he said. "I need to go." He turned to the door then paused. "Thank you for playing for me. Keeper is right, you're very good."

"You're welcome," she told him as he opened the door, "and thank you for supper."

Vi ate as she worked on her music. She really needed to keep her mind occupied until Keeps could wipe her memory. She had been taught how to deal with isolation and had no problem with it, but what she had endured at the hands of Ziafat's flunky wasn't even close to humane and it had left a scar in her mind that she needed to be rid of.

Eleven o'clock and Vi stood at Keeps' door. It was not shut all the way and she didn't even knock. She just went in and shut it behind her. Keeps was sitting at a computer at the desk in his room.

"Do you ever stop working on them?" She asked.

"Not really." He closed the top on the laptop and got up to face her. "Why do you want your mind wiped?" he asked.

"I just want you to take out the months after I was taken until I was given to Ziafat."

"That didn't answer my question. What did they do to you?"

"When you go through my mind you will have your answer," she told him.

"Alright." He moved the chair from the desk in front of him. "Sit down."

Keeps rubbed her shoulders. "You're tight." He worked to hit all the right spots on her neck and back. "Tell me what happened after you were taken from John."

Keeps listened as Vi told her story. "I woke in a dark room; there was no light and no sound. I had no clothes." Hours went by as Vi told him of the abuse she had endured from the man with the scar she called 'him'. He had never spoken a word to her, but beat her to the very point of death and had all but had sex with her. He used her in ways that were sickening to Keeps' stomach. Tears came to his eyes as she described being burned with knives for no reason, other than for just looking at the man. This man had all but destroyed her. Hearing her story had shed light on the women that they had taken from the compound. Each of them were healthy, but disfigured. Now he knew why. Ziafat had them each broken to the point of death, then brought back for only one purpose: to bear children for his trade. No wonder it had taken Vi to get them out; they were absolutely terrified of looking at anyone.

Keeps looked at Vi; there wasn't a mark on her physically. When they had pulled her out she was in bad shape, but not anything like the other women. Her genetic alterations had kept her from turning out like them. And once she was back, and they gave her the right medication, she healed perfectly, as if nothing had ever happened. But it had. It had affected her enough that she wanted it out of her head, out of her memory. He didn't blame her; she had lived through hell.

Keeps gave her the alteration of being held in a room and beaten, but made it very mild in comparison to the truth; after she repeated the story back, he gave her a recovery phrase and then woke her with another.

"You are so tense. Don't you ever relax?"

Vi blinked as Keeps rubbed her shoulders. She got up out of the chair and looked at him.

Keeps saw her slight confusion. "I told you when you got here I would have your stuff ready in the morning. Why are you so anxious to get to Nashville?"

She played off her confusion well. "I am ready to get back to music."

"So, is that the only reason you came to my room?" Keeps was trying to get her mind back to the last time she was here. Playful and light, he stepped close to her.

Vi stepped back; Keeps almost hesitated before he stepped close to her again. What he knew now had affected him, too. "You wanted to share my bed last time." He slid his arm around her and pulled her to him.

"I did, didn't I?" She said as she took his shirt off of him. "You are not in the right attire for what I had in mind."

Keeps mind and heart went to war. What he knew and what he wanted. "Alright." Keeps stepped back from her. "Stop playing with me, I know you just don't want to sleep alone."

"You started it." She smiled, and threw his shirt at him.

"Yeah I guess I did, but you are so . . . never mind."

"So what?" She backed him to the wall. "I'm so what?"

He grabbed her arms and flipped her to the wall and put his lips to hers, then kissed down her neck.

"Just say it Keeps. You want me, don't you?"

"You have no idea how hard it is for me to be around you." He was being honest. "Do you?"

Vi knew she affected Keeps and she loved playing with him, but she didn't have any clue just how much it really affected him until that very moment. He was standing in front of her with want in his eyes.

He stepped back. "I'm sorry." He turned and went through a door at the back.

Vi heard the shower turn on. She looked around his room then left.

Chapter 9

Nashville

V I WALKED TO Keeps' office slowly the next morning. She stopped when she got to his door. He was sitting where he always was behind—his computer.

"Are you coming in or are you just going to stare at me?" He asked her.

The Handler walked into the office behind her. He gave her the once over. "Interesting. You ready?"

Keeps handed her an envelope.

"Yep, I just need to go get my laptop. Thanks, Keeps, you're still the best."

He looked up at her and smile. "Yeah, yeah I know. Now get out of here."

Once they picked up stuff at her room, she followed him to a chopper.

"I am going to drop you at the airport. Your flight will leave in about 30 minutes," he told her as they took off.

Vi waited till she was on the plane to look at the contents of her envelope. She was in first class and all alone. Her full name was Violet Elizabeth Patterson. Her mom had overdosed four years ago, she never knew her dad. She had been working as a bartender in Vegas the last five years and had decided to make a change, so she had moved to Nashville. The car would be a present from a Casino owner that liked her.

Keeps had written down two bar names with a note for her to get a job at one of them. He had an apartment waiting for her; not in the best part of town, but not in the worst either. Her bank account had ten thousand in it. She laughed, not a rich kid this time. Not like she couldn't get anything she wanted, anyway.

The plane landed and she caught a cab to the address Keeps had written down for her apartment. She stopped by the office and got her keys.

She was on the 5th floor, E12; it was a corner room. The place was empty. Her new phone vibrated in her pocket.

"Your furniture will be delivered in about three hours. I hope you like what I picked out."

Vi smiled. "I'll love it," she texted back.

"There is a Hot Topic over about three blocks. May be a good place to pick up some clothes to go with your new look. There is a place actually called Grunge over on Fifth."

"Thanks."

Vi put her guitar and laptop in the bottom of the closet in the bedroom then headed for Hot Topic. Once there she found some great boots and a jacket. She also picked up black lipstick, eyeliner, black nail polish, and some earrings. She stopped by a Wal-Mart store and picked up some black tank tops, black bras, and some black undies. She added a few red items, but mainly stayed with black.

She got back to the apartment just as the furniture arrived. A large black couch and red arm chair. The bed had a black headboard. The table was glass with black and red chairs. The lamps were polished silver with satin red shades. Perfect. She signed the delivery paper as they left. Now all she needed were a few pots and pans, a set of sheets and curtains for the window.

She headed back down to the local Wal-Mart and got a set of black sheets, two red pillow cases, and a set of black curtains. She also picked a red pan and skillet along with a set of black dishes and a red tablecloth. By nightfall she had the place looking good. Tomorrow would be the day to find a job; she would check the two places Keeps wrote down first thing. She climbed in bed, closed her eyes, and slid off to sleep.

The sun coming in the window woke her up. She stretched and climbed out of the bed. She got dressed in her jeans with her new black lace up boots. A red bra and black tank top, that way the straps showed up nicely.

She painted her nails, added the black eyeliner and lipstick and then the large silver hoops in the bottom holes. She looked in the mirror and smiled.

Most bars wouldn't open till noon so she had time to go get some groceries and a few more things she needed that she hadn't picked up yesterday.

Out on the street she hailed a cab and headed to the local market. She took the groceries home, then headed for the local florist to pick up some silk roses. Next she went to a music store to get a few posters to hang up. She ate lunch and then headed for the first name on the list, The Wild Mustang.

Vi walked in the front door and up to the bar.

"What can I get you?" The bartender asked. He was big, looked like he spent a lot of time in the gym.

"Who do I talk to about a job?"

"That would be Mitchell, go down that hall and to the office." He pointed toward the hall over at the other end of the bar.

"Thanks," she told him. The door marked 'Office' was at the very end of the hall; she knocked on the door.

"It's open," a voice came from the other side. Vi opened the door and walked in. The office was big and decorated nicely.

"What can I do for you?" A tall young man said from behind a large desk.

"Looking for a job," she told him as she walked to the desk.

"I really don't need any waitresses right now."

"I don't waitress, I tend bar."

He smiled at her. "I could always use a bartender; that is, if they're good."

Vi smiled. "I am."

"Prove it. Come on." He got up and led her out front.

Vi walked behind the bar.

"Well, give me a top hat shooter."

She laughed. "Come on, make it harder than that."

She slid the glass down the bar with the drink in it.

"Alright, how about a Russian Roulette?"

"Better," she said as she mixed the drink.

He laughed as she added some vodka. "It doesn't have Vodka in it."

She smiled. "You don't know what a real Roulette is then. Most all Russian drinks have vodka in them." She sat down the drink on the bar in front of him.

He took a drink. "Nice. I'll try you a week, then we will go from there."

The other bartender looked at Mitchell. "You think she can handle it?"

"I'll keep her paired up for now, then we'll see."

Vi smiled, but didn't say a word.

"Come back tonight at six and I will have you a schedule made for you." He smiled, "You got a name?"

"Vi Patterson." She stuck out her hand.

"Nice to meet you Vi. I'm Mitchell and this Tommy." She shook both their hands.

"You got any problems with people I should know about?" Mitchell asked.

"No, not really."

"Good. Come back down to my office, and I'll get you some papers to fill out and bring back tonight." Vi followed Mitchell back down the hall. "You will be on a trial period this week. If it works out then we will talk full time job."

"Sounds good." She shook his hand and left the office. She sat down at the bar.

"You got a pen?" She asked Tommy.

"Sure." He reached behind the bar and got one and handed it to her.

"Where are you from Vi?" He asked.

"Vegas."

"So, what are you doing here?"

"Needed a change of scenery. I really hate the desert," she told him.

He laughed. "Nice tats."

She looked up at him and smiled. "Thanks."

"Let me give you a little advice. Mitchell is quite friendly with all the female help, so if you want the job, just be friendly back."

Vi looked up, and then put her pen down. "I probably won't make it the week, then."

Tommy looked at her. "How bad do you need the job?"

"Not that bad." She picked the pen back up and started writing again. "I'll just see how it goes for now." Tommy smiled at her. She finished the papers and handed back his pen. "Can I leave them here? I don't want to take a chance on losing them."

"Sure, I'll put them in this drawer."

She looked over the bar to see where he was talking about. "Thanks, I'll see you later, man."

Vi turned and made a quick survey of the bar before she left. There was the bar area, then a lower level with a stage. Altogether it was a pretty big place. She left and went back to her apartment.

Back at her building, she passed a young girl with a small child in the hall. She heard a lady yell when the girl opened the door.

"What are you doing here? I don't want you this week; that's why I sent you to your dad's."

Vi felt sorry for the girl.

"Mom, dad is sick, and we can't stay there." The door shut. She could hear muffled yells from behind the door. Vi put her key in the door; a loud crash turned her attention back to the door. The girl and kid came back out in the hall. The girl had blood running down her arm; Vi could see a piece of glass sticking out of a cut on her arm. Vi took a deep breath and turned to the girl.

"Hey." The girl looked up at her. "Let's get that cleaned up." The girl followed Vi into her apartment. "I'm Vi." She smiled at her.

"I'm Heather and this is my brother, Ben." She took a deep breath, "My mom's drunk, but she's fine when she sober."

"Is she drunk a lot?" Vi pulled the glass from the girls arm and cleaned all the blood off.

"No, just once a month, when we are at dad's; but he's sick with the flu and we couldn't stay. She will be fine by Sunday."

"You have anywhere else to stay?"

"Yeah, my aunt. She's really nice and won't care if we stay with her."

"Here, you can use my phone."

Heather took the phone and called her aunt.

"She will be here in 20 minutes."

"You have a nice place," Heather told her; the little boy held her hand and hadn't said a word.

"You're awfully quiet," Vi leaned over and patted Ben on the head.

"He is shy around strangers."

Vi smiled at Heather. "That's a good thing."

Heather smiled. "Yeah, I guess so."

"You guys have a seat while you wait for your aunt."

Heather walked over to the couch and sat down; her brother climbed up in her lap.

Vi walked into her room and brought back her guitar. "Do you guys mind if I play for a bit?"

Heather smiled. "It's your apartment."

Vi pulled one of the table chairs over by the couch and sat down to play. She hadn't played much in the last four years; she tuned and strummed a tune.

"I'm a little rusty; it's been a while since I played."

Vi played a little; as she did, Ben got down and walked over to her and watched. "You want to help me?" She asked him, he lit up. Vi moved the guitar and let him stand between her and the guitar. She then gave him the pick and showed him how to strum.

"Don't do it hard, do it real gently, like this." She took his hand and moved it back and forth over the strings. She changed chords as he strummed. "You're very good at that," she told him. A knock at her door brought her out of the chair.

"I'm looking for my niece and nephew," the lady said.

"Come on in."

Ben was standing beside the guitar and Heather had already stood up.

"Thanks for looking after them."

"No problem." Vi noticed the lady seemed to be a little nervous.

"Come on you two, let's get home and leave this nice lady alone."

Ben walked up to her and pulled on her pants leg. "Can we play again?"

Vi leaned over. "Anytime, sweetie." He smiled.

"Thanks, again," the lady said as she went out the door.

Vi closed the door and went to the bathroom. She glanced in the mirror as she walked by it, she had to laugh. No wonder the lady looked nervous; she looked quite evil.

Vi had several hours before six, so she decided to go down to the store on Fifth and see what they had. She returned at five with lots of new clothes. She found a short skirt and striped tights. The skirt was black; the tights were black and white. She got a white blouse to go with them; it was cute. She also got a pair of those big baggie jeans that had chains all over them and a pair of dark green cargos. She changed into the cargos for work, but left the same top on. She spiked her hair a little and refreshed her eyeliner and lipstick, then headed back to the bar.

Tommy was still behind the bar and handed her papers to her when she walked by. The bar was pretty full now. She walked down to the office and knocked.

"Come in," Mitchell yelled over the roar of the music. Vi opened the door and went in. He got up and walked around the desk and sat on the front.

"You will be working with Tommy for the next five days from 6 p.m. to 3 a.m."

She handed him her papers.

"I better get out there and help him, then." As she turned to go, he walked up behind her. She turned quickly, his eyes ran up her.

She took a step toward him. "Are we going to have a problem?" The question took him by surprise.

"What?"

"You asked earlier if I had a problem with people. The only problem I would have would be with you. That is, if you couldn't keep your hands to yourself." He smiled, but didn't say a word. "Let me just say one thing. I am a good worker and take my job seriously, but if you step out of line on me, you will regret it."

"I'm trying to give you a job and you threaten me."

She smiled. "No, just warning you."

She turned and went out of the office. She joined Tommy behind the bar and started serving drinks to the nearest person. The bar stayed busy till closing time at 3 a.m. They cleaned up the bar when Mitchell locked the doors.

She had met the four waitresses in the first hour. Holly was the blonde, Jasmine the one with the attitude and short black hair, Candy was the big-chested bleached blonde, and Mia was a fiery redhead. They all counted up and turned in their money. The girls really hadn't said much to her besides getting drinks from her.

"So what did you think?" Tommy asked her

Vi smiled at him. "Vegas was busier."

He laughed. "What did you bring in, Candy?" Tommy asked.

"$500 in tips." She raised the money overhead in victory.

Mia laughed. "I need to get a boob job so I can bring in that kind of money; I only got $300."

Both Jasmine and Holly had cleared just over $250 each.

Vi didn't say a word as she slid her tips in her pocket.

Tommy saw her. "What did you get?" When he said it, all the girls looked up at her. She pulled the money back out of her pocket and handed it to Tommy; he counted it.

"You got $375 in tips."

She looked at Tommy.

"Crap," Tommy said, "how did you manage that?"

"Pretty sad, isn't it? I have never made less than a thousand."

"In tips?" Tommy looked at her, "I need to go to Vegas and work. If I get $250, I'm doing good."

Vi smiled. "So $375 isn't bad for here?"

"No, it's good, girl."

"Well, that makes me feel better. I thought I must really have sucked tonight."

Jasmine looked at Vi. "How in the world did you do better than me?"

Vi smiled. "No clue."

She and Tommy finished cleaning up and left.

By the time she got home, showered and climbed into bed, it was going on four. By one in the afternoon she was awake and hungry. She ate and cleaned up, then sat down at her laptop and checked on their business. She answered a few emails from Joe, then logged back off. She put her jump drive in and looked at the pictures she had of Brandon and her; man, she missed him. Keeps had sent her here for a reason, so she was hoping Brandon was the reason. She got dressed and ready for work. Tonight she was wearing the little skirt and white shirt.

She got to work ten minutes early. It was Saturday night; live band night. The band was already on stage warming up when she got there.

Tommy was sitting on a bar stool. "Cute, Vi."

She smiled as she walked past him. Mitchell saw her come in and came over from in front of the band. She walked behind the bar and put her purse under the curtain.

Mitchell walked up behind her. "Had a lot of compliments on you last night." She turned to face him. He reached out to touch her arm, but she pulled it away. "You know, I can make working here really nice for you." He reached for her arm again.

She stepped back again. "I'm only going to say this once more: you better keep your hands to yourself."

"You know, you don't have to work here."

"No, I don't." She bent back over and pulled her purse back out.

"I was just teasing you. No need to get defensive." He backed away from her.

She put her purse back and stood up. Mitchell walked off. Tommy smiled at her.

The band that was playing had quit and was walking up to the bar. "What do you guys need to drink?" She asked them.

The singer smiled. "Five beers."

Vi pulled five beers up and popped the tops. "Here you go."

"You're new." One of the guys said as he sat down.

"Second night." She told him.

"Mitchell already making his move?"

Tommy laughed. "She has him shut down."

"I'm Todd," the singer said.

"Vi."

"You look like you belong to some kind of band."

Vi laughed. "I could out-sing you any day."

The guy smiled. "You want to bet on that?"

Vi smiled. "You serious?"

"Sure," he said.

"How about it?" Tommy said, "Three songs a piece, and let the crowd decide who wins."

Vi laughed. "You guys know any Flyleaf or Fireflight?"

"Sure," said the drummer. It was now five minutes till opening time.

"Let's give it a whirl," Vi said as she came out from behind the bar.

"Alright," Todd said as the band followed her to the stage.

"'Unbreakable', by Fireflight." Vi looked at Todd's guitar. "May I?"

"Knock yourself out."

Vi counted it off: 1, 2, 3, 4.

Tommy and Todd both were shocked, but it was nothing compared to Mitchell's reaction when he walked out and heard Vi singing and playing.

"Holy crap!" He walked up beside Todd. "She can sing."

"And can play," Todd added.

Tommy smiled. "So are you up for the challenge?"

Todd smiled. "Oh, yeah."

"What are you talking about?" Mitchell asked.

"Both of them are going to do three songs, then we are going to see who the audience likes best," Tommy told Mitchell.

"Ok."

The song ended and Vi walked off the stage. "We on?" She asked.

"Oh, yeah," Todd said.

"You go first, so I can help Tommy at the bar."

"Alright," said Todd, "but this is war."

Vi smiled. "Wouldn't have it any other way."

The guys in the band all laughed.

"You guys are going to be fair, aren't you?" Vi asked them.

"Todd sinks or swims on his own tonight. We are just the band in the background," the drummer said.

"It's time to open the bar," Mitchell said as he got up and walked towards the door.

Todd smiled at Vi. "Where did you learn to play like that?"

Vi smiled. "I lived above a bar most my life; bands were always going through."

The bar started filling up with people.

Mitchell got on the stage, "Tonight, of course, is band night and Fire Water is here." Cheers went up all over the place. "But tonight, we have a special treat for you. Todd, the lead singer, is going to be battling another singer tonight and you guys get to pick the winner. Todd is taking the stage first for the first three songs, then you will get to meet our second singer."

Some boos went up until Todd took the mic from Mitchell.

"No boos, it's all for fun. Now let's get rocking."

Vi had her end of the bar waited on and was filling drinks for the waitresses. Tommy watched her as she talked and laughed with the customers. She was good at her job. Vi only stopped and listened a moment when one of the guys at the bar made a comment about who could be stupid enough to take on Todd in a singing contest. Vi laughed, but never said a word. Vi noticed the bar was full of women tonight. Todd was good looking, so she was sure that's why most of them were there. Todd had made it through two songs and was starting a third when a man came to the end of the bar.

"You Vi?"

She stopped and looked at him. "Yeah?"

"I'm Hank Michaels. I own the bar." Vi shook his outstretched hand. "Mitchell called me; says you're full of surprises."

Vi laughed. "Only if you don't know me."

Hank smiled. "I'll talk to you later."

Vi smiled and went back to serving drinks. Todd's song finished.

"All right, now that you have heard me, it's time for the competition. Come on Vi, your turn." Vi went around the bar and made her way up on stage. "Come on guys, let's hear it for the new bartender here." Todd handed her his guitar and left the stage.

Vi turned to the band. "'Decode' by Paramore, first."

The song started; she belted out the first few words and cheers went up all over the bar. Her second song was 'Fully Alive' by Flyleaf. The crowd cheered louder and by the time she sang 'Unbreakable', the bar was a roar.

Todd and Mitchell walked back up on stage. "Let's hear it for Vi!" The place went crazy. "All right, now it's time to see who the winner is going to be: Todd?" The bar roared. "Or Vi?" The crowd roared again. "Todd?" The crowd roared. "Vi?"

Todd took the mic. "I think Vi has it." The bar went crazy. Todd handed the mic back and bowed before Vi.

"There you have it," Mitchell announced.

Vi took off Todd's guitar and handed it back to him as Mitchell put the mic back in the stand. Vi headed back to the bar; it took her a few minutes to get there, everyone was congratulating her.

"Let's hear it for Vi one more time," Todd said before he and the band went back to playing.

She had lots of offers of drinks, and lots of guys wanting to take her out after work. She thanked them, but always said no. The night stayed busy till about one when the band stopped playing and the dance music started.

Vi grabbed a bottle of water and sat down for a few minutes break.

Todd came up and sat beside her. "Well, we never did say what the loser had to do for the winner."

Vi smiled. "That's ok, I really wasn't doing it to win. I just love playing every once in a while so I don't forget how."

Todd laughed. "We usually play here twice a month. How about you taking a song or two every time we come?"

Vi smiled at him. "I would love that."

"Good," Todd said, "did you say this was your second night working here?"

"Yeah."

"So, how long have you lived here?"

"Three days."

Todd looked at her.

"Where did you live before?"

"Vegas."

"Why would you move here?"

"I hated the heat; looking forward to maybe some snow around Christmas."

"Oh, don't wish for too much."

"You don't like snow?"

"No, I love snow; I just hate the people trying to drive on it. They have no clue how."

"And you do?" She asked.

"Yep, been driving on it since I was ten, working on my granddad's farm."

"So you're from around here?"

"Oh, yeah, I grew up in Kentucky, so I'm not far from home, a couple of hours."

Vi got up. "I have to get back to work."

"Ok," he said.

Most of the crowd had left by 2:30, and she and Tommy were mainly just standing there. Vi started dancing behind the bar, Tommy joined her. Mitchell and Hank came up the hall and stopped and watched them. Vi looked up and laughed when she saw they had been caught. Hank smiled and started to leave; Vi caught him before he got to the door.

"Mr. Michaels?"

He turned. "Call me Hank, sweetie."

"Can I ask you something?"

"Sure."

"Do you think I am going to get the job?"

He looked at her surprised. "You already have the job."

"Oh. Mitchell told me I was on probation for a week."

He smiled. "That's just to weed out the bad seeds, but you're most definitely a keeper."

She smiled at him. "Thanks. One other thing. Mitchell has a bad rep for … well … being a little too hands-on with the girls that work here."

Hank smiled. "I know, and one of these days one of the girls will get fed up with it and put him in his place."

Vi smiled.

"Does that answer your question?"

She smiled.

"You won't lose your job if you beat the crap out of him." He smiled. "Tommy told me you didn't care for him, and had already warned him to keep his hands off. I have no problem with that, as long as you're a good bartender and do a good job."

"Thank you," she told him.

"By the way, you've got a great voice. You did great tonight."

She smiled. "Thanks."

"Have a good night, Vi," he said and left.

Vi walked back to the bar and went back to dancing with Tommy. Tommy may have looked like a jock, but he had rhythm and could dance. Tommy wore a wedding ring, Vi had noticed, and he hadn't come on to her, so she didn't mind dancing with him.

Todd and the band were putting away their stuff while Vi and Tommy cleaned up.

"You married?" She asked Tommy, "I noticed the wedding band."

"Yeah, ten years, have two little girls." He pulled out his wallet and showed her a picture.

"Wow, you wife is gorgeous and the girls are cute."

He smiled. "I work here so I can spend the afternoon with them every day after school."

"What a great dad."

"Hey, Vi." Todd came up to the bar. "We are all going to get breakfast. You want to go?"

Jasmine was counting up her tips on the bar. "How about me, do I get an invitation?"

Todd looked at her. "You know you're always welcome to come. I was just giving an invitation to the new girl."

Jasmine gave her a hateful look.

"I don't know. I would really just like to go home and go to bed. I am still not quite used to this shift. Maybe next time; but thanks for the offer."

"Alright, then." He turned and started to walk off, but then turned back. "Would you want to have lunch sometime?"

Vi smiled. "I'll think about it."

He smiled. "Ok, could I maybe get your number?"

Vi laughed. "No, I just met you." He dropped his head. "Playing the sad puppy won't get it, either," she told him.

He looked up then and smiled, "What will then?" he asked.

"Time."

"You ready?" The drummer walked up. "By the way, I'm Chaz."

She smiled at him. "Nice to meet you, Chaz."

"You coming with us?"

"Not this time, still getting used to the time. I might fall asleep in my eggs, but maybe next time."

"Alright."

The guys left, along with Jasmine, Mia, and Candy.

She and Tommy finished and closed up. Holly had left right when the bar closed.

"Can I give you a lift?" Tommy asked her as they exited the bar.

"That would be great; my car is being shipped out here, but won't be here for another week. It was being worked on when I left."

"Yuck, car problems; nothing will drain your wallet faster."

"I hear you, and my car is even worse. It's a classic and parts are hard to find."

"What is it?"

"68 Camaro."

"Sweet," Tommy said as they pulled up in front of her apartment building.

"Thanks for the lift."

"You're welcome."

She shut the door and walked to the stairs. She hadn't been running, so the stairs would be good for her. She showered and crashed on the bed.

CHAPTER 10

New Feelings

ONE MONTH LATER . . .

Vi had had the day off and had spent most of it working on music, but had fallen asleep. She wasn't used to being up in the daytime.

Someone knocking on her door woke her. "I'm coming." She got up off the couch and went to the door.

"I have something for you." Keeps said as she opened the door. He was dark-skinned and had dark brown hair and eyes, but his features were normal.

"Come in." She moved to let him by. "What are you doing here?"

"I brought you something." He held out a set of car keys.

Vi couldn't help herself and gave him a huge hug. "Where is it?"

"It's in the parking garage." He smiled.

"So, where have you been that you are so nice and tan?" She asked.

"I have something else for you, too." He walked over to the table and her laptop. "Sit down; I need to show you something." He looked back at her to find a strange look on her face.

"I promise you will like it." He then smiled at her.

"Alright," she walked over and sat down.

Keeps pulled a jump drive from his pocket and plugged it into her laptop. "Oh, yeah, I forgot." He turned back to her. "You are my Dagger, and I am your Cloak."

Vi blinked. "What did you do that for? If I wanted to remember, I wouldn't have had you wipe me in the first place." She stood up.

"I needed for you to remember or what I am about to show you wouldn't make sense. I can erase it again afterwards, if you want."

Vi sat back down and Keeps reached over and pulled up a video. He looked back at her then hit 'Play'.

The screen was black, then a light came on to reveal a man tied to a chair, naked; his hands were tied and his face covered with a hood. Vi looked at Keeps, who pointed back to the screen. Keeps entered the room; he looked at the camera, then to the man. He held a baseball bat. Keeps knew this would bring back lots of bad memories of the months she spent in the dark being beaten. Vi shivered in her chair and Keeps pulled another chair up behind hers and put his arms around her.

"You're, ok, I promise." He whispered to her.

She watched as Keeps beat the man till the ropes holding him to the chair were the only thing holding him up. He was bleeding profusely from cuts and bruises. Keeps took a hot iron and burned the man, then cut him several times. The man passed out several times during the beatings and each time Keeps woke him with smelling salts. Keeps finally cut the ropes and let the man crumble to the floor. There couldn't have been a bone not broken on the man. Keeps leaned over and took hold of the hood. He glanced back at the camera then removed the hood. He stood up and moved from in front of the camera.

Keeps watched Vi closely as the man with the scarred face appeared on the screen. Vi fell forward out of the chair onto the floor. Keeps picked her up and held her tight. Vi buried her head in Keeps. An unmistakable scream of terror brought her back to face the screen. The man lay on the floor, his manhood lay beside him. Vi stared as the man bled out and died. But Keeps wasn't through with him. He walked back on to the screen and put two bullets in his head, then the screen went black.

Vi turned to look at Keeps. He had killed this man for her. He had gone and found him and tortured him for her. She put her lips to his and kissed him for all she was worth.

Keeps pulled away and stood up. "I have to go."

"No." She stood up and put her arms around him. She looked up at him. "Stay."

He looked down at her. Was that want he saw in her eyes?

"I can't." He pulled out his jump drive.

Vi turned the chair and pushed him in it, then climbed up and straddled him. Her lips found his, her hands slid up into his hair.

Keeps took hold of her arms and pushed her back. "Stop!"

"Why won't you let me thank you?" She asked.

Keeps just looked at her. How tempting this was, he wanted it more than anything in the world, but ...

"You can't do this." He stood up and let her slide off his lap.

"Why not? I have no reason to stay pure anymore."

"You have a vow and a promise not to break."

"No, I have what they brainwashed me with," Vi said angrily. "My decisions have never been my own. They have always been there in the background pushing me into every move I have ever made. They were the ones that put the 'stay pure' in my head, and for what? A mission? No, this time it is my choice. I will give myself to whomever I want, and I want you!" Vi pulled her shirt and bra over her head and dropped them to the floor. "Do you not want me?"

Keeps scooped her up and took her to the bedroom and dropped her on the bed. His heart was pounding in his ears. "More than anything." He pulled his shirt over his head and dropped down on the bed. He put his lips to hers.

Keeps looked at Vi as she kissed down his neck. What was he doing? She was not his. He grabbed her hands as they were undoing his pants.

"Stop," his voice was ragged. "Please, Lindz," he looked her in the eyes, "I know you better than you know yourself. I know you believe in your vow and I also know you're willing to break it to say thank you, but you don't have to. Please don't. You are the one that has control of you. I know we have been raised for a purpose and we are good at our jobs, but they can never have this." He touched her tattoo of Brandon's heart. "You have already given it away and they can never take that from you."

A single tear ran down Vi's face. He had called her Lindsey. She looked up at him. "I give myself freely; no regrets," she told him.

"As much as I want you, and I do." He shook his head. "You're not mine; you already belong to someone else." He looked down at the tattoo on her chest and then got off the bed and walked towards the bedroom door.

"Keeps," she said from behind him. He turned to find her standing right behind him.

"Thank you." She put her arms around him. "You are too good to me."

"I love you," he whispered.

Vi heard him and it broke her heart to think of him loving her that much to kill for her, and still not wanting to ruin what she had with Brandon. Her mind then thought of something else.

"Keeps." She looked up at him. "How did you find him?"

"He was one of the men taken while you were there."

"But how did you get to him?" She asked.

"I asked King for his life."

"What . . . what do you mean you asked King for him?"

Keeps walked over and picked up his shirt from the floor. "Put this on and come sit down." He sat on the edge of the bed.

Vi took the shirt and slid it over her head, but stood in front of him.

"I recorded you the night I wiped your mind."

"You did what?"

"I took it to King; he needed to know."

Vi was furious. "How could you? That was between you and me. If I would have wanted him to know, I would have had you put it in some report or something."

"Listen, Vi, what that man did to you was unforgivable."

"You think I don't know that? I was the one there."

"It was the only way I could get to him."

"Don't you think that raised a little suspicion?"

"No."

"How can you say that? He now knows you care for me."

"No, you have to understand King and what he asked me to do, when he brought me your file."

"Explain it to me, why don't you?"

"Sit down and I will."

"Fine." She sat down.

"A few weeks before you came into my office, King came to see me. He handed me a file and told me to protect it with my life. Do whatever it took, no matter what it took. Mind wipes work for so long, but eventually your mind will recall the memories, and at that point you would have been ... well, I think you get what I made him think. Anyway, when I took him the recording I reminded him of his words, and he told me to do what I needed to do, and I did. But not totally for the reason I told them."

Vi couldn't have stayed mad at him if she wanted to.

"I have never wanted to kill someone more in my life," he admitted. "The very thought of that man touching you." He clenched his fist. "If I could have tortured him for years I would have." He looked up at her.

Vi climbed in his lap and threw her arms around his neck. "My knight in shining armor," she told him.

"You're not some damsel that needs rescuing," he told her.

She sat back and looked at him. "I was this time." She ran her finger down the side of his face. "How did I get so lucky?"

"I don't think luck has anything to do with it."

"Promise me something."

"What?" he asked.

"If for some reason I am given a mission that requires me to break my vow, will you break it for me before I am forced to break it with someone else?"

"You know how to make a man think he has had sex with you without him ever touching you."

"You know that doesn't always work. Now promise me."

"It's not going to come to that, but I promise."

Vi kissed him gently on the lips. "Keeps?"

"What?"

"I love you, too." She put her arms back around his neck.

Keeps held her tightly for a moment. "I need to go, Lindz; Handler is waiting for me."

Vi got up. "Let me change shirts so you can have yours back."

Keeps waited in the living room while she changed. He took the shirt and put it on when she brought it to him.

"Tell Handler I said hi."

"You know he has been watching you for me while I was gone?"

"Well, that explains the eerie feeling I keep having." She stood in front of him.

He pulled her into his arms one last time, then left.

CHAPTER 11
Clearwater Band

T WO MONTHS LATER ...
"I can't wait, the band's getting better every year," Todd was telling Vi.

"This year is supposed to be even better, because we have two bands that just got signed hosting," Chaz added.

Mike, the bass player, chimed in, "The Clearwater Band and Charger."

Vi looked up.

"The lead singer for Clearwater is hot," Holly turned and told Vi. "I think he's an Indian or something; he has long black hair and eyes that can look through your soul." Everyone burst out laughing.

"Sounds like you have a thing for him," Vi told Holly.

"Her and every other woman," Todd added.

"I must admit he is hot," Jasmine said.

"So, they have been here before?" Vi asked.

"They came here last year just before they got signed," Jasmine answered her question.

"How many bands are coming this year, anybody heard?" Todd asked.

"I think I heard Mitchell say 20," Holly told him.

Vi smiled, so this is why Keeps suggested Nashville; he knew Brandon would be coming.

The battle of the bands was all that anyone seemed to be talking about. Next week, bands from all over were coming to compete for an opening spot on a tour with a well-known band. And so far, every band that had won had been signed and had gone on to make it big.

Five bars were hosting the bands; they had a friendly competition going themselves to see who could sell the most liquor. The battle took place at a local arena and each bar had a make-shift bar set up. The arena was divided into equal space and each bar got a section. The winning bar got to host the winning band for three nights. It was all in good fun, or so they said.

They all left the diner about 5 a.m. Vi went straight home and showered. She lay down, but her head and heart were both racing. Brandon was coming!

She finally got back up and sat down with her guitar. She had been playing with Fire Water every time they came to the bar. She had loved the opportunity to play and sing. She had even started working again on the song she started. She opened her laptop and looked at the last thing she had written down. She played over it, then added a few notes and wrote them down. Vi worked on music till noon then lay down and went to sleep.

She woke at five, got up, got dressed and ready to go to work. She grabbed a sandwich at Subway on her way. She and Tommy were always 30 minutes early; he was her closest friend at the bar. She had spent a couple of her days off with him and his family. Valarie, his wife was a very successful lawyer. Tommy worked at the bar because he loved bartending, so everything worked out good for them. He was always critiquing her music for her, so she would come in a few minutes early and play for him. Tonight was no different; she had her guitar and was waiting when he walked in.

"I think I am almost done with the song. I did a lot of work on it today."

"Let's hear it, then." He sat on the edge of the stage. Vi played and Tommy listened. "Are you ever going to sing it for me? I know you have words."

She took a breath. "I am not quite finished with the words; just the music."

"But the song is empty unless you sing; your humming doesn't count."

"Alright, I'll sing what I have." She started over, this time adding the lyrics. "Could you whisper in my ears, I'll give you anything at all." Tommy smiled at her as she sang. "I want to wake up where you are," the song ended.

"So who is the song for?" Tommy asked her.

Vi smiled. "That's why I hadn't sung it for you. I knew you would start asking that."

"You're not going to tell me are you?"

She smiled at him. "Nope."

"Well, it sounds good."

Vi put her guitar in its case and set it over to the side of the stage.

"Hey, Vi." Mitchell came in.

She looked up.

"Can you be here early all this week to let the bands in to practice?"

"What time?" She asked.

"Around two. We are hosting six bands, and all of them will be in to practice a couple of hours."

"Sure, no problem."

"We are also letting one of the host bands practice here. They get tomorrow all to themselves, and the other bands have to share days."

"Who did we get, the Clearwater band or Charger?" She asked; she almost held her breath.

"Clearwater, they have played here before."

Vi smiled. "Great!"

"I talked to Brandon earlier today, that's the lead singer. He said they are already in town. They may even stop by tonight."

Vi's heart about stopped, maybe she would see him tonight.

"You ok, Vi?" Tommy asked her.

She looked up and smiled at him. "Tonight may be the night."

"For what?"

"You'll know when you see it."

"You're acting weird, Vi."

"I feel like a little kid getting ready to go in the candy store."

"What has got you stirred up?"

She grinned at him and shook her head. "Bring on the night."

Tommy laughed at her as Mitchell opened the bar for business.

The DJ cranked up the music and Vi danced as she served drinks. She watched as people entered the bar hoping one of them would be Brandon.

She didn't have to wait long, about 30 minutes after opening he walked in along with James, Todd and the other two guys from the band. Her heart was pounding so hard, her hands shook.

Brandon walked towards the office as the rest of the guys found a table. Vi turned her necklace backwards and went on serving drinks. She watched for Brandon to come back out. Mitchell and he both came out about an hour later.

"Hey, Vi," Mitchell yelled over the crowd. She walked to the end of the bar to where Brandon and Mitchell stood. "This is Vi; she will be letting you in tomorrow."

Brandon stuck out his hand. "Brandon."

She took it, his necklace hung around his neck.

Vi smiled. "Let me know if I can do anything for you."

"Thanks, I will."

She smiled, then turned and went back to work. Vi heard Mitchell from behind her.

"Couldn't talk you guys into playing tonight, could I?"

Brandon laughed. "No instruments, sorry."

"Vi's acoustic is up there," Tommy told them. "I am sure she wouldn't mind you using it."

"Maybe later I'll play something."

He looked at her. "So you play?"

"She can play and sing probably better than half the bands that are going to be here next week," Mitchell told him. Vi never broke eye contact with him the whole time Mitchell talked. "She won a bet with a local band and plays with them every time they play here."

"Does she now?"

Vi smiled. "I better get back to work." She turned and walked back to help Tommy.

An hour later, Vi noticed Brandon picking up her case on stage. She froze; his heart was on the front. She may have looked differently, but the heart . . . He opened the case; he turned all of the sudden and looked at the bar. Vi just stood there smiling.

Mitchell grabbed a mic and a stool and sat it up for him to play. Brandon played two songs then left the stage, carefully putting her guitar back.

Vi watched him say a few words to Mitchell then watched him walk back to the end of the bar.

"Can I talk to you a minute, Vi?" He yelled from the end of the bar.

"Sure," she yelled back.

Brandon's mind was racing. Could she be Lindsey? He knew she could change her looks, he had seen it. He motioned her to follow him; they went to Mitchell's office. He opened the door and let her in, then followed her. Brandon stared at her for a minute as if to ask if it was really her. The necklace! He reached up and flipped her necklace over to reveal the little ruby and waves of silver.

"Miss me?" She asked. His lips found hers at once. "I'll take that as a yes," she said when their lips finally parted.

"You look wild!"

She laughed. "Yeah, I know. When did you get in town?" she asked him.

"Last night. You?"

"Over three months ago," she told him, "Oh, I have something to show you." She pulled the front of her shirt down to show him her tattoo of his heart.

"Nice."

"Permanent?" He asked.

"No, it's like the skin color."

"Amazing."

"Not really," she said. "I better get back to work before Tommy is over run and Mitchell has a fit."

"What time do you get off?"

"Three, closing time. You going to stick around?"

He smiled, "I am not letting you out of my sight."

She smiled and kissed him. "I was hoping you would say that."

He opened the door for her.

They both walked back up to the bar. She went behind and went back to serving and he went to the table and joined the guys.

Vi couldn't keep the grin from her face. Tommy noticed. "I see what you mean now."

She laughed and served another drink.

Brandon and James came to the bar when the other guys from the band left around one.

"You want anything?" She asked Brandon.

"Water," he answered.

"I finally get you to stay at a bar, and you won't even have a drink."

Vi pulled a water out of the cooler and handed it to him.

"You know I don't drink," he said.

"I know, but I just can't figure out why."

Vi smiled.

"Maybe he wants to keep all his brain cells." Vi told James.

Brandon laughed.

James looked at her. "Can I buy you a drink?"

She laughed. "Nope. Don't touch the stuff."

"You work at a bar and don't drink." He turned and threw up his hands.

The bar started emptying out after two. Tommy gave her a nudge. "Go dance." She smiled.

"You want to dance?" She walked up in front of Brandon.

James just looked at her. "It's because he doesn't drink, isn't it?"

Brandon followed her to the dance floor. Vi smiled as she put her body against Brandon's and they moved together. *Sex on the dance floor* went through Brandon's head, that's what she had called it before. She wasn't kidding; moving with her body was intoxicating. They danced three songs before she pulled him back to the bar.

"Tommy, this is Brandon."

Brandon smiled and shook his hand.

"Nice to meet you."

"You, too."

James turned and looked at her.

"This is James," Brandon told them.

Vi smiled at him. "Hey, James."

"Now you talk to me."

"I think he has had enough to drink," Brandon told Vi.

"I think you're right."

"I better get him a taxi."

"I can drop him off, if you want to wait till I get off." She looked up at the clock. "Fifteen minutes."

Brandon smiled. "Alright."

Vi walked back down the bar and served a couple of more drinks then started cleaning up.

"Not going home alone tonight, are you?" Tommy came up beside her.

"Nope."

Tommy chuckled. "Wait till I tell Valarie you took some guy home with you, she won't believe me. How long have you known him?" Tommy asked.

"Not near long enough."

As the bar closed, Brandon and James sat talking to Mitchell as Vi cleaned up.

"Can I give you two a lift back to your hotel?" Mitchell offered.

"No thanks, Vi is dropping us off." Mitchell looked up at her. "You're giving them a ride in your car? You have never offered to give me one."

"Stop whining, Mitchell," she told him. "You guys ready?" Brandon looked at Vi. "Mitchell is in love with my car."

The three of them walked out the back door. Her alarm beeped and the doors unlocked.

"No wonder!" Brandon said as he ran his finger up the fender.

James just stood there. "I want one of those."

Vi laughed. "Come on, let's get you home." She stopped just before she got in. "You want to drive?" She threw the keys to Brandon.

"I want to drive!" James yelled.

"You're drunk," they both said at the same time.

James got in the back and Brandon slid into the driver's seat.

"Nice." He turned the key and the engine came to life. "Sweet!"

Vi laughed. "It will take off and leave you if you're not careful," she told Brandon.

He eased off the clutch, and it still peeled out.

The band's hotel wasn't far, so it didn't take long to get there. Vi let James out of the back seat; he staggered to the door and went in.

"Let me go tell the guys I will see them tomorrow, and grab some clothes." Brandon got out and went in. He was back in no time.

"Any problems?"

He laughed. "I think they are all in shock. I don't go out at all, and then all of the sudden one night I go home with a bartender."

Vi laughed and slid over into the driver's seat. Vi took out with a nice squeal. She pulled into the parking garage next to her apartment ten minutes later.

"This is it," she said as she opened the door.

Brandon walked in and looked around. "Nice."

Vi closed the door and locked it. She walked over, kicked the radio on low and sat her phone down next to it.

"I'm going to shower, make yourself at home." He put his bag on the couch.

Brandon noticed her computer sat on the table beside the couch. He saw the screen kick on. A familiar avatar popped up and waved. He walked over and sat the laptop in his lap. No voice came out of the computer, but words popped up on the screen.

"I told you that you would be seeing her soon. Now, are you sure you want to do this?"

"Yes."

"Alright, I will get you everything you need. Just give me a few days to get it all up and running."

"Thanks, man," Brandon typed back.

Brandon put the laptop back down as the screen went black. Brandon picked up his bag and went to the bedroom. He pulled his shirt over his head and took off his shoes and socks, then grabbed a clean pair of boxers and walked to the bathroom.

"You about done?"

Vi shut the water off and opened the shower door and stepped out. Her eyeliner and black lip stick was gone.

He stepped close to her and traced the heart on her chest with his finger.

She reached up and traced his. "You should have the picture filled in."

"No," he said, "she is the one who first stole my heart."

Vi smiled at him. "Get a shower; you stink."

She picked up a towel, wrapped it around her and then went out of the bathroom.

Brandon stripped and climbed in; he smiled to himself. Soon, very soon she was going to be his.

Vi went to the kitchen for a drink. She so wanted to break her vow, but she knew Brandon wouldn't allow it. Her mind wandered to Keeps; she had tried to break her vow with him and he wouldn't let her. He had already known she was going to be seeing Brandon again.

"I love you," he said as came up behind her and kissed up her neck.

"I love you, too." She turned to face him. She glanced at her phone sitting in front of the speaker.

"What's wrong?" Brandon noticed her look.

"Nothing, I was just thinking."

"About what?"

She grinned, "About a serious making out party."

Brandon laughed and gathered her up in his arms and dropped her on the bed.

"I was thinking the same thing."

A knock at the door brought Vi out of sleep. She glanced over at the clock; it was past noon. She climbed out of the bed and went to the door. She opened it to find Ben standing there all alone. He was in tears.

"What's wrong, Ben?" She scooped him up in her arms. "Where's Heather?" Vi looked up and down the hall. She walked down to Ben's door; it wasn't shut. Ben started shaking in her arms when she reached out to touch the door. He buried his head in her shoulder. She stepped back from the door and went back to her apartment.

"Brandon?"

He came to the bedroom door.

"What's wrong?" He looked at the boy in her arms.

"This is Ben; he is my neighbor, I need to go check on his sister. Can you watch him a few minutes?"

Brandon smiled. "Sure." He looked at Ben. "I'm hungry, how about you?" Ben just looked at him.

"He is my friend, and he will take good care of you, I promise."

Brandon held out his arms. Ben hesitated, but then went to Brandon.

"I'll be right back."

"Let's see what Vi has in the fridge," Vi heard Brandon tell Ben as she left.

Vi went back down the hall, the door still stood ajar; she pushed it slowly open. Vi could see feet on the floor first. She hurried in. Ben's mom was lying on the floor, a bottle still in her hand, but only the neck, the rest was shattered and gone. Vi bent over and felt for a pulse, there wasn't one. Blood was everywhere; a noise coming from the other room caught her attention. She carefully stepped over the kids' mom and walked down the hall to where the noise was coming from. Vi could hear a man.

"Come on, sweetie, you're going to love it."

Vi opened the door with force. Heather lay on the bed tied, and a man with no pants on was standing at the end of the bed. Vi was furious; the man came at her with a knife. Vi had the man dead in seconds without hesitation. Heather was sobbing on the bed. Vi untied her, picked her up and carried her out of the room. She flipped over the phone in the living room and dialed 911.

"911, what's your emergency?" The lady on the other end said.

"My neighbor's apartment has been broken into. She has been killed and her daughter assaulted. I have the girl and her brother in E12; please send some officers." She put down the phone, but left it off the hook and took Heather from the apartment. Ten minutes later police were beating on her door. Brandon opened the door and let them in. Vi was still holding Heather on the couch.

"Are you the one that called?"

"Yes, sir," Vi told them. "I also called their aunt. She should be here in a few minutes."

"I need to take a statement from you."

"Can it wait till her aunt gets here, then I will show you what I found."

"That will be fine. I will return in a few minutes." A female officer stayed at the door.

"Heather!" Her aunt came rushing through the door.

"Where's Ben?"

Ben came out of the kitchen. "I here," he said.

Vi passed Heather off to her aunt.

"You can go back; Officer Cahill is waiting for you," the female officer told her.

Vi walked up the hall; Officer Cahill opened the door. Heather's mom was still lying on the floor, but a coroner stood over her.

"She was dead when I got here. Ben came and got me, the guy must have not known he was here. I did check her for a heartbeat." The officer wrote in his notes.

"What happened next?"

"I heard something coming from the back room when I got here," she stopped near the bedroom door. "I heard a man; he was telling Heather she was going to like it. I got so furious I burst in the door without thinking. Poor Heather was tied to the bed, and he was standing there half naked," she pointed to the end of the bed.

"So, you killed him?"

"He came at me with the knife; I reacted." The man lay on the floor with his throat slit open, blood everywhere. "I untied Heather and called 911, then went back to my place to wait." The officer looked at the dirty man on the floor.

"Glad he didn't get away; sorry their mom was killed, though."

Vi looked up at him. "Can I go back to my apartment?"

"Sure, you need to give Carla your name and number in case we need to call you."

"No problem." Vi walked back to her apartment.

Heather was talking to the lady officer. "Mom just didn't get up, then he grabbed me and pulled me to mom's room. He tied my arms to the bed and took off his pants then Vi came in; he tried to cut her like mom, but Vi killed him."

Brandon walked over and put his arm around Vi.

"Did he touch you anywhere?" The officer asked.

"No, he hadn't got that far, yet."

"You're very lucky, but they will still want to check you over, anyway." Heather sat up, "Alright." Heather gave Vi a big hug before they left with the officer. "Thank you."

Ben kissed her on the cheek. "Can we play your guitar, sometime?"

Vi smiled. "You have your aunt call me, and we will set up a time to do just that."

Ben smiled.

"Thanks so much." Their aunt hugged her.

Vi closed the door behind them. It was now going on four o'clock. Brandon was standing in the doorway. He had put on his jeans when she brought Heather in, but he still didn't have on his shirt. Vi looked down and laughed; she was in her shorts and sports bra.

"I need a shower and a nap."

"I could call Mitchell." She looked at him.

"I was just kidding." He told her.

Vi went to clean up; she showered and got dressed. She left off the lipstick and eyeliner. Brandon was in the kitchen when she finished.

"Hungry?" He held out an omelet.

"Starved." She sat down at the table and ate. He sat down across from her and watched her. "I ate with Ben."

A phone ringing got her attention; Brandon jumped up and went into the other room. He came back talking on a phone.

"I'm sorry guys, there was an emergency."

"Crap!" Vi said. "I was supposed to open the bar for you and the band to practice at two. And that is when Ben woke us. Mitchell is going to be pissed," she said.

"Vi's neighbor was killed and she had the lady's kids till their aunt got here to get them."

"Tell them I'm sorry."

"Don't worry about it, Vi." He looked at her.

"We will be fine. It wasn't her fault, and, yeah, I do take offense to you saying that. I will be there just as soon as I can."

Vi put on her lipstick, eyeliner, and boots.

"We better get going."

Brandon grabbed a shirt, and put on his shoes and socks. "Don't worry about them," he told her, "I will take care of them."

"They're not the ones I'm worried about. Mitchell is going to be majorly pissed at me." They got to the bar just before 4:30. The rest of Brandon's band was already playing when she and Brandon went in.

"Vi!" Mitchell yelled as he came out of his office. There were security cameras everywhere, so he knew the minute she got there.

"There was an emergency, and I completely lost track of time," she told him.

"What could be more important than your job?" He yelled at her.

Brandon had made it halfway to the stage, but turned back when he heard Mitchell yell at Vi.

"Maybe the girl that she saved from being raped, or the druggy she killed to save the girl." Brandon got in Mitchell's face. Mitchell took a couple of steps backward.

"It was your practice time. If you're fine, I'm fine." He held up his hand.

"The life of a child is more important than this, any day," Brandon growled at him.

"You should have called, Vi." Mitchell backed away from Brandon farther.

"Sorry, Mitchell."

"Don't you apologize to him; he should be apologizing to you." Brandon looked at her. Vi just looked at him; she had never seen him mad.

"Sorry, Vi." Mitchell was doing some major back peddling, but no wonder. Brandon stood a head taller and he looked fierce. Brandon was looking at Mitchell again.

Vi put her hand on Brandon's arm. "It's ok. Mitchell, I would have called if there would have been time, but things just happened so fast and the last cop didn't leave till four." Vi looked at Mitchell, he still had fear in his eyes.

Brandon turned and walked back towards the stage.

Vi whispered to Mitchell, "Sorry."

Mitchell turned and went back to his office.

Vi went behind the bar to put her purse up. She could hear the band arguing on stage, then it all seemed to just stop and they started playing.

"So, how was your night?" Tommy came in behind her.

"Great would be an understatement."

Tommy laughed. "I figured they would be done by now," he looked up at the stage.

"They just got started."

Tommy looked at her. "What happened?"

"You remember my neighbors Heather and Ben?"

"Yeah," he answered.

"Their mom was killed this morning."

"Are they ok?"

"Yeah, they are with their aunt now. But they stayed with me till she came, so we just got here."

"You look tired."

Vi smiled. "I didn't get a lot of sleep."

Tommy smiled. "I didn't figure you would."

Tommy went to get the cash from the office and got the register set up, as Vi wiped down the bar.

"What's wrong with Mitchell?" Tommy asked as he put the cash drawer in.

Vi looked at him. "He and Brandon got into it."

"Over what?" he asked.

"Me being late."

"He tried to bust you? I would have been all over him, too." Tommy laughed when he looked up at Brandon. "I wish I could have seen it. I may be big, but I wouldn't want to get him pissed at me."

Vi smiled.

"Time to open." Mitchell came around the bar.

Brandon and the guys were still on the stage playing when Mitchell opened the doors. The bar started filling up before Brandon and the band quit and put their instruments away.

"Hey." Brandon came to the bar, Vi met him at the end. "We have to make some rounds at some other bars."

Vi pulled her keys out and gave them to Brandon. "Take my car; just don't forget to pick me up at three."

He smiled, then gave her a kiss on the cheek. "Thanks, I'll see you later." Brandon and the band left.

About nine, Hank came in and went to Mitchell's office. Vi had to wonder if Mitchell hadn't called him to tell him of her not coming in. Hank came out and sat at her end of the bar.

"Can I get you anything?" She asked him.

"You pick, I need something different."

Vi fixed a Red Hot Mexican and handed it to him.

"What is it?" He asked.

"Try it first; then I'll tell you."

He knocked it back.

"Wow, it's hot!"

Vi laughed. "Red Hot Mexican."

"Nice. It has a kick," he paused. "I got a call about you earlier."

"And?"

"It was from a local reporter."

She looked at him; she figured Mitchell had tried to get her into trouble. Great, all she needed was to be in the local paper. "He got a tip about you saving a girl's life and wants to interview you." Vi rolled her eyes, she did not need publicity. "I thought maybe you could put a plug in for the bar."

Vi laughed. "Don't plan on talking to any reporter."

"Why not?"

"Don't have any use for them. I don't want or care for the attention."

"I don't think you're going to get away from Chuck, he is the reporter that called. He does all the news that has to do with the bars, and if a bartender did something heroic he is going to have a story on it."

Vi just shook her head. "I'll think about it." Hank smiled and turned around to watch the people on the dance floor.

Several bands had come in and talked with Mitchell during the night. She knew they would be the ones she let in to practice all week. The rest of the shift went by quickly. Brandon came back in around two a.m. and sat at the bar. Hank had gone back to Mitchell's office, but came back out when Brandon came in. They went back to Mitchell's office and Vi didn't see them again till it was closing time.

The girls were all adding up their tips when he came back.

"Hey, Brandon," Jasmine walked up to him.

"Hey." He sat down at the bar to wait. "Last time you were here you said you had a girl. What happened to her?"

Brandon laughed. "You know how things go, you lose one you pick up another."

Vi could hear them talking, but went on and cleaned up.

"You could have picked me up."

Brandon smiled at her. "You ready Vi?" he turned and asked Vi.

"Almost."

Jasmine sulked off.

"You knew she liked you last time you were here, and you pass her by for the new girl," Candy told him.

"Sorry, but sometimes people click and sometimes they don't, and we didn't," he told her.

"I'm ready now." Vi walked up. They walked out to her car. "I hope Jasmine doesn't get totally pissed at me. She hasn't liked me since I got here."

Brandon laughed. "You're just worried she'll key your car or something."

Vi smiled. "You know me well." They both laughed. "How's Jacob and Michelle? Last time I saw them, she was getting ready to have a kid. What did she have?" Vi asked as they headed for her apartment.

"She had a boy, Seth. They are all great."

"How did your mom take the name? Wasn't that Beth's little boy's name?"

"Yeah, it was hard at first, but I think it has helped her a lot."

"They are not all living in one of those little cabins, are they?"

Brandon laughed. "No, he is not a Ranger anymore. He is the Sheriff on the reservation."

"How does he like it?" she asked.

"He loves it. Michelle is working at the hospital and mom watches Seth. She had to retire to do it, but I think she was glad to do it."

"Who wouldn't want to stay home and watch their grandkids?"

They walked up to her apartment. There were three cards sticking out of the door frame. Vi pulled them out and looked at them.

"Great."

"What is it?"

"Newspapers wanting to do stories on me." She opened the door and went in; Brandon followed her.

"That's not a real good thing is it?"

"Not really." She walked through to the bedroom and headed for the shower.

Brandon sat on the couch. Someone knocked on the door and Brandon answered it. It was a delivery. Brandon took the box; it was addressed to him. He sat down and opened it. It was from Keeps. Inside were a small box and several papers. Brandon took the small box and opened it. The two rings inside were silver with a symbol on them; it was the symbol for eternity. Brandon smiled. He pulled out the papers; they were all legal papers, a new identity for her and one for him if he needed it. Brandon put the papers back in the box and took the rings and headed to the bathroom. Vi was getting out of the shower when he went it.

"What's up?" She asked Brandon. He had a big grin on his face when he entered the bathroom.

"I have to ask you something."

"What?"

He dropped to one knee and held up the box. Vi stepped backwards. "Marry me."

She looked at him, and then at the box. He opened it; the two rings shined. "Before you answer you have to see something else." He handed her a towel.

She pulled it around her and followed him to the box he had left on the couch. He handed it to her. She pulled out the papers and looked at them.

"Are you sure you want to do this? You have a contract and a band."

He smiled at her. "I have been working with them a lot, and now Todd is doing the most of the singing. It won't take them long to find a replacement guitar player."

"But this was your dream."

"My dream is to spend the rest of my life with you." Tears surfaced in Vi's eyes, "I know what I would be getting into. You know I couldn't do all this on my own."

Vi smiled.

"I know," she said.

"The only reason I accepted the hosting job next week was to find my replacement for the band."

"What is the band going to say?"

"It doesn't matter. All that matter is this." He held up the rings.

"And you're really sure about this?"

"I have never been surer of anything in my life."

"And your family?"

"It's all going to be taken care of. We have plans standing by, if we need them."

"Really, really sure?" She asked again.

He laughed. "We have been working on this for the last three years, so I am pretty sure."

"That little sneak! He was working on this when we were together."

Brandon smiled. "Yeah, you know he loves you almost as much as I do."

Vi smiled. "I know he does. So when is all this supposed to take place?"

He smiled. "So is that a 'Yes'?"

She smiled at him. "Yes."

He lifted her into his arms and kissed her.

Fireworks exploded on her computer screen. They both laughed.

Keeps' avatar popped up on the screen. "You know this is going to take some time for you to heal? Your facial alterations don't work anymore; they use a bone sensor now."

"I know, but if it keeps us safe, then I have no problem with it."

"I will get you an appointment with the doctor very soon. But as soon as I do, Vi needs to move."

"I know. I will wait for the battle of the bands to end and Brandon to head back home."

"Then you will have a clean break, again," Keeps said.

Brandon looked at Vi. "Are you sure you want to go through the pain?"

"Pain only lasts a little while." she smiled. "What's the timetable?" she asked Keeps.

"It will take at least a year to get your surgeries done and you recovered, then get you set back up for a meeting."

She looked at Brandon. "You know this can go badly?"

"That's why there is a new identity in there for me, just in case."

"If they find out about Keeps, they will kill us both off. And you're sure you're ok with that?" Vi asked.

"Give him a break." Keeps told her, "he's sure."

"If you were here I would hug you," she told Keeps, "maybe a kiss, too!" She laughed.

"Sure," Keeps said and had the girl avatar that looked like Lindsey come out and kiss him. Brandon laughed.

Vi sat down on the couch. "I have a small problem."

"What is it?" Keeps asked.

"I have a newspaper wanting to do a story on me. I helped a little girl out the other day, and now I am getting calls at work about it."

"She saved the girl's life," Brandon added in.

"It will be better if you agree to do the interview and let them take one picture instead of them hounding you and taking lots and them ending up everywhere. I can corrupt their picture file with a virus as soon as they post it online," he paused. "You just can't help it can you?"

"What?" She asked.

"You can't help helping people, can you?"

Vi laughed.

"No," Brandon answered, "she can't."

"You make it sound like it is a bad thing to want to help."

"It's only bad when you need to stay hidden and out of sight. I will get to work on this from my end and then I will talk to you again when I get your appointments and stuff lined up." The screen went black.

Vi looked at Brandon; he was ready to give up his whole way of life if necessary to have her as his wife.

"I have given it a lot of thought and I'm ready, I promise," he told her.

"I wish you could stay in your band."

"You don't need the publicity, but who knows, maybe when all the surgery is done. Well, Keeps said if it went well I might be able to stay playing, but I don't think I want to. I would rather stay with you than have to be out on the road and stuff like that."

She smiled at him. "You don't ever have to work; your restoration business is a total success."

"So, that's what our business is?"

"We restore old houses; well, we front the money for a contractor who does it for us."

He smiled. "Maybe they can do a house for us."

"I was thinking the same thing." They laughed.

It was going on five a.m. before Brandon got in the shower. Vi lay down on the bed and dosed off. She woke when he climbed into the bed beside her. He pulled her close and she fell back to sleep.

Soon, he thought, she would never have to leave and they could be together forever. "I love you," he whispered in her ear as he closed his eyes.

Vi was awakened by a noise. She listened. Regular noises didn't ever wake her, but the sound of something or someone trying to be quiet always did. She pretended to toss in her sleep in the bed, but really she got the knife from the hole in the side of her mattress. She sprang up and had the intruder on the floor with the knife at their throat in seconds. Brandon woke when she jumped up. He reached over and flicked the light on. Vi sat on top of Keeps on the floor.

"I could have killed you!" She stood up.

Keeps smiled. "I knew you wouldn't, you love me too much." She smiled at him and gave him a hug, then kissed him gently on the lips.

"I do love you."

Brandon stood up and walked around the edge of the bed and stuck out his hand. "You have to be Keeps."

Keeps smiled and shook his hand.

"What are you doing here?" Vi asked.

"You're not the only one leaving." He laughed. "I am couriering some Intel. I thought I might stop by and say hi on my way through."

"I am glad you did."

A loud sharp noise went off, and then quit.

"They are coming online to monitor. I'm not here."

Vi walked back to the bed and sat down. Brandon followed Vi; Keeps motioned toward the bathroom then went in and shut the door. It was almost noon.

Vi got back up and went to the kitchen and started making them some lunch. Brandon pulled his jeans on and followed her.

"Can I help you?"

She smiled, "Can you get out the tomatoes and cut them up?"

"Sure." He opened the refrigerator door.

"What are you fixing, anyway?"

"Just some burgers."

"Sounds good to me; thanks for inviting me to lunch."

"You're welcome," she said. Three fast beeps told them the monitoring had stopped.

"They always do it at the strangest times." Keeps came into the room.

"Where are you supposed to be?"

"I have a layover at the airport for three hours, so it's not that I am not supposed to be here. It's just I am not supposed to be here with you."

Vi smiled. "How convenient your layover to be here in Nashville."

"Coincidence." He laughed. "I wanted to meet Brandon." He turned to look at him.

"You really just wanted your kiss," Brandon told him.

"Yeah, that, too." They both laughed.

"You guys hungry?" She flipped the burgers in the skillet.

They all sat down when Vi set the plates with burgers on the table.

"How come you didn't tell me you had been talking to Brandon?" She asked Keeps.

"I needed your head in the game, not following Brandon around."

She smiled. "Ok, I'll give you that one." She turned to Brandon. "You didn't tell me, either."

He laughed. "I wanted it to be a surprise. You're not mad at me that I didn't tell you, are you?"

"No, but I will make you pay for it, later." She grinned.

Keeps smiled at her, "Your honeymoon is going to be wild."

They all laughed.

"Oh, you can count on it," Vi told them. Brandon blushed and Keeps laughed at him.

"I have to get ready for work." Vi got up.

"I'll clean up, go ahead," Brandon told her.

Vi headed for the bathroom. Brandon filled the sink with water and started washing the dishes.

"So you are you getting out, too?"

"Once I know you guys are safe. But it may take a year or two. If I have things planned right, they will send me after her. That way I won't be under suspension of helping her. Then when the trail is good and cold, I will get out," Keeps told him.

Brandon finished the dishes and put them away.

"Thanks." He turned to Keeps.

"You're welcome. You know you're right about one thing. Keeps got serious. "I do love her."

"I know you do." Brandon smiled.

"If you ever hurt her . . ."

Brandon finished his sentence, "You'll hunt me down and kill me."

"With no mercy."

Vi cleared her throat, she was standing in the doorway. "That's enough." They both smiled at her. "I have to get to work." She gave Brandon a key to the apartment. Then turned to Keeps. "I'm glad you stopped by." She gave him a hug and kiss. "Be safe."

"I will."

"I'll see you later; I'm taking the car." Vi walked to the door and looked back at them. "I love you guys." She opened the door and left.

Keeps watched Vi shut the door, then turned back to Brandon. "I wasn't joking."

"I know you weren't." Brandon looked at him.

Vi got to the bar just before two. The band was already sitting in the parking lot.

"You guys are early," she told them as she unlocked the door.

"We need all the practice we can get," one of them said from behind her.

"My name is Vi; let me know if you need anything."

"How about your number?" A tall thin guy with drumsticks said.

Vi smiled. "Well, almost anything."

"Hey, Vi." Mitchell came up the hall.

"Checking to see if I was coming?"

He smiled. "No, the bar opens at noon. Well, the business of getting stuff delivered and stocked does. We are expecting a big order this week and the next week, so I thought I'd better come in and check to make sure we get everything. Checking to see if you made it was just a bonus."

The band made their way to the stage and set up.

"Can you help me a while?"

"Sure." She followed him to the back room.

It was full of boxes and bottles everywhere; you could barely walk in. They began to move and stack boxes out of the way. An hour later they were still working.

"So what's going on with you and Brandon?" He asked.

Vi laughed. "Like it is any of your business."

He put the box down. "He is my business. I am the one that is in charge of keeping him and his band happy while they are here."

"Does he not seem happy or something?" She asked.

"I am just warning you to keep him happy. If something goes wrong it could hurt the bar."

Vi shook her head. "Don't worry about that."

He stopped and looked at her. "I have to; it could cost me my job if something goes wrong."

Vi put her box down and faced him. "I promise you he is happy and will stay that way till he leaves. No matter what."

"He better be."

She laughed. "You ask him."

"Are you crazy? I'm not asking him anything concerning you." He turned and went back to work.

They finished up and went back out front. Brandon was sitting at the bar. Vi walked around it and gave him a kiss.

"Hey, what are you doing here so early?"

"It got lonely back at your apartment."

Vi looked at Mitchell and smiled. "Told you he was happy."

Brandon looked at Mitchell; Vi took the opportunity to kiss him again, this time a little longer and with more passion.

Mitchell retreated to his office. Vi laughed when she saw he was gone.

"What was that about?"

"He doesn't want me to get you mad, then you take it out on the bar."

Brandon looked at her. "Why would I get mad at you?"

"I think he just wants you happy and satisfied."

Brandon laughed. "No one could satisfy me more than you."

He pulled her into his arms and kissed her again.

Brandon's phone rang.

"Hey, what's up?" He answered it. "No, we haven't done anything much, yet. How's Seth?" Vi smiled, it was Jacob. "No, we are not really supposed to do anything till next week." Brandon smiled at Vi as she walked around the bar and started wiping it down. "Yeah, tell them I miss them, too. Ok, then, I'll talk to you later." He closed the phone and put it back in his pocket.

"Hey, Vi, there is a phone call for you on line two." Mitchell stuck his head around the corner. Line two was a private line.

"Hello."

"This is Chuck Haslow with the Times. I wanted to ask if I could talk to you some time." Vi took a deep breath. "I have already talked to Heather and Ben and would now like your side of the story."

"I'll tell you what, I am here watching bands practice the rest of the week from two to six. If you come by here, then I will talk to you."

"That would be great. Is today ok? I am not far from there now."

"Sure," Vi told him, "the doors are open." Then to Brandon, she said, "I suggest you make yourself scarce, the press is coming by."

Brandon laughed. "I will go talk to my band; I seem to be avoiding them lately."

"You want the car? I am not going anywhere."

"Sure." She reached down and got her keys. He leaned over the bar and kissed her. "See you later." Vi walked around the bar and sat down.

The second band came in and started their practice session. The other five couldn't stay while the other practiced so they left right away.

"You Vi?" A young man with short brown hair came in.

"Yeah."

He smiled and stuck out his hand.

"Chuck Haslow." Vi smiled and shook his hand. "So I need your side of the story. Heather and Ben told me what they knew; now I want what you know."

"Not really much to tell. Ben came to my door and I went to check on what was wrong. I found the door still open, his mom on the floor, and Heather tied to the bed. The man in the room came at me and the rest is history."

He looked at her. "There was more to it than that."

"Not really."

"So, how did you kill the man. What was his name? I have it here, somewhere, oh, yeah, here it is. A Mr. John Miller. So how did you kill Mr. Miller?"

She looked up at him. "You act like it was something done so easy. Taking a life could never be easy. I really don't even remember it. I just remember him coming at me then looking down at him on the floor with the knife in my hand and blood being everywhere." She shuddered for a visual effect.

"But you're a hero; you saved a little girl from certain rape and death."

"Well, I don't feel like one."

"I need your whole name."

"Violet Patterson."

"Can I get a picture?"

"You should take one of Heather and her brother. They are the survivors, that's more important."

"I have one of them. I wish I had one of you with them, but this will have to do. Their aunt wasn't too happy about me writing the story."

Vi sat still while he took a picture of her. "You haven't worked here long have you?" He asked.

"No, a few months."

"I knew I didn't remember you. But I don't come in here very often, usually just around Battle time. Well, I guess I will see you around next week. Thanks for talking to me." He shook her hand and left.

That wasn't as bad as she had expected. The band playing wasn't bad, either. Vi got out the schedule and looked for their name, Mile High. Interesting name. They sounded lots better then Bay Bridge, the band before them. The band quit just as Van walked in. Van worked the days she and Tommy were off; Van and Tony worked together like she and Tommy.

"Tommy's sick," he told her as he came around the bar. The guys from Mile High walked up and sat down at the bar.

"You guys sounded pretty good. Can I get you a drink?"

The lead singer was the first one to answer. "Shot of JD would be great."

"I'll just have a beer," another one answered. The rest all grabbed a beer and went and sat down at a table just as Mitchell opened for bar business.

"Hey, Vi." It was Todd; she hadn't seen him since the night in the diner.

"How does the competition look?" He asked.

"You guys will blow them all away," she told him with a smile.

"Has Clearwater been in?"

"Yeah, they were here Sunday night, then back to practice Monday."

"They're good, aren't they? I knew when they were in here last year they would get picked up."

Vi laughed. "Sure you did." She gave him a beer and went on down the bar.

"Remember me?"

She turned to find James sitting beside Todd looking at her.

"The drunken fool? Who could forget you?"

"I wasn't drunk," he said sarcastically.

"Yeah, and that's not Todd and you're not in a bar, either."

He smiled. "Ok, so I was a little drunk, but it was your fault."

"How do you figure?" She asked.

"I had to keep ordering drinks so you would talk to me."

"You were drunk when you came up to the bar."

Todd was laughing. "You better not argue with her, she is going to win."

James looked over at him and smiled. "James."

"Todd."

They shook hands. Vi went back down the bar to wait on someone.

"Don't take offense to this, but you don't have a shot with her. She hasn't given any guy the time of day since she's been here."

James laughed. "You weren't here Sunday then, because she left with Brandon. Matter of fact, he has been staying at her place ever since we got here."

Todd looked shocked. "Brandon who?"

"Clearwater."

Todd looked at Vi as she came back down the bar.

"You're sleeping with Brandon Clearwater?"

Vi was taken aback a second by his question. She took a breath.

"Well?"

Todd turned and left the bar and sat down at a table.

James gave her a strange look. "Boyfriend?" He asked, she laughed.

"No, just a friend that wants to be more than friends." She gave Candy a beer to take to Todd from her. She felt bad about hurting him like that, but she had never led him on. He was a great guy who deserved a great girl; she just wasn't it.

The bar was really busy and she stayed busy most of the night. Brandon came back in around midnight. Todd still was sitting over in the corner.

"I'm taking a ten minute break," she told Van as she left the bar area.

"Come on, I want to introduce you to a friend." She grabbed Brandon.

"Todd." She stood behind him. He turned to look at her. "This is Brandon, Brandon this is Todd." Todd stood up, Brandon stuck out his hand.

"Hey, nice to meet you." Todd looked at Vi and shook Brandon's hand.

"His band, Fire Water, will compete next week."

"That's great, I love meeting all the bands. When is your band practicing? I would love to stop by and hear you."

Todd smiled. "We are here tomorrow at four."

"Fire Water . . . You're the band that plays here all the time, aren't you?"

Todd smiled. "Yeah."

"I have heard you guys are pretty good; can't wait to hear you."

Todd smiled at Vi.

"I'll let you guys talk. I have to pee before I get back to the bar." She left them standing and went to the back.

When she came out, Brandon and James were sitting with Todd talking. He would forgive her now, she was pretty sure.

Several bands came in and out. Brandon made sure to talk to them all, but he went back to Todd's table after talking with them every time. The rest of Fire Water came in once while Brandon was talking to another band. Vi was sure Todd had called them all.

Around two, the bar started emptying out. By three, Brandon, James, and Fire Water were the only ones left in the bar.

"You guys want to join us for breakfast at the diner? We all usually go," Todd told Brandon. Brandon looked up at Vi, "You going?"

"Yep."

"Sure, you coming, James?"

"Yeah, I'll go."

Van and Vi cleaned up, as the girls counted up their tips. Candy was still ahead as always. She had pulled in over $700. She loved the bands coming in. Jasmine was even in a better mood and had $550. Vi never counted her tips; she just put them in a large jar when she got home. She really didn't care how much she made.

There were thirteen of them that went. Brandon and Vi sat together along with Todd and Chaz. James sat with Jasmine, Candy and the rest of the band.

"You guys have matching necklaces." Todd noticed.

James leaned over from behind Todd and looked. He gave Brandon a strange look.

James opened his mouth and Brandon got up and grabbed him, "We need to talk." A few minutes later they returned. James didn't say a word, but went back to Jasmine and Candy.

"Everything, ok?" Todd asked.

"Yeah, I needed to clear the air on something before he opened his mouth and inserted his foot."

Vi looked at Brandon; she wondered what he had told him.

The night finished out and James never said a word.

"What did you tell James?" She asked as soon as they got in the car.

"I told him Lindsey had given it back when we split, and I had given it to you."

Vi's phone vibrated, she pulled it from her pocket and looked at the screen. "Something is happening. I found some bone recognition software combing over pictures on the web. I think I have corrupted every picture file of you, but if I have missed one and you're found again, you will be changed by the agency permanently. That will mean our plans will have to be moved back." Vi put her phone back in her pocket and took a deep breath.

"What's wrong?" Brandon asked her.

"Someone is searching the web for me. Keeps thinks he has it under control, but he says be prepared if plans have to be moved back some."

Brandon pulled into the parking garage. "I thought people didn't know who you were."

"People are getting wiser and the software better. It's not good enough to just change your appearance anymore; you have to change your bone structure."

Vi started thinking about how being near him was putting them both in danger. If anyone found two pictures of her that had Brandon in them, but her appearance different, they would know how to find her. Just find Brandon, and know that he was in an upcoming band . . . she shuddered at the thought.

"What?" He said as he opened the door.

"I can't believe," she said as she looked at her phone to make sure it was safe to talk, "that I have put you in this danger. What was I thinking?" She shook her head as they walked up the stairs.

"I hope you were thinking you loved me."

"That is the whole problem. I do love you, and it could easily get you killed," she was half whispering.

"Just stop. I know the risk you take every time you find me. I gladly take the risk."

"You may take the risk, but it's different for me than you. I am trained for risks and what might happen, you're not."

Brandon pulled her into his arms as they got to her door. "Let it go, it's not going to do you any good to beat yourself up about it. It will all be over soon, anyway."

Vi gave a cynical laugh. "No, it won't, the minute we leave the grid it will just be starting. Long nights on the run. It won't matter what I look like, they will always be looking."

Vi pulled out of Brandon's arms. "I am going to shower." She left him standing there. Brandon watched as she unlocked the door and went in.

He went in, sat down on the couch and pulled her laptop into his lap. "Come on, Keeps, I need to talk to you." The screen lit up and Keeps' avatar popped up.

"What's up?"

"How can you ask that. You heard her just now."

"She's just worried about your safety; she would be a fool if she wasn't. And we both know she is no fool."

"She said someone was looking for her."

"Someone is looking for someone. I am not sure if they are looking for her, but someone is definitely looking. I just took a few precautions, just in case. I wanted her to be aware of things, not like last time; if they were to find her with you again . . . . things might not go so well."

"What do you mean?" Brandon asked.

"You were with her when she was found last time, so if she was found again and with you . . . well . . . she might never come back."

"I am going to find my replacement next week; then I can disappear into the background noise."

"It seems an awful shame for you to do that, after all the schooling and stuff."

Brandon shook his head and smiled. "She is so worth it."

The avatar that looked like Lindsey walked out and stood beside Keep's avatar. "I agree with you." The two avatars kissed.

Brandon heard the shower quit. "I'll talk to you later." He put the computer back on the table and got up. The screen went black as he sat it down.

Vi came out of the bathroom as he entered the bedroom. Brandon headed into the bathroom to get his shower. She still looked half upset and he wanted to give her time to settle down. Vi sat down on the bed. Her mind was racing in a million different directions.

Vi got up and went to the computer. Who was looking for her? She started hacking into the network that Keeps computer was linked to. She wanted to know what was going on. It didn't take long to come across the Nutria spyware. It was on every computer on base. She started tracing it; it had a good encryption and was trying to hide. But she was one of the best at finding the unfindable. When she heard the shower quit, she put her search in a folder and let it keep running, but hid it from sight, so Brandon wouldn't see it. She was going to find out what was going on before she was found, or even worse, Brandon was found with her again.

She went back and climbed into bed before he came out of the bathroom. Brandon didn't say a word as he shut off the light and climbed into bed beside her. She slid over and put her head on his shoulder. He rubbed his finger gently across her cheek. Vi put her hand on his chest and slid it up and touched his shoulder. Vi leaned up and looked at him. She hated to knock him out, but she needed time to search and didn't want him in the way. She climbed out of the bed and went back to the computer. She opened her files and started typing some code in. A black box popped up as she typed.

"Someone is searching like I have never seen. It is the most aggressive and I can't catch it."

"It's me," she typed back. Her line of code came to a halt. IP found she had hacked into the computer and kicked on the computer camera. The screen popped up and the camera kicked on. She sat there looking at the screen; it was Keeps' office. But no one was in the office.

"Any luck?" Popped up in the box.

"Where are you?" She asked.

"In my room, why?" The thought of Keeps doing the search or helping them find her came into her mind. But he knew what was going on. He couldn't be doing it. Not unless . . . he didn't know he was.

"Vi, what is it? What did you find?"

"A mole," she typed back, "did you know that Nutria spyware is on your computer in your office?" She typed.

"Yes, I found it two months ago. Someone has it on every computer here and they are monitoring closely."

"Keeps?" She was debating on asking him, or telling him it was all coming from his computer. "What?"

"Watch yourself."

"I will. I am currently wiping this computer, now. I don't want anything found."

Vi smiled; she knew it couldn't be him.

He had been couriering lately. They must use his computer then. The window disappeared. Vi put two encryption codes on her computer and set up a link to the Nutria system that kicked the camera on and recorded the whole session of the mole using Keeps' computer. Vi closed the computer. Her alarm would be going off in three hours. She climbed into bed and fell asleep in Brandon's arms.

The alarm sounded like a screaming siren. Vi was so tired. She was still lying on Brandon's chest.

"Morning," Brandon said.

"Man, I feel like I haven't slept at all," Vi told him.

Brandon climbed out of the bed and headed to the bathroom. Vi got up and opened the laptop, but closed it back when she heard the bathroom door open.

"I better get dressed and get to the bar before the band beats me," Vi told Brandon, as she passed him going into the bathroom.

"Todd said his band is practicing at four. If you don't care, I am going to do bar hopping until then."

"If you drop me off, you can have the car."

He smiled at her. "That would be great."

She must be feeling better this morning, Brandon thought to himself as he got dressed. They grabbed a muffin and a cappuccino on their way to the bar. He dropped her off at 1:30 and headed to one of the other four bars to listen to some other practices.

Vi opened the door and went in. Her mind was still going crazy with thoughts about Keeps' computer. She walked up and got out her guitar. Music flowed as the thoughts of maybe moving on and getting away from Brandon filled her mind. She could not take a chance on someone finding them together again. She knew what she had to do. Brandon was not going to like it, but safety was the highest priority—his safety. Keeps' safety, too; she needed to see him in person.

"You're good." Brought Vi out of her trance.

She opened her eyes to find five girls standing in front of her.

"We are here to practice," the tall blonde told her.

Vi got up and put her guitar away. "I'm Vi, if you need anything just let me know."

"How about another lead guitar?" One of the girls said.

Vi smiled and walked back towards the bar. Vi got out her band schedule; Fast Cars was the name of the band on the schedule for practice. Where did they come up with these names? Vi laughed to herself.

The girls got hooked up and started practicing. They weren't bad, but she knew they didn't stand a chance. The music was like their name; fast, but it had no meat. The bass player was having all kinds of trouble. She seemed a little out of place, too. The other girls looked hard core grunge, but the bass player was different. She had an elegant grace to her that was really out of place.

Vi walked back to the front to hear a little of the conversation going on.

"You know, I am not much good at this and this is making me extremely nervous," the bassist was telling the singer.

"Come on, Kay, you're good at bass, you can do this."

Vi watched the bassist as she played. She knew what was wrong. They stopped the song half way through, again.

"Kay, you're killing us."

Kay looked up as Vi walked up beside her.

"Why are you playing this? You're a cellist, aren't you?"

The girl smiled. "Yes."

"Then, play it here. Do you have it with you?"

"I always have it." She smiled at Vi.

The blonde came up behind Vi. "What are you doing?"

"You want to be good, don't you? Then, let her play the cello." The girl looked at Vi and Kay got up and went out.

"We need an electric bass, not an upright."

"Why?" Vi asked her. "If she is half as good as I think she is, you can blow half these bands out of the water. But you're not going to with how you're playing now." Kay came back in with a very impressive cello. Vi went and got a mic and hooked it up and sat it in front of Kay.

"Now try the song."

The song sounded so much better. "Much better," Vi told them.

"It was better," the blonde said.

Vi looked at Kay. "Don't hold back, let it fly; you're better than what you're playing."

By the third song, Kay was adding in and filling up all the empty space. She had given the band an edge.

Vi walked back up and sat at the bar and listened. Brandon came in around 3:30.

"They're not bad."

"Nope, not bad at all." She smiled at him.

"Love the cello in the mix," he added.

By 2:45 the girls had put away their instruments and got ready to leave.

"Thanks for the help." Kay came up to the bar.

"No problem."

Kay looked at Brandon. "Aren't you Brandon Clearwater?" She asked. He stood and stuck out his hand.

"That's me."

"Hey, Jonnie," she yelled over her shoulder.

The blonde looked up as she was carrying her case towards the door. She sat it down by the door and walked over. "You were right, it is him."

Brandon smiled. "Jonnie Thompson." She stuck out her hand.

"Nice to meet you ladies," he told them. "You guys sounded really good, the cello in the mix is great."

Vi smiled at Kay and Jonnie. They both smiled back at her.

"It's four, can we come in?" Todd yelled from the door.

"Come on," Vi yelled back.

"You guys need to head out, so the other band can come in," Vi told Jonnie.

"I look forward to hearing you play again," Brandon told them as they left.

"Hey, Vi," Todd said as he walked by the bar.

"Hey, Todd."

"Can I help you guys set up?" Brandon asked.

"Sure." One of the guys handed him a case and headed back out for another.

Brandon headed towards the stage.

Todd set his guitar down on stage and walked back to the bar. Vi could see the hurt and questions in his eyes, as he stopped in front of her.

"Why not me?" He asked.

Vi couldn't tell him the truth, but she hated that she had hurt him.

"I wish I had a good answer for you, Todd, but I don't. I'm sorry." Vi walked around the bar and stood face to face with Todd.

"We're ready," Chaz yelled.

Vi reached for Todd's arm, but he turned and left her standing there. Crap, introducing him to Brandon hadn't helped after all.

"What was that about?" Brandon came up beside her. Vi looked up.

"Were you going out with Todd?"

Vi sat down on one of the bar stools. "No."

"He wanted more?" Brandon questioned.

"Yeah." Vi smiled.

"And then I met you one day and am staying at your place?"

"Yeah."

"Sorry, if I screwed up a friendship."

Vi's phone vibrated in her pocket. "Another mission is pending; I left Intel on your computer." Vi put the phone back in her pocket; she noticed the blue light on.

"Anything wrong?" Brandon asked; he had noticed the light, too.

"My cousin Greg is in jail again. My aunt Joan wants money to bail him out."

Brandon laughed. "Shame we can't choose our family."

"I hear you," she told him. He tilted his head as if to ask if anything was wrong. Vi shook her head no.

"Hey, man." Mitchell came in.

"Hey, Mitch, would you care if I ran home and grabbed something, since you're here?" Vi asked before Brandon had a chance to ask what was wrong. "No, go ahead."

"Thanks, I will be back by six." Brandon put her keys on the bar so she didn't have to ask for them. Vi grabbed them and left.

"Todd and them are sounding pretty good," Vi heard Mitchell saying as she went out the door.

Keeps is a little more casual when he talks, something must be up, Vi thought, as she headed for home.

She ran up the stairs and opened the door. Keeps was standing there. She pulled out her phone; the light was off. Something was wrong.

"What are you doing here?" She played it safe.

"I have been sent with some Intel; something that could not be sent over the line." Yes, something definitely was wrong; Keeps would have said web.

"Alright, what is it?" He held out a large envelope, she took it. Inside was a disk and player. Keeps just stood there.

"Anything else?" Vi asked.

"I need your answer," he said.

"I have to get back to work; I will listen to it when I get home. Come back tomorrow at noon and I will give you what you need."

"You need to listen to it now and give me an answer now," Keeps insisted, but Vi knew better.

She knew they used these devices to get into your mind without you knowing. She had used it before and hypnotized a guy for info.

She would need a brainal beat implant before she could listen to it without it affecting her.

"I have no time, now. I will give you your answer tomorrow." Vi put the device in her purse and left the apartment. Where was she going to find an implant?

She unlocked the car door and got in. She drove back to the bar rather slowly. What was going on and where was Keeps? That was not him! Vi walked in and went to put her purse under the bar. A small package lay on top. Her name was written on it. She opened it. Three small things like hearing aids fell out in her hand; a note was also in it.

"You will have to tune them. I am couriering again. Something is not right. Layover, two a.m."

The note was signed, Seth. Crap, she needed to find him and wipe him clean before they got to him. They were getting him out of his office to use his equipment. And if they couldn't find it on their own they would use him, without his permission.

"You ok?" Brandon came up to the bar.

"Yeah, just have a headache."

"Did you take anything?" Brandon asked her.

"No."

She pulled a napkin from behind the bar and a pen. "Have to go check on something later; go home with the guys tonight. I am going to be sick!" She slid the note across to him.

He reached for the pen, "What's happening?"

"I don't know," she wrote back, "but I am going to find out."

"Be careful," were the last words he wrote. She smiled up at him. Vi tucked the note in her pocket as Mitch and Todd approached the bar.

"You got any Tylenol in your office?" Vi asked Mitch.

"Sure, it's in the top left hand drawer of my desk."

"Do you care if I get some? I have a killer headache."

"No, go ahead."

Vi went to Mitch's office and took two Tylenol. Next she stop was the bathroom. She flushed the note and headed back out front for a bottle of water. She made sure they all saw her take the pills.

"You ok?" Todd asked.

Vi was good at playing roles and playing sick was no big problem. "Yeah, I'm fine."

"You don't looks so good."

"It's just this headache. I'll be fine once the meds kick in."

The bar opened on schedule and Vi waited the bar. Several people made a comment about her not looking well. She told each of them about her headache and went on working. By nine she acted as if she was getting dizzy and took a break and went and lay down on the couch in Mitch's office for about ten minutes. Mitch, of course, came and checked on her. Brandon, however, didn't.

"I'll call Van; why don't you go home and get some rest? You look like crap," said Mitch.

"Are you sure?" She asked.

"Yes, go home; we don't need sick customers."

Vi finally agreed and left the bar.

As soon as she got to the apartment she set the brainal beat implants and listened to the disk. Of course, the Intel on a mission was all she heard, but she also hooked up a listening device and pulled apart the code, so she could see what was hidden underneath the normal stuff. She had been right about the hypnosis. They were looking into her brain and wanted to see if she was hiding anything. She had been instructed to answer all the questions in hypnosis, upon hearing the words *'Introducing Intelligence'*. She was sure that the man would return, upon her being sick, to question her. She was hoping it would not take long and she could meet Keeps.

She didn't have to wait long before there was a knock on her door.

"Did you listen to the disk?"

"Yes, but it will take me a day or two to go over all the Intel and get the findings back. I can't do it instantly," she told him.

"They told me Introducing Intelligence to you was very gratifying," the man said with a little smirk on the end of the sentence; she should immediately go into hypnosis on hearing the two words. "Why are you here?" He asked her.

"Rest and recovery," she answered.

"Why did you choose Nashville?"

Crap, she had to answer honestly; a slip up and she would be in trouble. "The Keeper suggested the music festival here."

"Why?" He asked.

"Because, I love music."

"Any other reason?"

"No."

"Are you involved with the Keeper?"

"We are friends."

"You're not sleeping with him?"

"Yes, I have once."

"You were instructed to keep your virginity intact."

"It is."

"You said you slept with The Keeper."

"Yes, I did sleep with him."

"Explain yourself." The man was pacing in front of Vi.

"I slept beside him in his bed."

"No sex?"

"No."

"What is your agenda here in Nashville?"

"To enjoy myself until I'm called back into service."

The man walked back to the spot where he had been standing before he started questioning her, "Introducing Intelligence was going to get results."

"I am not a miracle worker that can just wave my hands and have it, you know this, Keeps?"

"Sorry," he said, "this one is important to them." The man relaxed as if he was really playing a friend part now.

"Give me a few days; I will let you know when I have it ready."

"Ok." The man left.

It was going on midnight. Vi opened her Nutria file, the camera was activated. She opened the screen. Black, no picture, they had covered the camera. Very cautious of them! Vi turned on a ghost system on her computer. It made anyone looking think she was working, but she had it set with a recording if the camera was activated it went to a video of her sitting there working. She was more clever than the person on the Nutria system. If they had been smart, they would have taken video of Keeps sitting there working.

She washed and put her hair up and put on normal looking clothes, then carefully made her escape. She left her phone behind because of the GPS, but took a back up that Keeps had given her, in case she needed to be untraceable, but still be in touch. She also used the small pen device on her neck and left it lying by the computer. Just like what she had used in LA so if they turned on her tracker it would appear she was in her apartment.

The minute she turned the phone on, a message popped up; platform 32. She headed for the train station. She arrived at 1:30 and waited. Two a.m. and a train arrived on the platform. Five people got off, one was Keeps. He made his way to a local hotel and checked in for the night.

The radio was playing and the shower was on when Vi slipped into the room. She opened the bathroom door and went in. He was waiting for her.

"You ok?" She asked.

"Something is going on at base."

"I know," she told him, "I need to wipe you."

He looked up at her. "I know."

"You're not going to fight me?"

"No. I don't want anything to happen to you or Brandon. This is the only way I know how."

Vi dropped the toilet lid. "Have a seat."

He looked up and started to sit.

"Wait." She pulled him toward her, put her lips to his. He kissed her back with a passion she had never felt from him. He finally broke the kiss and sat down.

"Relax," she told him, she touched his shoulders and gently rubbed his neck.

"I need for you to think of the first day we met. Do you remember?"

"Yes," he said.

"Tell me about it."

"You had just come off from Mission and the Handler brought you in my office. I remember thinking you were one hot looking woman. I told you to call me Keeps and then I asked you for your number. You told me you were 23." Vi listened as he talked. She let him tell her all he knew about her. She altered the story in places. She left their friendship intact, but took away anything to do with Brandon, the knowledge that he knew, what she did and all of the conversations they had had. Anything that could lead anyone to knowledge of Brandon and her true relationship was gone. She then told him to stand. She stripped him down and put him in the shower with instructions to wake in ten minutes on the sound of the alarm she had set on his watch. She then went out of the room, went through his computer and wiped the last of his connections to her; other than what should be there. She slipped out just as she heard his alarm go off.

Vi got back to her apartment and set the ghost to where she would get up and leave the computer. Vi headed for the shower, then went back and worked on Intel till about five am, then lay down for some sleep. But it didn't come; she needed to wipe Brandon. But their lives were so intermingled she would need a full night to sort through all his memories. She was still lying there awake going over the things she needed to change when her alarm went off.

She should have wiped Brandon before Keeps, but it couldn't wait; now getting Brandon done without Keeps' suspicion was going to be a little hard. Vi got dressed and headed out; she needed to pick up a couple disposable phones so she could text Brandon and let him know what was going on, without letting Keeps know. Twenty minutes later she had two phones set up and was on her way to where Brandon and the band were staying. She turned the radio up in the car and rolled the windows down and let the wind blow her hair. She was hoping to have it loud enough they would look out the window without her having to go in. Brandon pulled back the curtain when she pulled up. Vi turned the radio down and waited. He came out in a pair of shorts, no shirt.

"Hey," he said as he leaned over on the car, "looks like you're feeling better." Vi handed him the phone and put her fingers to her lips to let him know not to say anything about it.

"Yeah, I am. I just wondered if you wanted to get some breakfast."

Brandon smiled. "Love to, just let me get dressed." Brandon turned and headed back to the hotel.

Vi began to texting him. "I wish we could talk, but things have changed. My brother Seth has had a bad brain injury and can't remember anything. I will have to go see him very soon." Vi hoped he got the picture correctly.

"Is Seth ok?" She got back.

"Yes, he is fine."

"Are you really feeling better?"

"Not really," she wrote back.

"What can I do?"

"I will let you know soon. You are not going to like it, but it is the only way at this point and must be done."

"That does not sound good," he sent back.

"It's not, now hurry up."

Brandon came out in five minutes.

"There is an IHOP over on 5th. You up for it?"

"Sure," Brandon said, "sounds great, I'm starving."

"Oh yeah, Mitch had to serve drinks last night. He never could get a in touch with Van."

"Oh, great; was he mad?"

"Actually, I think he liked it," Brandon told her.

Vi pulled in to IHOP and they got a booth. Brandon watched and listened for leads from Vi. But she kept things just simple and basic. The one thing he had noticed was that she wasn't wearing her necklace. He wondered what was really going on. What had she meant about Keeps not remembering things? And that things had to change, and the part about him not liking it. Something had happened yesterday when she got that text that sent her running home and then the pretending to be sick.

"Brandon?" Vi shook his arm. "Where are you?"

He looked up and smiled. "Sorry, I was thinking."

"About what?" She asked.

"This band competition is going to be hard to judge. I have heard some really great bands."

"I agree with you," Vi told him

"Todd's band really rocks, and that girl band I heard could really play."

"Glad I am not judging."

"Have you heard that band with the little freaky dude that can really sing?"

"You mean the guy with the horns?" Vi asked.

"Yeah."

Vi laughed. "No, but I have heard several people talking about him."

They finished breakfast as they talked. Brandon pulled his cell from his pocket when it rang. "The guys are heading out; they will meet me at Jose's," he told her.

Vi dropped Brandon off at Jose's then headed towards the Wild Mustang.

Mitch was opening the door as she pulled up. "I was wondering if you were going to make it in today," he told her as he held the door open for her.

"Sorry, I didn't call," she told him as they walked in.

"It's fine, I came on in just in case." Mitch headed back to his office and Vi wiped down the bar as she waited for the bands to come and practice.

Vi sat down as the band cranked up and started playing. She pulled out her regular phone and started typing Keeps, "I think I need to leave. I don't want to take a chance of either one of those guys recognizing me. Maybe it's time for Bethany Cline to make an appearance."

"Who?" Keeps text back.

"Oh, yeah, I forgot that was before you. Take a look back at my file. I did a couple of missions with some special OP's out of Cherry Point."

"I remember reading you did, but I didn't catch the name you were under. I'll see what I can do. Can you handle 24 hours more?" Vi smiled; that would be perfect.

"That's fine." Vi put one phone in her pocket, and got out the other.

"Four, here, we need to talk." She hit send. Before she could set it down, it vibrated. "I'll be there."

She put the phone back in her other pocket and sat pretending to listen to the band. But in her head she was making plans on how to get Brandon alone, without someone saying something about her absence.

Brandon came in before four and sat down beside her without saying a word. He just touched her arm, to let her know he was there.

She picked up a pen and wrote "Private bathroom, now!"

He didn't say a word, but got up and went to the back. Vi walked to the office and stuck her head in.

"Hey, I am heading to the restroom, my stomach is doing flips."

"Ok, I will go out front in a minute. Are you sure you should even be here?"

"I'll be fine, thanks."

Vi pulled the phone out and took it to the bar and sat it behind her purse. That way you could still hear the music, but it was muffled like she was really in the restroom. She then went back to the private bathroom behind the bar.

Brandon was standing behind the door.

"Hey." She was pulled into his arms.

"What's going on?" He asked her.

"I am not sure, but I think there is a mole on base. I saw Keeps last night and wiped him."

"You did what to Keeps?"

"I altered his memory; well, it is a little more complicated than that. He remembers you and me, but not talking to you and not that I told you what I do. And he doesn't remember you and him working together to get us out, or that I snuck off to see you when you graduated, or that he knew you would be here this summer and that's why he sent me here on purpose."

"Why did you alter Keeps?"

"Listen, I don't have time to explain all this." Vi looked up at Brandon. "I need to alter you."

Brandon pulled out of her arms. "What?"

"Listen, Brandon."

"No," he said.

"Brandon, just hear me out. I don't do this by choice, but there is no other way. Someone is tracking me and watching my every move. I have to take you out of the equation until I find out who is behind this. And altering your memory is the only way."

"Did Keeps agree to this?"

"He asked me to; he didn't want to be questioned under hypnosis and let something slip."

Brandon looked at Vi. "I don't want to forget you."

"You won't; you will remember everything except what I do and Keeps. You will also believe that when I left at Christmas that you haven't heard from me again. And you won't know that Vi is me. You will just know that we have become good friends." Brandon shook his head. "I promise that as soon as I can, I will return and return your memories. Oh yeah, one more thing: you don't know about the business. But, I will make sure you have plenty of money, if I see you getting low."

Brandon let a tear fall down his cheek. "Are you sure there is no other way?"

Vi pulled back up into Brandon's arms. "If there was another way I would do it, but with what is going on, there isn't."

Brandon pulled her up and kissed her. "I love you."

"I love you, too, and I promise to come back for you." Vi looked down at her watch they had already been in there ten minutes. "Stay here. I am going to run out front and then be right back."

He stepped back and let her go. Tears were running down his cheeks.

It shook Vi visibly, and she had to steady herself before she went out.

"Sorry," he said.

"No, I am the one that is sorry that I have to do this." She opened the door and went out. She walked to the bar where Mitch was sitting.

"You any better?"

She stood there a second or two, made a funny face and then took off back to the bathroom, as if she was getting sick again.

Brandon watched her leave the bathroom. His heart hurt. How could this be happening? He was going to leave the band and spend the rest of his life with her; now things were going so wrong. He wasn't even going to remember that. What if she never came back? No, he told himself; don't think like that, she has always come back. Not as Lindsey, but she always had returned. And she will again.

She opened the door and came back in. "Mitch thinks I am extremely sick." She smiled up at Brandon. "I really need to do this so you can pick up like nothing happened in the bathroom; with no one knowing you're here is ideal. I am going to go home again sick. I will let you out the back, and you can come in as I go out. Talk to Mitch a while, then come to my place; don't knock, I will leave it unlocked. Come in quietly, don't say a word. Got it? I have told Keeps I need to leave before you and James figure out who I am, so I only have a couple of hours left."

Brandon grabbed her up in his arms. "I don't ..." he started, but the tears were choking him.

"I know, I don't want you to forget me either, but it's the only way to keep you safe for now." They stood there just holding each other.

"We need to go." She stepped back as a tear fell from her cheek. He wiped it off. She stuck her head out and took a look. "Come on." She took him to the back door and let him out. She went back to the bathroom and put water on her face then wiped it off, which smeared her makeup. She looked in the mirror; that would do it.

She walked out front; Brandon had already come in and was talking to Mitch.

"You look like crap," Brandon told her as she walked up.

"Just go home, Vi," Mitch said, "don't come close to me, I don't want to be sick."

Vi walked to the bar and got her purse and phone. "Sorry, Mitch."

"Just go home and get well."

Vi left without another word.

Vi went straight in and turned on the TV. The phone vibrated from her pocket. "Playing hooky?"

"Yep, trying to keep everyone safe."

"Handler will pick you up tomorrow at noon."

"Thanks, man, you're the best."

"Yeah, yeah, so you're always telling me. Bethany will be heading out on a few missions in a week."

Vi sent a smile back.

"So what are you planning now that you're home for the night?"

Perfect, Vi thought. "A long hot bath and maybe a little guitar. Probably leave the TV on so people will think I have company, so I will most likely use my headphones."

"Yeah. You better take a long hot one, cause once Bethany's back you know there will be no chances for that for a while."

Brandon opened the door and came in as she was texting. He sat down quietly. She got up and headed for the bathroom and motioned him to follow. She turned the water on in the tub. Then pushed him to the wall and started kissing him.

"I am going to miss this."

She looked up at him. "No, you won't." She smiled at him.

"So how does this work?" He asked.

"Well, I will have to go back through all your memories of me and change them a little. Then, because you're here I will have to make you go out and the knocking on the door will wake you. You will be coming to check on me after seeing me so sick at the bar."

He shook his head. "I guess that will do."

"Brandon." She dropped the toilet lid, "Have a seat."

He sat down and looked up at her.

"I love you." She wrapped her arms around his head and hugged him and gave him one last kiss.

She pulled back till her hands were on his neck.

"I love you; never forget that." She smiled as tears started falling. "Relax and tell me about how we met."

He took a deep breath.

"Jacob brought you home. He picked you up at the airport and had to pick me up before returning to the park, so you stopped at the house for the night." Vi rubbed up his neck and started touching each point. She could picture every word he said. The night was long as she went through every memory of them, changing little details and adding a few things that would make other things make sense. She learned of all the plans he and Keeps had made from his point of view; she had already heard Keeps' view of it.

She gave him more strength in his will to stay pure till marriage. It was about two in the morning when she finally finished with him. She had to make up for the lost time he would have, so she would need to alter a few clocks and stuff and let him fall asleep in her apartment so when he woke, the time would be right.

She left him sitting in the bathroom while she changed times and closed curtains. Then she instructed him to go out in the hall and knock on the door and at the third knock awaken. And upon hearing the words *you look tired*, the need for a nap will take over. She would remove that when he passed out. She led him to the door and looked out. The hall was empty; she stood him in front of the door. She closed the door and knocked three times on it.

"Just a second," she called. "Brandon," she said when she got the door open.

"I just wanted to come and check on you. You looked horrible at the bar."

"Come on in." She opened the door and let him in.

"I won't stay long, I just wanted to check on you."

"At least talk to me a while. It is quite lonely being here two nights alone." Brandon sat down on the couch. "I may be sick, but you look tired."

Brandon yawned, "I am, all this band stuff has me worn out." He yawned again. "Sorry."

"Don't be, why don't you stretch out and take a quickie?"

Brandon laughed. "You don't know how tempting that is."

"Well?"

"It won't bother you?"

"No, go for it." Brandon stretched out and fell asleep. Vi walked over and touched his neck and leaned over and whispered a release in his ear. She also knocked him out with another touch. He should be out till morning or later in the morning. Vi leaned over and kissed him; changed all the clocks back and then went and climbed into bed.

Vi opened her eyes to someone knocking on the door. She climbed out of bed.

"Crap," Brandon said, "What time is it?" She heard him say as she came out of the bedroom.

"I'm coming," she said as the knock came again. Brandon walked back towards the bathroom as Vi opened the door. James was standing there.

"Sorry, to bother you, but have you seen Brandon? We can't find him and he is not answering his phone."

Vi opened the door.

"Come on in, he is here. He fell asleep on the couch last night and I didn't have the heart to wake him." Brandon came out of the bedroom.

"James," he said.

"Why is it that the singer gets all the chicks?"

Vi laughed.

He looked at Vi. "Why didn't you wake me?"

"You looked so peaceful that I didn't have the heart to wake you."

"Don't tell me you are still holding on to it?" James said.

"What?" Brandon asked.

"You still hanging on to your vow?"

Brandon laughed. "It may be silly to you, but is not to me."

Vi smiled. "It is nice to meet a guy with values."

"And here everyone thought you had finally given in," James said.

"You should know me better than that, James."

"We have been trying to get you all night."

Brandon pulled out his phone. "Sorry, I must have hit silent. What's up?"

"Mike wanted to meet with us last night."

"Crap," Brandon said.

"We got him to put it off till one today, so come on, we need to get moving."

Vi looked at the clock, it was already eleven. She was being picked up at noon.

"See you later, thanks for letting me crash, yet once again." He smiled at Vi. She walked into his arms and gave him a hug.

"Anything to let rumors fly." She had to laugh or she might just break down in tears.

"See you later."

As soon as they left, she got dressed and threw her clothes in a bag. Then she grabbed a pen and paper, wrote a couple of notes, put them in envelopes, then she grabbed her bag and headed out the door. She needed to do something with her car; the rest really didn't matter. She also needed to give Mitch an excuse. She jumped in the car and headed for Todd's. He opened the door before she knocked.

"I thought that sounded like your car."

"Can I ask you a big favor?"

"Come on in."

She walked past him onto his apartment.

"What is it?"

"I have to head home to Vegas; my cousin has gotten himself into some major trouble. Anyway, I wondered if you would take care of her for me?" Vi held out her keys. "Drive her; park her, just whatever, till I get back."

He smiled. "Sure." He took the keys from her. "I would love to drive that sweet little thing around."

"One other thing." She handed him an envelope.

"Would you give this to Tommy for me?"

"Sure, anything else?"

She smiled. "No, that's it." She stepped in and gave Todd a hug. "Thanks. I've got to run." She kissed him to seal the deal and she knew she at least owed him that. Todd smiled when their lips parted and Vi smiled back. Then she headed down the path as a black hummer pulled up and she got in.

Handler never changed; same dark suit and glasses, never a smile, he was just all business. "I have one last call to make, so be quiet," she told him. As if he was going to talk. She got out her phone and called Mitch.

"Hello."

"Hey, Mitch."

"Vi, you feeling any better?"

"Sort of, but that's not why I am calling."

"What's wrong?"

"I hate to do this to you, but I got a call from my aunt this morning and I have to go to Vegas."

"What?" Mitch said. Vi could hear the aggravation in his voice.

"I am sorry, man, I have to go; she is all the family I have left and her son has gotten himself into some major trouble."

"I can't hold your job," he said angrily.

"I don't expect you to. I am on my way to the airport now, so I left Todd with a note to give Tommy; the keys are in the note." She had put one in there for Brandon, too, but he didn't need to know that.

"Fine."

"I am so sorry, Mitch."

"Yeah, yeah, whatever," he said and he hung up on her.

Vi smiled. "You know, he wasn't very happy with me," she told Handler, who, of course didn't say a word. Vi sat quietly and went over the note to Brandon in her head just to make sure she hadn't said anything she wasn't supposed to. Like it would matter now that she was gone.

> *Brandon, I had to go out of town. My Aunt called and needs me. Here is the key to my apartment; you are welcome to stay there. Just leave the key on the table and lock the door when you leave. It was great to meet you and I hope we cross paths again one day. I wish you and the band success. Love, Vi*

CHAPTER 12
A New Old Life

BACK IN HER room five minutes and she wanted to leave. The stark white walls and silence was murder. She missed Brandon fiercely and not being able to talk to Keeps about it was going to be hard. She paced her room and finally got a shower and lay down on the bed. Sleep would not come; she felt hollow inside and all alone.

The clock read three am, as she closed the door behind her, went down to Keeps' office and to his room. She tapped quietly on the door. He opened it, and just like before he was still asleep. She giggled as she climbed in the bed beside him and laid her head on his shoulder. She slid up against him; his chest had filled out a little, she noticed. Her eyes started getting heavy and she slipped off into slumber.

"Why am I not surprised to find you in my bed?"

She awoke when Keeps had let out a loud sigh. She smiled as she sat up and pulled the cover from him.

"You've been working out?" She rubbed her finger across his chest. His body reacted instantly, and there was no hiding it in his boxers.

"Just stop right there." He took hold of her hand, "Go back to your room before you get us into trouble."

"I thought you liked me here." She smiled and looked down.

He grabbed the cover and pulled it over himself.

"You are going to drive me crazy. I try to keep you safe and you put us both in danger."

She got up slowly and walked to the door.

"Sorry, Keeps, I don't mean to." And then she left.

The next morning, she was back in his office.

"The team I have you with will be heading out tomorrow morning. Their communications expert got sick and you're the replacement," Keeps told her as she sat looking at him, "Ok. What is up with you? You have been looking at me strangely ever since you got back." He stopped typing and looked up at her.

"I've just been thinking." She tried to play off the sadness that had been trying to consume her for the last three days she had been back. "Why I got all that Intel, if they are not going to let me do the job? I am ready to go."

Keeps laughed.

"Is that what's been bothering you?"

Bethany smiled. "I don't like knowing what needs to be done, and having to sit on my hands and not do it."

"Well, maybe this will get your mind off it for a day or two. You will need to be at Cherry Point at six am. Your flight is leaving at six tonight." Keeps went back to typing. "I will have your dog tags and uniforms here by four so come back, then."

Bethany got up and walked back towards the door.

"Hey, Keeps."

He looked up. "Yeah?"

"Could you check and see how the band competition is going?"

He laughed. "Grab a chair and check it yourself." He motioned towards his other computer.

Bethany pulled her chair around and sat down in front of the screen and began typing.

"So, how's it going? Any band you liked winning?" Keeps asked as she read an article by Chuck Haslow.

"Looks like Fire Water is doing well, and Fast Cars, too. They have a cellist in their band," she told him.

"Oh, yeah, that band you helped where that girl was trying to play bass and sucked."

Bethany laughed. "Yep, that is the one." Keeps took notes and followed her very well.

"So, are you hoping Todd and Fire Water wins?" He asked.

"Yeah, they are a great band."

"They were better when you did the singing."

Bethany smiled. "Thanks," She got up and moved the chair back.

"I sent you the specs of the mission to your computer. Just remember, you're not the lead so . . ."

"Yeah, yeah," she said as she left the room.

This would give Bethany a chance to do more snooping. She opened her laptop and opened the file Keeps sent her. Then she moved ever so slightly to the left, so the camera over her left shoulder that she had discovered the second night back, could not see the small box she opened at the bottom of the screen. She again worked on the Nutria file. She had worked on it twice since being back. She was limited to the few times she could get on her computer.

Bethany first went over the page she was supposed to be looking at; then she went to work breaking into the file that all the Nutria information was filtering into. It was one of the best encryptions she had come across, but she was sure she could break it; it would just take some time. Two hours later she got up from the computer and stretched. She had made it through another block, but there were five more in place. The mission she was going on tomorrow was a simple smash and grab. So, her sitting at the computer any longer would raise too much suspicion and the two hours was a little long.

The afternoon crawled by. She went and took a long lunch then came back, played with her guitar, did a few crunches and pushups. Finally she went back to Keeps' office.

"This waiting game is for the birds," she said as she dropped down in the chair in front of his desk.

"Did you go over the Intel I sent you?"

"Yes, and they are really going about it the wrong way." She stuck up her hand before Keeps could say a word. "But I know I am not the lead, so whatever."

He smiled. "Just play a good little soldier. You just remember this was your idea. I could have just moved you to a different place."

"I know," she told him, "I guess I just didn't want to take another chance on seeing someone I knew again."

Keeps smiled. "Sorry about that; I really had no idea that Brandon's band was going to be there. I guess from now on I better do a little up keep on people you have met, before I let you back in the real world."

"I am just glad I had made a drastic change to my appearance or he might have recognized me."

"It didn't help that you made friends with him immediately."

"Yeah, I know, but I wanted to know how he had been."

A man in a black uniform came in with a box, set it on the floor, then left without a word.

"See if that is your uniforms." Keeps opened his desk and pulled out a box cutter and handed it to her. Bethany opened the box and handed the knife back to him.

"Well, let's see," she said as she pulled out three pairs of camo's and two pair of boots, a sea bag, a radio, maps, dog tags and a field knife. "Nice," she said as she pulled the knife from the sheath.

"Go make sure they fit." He got up and opened the door to his room.

335

Bethany grabbed one set of camo's and a pair of boots, went in and closed the door. A few minutes later she emerged fully dressed.

"Well, do I look gung ho?"

He turned his chair to look at her.

"You look just like any other soldier," he told her.

She saluted him. "Thank you, sir."

Keeps smiled. "Go pack your gear and get ready."

"I want to mark a few things on the map from the Intel I have, then I will." Bethany picked up the box and headed back to her room.

"Bethany 'Wildcat' Cline."

A large black man stood up as she entered the ready room to meet the rest of her team. Anthony "Tiger" Fergus; she would know him anywhere. He had been on her first OP's mission years ago.

"Tiger, you're still here. I thought you would have retired by now, old man." Tiger grabbed her and gave her a bear hug and they both laughed.

"If you two don't mind, we need to go over some things," a tall well built man said.

"Sorry, Sergeant." Tiger pulled up a chair for Bethany and sat down beside her.

"This is Mac, Bull, Fargo and Steele," Tiger told her.

There was a map lying on the table. "Cline, I need you here; you are our eyes and ears," the man Tiger called sergeant told her, the tag on his uniform read Steele. "Mac, you and Fargo will have the left and right perimeter, and Bull you're on the wall." Bethany looked over their map. The plan was ok, but there were too many unnecessary risks she thought. "We leave in an hour," Steele gathered up the map and handed it to Bethany. "You better be good; I don't like my team being changed at the last minute." Steele walked out the door followed by Mac. Fargo and Bull were looking Bethany over.

"Tiny little thing."

Tiger laughed. "Don't let her size fool you."

Bethany smiled at Tiger. The mission she and Tiger had been on was her first mission as an adult; she had many before that, but she always went in as a child. But since it was her first adult one, they set her up on a trial just to see if she could take the heat and hold her own. She had passed with flying colors. She had never worked with anyone after that again.

"They must still have you buried in Coverts."

"The best of us are, you know."

Mac didn't seem to like that answer. "Or out of sight and mind in case you screw up anything."

Bull nodded his head in agreement.

"She doesn't even have a side arm issued her."

Tiger smiled. "If I remember correctly, and I do, she doesn't need one." Tiger got up from the table, "Come on, Wildcat, everyone needs to be packing in case." Bethany got up and followed Tiger from the room.

"They a good team?" Bethany asked Tiger as they headed for the armory.

"Yeah, been with Bull and Mac for four years; Fargo and Steele for two."

Bethany picked up a side arm and a sniper. "Always better to have two just in case," she told him.

"Tell that to Bull, he won't like it." Bull had been assigned the wall which meant he was the sniper.

"So when have I ever cared? But I will keep it in my bag unless I need it." She winked at him.

"Smart move."

The team dropped in ten miles out and had to hike in. Bethany had the ridge that was a mile out. Bull would get in closer for better sniping. Bethany set up as the team went on farther. As she set up she kept getting that feeling; the same feeling she got when something was wrong. She set up and checked all the Intel she had as fast as she could; she did not want her team walking into a trap. She had satellite access and checked all the guards' heat signature. They were where they were supposed to be. But the feeling still loomed over her. She got out her binoculars and went over the area to look for anything out of place.

"In place." Bull was the first to check in.

"In," Fargo's voice came across the radio.

"Check," Mac's voice was next. Bethany checked on each of the spots as they checked in.

"Alright," Steele came across.

"Ready," said Tiger.

Bethany could not get the feeling to go away, and she checked and double checked everything. Her gut had never been wrong.

"Are we a go?" Steele's voice crackled on the radio.

"We are a go," Bethany answered back.

The feeling kept her looking and checking all perimeters and scopes. A small noise behind her caught her attention; she looked at her monitor. There was no heat signature behind her.

Bethany closed her eyes, sometimes they could be unreliable. She sat still listening, but looked like she was watching the monitor. The feeling she had was growing; it was almost at a point she wanted to scream.

She turned and reached up into the air, her hand caught on something and she took it to the ground with her knife poised to kill. She couldn't see anything, but could feel a heartbeat in the neck she held. Bethany felt around and found a hood; she pulled it up enough to find The Handler staring at her. She didn't remove the hood, just lifted it enough to see who was under it, then she put it back down, but did not release him.

The Handler wrote in the dirt beside them: *Mole, looking, Maker, all agents, surveillance.* She understood that they knew someone was looking for her, and that all agents were under surveillance.

Only four people knew her identity: The Keeper, The Handler, The Professor, and The King. Handler wrote again in the dirt: *King seeking mole.* The Handler had been assigned her on purpose. She released her grip. Bethany rubbed out his words and wrote her own, *You lie you die!* Then she turned back to her team. The foreboding was gone; it hadn't been for the mission, and it had been just for her.

Wraith suits, Handler was wearing one. She knew they were making them, but she had not seen one until now. Bethany checked each member of her team. Fargo and Mac had already taken out the guards, and Tiger and Steele were nowhere in sight. Bull had taken out the high tower guards and now all they could do was wait for Steele and Tiger to get the target. Bethany felt a movement against her leg, so she turned to see words appearing in the dirt.

Hypnosis usage, were the words that appeared. This she already knew, she nodded her head as the two words were cleared away.

"Retrieved," Steele's voice came over the radio. Bethany looked through her binoculars as Steele and Tiger emerged with a young man from the large building to the left. She watched her monitor for any movement. A small flicker came from the right tower.

"Bull, right tower."

"On it."

The flight back to base was filled with chitter-chatter over the mission. The young man sat quietly. Bethany chatted with the rest of the men, but caught the young man staring at her several times.

"So, who are you?" She finally turned to the young man and asked.

"Michael Bishop."

Bishop, the name seemed familiar. She went over things in her head trying to find the name.

"Are you ok, Mr. Bishop?"

"I am now, thank you." He smiled at her.

"So why did they have you, what do you do?"

Bishop . . . Michael Bishop her mind came across some Intel off a mission several years ago. Scientist working on genetics for the faster healing and recovery of soldiers, missing from a base in Germany five years ago. He never answered her question, but just smiled at her.

This was way too easy of a rescue for a man of this magnitude. Something was going on, but she already knew that, didn't she?

The plane landed and the team and Dr. Bishop went their separate ways. Debriefing and rest was next on the order of business for the day.

Back in her room, Bethany went over things in her head. If the King knew there was a mole, he would be the one searching, but his searching was going to have to find her to get the mole. She pulled her laptop up on her bunk and looked over all the info she had on their mission. It was way too easy. Was she being tested to find out if she was The Maker? A knock on her door brought her back to the present time.

"We are heading down to the canteen for some R & R. You want to come?" It was Tiger. Bethany looked back at her laptop; she really couldn't do much snooping right now.

"Sure, give me second." She left the door standing open and put on her flip-flops. The two of them walked out of the barracks and down to the canteen. The rest of the team had already knocked back a few when they arrived.

"So, what will you have?" Mac asked her as she sat down.

"Just water," she told him.

"Oh, come on, where is the fun in that?"

Bethany laughed. She didn't drink but in have-to situations, and this was definitely not one. Not that she could get wasted anyway; they had made sure her genetics could handle liquor.

"You still move?" He motioned to the dance floor as the music played.

She smiled. "Better than most."

"Alright, then," he said as he took her hand and pulled her toward the other people moving on the floor.

She felt out of place in her shorts and tank top as the other girls around her seemed to be dressed for dancing. But where she lacked in dress she made up for in her dancing.

"Are you sure you're not half black?" Tiger asked her. "I still don't know any other white girl who can dance like you."

Bethany laughed.

"My turn." Fargo stepped in between them. He put his arm around her and pulled her up against him.

"Girl, you and I need to make some music of our own."

"You making moves on my girl?"

Bethany knew the voice instantly. Keeps was taller than Fargo by at least six inches.

"Come on, baby, we need to talk." He took Bethany by the hand.

"Hey, she's with me." Fargo grabbed Bethany's other hand.

"Just a minute," she told Keeps.

She then turned to Fargo. "If you are wise, friend, you would let go and never grab me again."

Fargo held tight to her. "We were dancing."

"I am not going to tell you again." she looked down at her hand. He glanced over at the team watching his every move.

Tiger had come to his feet. "I'd let go if I were you," Tiger told Fargo.

Bethany didn't give him the chance. She knew exactly where to hit someone for the most damage with the least amount of force. Fargo hit the floor, out cold, and Bethany and Keeps left the bar.

"Did you miss me that much?" She asked him.

He smiled at her, "You know I did. So what was going on back there?"

"Drunken idiocy with the team."

"Great. That was your team?"

"Yeah," she told him as they walked back toward the barracks. "You realize Mac is following us?"

"Yeah, I knew someone was," Keeps told her as they got to her room.

"You might as well come on in." She and Keeps went in and shut the door.

Bethany stepped back and took a good look at Keeps. His sandy blonde hair was now cut in a high and tight and black. He had glasses and he was dark, almost as dark as Brandon. He was wearing jeans and a T-shirt. He was cute and now with his chest starting to take form, he was quite the catch.

"You know the girls are going to be lining up for you?" She saw Mac peer through the window. She walked up close to him and pulled his shirt out of his jeans and over his head. Keeps smiled as he slid her tank top off and threw it on the bed.

"How about a shower?" She asked as she unfastened her shorts and let them fall to the floor; then walked towards the bathroom in her bra and panties.

Keeps followed her. "I thought you would never ask," he said as he followed her, depositing his jeans on the bed beside her tank top.

Once the door shut, she turned the shower water on, she pinned Keeps to the wall.

"Tell me what you know."

"And, here I thought you wanted me."

She laughed. "I wouldn't want to get us into trouble. Now spill it."

"Oh, I will if you keep standing that close to me."

Bethany backed off and smiled.

"Sorry, I forget I seem to affect you."

"Seem to?" He turned and pinned her to the wall with his full body pressed against her.

"Does that feel like 'seem to'?"

She laughed. "What has gotten into you? They let you out for a mission or two, and now you're mister macho. Where is my computer geek I love?"

He backed away from her and laughed. "I'm still here." He smiled at her. "I know all the people I was keeping were reassigned and the main agents were assigned to other Keepers and all of us were sent to the field to watch over our assignments."

"Other Keepers? I thought you were the only one."

"No, there are five of us in all, but I kept you and a few others. But they took us all, gave us one assignment and sent us to the field to watch over the agent that had been assigned us."

Bethany smiled. "I am glad you got me."

"You know it was no accident?"

"Yeah, I know. Just like I know the others watching me was no mistake."

"I figured I wasn't alone."

Bethany pulled Keeps to her.

"So, who are you these days?" She asked.

"Mark Anthony Walters, at your service."

"Seth, you know I love you with my very soul, brother."

Mark blinked a couple of times. "Crap girl, you're good! What have you found out?"

Bethany had released her wipe of his mind, and now he remembered everything.

"There are agents in Wraith suits watching us. The Handler has been watching over me. He told me there was a mole trying to find the Maker, and King was trying to find out who it is."

"He is one of the ten, so he is now in cover with the rest of us. I was told we would be off the grid and on our own. The only thing that mattered was that I guard you with my life."

"We are off the grid?"

"King set this up and made us all disappear, but figures it is one of the ten that is the mole."

"Who is the King?"

"Now, have you had any luck with the Nutria system?" He skipped the question altogether.

"I haven't had much time; they have almost everywhere wired. I have managed to get through several blocks, but there are five left. You're not going to tell me who he is, are you?"

"No, not unless I have to; it is safer you don't know." Mark looked down at Bethany.

"This is going to kill me."

"No, you will just be very convincing."

He put one hand on each side of her and stepped close to her.

"Convincing others will be no problem; but convincing myself that it's all an act, will be."

Bethany ducked under his arm and walked around and stepped into the shower.

"Come on."

Mark took a deep breath and stepped into the shower with her. She smiled at him as the water poured over him.

"If we are off the grid, I guess there is no reason to wipe you again." She slid her bra off and dropped it over the top of the shower.

"I can help you if you don't. Maybe together we can break the blocks and find the mole." He looked down at her.

"Fast." She laughed. She shut the water off and grabbed a towel. "You coming?"

"Not, yet," he said as she stepped from the shower. He removed his boxers as she turned to go out of the bathroom.

She heard the shower come back on as she shut the door behind her.

This was good and bad news; good that now she could do more work on the computer and Keeps could help her, bad that now they were on their own in the Marines and were at their whim—even worse that she just knocked Fargo out.

Bethany checked to see if Mac had left; then, went carefully over to her room just to make sure there was no listening or video devices. Mark came out as she was making the sweep.

"It's clean; I checked it when I arrived on base earlier. Right before I came to the canteen."

She finished her sweep. "You got your laptop?"

"Of course, it is in my room. I'll get dressed and go get it." He turned and faced away from Bethany as he dropped the towel and grabbed his jeans. Bethany laughed.

"So why are you playing modest, now?"

Mark dropped his jeans and turned and walked straight at her. Bethany laughed and darted around to the other side of the bed. Mark stopped and went back and got his jeans and put them on. Bethany crawled over the bed and stood in front of him. She still had her towel on, too. He grabbed the front and ripped it off her; she never flinched.

"You know there is not a modest bone in me." She took a step closer to him. His eyes wandered slowly down her and back up to her eyes.

"You are going to be the death of me." He told her as she ran her finger across his still bare chest. He scooped her up and dropped her on the bed and pinned her there.

"Please, Lindz, don't tease me. You know how I feel about you."

She reached up and rubbed across his cheek. He had used her name Lindsey again.

"Sorry, Keeps, I needed to know just how far I could push you before you'd break."

He leaned in and kissed her gently on her lips. "It's a very thin line," he told her as he got off of her.

"I will try not to push it, but with this situation it is going to be hard not to cross that line."

"I know," he said as he pulled his shirt over his head.

"I'll be back in a few minutes and we can do some work." He opened the door.

"Mark?"

"Yeah?" He turned to look at her.

"Watch out for Fargo and Mac."

"I will." He turned and shut the door.

Bethany got dressed quickly and got to work on her laptop. She needed to get through the last five blocks and find out what they knew about the Maker before it got agents hurt or killed.

Time passed quickly while she worked and two hours later she looked up at the clock. Mark hadn't hadn't returned. "Crap." She got up and headed for the door. She should have put the wipe back on him just in case. As she headed for the men's barracks she was hoping Mac and Fargo had just caught up with him, but as she got closer, fear for him started creeping up in her. She had no idea what room he was in as she looked at the three story building. Since females were not supposed to be in the rooms, and vice versa, there was always a guard on duty so you could call up to a room or at least let them know you were going up to get someone. Of course, there were always guys and girls sharing a room, but everyone including the guard just let it slide unless there was a fight or something.

"Hey," Bethany said as she approached the guard, "I am looking for a friend that just transferred in."

"What's his name?" He said as he walked over and picked up the roster.

"Mark Walters."

"Oh, yeah, he is in 325. Mac and Fargo asked about him earlier. New to their team, you Cline?" He asked.

"Yeah."

"They are a good team."

"Yeah, I agree." She smiled. "Thanks for the info."

He smiled. "Have a good night."

Bethany had to keep herself from running for the stairs. She walked up the first flight and as soon as the guard was out of sight she sprinted up the last two.

Room 325, she ran along looking at door numbers. She stopped and listened, when she found the door then knocked.

Mark opened the door. "Hey." He opened the door so she could go in. Mac, Fargo and Tiger were sitting in the room. Fargo looked up at her, but didn't seem drunk.

"Hey, girl." Tiger got up as she came into the room.

"Sorry, I had company," Mark told her.

She smiled at him. "That's ok."

She looked at Fargo, "Sorry for dropping you earlier. I don't like being touched."

"I beg to differ," Mark said from behind her.

"Ok, so I don't like being touched by anyone but you."

"Serves me right for getting half drunk; I know better."

Bethany felt relief wash over her. Fargo got up. "You should have told me she was expecting you back." He looked at Mark.

"I figured she could wait. I better stop and make up for getting her mad at you. I didn't know you were from the team till she told me."

Fargo laughed. "Never keep that woman waiting."

He smiled at Bethany. "That's ok, I know how to make her smile and purr like a kitten," Mark smiled.

Bethany looked at Mark, "We'll see who is doing the purring."

"I think that's our cue," Tiger said as he headed for the door.

Mac and Fargo followed him.

Mark grabbed his computer. "Ready." Bethany held the door as they left.

"Sorry," he said as they walked out.

"No, I am glad things worked out. I had started to really panic when the guard told me Fargo had asked for your room number."

"So you were worried about me?" He smiled.

Three a.m. and one block was all that was left. Bethany closed her computer and lay down on the bed. Mark climbed up beside her. She scooted over against him and he put his arm around her waist. Mark pulled her tight against him. Bethany closed her eyes and fell asleep.

Mark could smell Bethany and was having difficulty being this close to her. He knew she loved Brandon more than anything, but he also knew she loved him, just not the same way. But he did love her and would give anything for her and if this is the way it was, then that's what it would be. He would love her with his very soul and take what she gave him. Mark closed his eyes and tried to sleep, but all he could see was from earlier in the night and it was getting very difficult just to lay there with her. Why couldn't it be like when she always came to his room?

Without warning Bethany shifted around to face him, but her eyes were still closed and her breathing said she was still asleep. Her hand wound around his waist and pulled him back close to her. She snuggled up against his chest. His heart was beating out of control and he was now having trouble breathing quietly.

Bethany opened her eyes and looked up at Mark. His eyes were focused on the ceiling and she could tell he was trying to regain control of himself. Bethany pushed him to his back and straddled him. She looked into his eyes; she couldn't believe she was going to do this, but he wasn't going to get any rest otherwise. She rubbed her hands up over his chest and up around his neck. She leaned over and kissed him gently on the lips. He was out cold.

She so loved Mark; not quite like Brandon, but loved him none the less.

"Wake up." Bethany poked Mark in the side. "We have to go report in." Mark rolled over. "You have to go clean up and get in uniform."

He turned back and sat up. He couldn't remember how he had fallen asleep last night. He looked at her, she had already showered and was in uniform. He looked at her as he was standing there.

"Come on, Mark, get moving." He slowly walked towards the door.

"I went and got your stuff this morning; you can shower and change here." His bag was lying beside the bed. "Sorry about last night. I couldn't think of any other way . . . well, yeah, I could, but knocking you out was the only sane thing."

He smiled. "So, that's what happened."

She smiled at him. "Get going soldier."

Mark perked up and strolled into the bathroom.

Bethany laughed, then got a thought. What if he did dream something else happened? She smiled; she wouldn't put it past him to dream more. She sat down a few minutes in front of the computer and worked on the last block. It was a big one; it might take them a whole week to hack through it. Mark came out of the bathroom and got dressed.

"You look nice in uniform; love the dark skin and eyes," she told him as they headed for the parade ground.

He smiled at her. "You look good in anything." They arrived just in time for formation.

"We have Intel coming in for our next mission. Cline, you and Walters will need to go over it and then get with me to get it ready. Everyone stay on base, I don't want to send out scouting parties to find you. You're dismissed."

Steele handed them a jump drive. "Everything is on here. Now get to work."

"Yes, sir." Bethany took the jump drive from him. Well this was going to put a damper in their work.

They headed to the communications building to work on the Intel. Bethany plugged in the jump and went to work. The Intel was on Intel; it was an Intel retrieval mission. A large summit would be taking place and they needed to get in, get the Intel and get out. Mark looked at her as she typed and smiled.

"You're not the lead."

"Who says?" She kept typing.

"-Ebil u nerede turaletler bulunmaktardir soyler misiniz," Bethany asked a guard where the restrooms were while holding her stomach and wearing her best sick face.

"Salonu ve sola asagi." He pointed and told her, "down the hall to the left."

She told him thanks, "U tesekkur" as she headed down the hall at a fast pace.

Bethany went into the restroom. The restroom had an air duct running up the building and to the offices three floors up. Right where she needed to be. Her purse looked small enough, but looks could be deceiving. She pulled her pants from under her party dress and her gear from her purse. Once the dress was hung up in the stall below the vent, she carefully undid the screws, put dummy heads in their place, and shimmed up the vent carefully shutting it behind her.

There were four sets of lasers in the vent system which would be no problem. The room was going to be trickier, however; two guards outside the door and two on the terrace. There were also three lasers in the room and motion sensors.

Each laser was rerouted as she came to it, then on to the room. The motion sensor had been carefully placed and would be a little more challenging. Bethany opened her small bag of tools and retrieved a small pack to override the sensor once she found the wires. Carefully, she sliced the sheathing back from the wiring. Timing was everything; she had set the wire and hit the failsafe to override the signal that would be sent the minute she moved the ceiling panel, but once the override registered, it would start recalibrating for reset. She should have seven minutes before it came back up.

Once she hit the button, she slid in the room careful not to step into any of the other laser beams. She linked her small handheld and the computer. The hacking of security took three minutes, the retrieval took three. She had one minute to get back over the lasers and back in the ceiling. The reset took place as she set the ceiling tile back in place.

Back down the vent to the restroom. It had been ten minutes since she went in. Now all she lacked was to go back to the main room with the guests.

"Herhengi daha iyi hissediyorsun," one of the guards asked if she was feeling any better.

"Gercekten ben geri dondum otele gitmek gidiyorum dusunmuyorm," she told him 'no', and that she was heading back to her hotel and thanks for asking. "Sordugunuz icin tesekkur ederim."

Back with the guests, she retreated to the exit and went out. Her limo was summoned and Tiger drove her out of the gate.

"Oh girl, you are good. Why did they ever bring you off coverts?"

"I needed a change of scenery." The rest of the team joined them up the road a bit. They had been on standby in case anything went wrong.

Back at base the guys all celebrated in the canteen. Bethany was the one the cheers were going up for, so she downed a few shots with her team, and then left the rest of the celebrating to them. She wanted to get the last block broken and headed straight for her room. Ten minutes later and Mark was right beside her, working as hard as she was.

"You know you shouldn't have done the mission like that. It will be noticeable and make you stand out." Mark really cared for her and she knew it. And he was right, but it just made the most sense.

"I know." She kept typing. "Got it. Now, let's see what they know." The file opened in front of them. A list of missions, dates, and names were listed along with things they had in common and things different. Then a list of things they knew for sure.

"Some of these missions aren't mine."

"No," Mark said. "That is 25 and this one is 35. But the most of the rest are yours. Crap, they are narrowing down. Look," he pointed at the list under things known about Maker.

"They have your age down pretty close 20-25 and they know you mainly work alone. You're very fluent in over forty languages. Your weapon of choice is no weapon, but you know how to use most every kind. They even know you are good at computers." As the two went over the list and some of the info in the file, new info popped in. It read: *Most likely woman.*

"Crap!" Mark stepped back and dropped on the side of the bed. "If they know that, then it won't be long till they find you."

"Why do you say that?"

"There are only three women out of the ten, and I know 15 and 25 will not be hard to dismiss." Mark put his head in his hands. "This is not good."

Bethany walked over and knelt down in front of him. "It will be fine, Keeps; now maybe we can pull them out in the open."

More information popped up: *Kill on sight.*

"Maybe we can make them think they have that info wrong."

Bethany got up and walked back to the computer and sat down. "Mark," he looked up, "What about your files? The ones you keep on me."

"I am not stupid; I infected them with the Newbie virus."

"That's it, Keeps! You're a genius." She jumped up and kissed him.

"Let's let it go in the Nutria File."

"But it will wipe out everything that it is in, all the computers, not just the one it originated from."

"I know, that's the beauty; they will have to start from scratch and most all the data will be wiped out. And I know it will wipe out everything we have gotten, but maybe we can save the major Intel and funnel it just into the Nutria itself."

"It will take a few days to get all that done, even with the two of us working. They could find you by then."

"Alright then, let's let it go in the whole system and wipe everything out."

"But agents could be hurt if they don't have the back up and stuff they need. Most missions will be fine. It won't affect those out in the field; they already know what they're doing. The only ones it will mainly effect is the computer geeks like us trying to go through and analyze all the info and, of course, anyone looking for anything."

Mark got up and paced across the floor several times. "The only thing it will stop is what they don't know, and they know almost everything now."

Bethany smiled. "Let's feed them some inconsistencies first so they will question if the info is right."

"That might work." He stopped behind his chair.

"But they still kill all . . ." Bethany stopped him.

"We will deal with that later; let's get some Intel going."

The two of them worked all night putting discrepancies in files and little things under Keepers' notes that left a question when you read it. By six am, they were both wiped out.

"We better get a little shut eye before we have to report in." Bethany climbed up on the bed.

"Noon, right?" Mark asked.

"Yeah," she answered as he dropped beside her. He pulled her into his arms.

"I promise to do whatever it takes to keep you safe," he said as he drifted off to sleep. Bethany took a deep breath and drifted off to sleep.

The alarm screaming woke her. It was eleven and they both needed to shower and change. She turned over to find Seth staring at her.

"What?" His eyes almost looked glassy.

"I let the Newbie go this morning."

"Ok, so what's wrong?"

"The last thing that was listed this morning was Cherry Point and ..."

"And what?"

"Virgin."

"What time did it post?"

"Thirty minutes ago."

"Alright," she said.

"No time to waste then, come on." She climbed out of the bed and stuck out her hand. He took it and she pulled him off the bed. "I need a big favor from you."

He looked at her. "Anything."

"Promise?" She started pulling her shirt over her head along with her sports bra.

"No, I can't." He backed away from her.

"I know you better than that; you have been dreaming of this for a long time."

"Maybe, but not like this."

Bethany closed the distance between them.

"Oh, please, don't ask me to do this."

"You promised me." She pulled his shirt over his head.

"This is the only way they will question their Intel," she told him.

"No, the orders are to kill on sight."

"You think they are not going to check? They will but maybe not until they're dead, but they will. If we or King have any chance of finding them, I have to appear just like the 15 and 25."

She pulled his hand to her waist. He stood there frozen.

"There has to be another way," he told her as she undid his pants and let them fall to the floor. His boxers were the next thing to hit the floor, then she pulled him back towards the bed.

Her heart was screaming for Brandon, but her head told her this was the only way they would find the mole. If they did find her to be a virgin then they would know their Intel was right, but if they didn't find her a virgin then just maybe they would think they had it all wrong. She just hoped Brandon would forgive her.

"Mark, please."

He stopped her before she could get him on the bed.

"He will hate me for this and after it's over, you will, too."

"No, he won't." She knew he was thinking of Brandon, too. They had become pretty good friends while they were planning her and Brandon's escape.

Bethany turned him and pushed him off balance and he fell on his back onto the bed. She pinned him there with her body.

"I can do this myself."

With her being that close to him, his body was reacting on its own.

"But I would rather you . . ."

He managed to get the upper hand and flip her. He looked her into her eyes. "I can't believe I am going to do this." He ran his finger down the side of her face. "I promise to try not to hurt you." She smiled up at him and he leaned in and kissed her ever so gently. She ran her finger up his back and the affect it had on him was instant as his kiss became heated.

A sharp pain suddenly wracked her whole body. Mark got still to let it pass before he moved again. An ignition of sorts took place where the pain had been and a moan escaped from her that shocked her. A sudden need took control of her and she wanted more. She never wanted to stop, never wanted it to end. Mark's moans only made her want even more. Her head was spinning and her heart soaring; the sudden climax had spilled over, left her breathless.

"Are you ok, did I hurt you?" Mark looked at her. Before she could find her voice her lips found his. He suddenly pulled away from her.

"We've got ten minutes." They both jumped up, threw on their uniforms and ran from her barracks.

They hit formation just as Steele called them to attention. Bethany suddenly realized that there was warmth running down her legs. Crap, she had forgotten you were supposed to bleed some after your first time.

Steele seemed to be taking his own sweet time this morning. He walked back and forth in front of them talking about how successful the mission had been and how it was good to play to the strengths of each member of their team. Bethany wasn't hearing much of his speech she was hoping since her camo's were so baggy that the blood was drying on her legs instead of soaking into her pants.

"You're dismissed!"

She glanced down. No sign of blood, but she wasn't going to stick around and let it soak through.

"Hey, where are you heading?" Tiger stepped in front of her.

She leaned close to him. "I think I started, so I have to get back to my room, quick."

He laughed. "You better get moving, then."

She smiled and took off at a run.

"Something wrong?" Mark asked Tiger.

"I think she has some plumbing issues this morning."

Mark smiled at Tiger, but in his head he was wondering if he had really hurt her. He chatted a few minutes then headed back to check on her. He could hear the shower going.

He needed one, too, he was nasty. He opened the door and stuck his head in. "You ok?"

Bethany stepped out of the shower and pulled him in the bathroom.

"I will be," she pulled his jacket and T-shirt off him.

He spun her around and pinned her up against the wall. "Are you sure about this?"

Her lips found his and told him all he needed to know.

"You're going to kill me," he told her as she smiled down at him, two hours later.

"Sorry." She moved from off top of him to a sitting position beside him on the bed. Bethany looked at Mark. How could she be so in love with Brandon and want Keeps as badly as she did. Just looking at him sent flames up her.

"Are you sorry?" He asked her.

"Yes and no," she was honest with him. "How about you?" she asked.

"Same," he told her. "Do you think he will forgive us?" Mark asked her.

"I hope so, but to tell the truth, I don't know if I can forgive myself."

Mark sat up and wrapped his legs and arms around her. "If he loves you like I know he does, he will. But you know you could always stay with me. I will always love you."

She leaned her head back on his chest and looked up at him. "I know that you do, and that I could," she took a deep breath, "you will always have part of my heart."

He kissed her on the nose. "I will take what I can get." Bethany smiled up at him.

How unfair she was being to him; she loved him, but not like Brandon. But now, what if Brandon wouldn't want her? Mark would love her forever. Her heart seemed to hurt, tears surfaced and slid down her cheeks. Mark held her close and didn't say anything. He was a great friend ... well, more than just a friend.

"I need to pick up some stuff from my room before it gets late. I brought a few gadgets with me. I always like to be prepared." Bethany got up from the bed and went to the shower.

In the shower she let the tears really flow. This was insane; how could you love someone so much it hurt, yet want someone else? Her heart ached for Brandon; her body for Keeps. Could she ever want Brandon that way, would one night with him change it all or would Keeps be the one she always wanted? This was why she had decided to wait till she got married. She didn't want to be comparing Keeps and Brandon. She also didn't want to catch any kind of disease from someone. What about Keeps? Who had he slept with and were they clean or did they have something, and now she had it? Bethany sat down on the floor of the shower and wrapped her arms around her legs; this was definitely not where she wanted to be.

Mark opened the shower door. "You ok?" he asked.

Bethany stood back up. "I am exactly where I never wanted to be. I have had sex before marriage, and don't take this the wrong way, but I hope you have been careful not to get anything from anybody else, and then there is the comparison thing."

Mark stepped in the shower. "This was your idea, not mine. Remember, I said no, but you insisted. And as for catching anything, you were my first, also. So that takes away any comparisons."

Bethany looked up at Mark. "What about the hooker I got you in Los Angeles?"

Mark laughed. "I just paid her to leave." He smiled down at her. "I guess you rubbed off on me."

Bethany pulled Mark to her and hugged him tightly. "I would have not given it away so quickly if it had been anyone else."

Mark just looked at her, "Only one other person I know of, and I know you tried and he said no. I guess I am not that strong when it comes to you."

"I am sorry, Keeps. Will you ever forgive me for being so selfish?"

"You're not selfish; your life is more important than anything. And I would do whatever it takes to help you."

Bethany was glad she was in the shower, that way Mark could not see all the tears that were falling down her cheeks.

"We better get showered and out, I need to do a little work before it gets dark tonight," Mark told her as he reached past her to the soap.

Bethany and Mark walked over to the guy's barracks late in the afternoon. Mark needed to pick up some of his stuff. So, of course they acted like they were seeing what was going on with the rest of the team. Mac and Fargo were playing Halo down in the common room. Steele and Tiger had gone out on town on a little R & R trip.

Fargo had told them, "Looking for ladies."

Mac laughed. "Tiger will have no problem, but Steele is like his name: cold."

"And most of the ladies don't like him," Fargo added.

"So you two are not looking for any company tonight?" Mark asked.

"Already meeting some fine ladies later at the canteen." Mac puffed up and smiled big. Mark laughed and Bethany shook her head.

"You're nuts."

"What about them?" Fargo asked as he stood up.

"I would love to show them to you some time, but in the interest of the team and Mark," he smiled, "I won't."

"Oh, I am so deprived." Bethany laughed. "Not!"

"I am heading to my room to grab my stuff. You staying with them or going with me?" Mark asked Bethany.

"I'm with you."

"Oh, come on," Fargo said, "I promise I'll behave. You can even join the game."

Bethany laughed. "Thanks, but no thanks." She knew she sucked at Halo and they would slaughter her. She really didn't want to let Mark out of her sight unless she had to.

"You just don't want to get your butt kicked," Fargo said as he flopped down on the couch.

"I like to kick butt for real, not on some game. You want to meet me on the mat and I will show you a butt kicking; but as for games, you can keep them."

"She's just chicken," Fargo told Mac.

"Whatever. You ready?" She turned to Mark.

"Yeah," he told her, and they headed for the door.

Once they had Marks's bag they headed back to her barracks. "So what kind of good things did you bring?" She asked as they walked.

"Motion sensors, grid locks, jammers, blockers, cameras, you know, just the fun stuff."

As they walked, both of them watched closely for changes or anything out of the ordinary.

Once they got to her room, Mark started setting up things. He placed three spider cameras outside. Sensors were put on the door, window and ceiling of Bethany's room.

The blocker was also used. It was better than a jammer any day, but he had brought both. Blockers couldn't be traced, where jammers could. Mark had the place wired, videoed and on lockdown by nightfall. Bethany had asked to help, but Mark was intent on doing most of it himself. Bethany's stomach had started growling about three hours before he finished and was now demanding something be done. Mark handed Bethany an earpiece as her stomach growled loudly.

"Here, this will let us know if anyone is around or . . ."

Bethany smiled.

"Sorry," he told her, "when I get started on something I lose track of everything else."

"That's fine. I am used to going without, but for some reason my stomach's throwing fits. How about a pizza. You know they deliver here on base?"

"That sounds great." Mark went and picked up the phone.

"Yes, I want a large pizza with the works and extra cheese. Cherry Point, women's barracks, room 125. Thanks," then hung up the phone. "It will be here in 30 minutes."

Bethany's stomach let out another large growl.

"Are you going to make it?" He laughed.

"I hope so." She smiled.

A small noise would go off every time someone walked by the room and they both would look at the computer to see who it was. Most of them she had seen, but every once in a while it would be someone she didn't recognize, but she hadn't been there long.

As each person walked by and the software recorded their face, a program would then kick in and the person's name, rank and how long they had been at Cherry Point would pop up.

Soon the pizza arrived and they sat down and ate.

"My gosh, I don't think I have ever seen you eat that much," he told her as she ate her fifth piece.

"I don't think I have, but I felt like I was starving."

A woman walked by as Mark was finishing his last bite on his third piece that the computer recognized as Corporal Maria Martinez, she had just been transferred in. Mark was watching the names, but since she was new he popped up her record and picture.

"Crap," he said.

"What?" Bethany asked.

"It's 25. What is she doing here?" He flipped open Bethany's laptop and opened a secure site.

"What are you doing?"

"I am going to ask the King if she is supposed to be here. If she's not, then we have our mole."

"You can't; you'll infect my computer with Newbie."

He laughed. "I am going to his other secure site; the two are not linked in any way, so no one knows who he is. But I need to know, and he needs to know." Mark wrote out an email address and sent a small message, *Seen the number 25. Is it in the right place?* Then he hit send.

"Who is it?" Bethany asked Mark.

"No, I told you I am not telling you." A reply came back almost instantly. *Out of place, I will send someone to fix the problem.*

"Well, we know who our mole is, anyway. I wonder who got to her."

Bethany sat down beside Mark. "Let's find out. Where has she been lately, do you know? Were you her Keeper?"

"Not lately, but she has been on a continuing Intel-gathering mission for the last five years. She comes in for a month, then goes back out for eleven. She's been in the Middle East."

"Well it looks like she either switched sides, or they have something on her. What else can you tell me?"

Mark closed his eyes. "Let's see, she has been with the Shadar family the whole time, a tutor for their sons. Shadar has terrorist ties, and she has been bringing us great Intel." Mark turned and did a little surfing. "Here is Shadar and his family."

"Looks like he keeps several wives and has lots of sons."

"Yes, he is a prominent man in his culture. He has lots of daughters, too, but you know what they do to their daughters."

Bethany knew all too well. She had spent several years there breaking down a human trafficking ring. And it turned out to be a man selling his own daughters. He wasn't selling them anymore. Bethany thought of Kalahari, and how he was the reason she had had to leave Brandon the first time.

"Is there any way you can get me to Shadars? I could see if they are holding something over her, or if she is just a betrayer."

Mark looked at her. "I will see what I can do."

He turned back to the computer and started typing.

Bethany went and laid down, she was so tired. She closed her eyes as she slid off to sleep hearing Mark type.

The small squeal in her ear woke her. The room was dark and Mark was lying beside her.

"Shh!" He whispered. He pointed to the monitor on the computer showing the cameras outside. 25 was standing outside looking at the door. Mark pulled a gun from under the mattress. Bethany grabbed her knife. They both moved to either side of the door. A small camera poked its way under the door. Seth carefully put his gun on one side of it, and Bethany her knife on the other so it could not turn enough to see them. The camera looked carefully around the room. Mark and Bethany stayed still and plastered to the walls. The camera finally pulled back under the door. Neither one of them moved for a minute. Mark stepped over and turned the computer around so they could see. She was at the next door. Mark walked back to the bed.

"If she finds me, she finds you. I don't have your genetics."

Bethany knew what he meant. He wasn't able to change his facial features as much as she could. She sat down on the bed beside him. "Tomorrow morning Tiger is going to escort you to breakfast, then to Handler who will be arriving at ten a.m. I won't leave this room till I know you're safely in Handler's hands."

"Tiger?"

"Yes, this morning at five a.m., all of the team will get letters and in those letters will be info about you. It will say something like you had been in coverts and now someone is here on base threatening you. Each letter contains a pic of 25. They are being called in to help here on base; find and detain 25."

"And where am I heading?" She asked.

"The King didn't like your plan, but agrees that there is someone else pulling her strings, so he has agreed to sending you in. Handler will get you everything you need and make sure you get to your destination. Then he will come back and pick me up, and hopefully 25 as well, to take us back to headquarters for questioning."

"I don't like it you're staying here."

"Don't worry, I will have the team with me at all times."

Bethany climbed back on the bed and sat up against the headboard.

"What?" Mark asked her.

"Did I throw it all away for nothing?"

Mark climbed up beside her. "We had no idea it would turn out like this."

Bethany didn't mean to hurt him, but she could see the hurt in Mark's eyes. "Sorry, Keeps, I didn't mean . . . well, I didn't mean to hurt you."

He smiled at her. "Don't be silly, I never expected any of this, and I am sorry that you regret it. But I would be lying if I said I regretted it."

Bethany slid over into Marks's arms.

"For what it's worth, I can't even look at you without getting all hot and bothered," Mark laughed.

"I know what you mean. It's crazy isn't it, to just look at someone and want them so badly?"

Mark looked down at Bethany and gently kissed her on the forehead.

"You trying to start a fire?" She asked him.

"Only if you want one set." She did want him, but every time she did, guilt ripped through her.

"You know I want you . . ." she paused.

"But?" He asked.

"But I feel I am betraying both of you."

"I understand why you would feel that way about him, but why would you feel that way about me?"

She smiled at him. "I don't want to lead you on."

He laughed. "Who's leading whom? I know what this is, and I also know if you had it the way you wanted, it would not be me."

She knew he was right and that he understood, but she still felt guilty. The extreme emotions that were pulling them together wasn't doing anything but making it worse.

Her heart was racing and her insides ached for him. She looked at him; his eyes seemed to be calling to her. Her heart raced harder and she pulled him down till their lips met. She smiled at him when their lips parted.

"You started a fire, now put it out."

He laughed. "I will do my best."

By eight, Bethany had showered and dressed. Keeps still was lying in the bed; he had fallen asleep when she went to the shower. She sat down and waited for time to pass. How could she do that to Brandon again? How could she do that to herself and to Keeps? Things she knew and had planned seemed to be slipping away.

She hadn't checked in with Jeff and the business in weeks. She wasn't even sure she wanted to go back and face Brandon now that she wasn't pure. What if he wouldn't want her, what if . . . What if she just never went back? He didn't remember her well. He remembered Lindsey, and that they loved each other, then got in a fight and she left. And unless she recalled anything else, that's all that he would remember. Maybe it would be best this way. She looked over at Keeps. There was no way that their relationship could continue once everything was back to normal. Tears came to her eyes and spilled out onto her cheeks. She pulled her knees to her chest and cried quietly. An arm suddenly around her made her jump.

"What's wrong?" Keeps had woke up.

"I feel so out of control."

"It's not, I promise. You go and do what you do best. I will be here doing what I do best, straightening everything else out so when you return everything can go back to normal and maybe you can go find him."

She smiled up at him. "You're so good to me. But what if I decide not to go back to him?"

He smiled at her, "That would sound great, if it meant you were going to stay with me. But I know you would always be thinking of him, and it would end up getting the best of you."

"How can you be so understanding? I have used you."

"No more than I have used you."

A knock on the door brought Keeps to his feet.

He checked the camera. "It's Tiger."

Bethany threw herself into Keeps' arms. "Be careful Keeps, I love you."

He smiled and kissed her. "You are the one going into the danger zone. Come back to me safely and we will go from there. Whatever happens, I love you, too." Keeps stepped behind the door so she could open it. Her eyes filled with tears all over again.

Bethany looked at Mark. "Seth, I love you with my soul, brother." She put his wipe back in place, although the last few days she hadn't gone through it and it would be confusing to him, but just in case.

Mark blinked a couple of times.

Tiger knocked again. "Wildcat?"

"Be right there," she called back to him.

"I know the last few days may not make sense to you, but trust me and block out what you don't understand, ok? Just trust me and bury it deep." She could see his confusion already. She laid her hand on his arm. "Trust me, I promise I will remove the block as soon as I see you again, but it's needed to keep you and me both safe. Please."

He looked at her. "Alright."

She put her hand on the doorknob, looked at Mark once more, took a deep breath, dried her tears and opened the door.

"Hey, how about some breakfast?" She smiled as she stepped out.

"Sounds great, I'm starving."

Keeps stood behind the door for a moment. What was going on? He thought back over the last few days. He had slept with 23; no, he had slept with her before. This time he had actually had sex with her, and more than just once. His mind shifted to 25, the mole; they had found the mole, let the Newbie go in the system and now . . . what did she mean bury the last few days? What had happened that he could not remember; what had scared her enough to wipe his memory? He sat down on the edge of the bed. He had to trust her; he tried to clear his mind. If she wanted him to bury the last few days, then he would. He closed his eyes, relaxed, and focused on the last thing he knew he was supposed to do: Capture 25.

Bethany noticed 25, as she exited the chow hall. She held the door as they entered.

"Gracias," Bethany told her as they walked by her.

"Bienvenida," she replied as she let the door close behind them.

Bethany walked on like it was just any other person. Tiger, however, looked at Bethany with wide eyes as soon as the door closed.

"Just keep going, she doesn't know who I am, yet," she said with a calm and quiet voice.

"The team will take care of her as soon as you're safely on your flight," he smiled at her.

"Can I ask what you were into that got her on your tail?"

"Now, you know better than that. If I told you I would have to kill you." She gave him a big grin. "So what's for breakfast?" She asked as she entered the line.

"Looks like pancakes and sausage, today," a guy in front of Bethany said. He turned and smiled. "I think they have some waffles if you don't like pancakes."

Tiger smiled at the guy.

"Hey, man, haven't seen you in a while. Where you been hiding?"

The young man smiled and looked back at Bethany and stuck out his hand. "Cutter."

"Cline." She shook his hand.

"I am not the one that keeps running all over the world, that's you." Tiger smiled.

"I guess that's true."

"So, Cline." Cutter looked at her. "How did you get messed up with Tiger?"

"Had to fill in for . . ." she turned and looked at Tiger. "Who is it that I am filling in for?"

Tiger laughed. "Calhoun, his granddad died or is real sick or something, so he had to go home on emergency leave."

Bethany got herself some pancakes and two sausages.

"How about you guys join me for breakfast?" Cutter asked as they picked up some milk.

"Sounds good to me," Bethany told him.

"Sure," Tiger agreed. The three of them found a table and sat down to eat.

"I am sure Fargo is loving you being on the team."

Bethany nodded her head.

Tiger laughed. "The first time he tried to make a move on her she knocked him out cold. It was great."

Cutter looked at Bethany.

She just smiled. "He asked for it. He was drunk and acting stupid."

"Ouch, that hurt his pride."

"You know it did. He played it off on being drunk, but he wasn't all that drunk. Not for Fargo, anyway."

Bethany ate her pancakes as Tiger and Cutter got caught up on who was seeing who and who was messing around on whom. Bethany had to smile at the gossip that was going on. And most guys thought girls were bad at gossip; they should hear these two.

"We need to go," Tiger told Cutter about quarter till ten. "We will have to go get a drink."

"Sounds good," Cutter told him. "Nice meeting you, Cline."

"You too," she told him as she got up from the table.

She and Tiger dumped their trays and put them on the conveyer belt and headed towards the airstrip.

"You two were worse than a couple of old ladies gossiping. So is he gay?"

Tiger looked at her. "Most people don't know that about him. How'd you guess?"

"He just had a certain not normal quality about him."

A helicopter flew over them towards the airfield. As they approached, she could see Handler standing beside it. Tiger walked her all the way to Handler.

"You ready?" He asked as they got close.

"Yes." She turned to Tiger.

"See that Mark is safe for me."

"No problem, I will make sure he gets off safely, too."

"Thanks." She gave him a hug then climbed in the door that Handler opened for her.

"Keeps left a bag of stuff you would need; they will be waiting at our next flight stop. You can go through and see if you need anything else."

Bethany sat beside him.

"Do you know the King, as well?"

He smiled. It was the first smile she had ever seen on him. "Yes, I do."

She shook her head. "Am I the only one who doesn't?"

"Only The Keeper and I do."

Bethany was so tired. She hadn't slept much and she knew the next few days and months would be crazy. "Do I have time to catch a few winks?"

"The next flight will be better for sleeping, but go ahead. I will wake you when we land."

Bethany closed her eyes and leaned over towards the window. Then she scooted the other way and fluffed up Handler's shoulder. He scooted over and pulled his hands back and patted his lap. Bethany lay her head on his leg and fell asleep.

"Wake up; we need to change to a jet."

Bethany stretched as they exited the helicopter and ran across the airfield to a jet. Bethany sat down in one of the rows that had four seats and buckled up for takeoff. As soon as they were in the air, Handler brought her a duffle bag.

"Let me know if you need anything else, and I will have it waiting at our next switch."

She nodded her head and unzipped the bag. A paper, with a manila envelope attached, lay on top with a list of the bags contents.

1 Hair syringe

1 Skin syringe

1 injection

6 structural syringes

2 nine millimeter guns

1 K-Bar

1 widow maker

10 spider bugs

10 micro sensors

10 micro cameras

2 stripe jammers

2 stripe blockers

5 gum explosives

1 shield

1 Bible—hollow back flap for storage

3 sets clothes

Bethany read, and pulled out each item as she read it off the list. She had dealt with most all of the things before, but these were the smallest versions of them she had ever seen. The shield, however, she had never seen before, but had heard of. It was a small three inch by four inch handheld computer. It was internet and satellite ready. It was as thin as a panty shield, hence the name shield. Bethany pulled out the Bible; it was typical book size. It looked well used. She flipped through the pages. There were notes scribbled in, passages highlighted and the cover was leather. The back cover had a map on the inside; she took one of the knives and peeled the map up to reveal a tiny thin compartment. Most all of the electronics would fit nicely inside.

Bethany put everything back in the bag, but kept out the Manila envelope. She opened it and pulled out the paper and picture inside.

> *You know Kailia's main history, but when she was at school at Oakland City College she meet Seth McCallister and married six months ago. He died in a tragic car crash three days before you left the States. He was a missionary that wanted to help the people of war torn Iraq. He and his wife are supposed to be helping the Red Cross for a month. Report to Red Cross in Daharan and you will work with them for the month, then you are on your own. Also, I included a picture of your husband, Seth.*

Kailia looked at the picture; it was of Handler. He was wearing jeans and a T-shirt holding the Bible, reading. She had never seen

Handler in anything but a suit. He looked so normal and happy. It was almost surreal.

"Nice picture." She looked at Handler. "Who knew you were so cute?"

He never cracked a smile.

"How long do we have on the next flight?" she asked Handler who had sat down. A few seats up from her.

"We will have a couple hours' layover in the UK, then we will be in the air all night. Do you need anything else?"

"No, I think he has everything in here. How did Keeps do this?"

"Why don't you catch another nap before we hit the UK? You look like you haven't been sleeping well." He got up and came back with a pillow and blanket. He handed them to her and moved two of the rows to form a bed.

"Thanks."

He looked at her as she lay down. "You're welcome."

Kailia pulled her blanket up and closed her eyes.

"Time to move." A hand was shaking her. Kailia grabbed her bag and headed for the door. "We have 30 minutes to grab a bite to eat and get to our next plane."

"I thought we had a two hour layover?"

"We did, you slept through most of it. Come on, let's go."

Kailia followed him down to a waiting car where they were taken to a restaurant.

"We are getting it to go," he told her.

Within ten minutes their food was with them and they were on their way back to the airport. Kailia and Handler got on the plane and waited for takeoff. As soon as the plane was in the air, they ate. Then Kailia started changing. Not her clothes, but her skin, hair, eyes, and face. It took her three hours to get her face back to what Kailia had looked like before.

She would have them drop her in Saudi Arabia; she knew a family there from the last time she had been in the Middle East. She would spend a few days with them getting herself set up to go across the border. Most of the people she had met in the Middle East were great, but just like the U.S., a few can ruin it for many.

"The Keeper said you would want to be dropped in Saudi."

"Yes, that is right, I do."

"He also said to give you the word Dagger and you would know what your password was for the shield."

She smiled, he didn't.

She pulled the handheld out and turned it on. The password screen came up. She typed in *Cloak n Dagger.* "ACCEPTED" appeared on the screen.

She laughed. "Oh, he is good," She locked it back and turned it off. Handler's phone rang.

"Yes, she is right here." He handed her his phone.

"Yes?"

"Maker, King here. This mission is important. I believe, like you do, that 25 is not acting on her own. Find who is pulling her chain and sever the link; do whatever it takes," the voice was an eclectic cold voice.

"Yes, sir, I will."

"Good luck," then the line went dead. She handed it back to Handler.

"You have six hours before you're dropped," he handed her a manila envelope.

"This is what we know about where she has been and what she has been doing. Or at least, what she was supposed to be doing."

Kailia took the envelope and pulled out the contents. Melina Corsican had been a tutor at the Shadar family. She had an Iraqi father, but she had an American mother who had sent her to America to be schooled. And when she returned, she was teaching children at a local school. That is where Shadar had come across her and hired her to tutor his sons and due to his status, she could not say no. He had ties with Al Quida and other terrorist groups.

Melina had been getting Intel out for over three years now. She would come back to the States once a year to visit her mother who had moved back to the States after her husband passed away.

Kailia had been in the Middle East several years ago and she knew how men like Shadar treated their family. Kailia keep getting the feeling he had to have something over 25. But what, she didn't know. Kailia read through all the information, then gave it back to the Handler.

"Does Shadar have any connections to anything I have worked on in the past?"

"I will find out," he told her.

She reclined her seat and closed her eyes. "Wake me when you do."

Kailia awoke when Handler touched her.

"Keeps says he can't find any, but he will keep looking. We are also thirty minutes out."

Kailia went and changed. Kailia Hasar McCallister was now ready. She had been silent for seven years, but today she would be back in the Middle East. Kailia checked her appearance in the mirror. Everything was covered and she was ready. She exited the plane and headed for a waiting cab. She gave him the address of some friends she had had in the country before. It was crazy how many Ziafats there were; the last one she had met, she killed.

Forty-five minutes later she got out of the cab in front of the Ziafats' house. She had met Afshim and his family when she was here before, when she went into Iraq. She had only written them twice since leaving. Now she needed them to make a trail, if anyone came looking. Kailia walked to the door and knocked.

"Kailia!" A small but beautiful woman answered the door.

"Jasmine!" She hugged the woman.

"Come in." She let Kailia pass her and shut the door behind her so the two women could remove the shaw from their heads.

"Afshim will be so surprised; we had just been talking about you the other day. Wondering how you were; you hadn't written in so long."

"Sorry, things got crazy. I went to work cleaning for the Kalahari family for a while, and then I went to the United States to school." The two ladies went in to the front room and sat down.

"So why are you back here?"

"Well, I got married while in the States, and my husband was a missionary. He wanted to come back here and work in Iraq with the many hurting families. But two days before our plane was to leave," she paused and gathered a few tears, "he was killed in a car accident."

"Oh, I am so sorry."

"I was not sure I would come, but I decided I would come this far and from here decide if I will go on or go back. Would it be ok if I stayed with you a couple of days?"

"You know you are welcome to stay as long as you like." Kailia got up and hugged her friend then sat back down.

"I knew you would say that." She smiled at her.

"So how is your family?" Kailia asked Jasmine.

"The boys have all married and left. It is just me and Afshim now."

"Wow, I have missed out on a lot."

"You can stay in the boys' room."

"Thank you again, Jasmine."

"Think nothing of it. Can I ask when it was your husband died?"

Kailia pulled tears to her eyes. "Three days ago. I buried him and got on a plane."

"Oh, my!" Jasmine got up out of the chair and went and put her arm around Kailia. A tear slid down Kailia's face. Kailia's stomach growled.

"Sounds like you're hungry. Come on to the kitchen, I was just getting ready to start lunch."

Kailia gave Jasmine a weak smile and the two of them got up and headed to the kitchen. Soon the two of them had good smells rolling as they cooked and prepared vegetables. Kailia snacked on a few raw veggies as she cut them up and handed them to Jasmine to cook.

"Afshim still comes home for lunch?" Kailia asked.

"Every day like clockwork." Afshim worked at an oil base and was ten minutes from their home. He had been coming home for lunch ever since he had worked there. The two of them were not your everyday Middle East couple. They had a life more like most Americans, but they were respectful of others that weren't as modern in their beliefs or habits.

"Smells good!" They heard Afshim yell as he entered the house. Jasmine turned and smiled at Kailia.

"Kailia!" He said as he entered the kitchen.

She gave him a big smile. "Afshim." She gave him a hug. "It is so good to see you," she told him.

"Where have you been hiding yourself? We have missed you," he told her.

"She has been in the United States going to school," Jasmine told him.

"That is wonderful."

"She is going to be staying with us a while," Jasmine added.

"That is even better news," he said.

"Thank you for your hospitality."

Jasmine handed Kailia the plates and she took them to the table.

"I am surprised you are not married by now."

Kailia stood still a second, then made a line straight for the bathroom.

"What?" She could hear Afshim say as she walked a little slower once she got out of sight of the two. Kailia walked into the restroom and washed her face, sat down for a minute, then walked back to the kitchen. Afshim's face said he was sorry before his mouth did.

"I am so sorry, Kailia."

"You didn't know, and I did not expect you to, but the statement still caught me so off guard." Afshim pulled out the chairs for both Jasmine and Kailia.

"Shall we eat?" Afshim sat down.

"I told Kailia she was welcome to stay as long as she wants."

"Oh, yes," Afshim agreed, "please stay as long as you want or need to. With the boys gone we have plenty of room, and I think Jasmine would love the company."

Jasmine nodded her head as she handed Afshim the plate of steaming vegetables.

"It is so lonely without the boys here," she said.

"I don't promise to stay long, but I don't think I am ready to move on yet, either." Kailia took the plate of vegetables from Afshim and put some on her plate as she talked. "I really feel like I need to go on and fulfill Seth's wish to help out with the many hurting from the war, but I don't think I am quite ready, yet."

"So, how long had you and Seth been married?" Jasmine asked.

"Six months."

"Oh, my, you were still newlyweds."

Kailia smiled at Jasmine. "You would have liked him. He had sandy blonde hair that was a little long, but I still liked it." She closed her eyes as if remembering.

"Do you have any pictures?" Jasmine asked.

Kailia opened her eyes. "You know, I don't know if I do or not. I packed and left so quickly, I am not sure what I even packed."

"What did Seth do?" Afshim asked.

"He was a missionary, but had been working with the Red Cross lately. He had signed up to work for a month in Iraq."

"My brother Kazim goes in and out with aid. It is hard and very dangerous. But he knows that not all people are for this war, and he is dedicated to help the ones that he can."

Kailia had only taken three bites, when she suddenly got sick and ran to the bathroom.

"Sorry," she apologized to them, "I guess I have gotten used to western food."

CHAPTER 13

Whose are you really?

TWO MONTHS LATER . . .

"Are you sure you want to do this?" Jasmine asked Kailia.

"Yes, I am and don't worry. Kazim said I would travel as his wife to be even safer."

"Kailia, you need to be thinking of your child. This is not an easy road. It is very dangerous." Kailia smiled at her friend.

"I know it is, but I know Seth would want me to continue to work here even without the Red Cross," Kailia hugged her friend and got on the truck.

"I promise to watch out for her," Kazim told his sister.

Kazim had taken an instant liking to Kailia. Jasmine had introduced them over a month ago just as she was finishing up her work with the Red Cross. Since then Kailia had begun helping him every day, preparing and gathering supplies to go back into Iraq and help its people.

"Thank you for letting me come with you," she whispered to Kazim as they sat together on the back of the truck.

"How could I deny you from honoring your husband and completing his work?" He smiled at her.

The truck bumped along as they went. Kazim had made sure Kailia had several blankets to set on so the bumps would be a little easier on her. The trip would be an all night one; they would be crossing the border in the dead of night. Kazim had told her that they had bribed a set of guards at the border so they could pass every month.

Kailia sat thinking of Keeps as the hours passed. How was he going to take her being pregnant? And Brandon, well, she had all but written off ever going to see him again, especially now.

What would they do to her? What would they do to them? She closed her eyes and leaned back on some of the supplies. She didn't need to be thinking of what was going to happen later, she needed to be focused on finding a way to get to Shadar. She would help out Kazim, then make up an excuse to stay and if he didn't accept it, she would slip away from him. Of course, she didn't want to do that; Jasmine would be worried to death over her disappearance, so hopefully she would find something to keep her there.

By two am, they had crossed the border quietly and were pulling into a small town. The supplies had to be unloaded and reloaded on a local truck so the other truck could get back over the border safely.

The truck was unloaded and the other loaded in thirty minutes. The four that had come with them all went back on the other truck. Only she and Kazim stayed to take the supplies on.

They took the truck full of supplies and headed on to the next town. They arrived just before sunrise. An elderly man waited for them with a place to hide the truck. They would take supplies from here in small bundles to each of the next five cities. Omar, the elderly man, had a small room for them to stay in. He never really spoke; he just shook his head or pointed. Kazim gave the small cot to Kailia and he slept on the floor beside her.

By noon the next day, the two of them had a bundle of supplies hidden in a chicken truck and were on their way to one of the five supply drops. It would take eight days to deliver all of the bundles. Two of the trips would take two days each. The next to the last was Kudash which is where Kailia wanted to be. Shadar lived in Kudash.

The trip to Miscal was not a long one, but the roads were not much more than dirt paths and were very rough.

By one they were passing out supplies to families, and by three heading back to Omar's. Kazim didn't talk much while he drove. He was more occupied with watching for military stops or check points. Having her along had put him on extra guard.

By the third day they were in a heavy war zone and not only did he have to watch for military he had to watch for roadside bombs. Kailia was probably watching more closely than he was but, of course, he didn't know that.

"When we get to Kudash, I am going to go on to Al Kish alone. The fighting there is very fierce right now," Kazim told her as they drove down the road. "You can stay with Omar and Ruth. They are a nice older couple. Ruth will love having you." He smiled at her.

"How long will you be gone?"

"You should only have to stay one night, but you never know. If the fighting is too bad, it may be two."

Kailia smiled; she really would like not being bumped along for a couple days and the fact that it would be in Kudash was even better.

As they got close to Kudash there was smoke in the air. Kailia could see signs of several recent battles. The road leading into the city was littered with blown up military vehicles. Kazim drove slowly and carefully between the carnage. Kailia caught sight of several armed men hiding behind the rubble. Kazim slowed when two of the man stepped out and blocked the road.

"Where are you heading and why?" The man asked.

"We are going to check on my Uncle Omar. We heard there had been some recent attacks and we haven't heard from them." The other man walked around the truck and looked in the back.

"What is in the back?"

"We have a few things for my uncle to get by on until we can visit him again." The second man came back around and gave the man at the window a nod.

"Alright, you are free to go in." Kazim slowly drove forward. Kailia had noticed one of the men had a large scar down his arm; he looked like he had been in a fire.

The houses were small, like all the other places they had been, but they also passed several houses with stone fences and guarded gates.

"We will go see Ruth first, then I will unload the truck down at the shelter."

"I'll help you," she told him.

"No, I would rather you didn't here. I will get Omar to help."

"Why not?"

"It's getting late and you don't need to be out when it gets dark. It's not safe."

"Alright," she told him.

It was getting dark as they pulled up to a small dwelling. There was a fire outside in a pit; an older man sat in front of it. Kazim parked the truck and ushered her past the old man, straight into the house.

"Ruth," he said as he entered.

"Kazim." A little old lady stood to greet him with a hug.

"How are you?" He asked her.

"I am good. Who is this?" She asked.

"This is Kailia; she is helping me this trip, but it is too dangerous for her to go to with me. Can she stay here with you and Omar?" He asked.

"Of course, she is most welcome here." She smiled at Kailia.

"Thank you," Kailia told her.

"You better go unload before it gets any darker. The streets are not safe at night you know." Kazim went back out the door.

"What brings you here, dear?" Ruth asked her.

"Fulfilling a dream." Kailia smiled at Ruth.

"Let's get you and Kazim something to eat. That trip is a long hot dusty one." Ruth pulled a few dishes out of her cupboard.

"So, you had a dream of coming here?" She asked as she scooped something out of a dish onto a plate.

"No, I have been here. It was a dream of my late husband to come and help out. I am just honoring him." Ruth sat the two plates on the edge of the old stove.

"They should be hot by the time the men return. Come sit down. Although, I am sure you're tired of sitting, but at least this seat is not as rough and bouncy."

Kailia smiled and laughed. "You are right; it was a very rough and bouncy road, so the stillness will be great."

Kailia sat down on the old chair. It wasn't much to look at, but it was comfortable. Maybe since she was staying here with Ruth she could find a way to stay. Helping out here would be a good way to find the Shadar family.

"The men are back," Ruth touched Kailia's arm. "You must be exhausted, you fell right to sleep."

Kailia smiled at Ruth. "Sorry."

"Don't be; you go get a plate and eat, then I will show you where you can sleep." Kazim was already eating at the table.

"How are you feeling?" He asked as she sat down.

"Fine, just a little tired."

He smiled and laughed. "You were snoring pretty hard, when I came in."

Kailia smiled. "I was not."

He laughed again. "You can help Ruth tomorrow pass out supplies at the shelter and Omar will go with me. He said I had to take a different road and he will go with me to show me the way. It will also take a few more days then I thought."

"That's fine," Kailia told him as she ate.

Ruth showed her to a tiny room on the back of the house. It was barely big enough for the cot in the corner, but it was a cot, and Kailia was happy not to have to sleep on the floor. Kazim slept on the floor in the small living room.

When Ruth came to the door in the morning, it was still dark. "Kailia, we need to get some things done before we head out. Would you help me?"

"Sure," she told her, as she sat up. "I would love to."

Ruth was in the tiny kitchen when Kailia cleaned up and got dressed. Ruth was kneading some dough, "There are two more batches; you can work on that one." She pointed at another big glob of dough.

Kailia worked on the dough, as Ruth worked on the other. Soon they had all of them in pans and set to rise for a while.

By this time, the sun was coming up. Ruth sent Kailia out the back to let out the chickens, feed them. and to gather the eggs, while she began making them breakfast.

The chicken coop was right out the back door to the left. Kailia had never gathered eggs before, and wasn't sure about it. The coop was small, with a little house up off the ground; in the middle the top hinged to the right. She opened the small door on the front and the chickens came out, then she opened the top and could see all six nests. She gathered the eggs and put the lid back down. A small barrel was right inside the coop door; it was full of feed, so she threw a couple of handfuls out on the ground for the chickens. That wasn't bad, she thought, as she went back to the house. Ruth had breakfast ready and they sat down and ate a piece of bread and an egg.

"So, what exactly are we doing today?" Kailia asked, as she ate.

"We will have to walk up town to the shelter. There will be a few men there to help us. But mainly there will be families coming in and out all day needing supplies. We will just need to help divide and pass them out."

"Alright," she told Ruth, as she finished. She took her plate, cleaned it and put it away. Ruth smiled at her when she took her plate and cleaned it and put it away for her, as well.

The two of them headed out as soon as breakfast was done. They had to walk about a mile to get to the shelter. Kailia really wished she could just run it, but knew it was a silly thought.

After doing all the riding, it was good to get some exercise. Kailia took her Bible; she had gotten to where she packed it everywhere, for her husband, of course. She and Ruth walked by a large gate with guards; the men stared as they passed. Ruth told her there were three guarded houses they would pass.

"Just to make sure you remember, don't even look their way," she told her. "If they even think you're up to something, they might shoot you."

Kailia did remember, but she was also prepared and used the camera on her shield to film each house as they passed it; she had it carefully concealed in the folds of her robe. As they arrived at the small building, three men arrived, too. Once inside Ruth introduced each of them.

"This is Kailia, my neice, she is here to help us the next few days. She has been in the States at University. She is here to help out while she mourns the loss of her husband. Kailia, this is Japtha, Maliacha, and David."

Kailia gave them a small smile. She was glad Ruth had thought to introduce her as a niece. This helped with custom, and her being a widow would help even more. Ruth was a very clever lady. She noticed two of the men were carrying guns, but they were concealed. Kailia followed Ruth to the supply room where she and Ruth started separating things into small groupings of stuff.

"There are several that come; we have to be very careful to spread it out as far as we can."

"Here they come," David called from the other room.

Ruth sat behind a table as people would come up and tell her what they needed. Kailia would get the supplies and Ruth would go through and make sure they didn't have too much or too little, then give it to them. By nine am the line was long and Kailia knew that there was not near enough.

"I have a few things coming in before lunch," David told Ruth.

Ruth smiled at David. "You are a good man, David," she told him.

"I have a lot to make up for." He smiled back at her.

By noon, almost everything was gone and the line had dwindled down until only a few remained, but they looked like they needed more help than some of the others. A truck pulled up in the back and unloaded several things. Ruth and Kailia quickly separated and handed out the supplies to the rest of the line.

"Was there enough?" David asked Ruth.

"We got all the ones that came in, but we don't have enough for the five families stuck at home." David smiled. "We will have. I will meet you back here after lunch. I will have all we need then." Ruth patted David on the arm.

"We will see you then." Ruth and Kailia headed back to Ruth's.

"Who is David that he feels he has a debt to pay?" Kailia asked Ruth as they walked.

"He is the son of Eli Shadar. His father was ... well, he was not such a good man. But David is trying to make up for the pain his father caused a lot of the people here."

"How long ago did his father die?"

"About four months ago; I think, it hasn't been long," Ruth told her.

Kailia walked on wondering about what to do now. She would have to check out this David.

"The people have not been so good at taking his help, but have been better since he started working at the shelter. His house is the third one with guards. People would still like to kill his family and he takes a big chance every time he comes to the shelter, that's why he always has two guards with him," Ruth told her. So Japtha and Mailiacha were his guards. At least, she knew now why they had been carrying guns.

Ruth and Kailia sat down for a small sandwich at lunch. They also put the bread in the oven. Lunch was good, but it didn't settle on Kailia's stomach and she had to excuse herself to throw up.

"How far along are you?" Ruth asked, when she returned.

Kailia smiled. "Just over two months."

"At least you will have a child to remember him by." Ruth patted her arm.

"I only wished he knew," she told Ruth.

She really wished she could tell Keeps he was expecting a child. Well, she wanted to tell him, but at the same time she was disappointed that it wasn't Brandon's. But she would still love it, no matter what or whose it was. And she was glad it was Keeps', in a way. At least, it wasn't some stranger. The thought of it made her stomach turn again. All those times she had been sent to bring down a human trafficking ring, she had come so close to being raped. Her emotions started showing in tears down her cheeks. Ruth patted her arm again. She gave Ruth a smile.

"Why don't you go lie down and take a nap? I will get you when the bread is done and we are going to head back to meet David."

"Thanks, I am tired."

Kailia got up and went to her room. But she really didn't want to take a nap, she wanted to check out the footage she had taken that morning. And now that she knew which house was his, she could check out the security. She pulled the small shield out of her pocket in folds of her robes.

Kailia sat down on the edge of her cot and watched the video. She put the shield in the Bible flap and laid back. It could easily be a trap, she thought, as she lay there with her eyes closed.

"Hey, Lindsey, where have you been?" Brandon was walking up to her on trail seven. Lindsey found herself in her Ranger uniform. Before she could open her mouth, he was standing in front of her looking down at her. Well, really at her belly; it was huge.

"Brandon," someone said from behind her. She turned to find Keeps coming up the trail behind her. Brandon looked hurt.

"What happened?" He asked her. "I thought you were coming back to me."

"I ..." Lindsey started.

"Sorry, Brandon, but it couldn't be helped," Keeps told him.

"Whose is it?" Brandon asked.

"Mine," Keeps told him.

"You slept with Keeps?" Brandon raised his voice. "How could you?"

"It was her virginity or death, which one would you have her give up?" Keeps raised his voice back at Brandon.

"Brandon," Lindsey started.

"No, I don't want to hear it." Brandon turned to leave.

"Please, Brandon." Lindsey grabbed his arm. "Let me explain."

"Brandon, listen to her!" Keeps added.

"And I thought you were our friend!" He jerked his arms from Lindsey's grasp and faced Keeps.

"It was either me or a stranger. Which did you prefer?" Keeps held his ground.

Brandon drew back and punched Keeps.

"Sweetie, it's time to head back." Kailia heard Ruth's voice as Keeps hit the ground.

Kailia opened her eyes, tears fell down her cheeks as she sat up.

"Are you ok?" Ruth asked her.

"Yes, just dreaming of my husband," she said as she wiped the tears from her face.

Ruth and Kailia went back to the shelter where David and his two guards were. David had brought enough supplies for all five of the families that still needed them.

"David." Ruth smiled. "Thank you."

"No one deserves to go hungry." He smiled at her.

"We will take them from here," Ruth told him.

"Are you sure?" He asked.

"Yes, I have Kailia and between the two of us we will be fine."

David turned and looked at Kailia. "You ok? You look like you're not feeling well."

Before Kailia could say anything, Ruth had already told David that she was expecting and that her husband had recently been killed, so she was doing as best she could.

"I am so sorry." David looked at Kailia.

"It's ok, I'm fine." She smiled at him.

"Are you sure?" He asked.

"Yes," she assured him.

She and Ruth spent the remainder of the day taking supplies one at a time out to families. Some were a mile or so out of town and the road was crowded with tanks and military vehicles going north. Most of the time they stayed to the edge of the road, too many land mines, Ruth had told her, to walk far off.

Kailia spent her time watching for signs of mines and looking over her shoulder for anything. By the time they got back into town from the last family, it was getting dark. David was waiting at the shelter.

"I was starting to get worried," he said as they entered.

"The road was covered in soldiers today; it was a slow trip," Ruth told him.

"I will make sure you get home safely," he told them, as he ushered them to the door, to a waiting truck.

The truck was huge and black. It looked to be armor plated and bullet proof.

"I don't like taking this thing, but it's getting late and you don't need to be on the street after dark," he told them. Ruth agreed about not being on the street after dark.

Kailia took the opportunity to feel David out.

"Ruth told me about your family. I hope that was ok?"

"My Dad was a tyrant. He did more harm to these people than I could ever even start to tell. I will work the rest of my life trying to make up for his stupidity." He shook his head in anger as much as shame.

Kailia touched his arm. "Sorry, didn't mean to stir up bad memories."

"It's ok; I am just glad I was out of the country for most of it. Although, maybe if I had been here, I could have tried to straighten him out."

"David, he would have pulled you in. It was good you were not here," Ruth told him.

Kailia and Ruth thanked him for the ride home, exited the truck and went in the house. Ruth went to get them some supper and Kailia went and closed the chickens back up.

After a small supper, Kailia excused herself to her tiny room and did some work on her shield. She needed to find out more about David. She searched for records on him and found that he had been at Princeton for four years and had graduated top of his class. He had come back just days before his dad had been killed by assassination, which had been now over six months ago.

David was the youngest of twelve brothers. Most were dead or fighting in the war. With David being in the U.S. so long, she was sure he would have satellite internet and she spent several hours finding the link to his computer. It was going on one in the morning when she finally broke into his laptop. Once in, she hid her tracks and closed out for the night. Luckily, the shield made its own energy by movement, but her, she needed rest.

The sun was up when she awoke and headed out to the restroom.

"Did you sleep well?" Ruth asked her. "I didn't have the heart to wake you this morning; you looked like you were sleeping soundly."

"I don't know about good, but better than the night before," she told Ruth. "So what are we doing today?"

"I need to go to the market and pick up a few things, then back to do some laundry and cooking," Ruth told her. "Why don't you just lie around here and take it easy. You need to take care of yourself."

Kailia normally would have objected, but the time alone would give her time to work on her next move. "Are you sure? I feel fine and don't mind helping."

"You take it easy today."

"All right then, I won't argue with you." Kailia gave Ruth a hug and returned to her room and lay back down on her bed to rest until Ruth left the house. Twenty minutes later she heard Ruth leave.

Kailia got out her shield and began to work on David's computer. He was logged in and online. She turned his camera on. He looked like he hadn't been awake long. His hair was a mess. He was on a secure server, but to her it wasn't that secure. She read all the mail that was in his inbox for the last four months. Most seemed normal, all but one. It was signed Karen, but it had a tone she didn't like.

Have got it in place, we will soon know. Karen.

Problem, but still getting lots done. Karen.

I almost have them. Karen

The last one was from three days ago; the rest were spread out over the last three months. Karen had to be 25, but if she was, then

David was in on the whole thing. A message popped in as she was still sitting there.

Problems, be a few more days. Karen.

Without warning her stomach sent her running to the restroom. This wasn't good. She was here on a mission, but the only mission she had going for sure was the one that kept sending her running to the restroom every little bit. She sat back down on her cot. Maybe she could use this to her advantage. Maybe ask David for help; she had yet to be seen by a doctor.

Ruth returned around noon, and to her surprise David was with her.

"David has some wonderful news," Ruth told her.

"Well, let's hear it."

"I was able to get the Red Cross here tomorrow for a clinic. I was just coming by to ask Ruth if she thought it would be ok to use the shelter."

"That's great. How did you manage to get them in?" Kailia asked David.

"Well, I used a little persuasion." He dropped his head. "Ok, so I used a few of Dad's old channels, but if it helps the people, it was worth it," he said and lifted his head back up.

"I want to help," Kailia told him.

"I was hoping you would. I am sure they will need translators." He smiled at her.

Kailia jumped up and ran to the restroom. She soon returned.

"Sorry about that, but I seem to stay sick," she told them as she entered the kitchen.

"It will pass in another month or so," Ruth told her.

"A month or so? Oh, good grief!" She sat down. "Can't it quit now?"

Ruth smiled and finished talking to David about the Red Cross. Kailia just listened and tried not to have to run to the restroom again before he left, but had no luck and had to make two more trips.

That night Kailia didn't sleep well; she kept dreaming of Brandon and Keeps fighting. When she awoke she felt like she hadn't slept at all.

"How did you sleep?" Ruth asked her as she entered the kitchen.

"Not good." She was honest. "What time is the Red Cross coming in today?" She asked Ruth. She had been in and out so much when David was there last night, she couldn't remember hearing a time.

"They will be coming in by ten this morning. David wants us at the shelter by nine to help get things set up for them before they get there," Ruth told her. "Are you hungry?"

Kailia looked at the plate of eggs towards her, then turned and ran to the restroom.

"I'll take that as a no," Ruth said.

"Maybe some crackers or something?" She asked when she returned.

Ruth laughed. "You won't find crackers here, but I will toast you up some bread. Maybe that will help."

"Thank you," Kailia told her.

After Ruth toasted some bread and wrapped it up they headed to the shelter. David was already there moving tables.

"You feeling ok?" He asked Kailia.

"Not a good night." She moved a chair to one of the tables.

"Are you going to be able to help today?" He asked.

"I'll be fine." She gave him a smile. By ten they had the shelter made into a makeshift hospital and people had already started lining up. The large white truck with the big Red Cross on the side pulled up just after ten.

"Kailia." The driver greeted her. He had been at the Daharan Red Cross while she was there.

"Jim, it's good to see you," she told him.

"You wouldn't happen to have any crackers, would you?" She asked.

"Going through the sick phase of pregnancy, are you?" He asked.

"Oh, yes," she said as he reached back in the truck and pulled out three packs.

A young man and woman got out of the other side of the truck.

"Kaila, this is Kara Johns and her brother, Kyle."

"Nice to meet you," she told them. Her stomach seemed to be calming as she ate the first cracker.

David, Kyle and Jim began to unload supplies and Kara set up at the front table.

"Are you Indian or from India?" Kailia had noticed how dark Kara and her brother were.

"Native American on my Dad's side." She smiled.

Kailia's heart suddenly ached for Brandon.

"I am here to translate," she told Kara.

Kara smiled. "Thanks, but I don't need one. But you can translate for Kyle if you want."

"Did he not take Arabic classes?" She asked.

"No, neither of us did." She smiled as she wrote on a paper.

"Ok, I am confused; do you speak Arabic?"

"I speak perfect Arabic." She looked up at Kailia.

"But you just said neither one of you took it."

"We didn't. I have the gift of tongues."

"Are you ready?" Kyle came in with an armload of supplies and sat down beside Kara.

"Ready," she told him. Kailia listened to Kara talk to each person as they entered. She spoke better Arabic than she did, and she was supposed to be from this part of the world.

"They're good, aren't they?" David came up behind her.

"Yes," she answered.

"I didn't know you worked with the Red Cross before. Jim says you served a month in Daharan."

"Yes, that is why I was coming back here. My husband wanted to serve and help here and I decided it was best to finish what he had started."

David smiled at her.

"You two going to just stand there and talk, or help?" Jim asked them as he walked by. The afternoon went by so fast. The line seemed to be endless.

Jim and David had worked out a few more trips for the next few weeks, by the time they had to leave at five. They didn't need to be traveling in the dark.

Kailia closed her eyes; that night she didn't get sick after she had eaten a few crackers that morning, and she slept soundly.

"It was a rough . . ." Kailia heard Kazim's voice as she walked towards the kitchen.

"You're back!"

"Yes, are you ready to go?" He asked.

"No, I want to stay." She looked to Ruth, "Can I stay here? I want to help the Red Cross when they come back.

"What?" Kazim looked at her. "You defy me? You have been in the States to long and have picked up their bad habits. But Since I am not your husband and am not a real relative, I will act like it never occurred."

"You are welcome to stay," Ruth told her.

"It is only a matter of time that the fighting we went through will be here," he stood up to face her, "and you don't need to be here when it does."

"I'm not leaving." She looked him in the eye.

"Stupid Americans and their ways." His anger was plainly written on his face. "And what am I suppose to tell Jasmine?" He asked.

"The truth, I want to stay here and help."

Kazim threw his hands in the air. "Fine. So be it, you are not my kin."

"That's right." Kailia smiled and sat down. Her stomach turned when Ruth sat some bread and eggs in front of her.

"I am not hungry." She left the table and went back to her room. She thought of Kara and what she had said about having the gift of tongues. She pulled out the big old worn Bible. She opened it to the concordance in the back. She came across Acts 2:4, *"And they were all filled with the Holy Ghost, and began to speak with other tongues, as the Spirit gave them utterance."*

Could Kara be talking about this Holy Ghost giving her the wisdom to speak other languages? She would have to ask her more about it. Kailia had been taught many religions and knew of this one, but it was mainly like all the others, just another bunch of people trying to find meaning to their life. She closed the Bible and lay back down. She didn't believe in a God; how could she? There was suffering in this world that was too horrible to mention. If there was a God, surely he wouldn't let all of that go on.

"Kailia?"

She opened her eyes to find Ruth standing at her door.

"Sorry, I didn't know you went back to sleep," she said.

"I didn't know I did, either." Kailia smiled at her.

"David is here. I thought you might want to hear what he found out today from the Red Cross."

"I do, thank you." She got up and followed Ruth back to the kitchen.

"Good morning," David told her as she entered.

"Morning." She sat down.

"I talked to Wameedh Majed."

396

"I know Wameedh. He runs the Red Cross at Daharan," Kailia told him.

"Yes," he said, "he tells me that the team can re-supply and come back in two days. This time they will stay for three days. They will stay at my house while they are here."

"That's good." Ruth smiled. "They did great work yesterday, but there are so many still hurting."

"I agree." David looked at her. "I hope I can get them coming in on a regular basis."

"Will it be the same team?" Kailia asked David.

"I don't know, but I hope it is Kara. She was so good with the people and her not needing a translator helped us see more people."

"Yes, it did." said Ruth, "I liked her and her brother."

"Well, I've got to go. Many things to be done before they come back. Mainly get my house cleaned up. Since Karen has been gone I have sort of let the place go."

"Karen?" Kailia questioned. The emails she intercepted were from a Karen.

"My wife," he smiled.

"I didn't know you were married."

"Yes, I married not long after my dad died. I guess it was silly, but she was my younger brother's tutor."

"She was there when no one else was," Ruth smiled at him.

"Yes, I guess that is what did it. I hated my father for what he did, but he was still my father and I mourned greatly when he was killed. I guess if it had not been for Karen . . . well, she got me through."

"How is her mother? Isn't that where she went?" Ruth asked.

"Yes, it was; she's not well at all. They only gave her six months to live and I couldn't deny her that time with her."

"Oh, I am so sorry." Kailia looked at David. "How long has she been gone?"

"Going on four months, now."

397

"Can I do anything to help?" Kailia smiled. She would love to get the opportunity to get into his house.

"Did you send everyone away?" Ruth asked, "I thought you still had a few servants."

"I couldn't see keeping them; father had been so cruel to them that I let them all leave."

"We will come and help," Ruth announced.

"No, you don't have to do that."

"Sure we do." Kailia said. "You have been providing for the shelter when no one else could. It would be an honor to help."

"Let's go," Ruth got up.

"Ruth, where is Kazim? I think I was a little rude with him earlier."

"He is already gone. He left right after you said you weren't going back with him," Ruth told her.

"Not going back?" David asked.

"No, I have decided to stay."

"Wonderful!" He smiled.

The three of them left the house. Omar was sitting in front of the fire outside as he was the first night she arrived. David told him Ruth and Kailia were going to his house and would be back later. He just nodded his head and went back to smoking the pipe he held.

Kailia carried her Bible on her back in a pack she made. David noticed it.

"Why do you always carry that?"

"It was my husband Seth's. It is sort of like carrying him with me." She smiled.

"You are already carrying part of your husband." He looked at her stomach. "Why add the extra weight?"

Kailia pulled the pack off her as they walked. She pulled out the Bible and opened it and pulled the picture out and handed it to David. "He read this every day; it went everywhere with him. And now it goes everywhere with me." She took the picture when he handed it back. She put it back in the Bible and returned it to the pack and slung it over to her back again. Luckily, the word Bible was worn off the front and most would not know what the book was; which was good, since most of them didn't believe in it anyway. She didn't need to stir up trouble for herself.

"I guess I can understand that." He pulled a round gold piece from his pocket, "This was my father's; he carried it with him, too."

When they got to the gate the guards opened it and let them in. The courtyard was large and open. David opened the door for them when they got to the house.

"Welcome," he said as they entered.

Kailia found that the house was not unlike the other Middle Eastern houses she had been in. Open and large, one of the benefits of being wealthy in a poverty stricken land. The house wasn't all that messy, just dirty, but in this sandy land, that was normal.

"Will you give them the Northern wing?" Ruth asked. She evidently knew the house.

"Yes. You can start there." David told her.

"Come on," she told Kailia. "I think I remember where the cleaning supplies are." She walked toward another room.

"Nothing has really changed, Ruth," David told her.

Kailia followed Ruth through a large open inner court into a large kitchen, "I worked here in the kitchen for his father for many years. He was a cruel and mean man," she said as she opened a large pantry. Inside were buckets, mops, brooms, dusters and lots of cleaning cloths. "We shall start in the North wing and work our way back to the kitchen."

They changed bed linens, dusted and cleaned every floor. Kailia took every opportunity to place spider bugs and cameras as they went. A woman appeared with their lunch around noon. Ruth knew the woman; she had been born in the house and had no family left, so she had stayed when everyone had left. Ruth knocked on a door and then opened it. David sat behind a large desk working at a computer.

"Would you like us to clean in here, too?" Ruth asked.

"Yes." He went on working as they entered. There were pictures of men along the wall of the office. Two caught her attention. Ziafat was one of them and the other was the man with the scar, but in the picture he had no scar.

"Who are all the pictures of?" Kailia asked David innocently.

"Mostly family." He pointed to one. "That one was my father." He pointed to several more. "Those are my uncles." Ziafat was one he indicated as an uncle.

"What about those?" She asked to the grouping that held the man with the scar.

"Brothers." He smiled.

Kailia went back to dusting while carefully placing a spider bug and camera on one of the pictures facing David's desk. They didn't go to the door at the side office, so when they left she asked Ruth about it. Ruth told her it lead to the bunker and to the many cells where David's father once held his many prisoners.

"Ruth." David stuck his head out the door of his office. "Saja has kept my room clean, so you don't have to clean it."

"Alright," she told him. The two of them spent most of the day cleaning and left just before dark. Omar was still sitting in the same spot when they walked up in front of the house. He nodded as they walked by.

"I better get him something to eat," she told Kailia. The two of them working together quickly had supper ready. Ruth took him a plate out to the fire and she and Ruth sat at the table.

"So you worked for David's father?"

"Yes, long before he was killed. I knew David when he was a small boy." She smiled.

Kailia finished eating and cleaned their dishes.

"I am calling it a night," she told Ruth, "it has been a long day."

"I hope you sleep well," Ruth told her.

Kailia cleaned up and went to her tiny room. She pulled her Bible out and got out her shield. She held it in the crease of the Bible, so if Ruth walked by it would look like she was reading. She activated her cameras looking at each one and what was going on in the rooms. Her first camera was set in the front foyer and she could see the inner courtyard. The second was down the corridor of the North wing; she had one in the east and west wings, also. The one in David's office was perfectly fixed on his desk and the door to the side of it. Most of the cameras had nothing going on in them, but the one in David's office did. David sat at his desk, he was on the phone. She activated the bug.

"I don't care, he is not the same thing," he was saying. "Then bring him in and let's get it done," he continued. "I will see you in two days then. Bye." He hung up the phone. David got up from his desk and went into the bunker door and shut it.

Kailia needed to get in there and look around. She went online; there was more ways than one to get it done. She would love to check on Keeps, but since the Newbie virus had that system she was not going anywhere near it.

She hacked into one of the many spy satellites the military wasn't supposed to have. Of course, to anyone watching it, it was all fuzz. She pulled in the country, then the village, then his house. She turned on the thermal imaging. Each guard had a red heat signature. There were three guards walking the perimeter of the house. There was someone walking toward the east wing. Where David's office should be, there was nothing. She zoomed back out just a bit, off to the south there were several images, but they were faint. She turned up the sensitivity. There were at least ten of them. They had to be in cells. Each one was alone, but they were all no more than ten feet from each other. There was one moving between them all. It moved back and then back towards the house. It came out into

David's office. The shield was too small to see several things at once so she closed the satellite out and turned on the camera. David was back in his office.

Kailia closed the Bible and lay down when she heard Omar and Ruth come in from outside. Soon the house was dark and quiet. Kailia pulled her bag out from underneath the cot. She quickly changed into a pair of black pants and shirt. They were made of a spandex blend and when they weren't on they almost looked like children's clothes, but they could stretch 40 times their size. She pulled the blanket up on the bed so it looked like she was sleeping. She slid two knives in her waist and carefully went out into the night. She stuck to the darkest of shadows. The guards at the front gate never saw her as she went over the tall stone wall. Getting to the house was no problem, either. The guards walked circles and she slid right between them. She had paid close attention while in the house, earlier. She knew the only security he had was quite primitive and she would have no problem bypassing the main circuit at the main electrical box. Once inside, she carefully made her way to his office. The light still showed under the door. She sat and waited. About midnight David left the office and went to his room. It was only three doors down the corridor. She opened the office door and went in. The bunker door had a keypad lock not unlike the security system on the house. It only took her a few seconds to bypass it and open the door. The smells that met her when the door opened were familiar. Torture had a smell, and she knew it well.

The steps from the door led to a small room. To the left and to the right were both a set of doors. She had seen images to the south so she went to the left. As she approached the door, the smell got stronger.

The lock on this door was more advanced, but still was child's play, and she had it opened in minutes. There were cell doors on both her left and right. She used her shield to carefully peer through the dark into each tiny door slot. There were ten girls. Each of them was disfigured, four of them were pregnant. Kailia shuddered; had he also been in business with his uncle? She could remember no ties to David's father being found. 25 must have hid the trail to David's father, or maybe the trail was to David.

There were five more cells, each was empty, but they probably hadn't been empty long from the look of feces lying in them.

Kailia made her way back to the small room before the cells. She then went to the doors on the right. They had no security. Inside were several rooms, this had to be what was considered the bunker; it was set up with bedrooms and an office. The office door was open; it looked similar to the one up in the house.

Kailia's *something is not right* feeling came over her as she got to the office door. She pulled out her shield from her pocket and held it up. She scanned the office from the door. The shield picked up laser sensors running throughout the room. The security had been nothing until now. There was a computer on the desk in the office. This one looked nothing like the older model that was in David's upstairs office. This one looked new and up-to-date. The blue light shining on the wall told her the computer was on. Kailia sat down with the shield. There was a Wifi network detected; she spent ten minutes hacking the code to get on it. Someone had set up a good security system and . . . Nutria, she found a Nutria trail. She was definitely in the right place. She pulled off the trail and got off the system fast. If this trail led to where she thought it did, then the Newbie virus was present and she wanted no part of it.

Kailia turned her cameras on and checked the area before she emerged into the house again. She reset the alarm and went back to Ruth and Omar's. She quickly changed and got into bed. She lay there awake, her mind going over things. In two days, someone would be coming to David's. The Red Cross would also be coming. Was there a connection, or was that just a coincidence? Either way, maybe she could use the Red Cross to get invited back into his house. And was the person who was coming bringing someone with them?

Kailia wished she could contact Keeps and let him know what was going on. Maybe she could; she pulled the shield back out and searched for her phone she had while at Cherry Point. The battery was still in and the GPS kicked on. It was in Indiana; she turned on the monitoring system.

"No one has heard from either of them," she recognized Handler's voice.

"I am sorry," a woman's voice said. "But when your two top agents go off grid, you can't help but get a little tense . . . And you can't get a reading on either of them?"

"No, ma'am. I have already told you both trackers are deactivated."

"But how did she know about hers?"

"Didn't you tell Keeper to deactivate her when you sent him to Cherry Point?"

"Yes," the woman sighed.

"Is there anything else?" Handler asked the woman.

"No, you can go."

Kailia listened closely. She heard a door shut then the echo sound of a hallway. She sent a message. *Amhed Ziafat and Ali Shadar are brothers. Traffic ring is linked but hidden by 25. Was she caught?*

A message returned: *No, three dead and one missing.*

She sent back a question mark.

One word returned: *Cloak.*

Handler was much smarter than she had given him credit for, but then again Keeps had told her on numerous occasions the Handler was the best at surveillance and evidently he had been paying attention, close attention. She had no doubt he knew about everything, and that included Brandon.

A question mark came in to her.

She sent back only one word: *Safe.*

Kailia lay awake most of the night. Did 25 have Keeper, or was he on her trail? Was it 25 that was coming and was she talking about

Keeper? Her stomach turned and twisted till she was sick and in the restroom throwing up.

"Are you, alright?" Ruth tapped on the door about six am.

Kailia opened the door and looked at Ruth.

"Oh, my! You look horrible; have you been in there all night?" She asked.

"Most of it," she told her.

"Why don't you try to get some rest?" Ruth walked her back to her room. "Take it easy today; you probably just over did it yesterday."

Kailia lay down and closed her eyes.

Keeps was crouched in a corner of a dark room. He was beaten and bruised. He looked half dead. She ran to his side, but when he looked up, it was now Brandon.

"You betrayed me," he told her as he stood up.

"Where is he?" She screamed at Brandon. "What did you do to him?"

"He deserved everything he got," Brandon told her. He looked behind him, they were now standing in a field, and he was looking at a fresh pile of dirt.

"No!" She screamed. "He's not dead."

"You just keep telling yourself that."

She looked to Brandon, but it was no longer Brandon, it was David's brother with the scar.

She dropped to her knees at the pile of dirt and screamed, "No! He's not dead! He can't be! He's going to be a father!"

"Kailia, Kailia! Wake up, sweetie." Someone was shaking her.

She opened her eyes to find Ruth kneeling beside her cot shaking her arm.

"What . . . What's wrong?" Kailia asked Ruth.

"You were screaming in your sleep."

Crap, what had she been yelling, she thought. Kailia closed her eyes a second then opened them. "What was I yelling?" She asked Ruth.

"I think you were dreaming about your husband. You kept yelling *He's not dead!* over and over."

Kailia's eyes filled with tears. "I was dreaming of Seth."

"It is all going to be fine." She patted her arm.

"No, it won't," she told Ruth, "my child will never know it's father." Tears ran from her eyes. Her thought went to Keeps again. Was he ok? Tears flowed like someone had turned on a water faucet.

"I know it doesn't seem like things are going to be fine, but they will be, I promise." She patted Kailia's arm again and then got up and left the room.

Kailia curled up in the cot. Her emotions were going crazy; she couldn't stop crying.

Keeps looked at 25 sitting in a chair to his left by an old broken down desk. She was smarter than he had given her credit for. How she got the upper hand on them he didn't know, but she had, and now three of the team had been killed and she had him. Where he was he wasn't sure, but it looked to be an old warehouse of some kind. His hands were taped palms together just like all ten of them had been taught. He was also taped sitting up in a chair.

25 suddenly got up and left the room. He could hear her talking, but it was muffled and he couldn't tell what she was saying.

"Tell me, is she 23 or 15?" She came bursting back through the door. She stopped in front of him.

"I have already told you I don't know." He looked up at her.

"Tell me where they are!" She backhanded him across his face.

"I don't know! How many times do I have to say it?" He yelled at her.

She dropped to her knees in front of him. "Come on, 22 you took care of us all, you know. You have to know."

"I know no more than you," he told her again.

"Please tell me; these people make the torture we learned child's play."

"I can't tell you what I don't know. I just kept you supplied with what you needed, sent 10 to get Intel from you, but that's it."

"But you're the one that hid them; just tell me where they are. Only they need die, not you."

"I didn't hide them, King did. I was sent out in the field to hide as well. King hid us all, and if you were good enough to find me, then you should be able to find them."

She looked at him and got up off the floor. "You weren't hidden; none of the males were hid hidden well enough that a baby couldn't find them."

"You weren't given orders?"

"How do think I found out that the Maker was female? My orders were complex and very detailed and specific."

Keeps looked at her and smiled; maybe she wasn't that smart. "Maybe that's what King wanted you to think. Hiding the Maker, but not hiding the Maker."

25 paced the room. "You're the best hacker in the business. If I get my laptop, will you break into a file for me?"

"I can try; I am not the best. There is someone out there better than me."

25 left the room and returned with her laptop. She set it down in her chair and pulled out her knife. "Try to get online or send a message, and I will gut you like a fish." She sliced the tape from his hands.

"Just give me the laptop."

She picked it up and handed it to him. He opened it and the desktop popped up. A file was on the desktop that read Maker.

"Break open the file," she pointed to it.

"Where did you get it?" He looked up at her.

"King's Computer. Now break it,"

Keeps began to type. "Got it," he announced thirty minutes later.

25 took the computer from him, and re-taped his hands.

"At least, let me read it," he told her. Keeps watched her closely as she read the file. In his mind, he went through report after report he had put in the file. Nothing gender specific.

She slammed the lid on her laptop. "Forget the Maker. Who killed Ziafat?"

"What?" Her question had taken him by surprise. Could all this be about Ziafat? He thought for a moment. He could keep Maker safe by giving 23 away.

"Who was sent to deal with Ziafat?"

"Ziafat?" He looked at her.

"Yes, who was sent to kill Ziafat?"

"23," he told her. "I couriered Intel for her, posed as her brother."

She marched over and stood in front of him. "Who took his life?"

"23 did. What has all this got to do with Ziafat?" He questioned her.

She turned and left the room. Keeps now wondered about what he had just done. Was it the right thing? He hoped that Lindsey had been successful in getting set up somewhere in Shadar's life. But what did Shadar have to do with Ziafat?

His thoughts turned back to Lindsey again; he wanted nothing more than to see her again and to hold her in his arms. Brandon flickered in his thoughts, too. Was this what he felt like every time he parted ways with her? No, he couldn't; he didn't know her like he did now.

25 came back into the room. "It's time to go." She reached toward him.

Kailia spent most of the day in bed, half sleeping, but mostly crying. Every time she would try to quit, it only seemed to get worse. Ruth had told her it was all baby emotions and not to worry.

Kailia could hear David and Ruth talking around supper time and she stood in her doorway listening.

"She has been crying all day and every time the poor thing goes to sleep she starts screaming something about him not being dead. I think she's dreaming about her husband; I also think I must have worked her too hard yesterday."

"Oh, my goodness, I never thought of that. I am to blame if anyone is. You worked for me."

"She will be ok," Ruth told him.

"Why is she missing him so much now? It has been months."

"She's pregnant, David; her emotions are in overdrive."

"Poor woman," he said.

Kailia went and lay back down. She needed to calm herself, get control again. She closed her eyes and took a deep breath. She then let her mind wander back, back to Mt. Rainer, back to walking trails, back to playing piano in the clubs room. The calmness of the forest, the feeling of the piano keys under her fingers soothed her. Brandon and his smile entered her head. She thought of the first time she had seen him. He had come up the hallway at the Clearwater's house and had gone straight to wrestling with Jacob. She thought of the first night he stayed in her cabin and how he had accidentally caught her towel and it hadn't fallen from her, his face had turned so red. A small twinge in her stomach sent her mind in another direction as Keeps entered her thoughts. Heat flooded her in the sudden want of him. She opened her eyes and took a deep breath. She then pulled herself up from her cot and left her room.

Ruth and David were still sitting at the table when she entered the kitchen.

"How are you feeling?" Ruth asked her.

"Hungry."

"That's good," Ruth told her.

"I am sorry about earlier," she told Ruth. "I have no excuse." She sat down at the table.

"Yes, you do." David looked at her. "You're pregnant, and you lost your husband."

"David," Ruth looked at him.

"I feel so lost," she told them. "What am I even doing here?" She put her head in her hands.

"Fulfilling Seth's dream," Ruth told her.

"He wanted to serve in the Red Cross here then move on to another country and serve. So, why am I still here. I served the month he wanted." She looked up Ruth.

"What is it that you want, Kailia?" David asked.

"I don't know. Is it worth the risk of losing my child to serve here?"

"Is something wrong with the baby?" Ruth put her arm on Kailia.

"I am over three months along and have yet to see a doctor." She looked at her.

"You should go back to the States," David told her. "They have the best doctors."

"Do you know when Kazim will be coming back?" She asked Ruth.

"He is scheduled to be back at the end of the month."

"I can make a few calls and get you across the border." David looked at her.

"No." She smiled. "I will go when Kazim comes back. I said I would help with the Red Cross on their next visit, and I am going to keep my word."

"Are you sure?" He asked her.

"Yes, I have made it this far and I will make it one more month. Then I will go home." She smiled.

David set his hand gently on her arm. Kailia looked at him; men didn't touch women that weren't their wives. "Sorry." He drew back his arm quickly. "If you change your mind let me know." David got up from the table and left.

Kailia looked at Ruth, who in turn was looking at her. "It is good his wife will be returning in a few days." She turned and pulled a plate from the cupboard.

"His wife is coming home? So did his mother-in-law die?" She asked. Kailia smiled to herself; she had gotten this man to actually care enough for her in the last week that he had broken a cardinal rule in his own culture.

"Yes, he told me earlier that Karen had called last night. Her funeral is today and then she would be coming home."

"That's good. Not that her mother died, but that she'll be home."

Ruth set a plate in front of her. "Yes, it will be."

"Thank you," she told Ruth.

"I'm glad you're feeling better."

Ruth and Kailia spent the evening doing laundry. Well, Kailia mainly watched, Ruth wouldn't let her do much.

Kailia went to her room when Ruth went out to sit at the fire with Omar. She pulled the Bible out from under her cot. It fell open when she sat it down. She looked down, there were several verses highlighted in bright yellow. One was in orange, she read it.

> *Others were given in exchange for you.*
> *I traded their lives for yours*
> *because you are precious to me.*
> *You are honored, and I love you.*

Kailia smiled then flipped to the back and pulled out her shield. She activated one camera, then another, and looked around David's house. She found him pacing in his office. He would sit down for a few minutes then get back up and pace again. She closed the camera and opened her connection to his computer. It was searching. A window opened results on Seth McCallister. He was checking her out. The list was long. He sat and went through name after name, picture after picture. He retyped in his search engine *'obituaries for Seth McCallister'*. The search yielded ten matches. He went through the first four before he found what he was looking for.

> *Seth Brandon McCallister was born March 13, 1988 to Markus and Betty McCallister of Puducah, Kentucky. Graduated from Oakland City College in June of 2010. Leaves behind wife Kailia Hasan McCallister. Services will be held at two pm at the Benton and Glunt funeral home.*

David closed the page, turned off the light, and left the room. Kailia quickly changed cameras, he was heading to his room. She turned off the camera and went back to his computer. She searched through all the files. Nothing but normal stuff. Everything had to be on the computer in the lower office, which she hoped was being wiped out by the Newbie virus. Kailia closed the Bible and put it back under her bed and went and washed up for the night.

Keeps woke with his head bouncing. His hands were still tied, but he now lying and from the sound of it he was in the back of a covered truck. He could see the sun as the back canvas flipped in the wind. Two men with rifles sat to the left and right of him. He wondered just how long he had been out this time. The thought of 25 putting him under hypnosis scared him. She could easily find out everything. He had tried to be as convincing as he could every time 25 had questioned him. He closed his eyes and worked on his mind. Each of them had been trained how to keep hypnosis from working, but of course it didn't always work.

Kailia woke early and for the first time in several days she had slept pretty well. She got up and headed to the kitchen. Ruth was already kneading dough.

"You're up early this morning."

"Yes, I think I slept better last night than I have in months," she told Ruth.

"Good; get to kneading." She handed a bowl of dough to Kailia.

The morning sped by with a trip to the market. David had asked Ruth to help Saja with the meals for the Red Cross workers. So they stopped by David's on the way home to drop off some of the fresh vegetables.

"Ruth?" A woman opened the door.

"Karen." She smiled.

"David said you would be dropping by." She held open the door. "You must be Kailia, I'm Karen."

"I am sorry about your mother."

"Thank you," she said, "she was sick a long time."

"When did you get in?" Ruth asked as they walked to the kitchen.

"Early this morning." She smiled. "How's Omar?" Karen asked.

"Same as always," she told her.

"Oh, yes, I wanted to thank you for cleaning the house."

"You're welcome," Ruth told her, "it wasn't bad, just cluttered and dusty."

David came into the kitchen eating an apple as they were putting the vegetables up away. "Good morning." He smiled. "You look like you're feeling better today," he told Kailia.

"I am, thank you," she told him.

"Morning sickness." Karen smiled at her. "David said you were pregnant."

"Partly, I think, but also think I took on more than I should have too soon."

"I think you're right," David told her.

"I am sorry about your husband," Karen told her.

"Thank you."

Kailia watched every move Karen made. Was this woman 25? Genetic altering was great if you wanted to hide, but when you were the one looking for someone else who could do it, it was not easy to find them.

"Jim and the Red Cross team are coming in tonight," David told them, "that way we can get started early in the morning."

"Wonderful," Ruth told him, "I better head back to the market." Ruth looked at the supplies she was putting away.

"I will take care of tonight," Karen told her, "make sure you come join us for supper."

"David, do you know if it's the same team or not?" Kailia asked.

"Yes, it is. Jim mentioned that this was going to be Kara and Kyle's last trip before they headed back to the States. They have evidently been serving for the whole last year."

"It's crazy that the whole time I was in Daharan I never met them; saw Jim plenty, but never them. I will have to ask him about that."

Maybe Kara was 25. It made sense; she spoke Arabic perfectly and her story about the gift of tongues was a little farfetched. Kailia noticed the look Karen got on her face. She needed to talk with Kara, if she wasn't 25 and Karen was, she had just put her in danger.

"That is crazy," Karen told her.

"We better get going, we have lots to do today," Ruth told them.

Kailia noticed that for Karen being gone four months, David didn't seem too affectionate towards her. But it wasn't the custom to show outward affection. But then again, he had touched her.

"Supper will be late, so I will have Japtha come get you in the truck," Karen told them as they walked towards the door.

She and Ruth walked back towards the house. Kailia put her mind to work as they walked. Kara was quite tall; 25 wasn't quite that tall, she didn't think. She remembered passing her at the cafeteria doors. No, she was more Karen's height. She smiled to herself, good and not good. She had just given 25 an excuse to suspect her. The other thing that now bothered her wasn't that Karen might suspect her, but there were still ten women in the cells below David's house and Kara was young and pretty.

"Anything wrong?" Ruth asked as they got to the house. "You haven't said a word since we left David's."

"No, just lost in thought." She smiled.

"About what?" Ruth asked.

Kailia had to think. "I was thinking of baby names. If it's a boy, it will get Seth's name, but if it's a girl, I am not sure."

Ruth laughed. "You'll have a name picked out long before you give birth, I promise."

Kailia hadn't really thought about names and now, well, she was having a baby. But what did you name a baby whose parents didn't even have real names. 45, she laughed to herself. Well, it was her 23 and Keeps' 22 added together. She almost laughed out loud as she thought about it, she could name a boy Colt . . . . Colt 45.

Keeps woke again, it was dark and the smell was horrid. His hands were still taped, but he could feel something on his wrist. He waited for his eyes to adjust, but they never did; there was no light coming from anywhere. Total darkness; he closed his eyes and listened closely. He could hear dripping water. Sounded like it was hitting rock; there was also a little movement somewhere, but nothing close. He wiggled around till he hit his head on something and his hands caught. He pushed with his head till he was in a sitting position. He sat still and closed his mind to the darkness and silence of his confinement. He wandered through time, his mind stopped on 23 and the few nights she had spent in his arms. It was probably the happiest he had ever been, but there was also a sense of dread. Knowing they had broken the one thing she was told to keep, no matter what. What would they do to them if they ever found out? But still that wasn't all of it; he had a horrible feeling they had done something else. No, don't think about that. He needed to get his mind elsewhere. He went to LA, to the week he had spent with Kally. They worked Intel and did some sightseeing; after all, they were supposed to be on vacation.

The truck pulled up and Ruth and Kailia got in. Omar just nodded like he always did, smoking his pipe sitting at the fire's edge.

Kailia could see the Red Cross truck as they pulled through the gate. David was standing at the door when they got out.

"I hope you're hungry," he told them as he opened the door. "Karen and Saja cooked enough for an army."

The smell that hit them in the face when he opened the door was heavenly. Kailia's stomach growled loudly.

David laughed. "Well, at least one of you is hungry."

David showed them into the dining room where everyone was already seated.

"Kailia, Ruth." Jim stood as they entered. The young man, Kyle, stood and nodded to both of them.

"Evening," Kailia said. "Karen, everything smells wonderful."

As they ate, the conversation stayed mainly between Jim and David. Jim talked about their trip to pick up supplies and how there seemed to be more troops on the road than ever. Kyle spoke on occasion, but mainly just exchanged looks with his sister, who would smile or grin as if they were having their own conversation.

"Kara," Kailia finally spoke, "why is it I didn't see you in Daharan a month ago?"

"Oh, we weren't in Daharan then; we were in Egypt. We have been serving all over the Middle East, not just here."

"Are you and Kyle the same age?" She changed the subject.

Kyle laughed. "We're twins, but I am older."

"Only by a few seconds," Kara said.

"What made you join the Red Cross?" Karen asked.

"Well." Kara smiled at Kyle. "I have a special a gift, and what better way to use it than helping others."

"Gift?" Ruth asked, "What kind of gift?"

"You mean the speaking in tongues?" Kailia asked.

"Yes, exactly." She smiled at them.

"Speaking in tongues?" Karen looked at Kara.

"She can speak any language," Kyle chimed in, "and the only ones we were taught were Spanish and French."

"So, you know Russian and Chinese?" David, who was now listening, asked.

"Well, I don't know. I have never heard Russian or Chinese, but so far every language I hear I have been able to speak."

"Wait, I don't understand," Karen said, "you have to hear the language?"

"Yes, I only need hear someone else speaking it . . . well, that's not entirely true. I usually don't realize there is a different language being spoken; all I know is I understand what's being said."

"Tak YTO Bbl noHNMaTe, YTO R roBoplO?" David asked Kara in perfect Russian.

"KOHeYHO R," Kara replied.

"What was that?" Kyle asked. Kailia was glad someone asked; she had understood him perfectly.

"Russian." David smiled. "I asked if she understood me."

"Where did you learn Russian?" Kara asked.

"School. I was sent to Princeton, but you have to study languages, so I took Russian."

Kailia noticed Karen watching her when David spoke Russian, so she tried to look confused like Ruth did.

"That's amazing," Kailia told her.

"I am just blessed." She smiled.

The conversations carried over into the lounge. Kara told quite a story about her and Kyle's faith. It was very interesting and it touched Kailia very deeply. She found herself with tears in her eyes several times.

Kailia sat on her cot holding the large worn Bible in her hands. She lay the Bible in her lap and let it fall open. She looked down at the first highlighted verse.

Love must be sincere. Hate what is evil; cling to what is good. Be devoted to one another in love. Honor one another above yourselves. Never be lacking in zeal, but keep your spiritual fervor, serving the Lord. Be joyful in hope, patient in affliction, and faithful in prayer. Share with the Lord's people who are in need. Practice hospitality.

That did sum up Kara and what she had told them. Maybe there was something to this God of Kara's.

She then turned to the very back and opened the back cover, pulled out her shield and turned on one camera then another. David was in his office, but no one seemed to be stirring in the rest of the house. She hacked into the satellite, again. There were several more heat signatures this time. Three in the North wing, and then there was David in his office. Saja was in the kitchen, but she didn't see Karen. She turned up the sensitivity and went down to where the cells were. There were definitely more bodies here, two in the bunker, two outside the bunker, and eleven in the cells.

The two in the bunker were together, almost one. If she didn't know David was in his office, she would think it was David and Karen. She should have placed a camera down there. Why she didn't, she didn't know. The two outside the bunker she was pretty sure were guards, and the eleventh cell occupant had to be whoever she brought back.

Kailia lay down and waited; she needed to get it and see what was going on. Omar and Ruth finally shut off the light and Kailia changed and left. Once inside the gate, she again deactivated the primitive alarm and entered the house. She pulled the shield from her pocket and checked the camera in David's office. He was no longer there. She used the satellite. He was in his room, alone. She went to David's office and let herself in. Back to the satellite. All the heat signatures were still where they had been. Save one, which was her.

She moved carefully as she descended the stairs. The two guards were sitting, leaned back in chairs against the wall positioned outside the bunker door; both looked asleep. She quietly walked over to the guards. She held her hands out so she could touch them at the same time. Carefully, not to disturb them she took hold of the nerve in their shoulders at the same time. She again checked the satellite feed. The two images inside were close, but not like earlier. There were three rooms on the other side of the door. The images were in the bedroom to the right. She pulled the door silently open just a crack. The bedroom door was almost closed; she could hear two voices, one she recognized as Karen, the other she didn't know, but it was male. She placed a small camera on the door facing the office as she listened to the conversation taking place in the other room.

"No, he hasn't, but every day I get a little closer," Karen was saying.

"Closer to what? We know who killed my brother," he told her.

"Yes, I know, we know who, but we need to find out if he knows where she is, or at least what name she is going under."

"I thought you said that your minds were unbreakable, if you wanted them to be. Is he not like you?"

"Yes, but . . ."

"But why not kill him and be done with it?"

"There is something more."

"Like what?"

"He reacts when he talks about her. There is something going on between them. I want to know what."

"You have a week, then I want him dead. I will need the cell space."

"You know your son has a thing for the woman, Kailia. You could easily use her to control him better."

"Fine, but I want the girl Kara."

"And you shall have her." She watched the screen as the two images merged as one.

She wanted to check on the new prisoner, so she took the opportunity to go to the cell area. She disarmed the lock and opened the door; the smell was almost unbearable. She placed a camera on the facing in the cells. She checked the satellite once more, then turned on the shield night vision and closed the door behind her. She checked each cell starting with the ones to the right. Each had a girl, but as she got to the very back she found a male. Her heart almost stopped as she recognized Keeps. He was still in his camouflage, but looked ok.

"I hear you, who's there?" He whispered into the darkness.

She whispered back. "Are you ok?"

"Yes."

"She has had you under hypnosis, did you know?"

"No," he answered her.

"Keep your head clear. I don't think you have given up any information yet, but she plans to keep working on you," she told him.

"Are you ok?" He asked her.

"Fine, I have to go. Stay strong, I will have you out soon."

"Don't worry about me, take them down."

"I will do both."

She placed one of the small cameras inside the small hole in the door, then turned and left very carefully and quietly. Her heart was beating so loudly she wasn't sure if she was even being quiet. When she made it to the street she sprinted between the shadows to get back to Ruth and Omar's.

Once inside she changed clothes and turned on her new cameras one at a time. The bedroom door was still mainly shut, but there was someone in the office now. Kailia recognized the man from the picture in David's office. So his dad wasn't dead after all. They were smart in killing him off so that there were no tracks to him, and having David play the son trying to make up for his father's misguided ways. Brilliant!

Keeps heard the door again. His heart was pounding. Why was she affecting him so? He sat back against the wall; he needed to clear his mind of her ever coming. If 25 had been using hypnosis on him, she had done a good job, because he didn't remember it. At least 23 had managed to get close. He had confidence in her that she was going to get the job done. He leaned back: ok, clear your mind.

Kailia turned on the cameras in the cell area, just blackness. She then shut them off and closed her eyes a moment. If 25 were smart, which she was, she would wait till the Red Cross was leaving to take Kara; maybe blame a roadside bomb on the death of the others. She had three days to get Kara, Kyle and Jim to safety. Not to mention she needed to get Keeps and those other girls out of the cells.

She set a vibration on her shield to go off if the lights came on in the cell area, then she put it under her pillow and tried to get some sleep.

"No, I don't want you anymore, you ruined yourself, gave it away, and for what?" She and Brandon were standing in Vi's apartment.

"I had to," she pleaded with him, "it couldn't be helped."

"Brandon, she's telling you the truth." Keeps was now standing there with them.

Brandon pulled back and tried to hit Keeps, but he wasn't near fast enough, and Keeps had him pinned to the floor in a matter of moments.

"I don't want to hurt you, Brandon," Keeps told him.

"How could you, Keeps? You were helping me plan to get her out and then you go and take her away from me!" Brandon yelled at Keeps.

Keeps got off him and let him up.

"I'm sorry, I was helping you, but I never meant to ..." Keeps got up and turned to leave.

"No!" Vi screamed. Brandon had a gun pointed at Keeps. She heard the gunshot and watched as Keeps fell to the floor. She rushed to his side and dropped to her knees; he looked at her.

"Now, maybe now, he will take you back," he whispered as the blood pool got larger around him. He was dying, and he was still thinking of me.

What ... Kalia opened her eyes. Tears ran down the side of her face. The shield's vibration had awakened her. It was going on three in the morning. She pulled the shield out and flipped on the camera. The lights were on. Karen and Saja were carrying trays of food to each cell. At least, they fed them well, but that was only because they wanted healthy babies. Karen also took Keeps some food. Kailia turned on the camera she had placed in his cell. He didn't look too badly, just filthy. She had thought he would be bruised and broken, but he just looked tired and weary. Karen stood in his cell talking to him, but Kailia had not placed a bug so she couldn't hear anything.

Twenty minutes and Saja was back to collect all the trays. Karen returned with the two guards and they took Keeps out into the room adjoining the bunker and the cells. The guards tied him to a chair and Karen walked back and forth in front of him talking.

Kaila quickly hid the shield when she heard Ruth get up and go to the kitchen. Kailia put the shield away and listened to Ruth stir around before she decided to get up and help her.

By nine they were on their way to the shelter. David and the others were already setting up when they got there.

"Morning," Kara told her, "You look tired, did you not sleep well?"

"Not really," she told her.

"David said you were leaving not long after we do."

"Yes," she told her.

"He's right about the best doctors being in the U.S.." Kara smiled at her as they moved tables around.

"Has she told you what it is, yet?" Kyle asked Kailia. He had been placing chairs at the tables they were moving.

"What?" Kailia looked at him.

"Has Kara told you if it's a boy or girl?"

"Kyle." Kara looked at her brother.

"How could she know such things?" She asked Kyle.

"She has a God-given talent, and I know because she has never ever been wrong."

"Never?"

"Nope, never." Kyle smiled.

"Do you want to know?" Kara asked her.

"What do you have to do to find out?" She asked Kara.

Kara smiled. "Nothing, I already know. But do you want to know?"

"You already know, but how?"

"Well, ever since I was little I see a small blue or pink spot on pregnant women. I know it sounds nuts, but right there," she touched Kaila's stomach, "is a small amount of color on you. The craziest thing is I usually know women are pregnant before they do."

"Well, do you want to know or not?" Kyle asked.

"Kyle." Kara looked at him again. "Sorry."

Kyle left the room to go help David and Jim.

"Sorry, about that Kailia, my twin forgets his place here. We better get done; it looks like the line is already getting long outside," Kara pointed to the door and the people outside.

Soon Kyle had the supplies ready and David, Ruth, and Jim had the small rooms ready for treatments. Kara and Kailia played nurses, Jim was the doctor, and Ruth, David and Kyle helped getting medicines and keeping order.

Kailia thought as they worked about what Kyle had said about Kara knowing if she was having a girl or boy. Kara was very different; she watched her closely. There was something about her that Kailia just couldn't quite put her finger on. As they worked, Kailia took every opportunity to talk to Kara but they were hardly around each other except in passing until they took thirty minutes for lunch. Karen brought food from the house.

"Have you got any names picked out?" Kara asked as she sat down by Kailia.

"I haven't really given it a lot of thought, yet," she told her. "Should I be picking out boy names or girl names?" She asked Kara

"Boy ones." Kara looked at Kailia. "Yes, definitely boy ones."

"So what are your plans when you get back to the States?"

"Well, I don't know." she smiled. "First thing I plan on is seeing my little brother."

"How many siblings do you have?" Kailia asked Kara.

"There are just us and my little brother, David; he will be seven this year. Man, I have sure missed him a lot. But as for real plans, no, I don't make plans because I have learned my life is not my own."

Kailia looked at Kara. "What do you mean?" She asked her.

"Each moment of this life is just like a mission, it has all been planned out for us."

Kailia was now glad Karen had already left. She would have been sure to think Kara was an agent, hearing that statement.

"Mission, what are you talking about?" Kailia really needed to understand Kara. She surely wasn't an agent being that blunt, was she?

Kara laughed. "Sorry, am I confusing you?" She asked Kailia. "Come on, let me show you." She got up and threw her trash away. Kailia followed her lead.

"I see your confusion and I understand things aren't always what they seem to be. No one understands that better than me." She smiled at her. "But what I am saying is not what you're thinking. Look around here, all these people, all this pain and suffering, it's not without a purpose."

"What purpose could there be in these people suffering?"

"If life were perfect and there were nothing to overcome, no challenges, what would there be to live for?"

"What?" Kailia looked at Kara.

"The Maker has sent me here for a purpose. I am here to help these people with medicine and supplies and you are here to help them in a whole different way."

Kailia was now more confused than ever. She herself was The Maker.

"The Maker I refer to is the Creator of the heavens and earth, Kailia."

"Oh, you're referring to God."

"Yes." She smiled.

"I find it so hard to believe He would allow people to suffer like this." She needed to keep her cover intact.

"That is just it, without suffering, people would not believe. Without evil, where is the place for good? Without need where is the place for help?" Kara placed her hand on Kailia's arm. "I see the struggle in your eyes every time we meet. I know you have been sent here to help in ways I could never help. Ways most of us couldn't help, but know that you were sent here for a purpose even if it is not what you understand to be. He did send you, make no mistake about it."

"It's time to get back to work," David yelled from the door.

"Ok, coming!" Kara yelled back.

"He is not all bad." She looked at Kailia. "He just has some bad influence. Now, Karen on the other hand, I would not trust at all."

Kailia was again taken aback by what Kara was saying. She had to be an agent to know all she did. Was she 15? Keeps said there were three females in the field. If she was, she was playing her part well.

"Come on, we need to get back to work; we can talk more later." She smiled at Kailia.

Kailia walked back into the shelter, her mind now going in five different directions. Kailia watched Kara and Kyle's every move. Kara was very good at communicating with the people of the town. Kyle worked diligently at helping Jim with medicines. Could they be a team sent in? Kailia knew when people were lying. She was good at reading people and Kara, well, she believed everything she said and that included the part about God.

Just before sunset, they closed the clinic and headed back to David's. Kailia and Kara walked at the back of the group.

"Kailia." Kara slowed to let the group get ahead.

"Yes?"

"I am sorry if I confused you earlier. I just have so many things going on in me that I forget that not everyone is ready to hear what I have been sent to tell them."

"Sent?"

Kara laughed. "Sometimes I forget that people were not raised like I was, and their faith is not as strong as mine."

"What do you mean 'sent'?" Kailia asked her again.

"Have you ever had a dream that affected you so much that you felt compelled to do something, because of it?" Kara asked her.

"No."

"Well, I did, and that's why I came here. I had a dream when I was about fourteen, of a woman. She needed to know that her life was more than what she had been taught, more than how she had been raised. She needed to know that her life wasn't her own, but it did not belong to whom she thought it did."

Kailia just looked at Kara. How could she know she thought that?

"She needed to know that God himself put her where she was." Kara stopped walking and looked at Kailia. "I have no idea what this is supposed to mean, but I know I am supposed to tell you ... oh, this sounds nuts, but here goes. Your gifts were given you for a reason, there is a reason you are the best in your field. Do not fear anything or anyone. You will succeed in the task at hand, but remember to call out to Him, for He hears the very desire of your heart."

"Call on whom?" She stepped closer to her. "No one knows I am even here."

"God does." Kara smiled. "And you have been chosen by Him to be a warrior."

"What are you two doing back here?" Kyle walked up to them.

Kara looked at Kyle, and Kyle turned and walked back towards the group.

"Come on." Kara started walking again. "Just think about it, Kailia."

Kailia slowly started walking. Kyle had slowed back down and was now getting close to her. Kara passed him without saying a word.

"Is everything, ok?" He asked as she caught up to him. "You look a little shaken."

"I think it has been a long day," Kailia told him.

"I figure she must have told you about her dream." He looked at her as they walked. "She has lots of dreams, and over the years I have learned never to question what she does. If she told you something, then know that it's true. Believe what she says and take any advice given you. I promise you that you won't be sorry." Kyle smiled at her.

"So, if your sister is so gifted, what do you do?"

He smiled. "I am full of surprises, but I am not here to help you, she is."

Kyle let her pass through the gate before him.

"So, you're a team?"

Kyle laughed. "I guess I never quite thought of it like that, but I guess we could be if the right problem arose."

"Like what kind of problem?"

"I am not that gullible." He smiled as they got close to the door. Everyone else had gone in so he opened the door for her.

The evening was like the evening before. They ate then went and sat in the lounge for a while. The men talked and the women talked, but Kailia didn't say too much. She just sat and listened.

"I think I better get Kailia home; she looks worn out." Ruth got up.

"I hope we didn't work you too hard," Kara told her.

"What?" David must have been listening. "Is Kailia feeling badly?" He now stood close to her chair.

"No, I am fine, just tired." She smiled up at him.

"Maybe you shouldn't work tomorrow," he told her.

"No, I'm fine. Maybe take an extra break every once in a while." She smiled.

"Are you sure?" He asked.

"You do look dreadfully tired," Karen told her. "Why don't you take one of the spare rooms here for the night?"

"Yes," David said, "Ruth, you're welcome to do the same."

"No. I need to see to Omar, but thank you for the offer."

"I am fine." Kailia got up to join Ruth.

"You should take Karen up on her offer." Ruth told Kailia. "They have beds here, not just an old broken down cot,"

"What? She has been sleeping on a cot?" Karen looked at her. "Well, that's it, you are staying here. A woman in your condition needs to be comfortable."

"Really, I'm fine."

"Listen to her." David gave her a gentle smile. "Please."

She looked at David. "Ok."

"Good," Karen said, "you can have the room beside Kara's. I will show you, follow me."

Kailia followed her to the North wing.

"If you need anything, let Saja know."

"Thank you, Karen."

"Don't think anything of it." She opened the door to her room. "And feel free to go to the kitchen if you get hungry," she smiled at her.

Karen turned and left Kailia in the room. This was a good and a bad development at the same time. She was closer to what was going on, but just like she could watch closely now, she would be closely watched.

Kailia looked around the room. It was nice, had more the feel of American living. The bathroom that was off her room was what she liked the best. She took her first hot shower in two months.

After her shower, she lay down on the bed still wrapped in her towel. She climbed in the covers and slid the towel out and dropped it on the floor. She reached over and pulled her Bible from the pack she had laid on the bottom of the bed. She opened it and pulled her shield out carefully. She needed to check the room for privacy.

The scan revealed she was alone. She needed to find a way to get Keeps and the girls out. She was not going to be able to do it alone. She turned on the locator on her phone. It popped up in Saudi; she turned on to monitor. It was quiet, but it was late. She sent a message.

"?"

"Checked on Shadar and Ziafat. Am I in the right place?"

"Yes."

"What do you need?"

"I need you."

"Where and when?"

"Tomorrow night, alone. You have ten seconds to retrieve location."

"Ready."

She turned on a GPS locator counted to ten, then turned it back off.

"Target acquired."

"Here, same time."

"I will be there."

"Thank you."

She turned on the satellite. Kara, Kyle, and Jim were all in their rooms. There was an image in the kitchen which was sure to be Saja, and two in David's office. She moved to the cells; still eleven and three others sure to be the guards, and Shadar. She turned on her cameras one at a time. David and Karen were in David's office. She turned on the sound.

"No, you can't do that," David was talking very loudly.

"Yes, I can, and when I do you better do exactly what I ask, or she will pay for your lack of obedience."

"Karen, please don't do this."

"I know you want her, David. Everybody that was in there tonight knows how badly you want her."

"I don't want her like that."

"You can thank me later."

"Please, Karen. I'll do anything, just leave her alone."

"Anything?"

"Yes." You could hear the defeat in his voice.

"I want four sons from you." It got silent for a few minutes.

"Alright," David finally said.

"Good."

Karen left the office and went into the bunker. David sat at his desk, his face was in his hands. Kailia felt a sudden twinge of sorrow for David. He was just a pawn in Karen's game. And she was being used to control David.

David got up and left the office; he walked to the north wing and just stood looking at her door. Kailia jumped up and put on a robe. She opened her door.

"Oh." She jumped.

"Sorry, I didn't mean to scare you," David told her. "I thought you were asleep. I didn't wake you did I?"

"No, I was going to the kitchen."

"Hungry?"

"Yes, I can't seem to stay full. I go from not being able to eat, to never getting full."

"Well, come on, we better get you something to eat then." He smiled at her.

"Karen asleep?" She asked as she walked with him.

"I think so. I just came from the office." He turned on the kitchen light and went to the cupboard. "So what are you hungry for?"

"I don't know, just something small. Do you have any pickles?"

David laughed. "I am sure we do, but I know we don't have ice cream."

That did sound pretty good, Kailia thought. "Just pickles will be fine; well, maybe some cheese, too."

David sat the jar of pickles out and got out the cheese and sliced it. Kaila snacked as David sat across the small kitchen table from her.

"Kailia." He looked at her seriously. "If I ask you to do something for me, would you?"

"What's wrong, David?" Kailia reached out and touched his hand that was on the table, then drew it back quickly.

He smiled at her then looked over his shoulder towards the door. "I need for you to leave."

"What?" She looked at him.

"Karen is ... well, she is jealous of you."

"Of me, why?"

He looked at her, his eyes told their own story. Kailia knew that look; she had seen it many times in Brandon's, as well as Keeps' eyes.

"Oh." She said. "I didn't mean to get in ..."

"No." He reached for her hand. "It's me."

Kailia looked at her hand in his. "I'm sorry." She pulled her hand back from the table and got up so quickly that she almost tripped over her chair.

David was at her side in seconds to steady her. She looked at him as he held her in his arms. She just stood there. She knew if she could get him on her side she would have a better chance to pull off their escape. But at what cost? Another hurt heart. She pulled from his arms.

"Thank you." She turned and left him standing in the kitchen.

Kailia sat on her bed for a few minutes, then got out the shield and checked on Keeps. The cell was dark. She turned on her camera facing Shadar's office. Both the office door and the bedroom door were shut. Kailia could not see light coming from under either. She turned on her one in the kitchen. David was cleaning up where Kailia had been eating. Once he finished he went to his room.

Kailia took off her robe and slipped into bed. How could she have done this to yet another man? What was wrong with her, how could she do these things? But wasn't that what she was taught to do, use, then move on? Kailia closed her eyes. She was not going to do this anymore. She put her hand on her stomach.

Kailia woke with that feeling; she knew someone was in the room. She didn't move; she didn't need to blow cover, no matter what.

"Kailia," she heard David whisper.

Kailia opened her eyes and blinked to get her eyes to focus. David was standing beside her bed.

"David," she whispered, "is that you?"

He sat down on the side of the bed. "I need to talk to you."

"What is it?" She sat up and tucked the covers under her arms since she had gone to bed with nothing on.

"I lied to you earlier."

"About what?" She asked.

"About Karen," he told her, "things are not exactly what they appear to be."

"What are you talking about?"

"Karen was my father's wife. I just sort of inherited her."

Kailia turned to face him. "But Ruth said she got you through your dad's death."

"Ruth doesn't know everything," he told her, "she may have worked here once, but when Dema ..." He paused, "well, she doesn't know everything."

"Who's Dema?" Kailia asked David.

"It's not important, but Karen and I are not ... well, we're only married in name. I don't love her, and she doesn't love me. We don't even share the same room."

"Why are you telling me this?"

"Because, Karen is using you against me."

"What, how? I don't understand!"

David dropped his head. "How could I let it get this far?" He shook his head.

"David." Kailia took her hand and lifted his face so he would look at her.

"My father is a horrible man, Kailia, and Karen is just like him."

"You mean was?"

"No, I mean is; he's not dead. He is in the bunker with Karen. My life is a lie, Kailia; everything I do is a lie." A tear rolled down his face.

"Then why are you doing it?"

"When I came back from the States from school, my uncle had been killed and my father was already in hiding. Karen said he needed to disappear so nothing would be traced to him. I didn't even know what she was talking about until I saw those girls." Tears were flowing.

Kailia slid over in the bed and put her arm around David's shoulder.

"He was getting them pregnant and selling the babies. He beat each of them so badly, that they are scared and disfigured."

"Why did you stay? Why didn't you just leave?"

"Karen had a plan, to pretend to kill father, then let him hide while I took over and make amends for father's cruelness to the town."

"And you went along with it. Why?"

"I made a bargain with them. I would stay and take care of the town and pretend to make amends on the condition he would take no more women. But now Karen is trying to control me even further and she is using you to do it."

"How is she using me against you?"

"Do you not know I care for you?" He looked up into Kailia's eyes.

"Yes, I know you do."

"Well, so does Karen. She will hurt you if I don't do as she asks, and I can't. I cannot do what she wants; I would rather die. So, please, let me get you out of here so she cannot use you against me."

"What does she want you to do?"

"She want me to . . . she wants four sons from me."

"How are you . . . oh, she wants you to . . . your father still has the girls?"

"Yes, but I can't."

Kailia looked at David. Was he telling the truth? Kara's words rang through her head. "You know he's not bad, just being influenced." She made a decision.

"David." she lifted his head once more to look at her. "I need to . . ." she paused. She didn't want to hurt him. "Let me try this another way. I never meant to make you care for me. I wasn't even trying to catch your attention. I would never want to hurt you."

"Hurt me?"

"Listen, I am just pretending to. I am not who you think I am, either."

"What?"

"You told me why you're pretending. Now it is my turn."

"Alright, then tell me."

"I am . . . the one who killed your uncle."

"You . . . ? And my brother?" He stood up from the bed.

"No, I didn't kill him, but I would have liked to. I spent three months in a dark cell being tortured by him."

David dropped to his knees beside the bed. "No."

"Yes. I have never felt so degraded and humiliated and worthless in my life." She fought back the tears that threatened to consume her. She closed her eyes and took a deep breath; she could see his brother clearly in her head, feel his hands. She shuddered. David put his hands on hers and she opened her eyes. She couldn't help the tears that fell from her eyes.

"I came for Karen, but knowing about the girls, I am now here for them and for Karen and your father's death. But David, I promise you I was not trying to make you care for me. I would never harm you."

"How could you have spent time with Ali and not have a mark?"

"The people I work for can hide anything physical. But the scars are still in my mind, still emotional and they can never be erased. David, I tell you this because you are willing to sacrifice your life to not harm these women. I plan to set them free. Will you help me?"

He stood up beside the bed and looked down at her, "You're planning on killing both of them?" he asked.

"Yes." Kailia reached for her robe slid it over her head and stood up in front of him. Kailia could see hurt and anger in his eyes. "David, I did not mean to . . ."

He pulled her into his arms. "Was it all a lie, every word?"

"No, not every word." She touched his face.

"But there was no husband, no pregnancy. You weren't really here to help these people?"

"I have no husband. I am pregnant, and yes I am here to help these people."

"You are pregnant?"

"Yes, I didn't know it till I got here, but yes, I am."

"And the father?"

"He has no clue. But that doesn't matter now. What matters is those girls downstairs and Kara, Kyle, and Jim. If you help me, we can get them all out safely."

"And if I say no?"

"Then I will try without you."

"And if you die trying?"

"Then I will die. I will hold nothing back."

"Alright, I'll help you."

Kailia leaned up and kissed him on the cheek. "Thank you, David."

"Do you know what happened to my brother?"

"Yes, he was killed." She looked at him. "By the father of my child."

David smiled at her. "Well, I guess I know how you said thank you." David looked down at his watch. "I have to get back in my room. Saja and Karen will be getting up to fix the girls' breakfast at two. I will see what I can do about getting you all out tomorrow," he told her and turned to leave.

"David, don't do anything, yet, but come in here after everyone is down for the night tomorrow."

"What do you have planned?"

"I will tell you tomorrow."

David left her room. Kailia took off the robe and climbed back into bed. She pulled out her Bible and checked to see if David returned to his room. She got the camera on just as he went in and shut the door. She closed the Bible and put it back on the nightstand.

Kailia scooted down in the covers and closed her eyes. All her training over the years, she was trained to handle anything. Trained to kill without feeling, trained to face death without fear, trained to keep going when others would give up, trained to follow orders without thought or consequence, so why did this mission have her worried? Her life was not her own; she now had another life to worry about, another person depended solely on her. She needed help, more than Handler could give, more than David could offer.

Alright, Kara's God, if You are who You say You are, then I need Your help. If You really sent me here, then I need to know. If You have a plan for me, then show me what it is.

The sun was bright, the house that was in front of her was an old two story. There was a boy standing on the porch.

"Mom, come on!" He looked just like a small version of Keeps with his sandy blond hair and blue/green eyes. "I have to pee." He was prancing as she walked up and opened the door.

Inside to her left was a piano and several acoustic guitars. She walked over to the piano, several notes lay there, one read.

> *Songs for Sunday—How Great is Our God, Glorious Day,*
> *Awesome God and Beautiful One.*
> *Practice—Tuesday, 5pm at church.*

"Kailia." Someone was knocking on her door. She opened her eyes.

"It's open." She looked towards the door and Kara opened the door and entered. She was smiling even more than she usually did.

"What are you grinning about this morning?" Kailia asked her as she sat up and grabbed her robe.

"This day is going to be the beginning." She sat down on the edge of Kailia's bed.

"The beginning of what?" She asked as she gathered up her clothes to get dressed.

"The rest of your life."

"What?" Kailia turned and looked at Kara.

"Did you not ask for the Maker's help last night?"

Kailia sat down in front of Kara. How could she know? "How did you know?"

Kara pulled Kailia in and gave her a hug. "Because of the verse that came into my head this morning. Isaiah 55:11, it says: *So is my word that goes out from my mouth: It will not return to me empty, but will accomplish what I desire and achieve the purpose for which I sent it.*"

"And that told you what?"

"That you heard what I told you, and that you accepted it as truth, and in doing so you had to have called out to Him."

Kailia smiled at her. "You are amazing."

"No, just blessed. Now hurry up, it's time to eat and get down to the shelter." Kara got up and headed to the door. "One other thing, I was also given this verse, Proverbs 3:25, which says: *You need not be afraid of sudden disaster or the destruction that comes upon the wicked.*"

"And what did that one tell you?"

"That I shouldn't be afraid. Things are getting ready to happen and people are going to die for their transgressions against God." She smiled at Kailia. "I told you that you were here for a purpose." Kara opened the door and left Kailia standing there.

Kailia dropped to her knees. *Alright, God, I hear you.*

"Good morning," Kyle told Kailia, as she walked into the kitchen.

"Morning." She smiled at him.

"Morning." David came in behind her.

Kailia turned and looked at him. "Thank you for letting me stay here. I think I slept better than I have since I got here."

"I wish I had thought of it sooner than last night." He looked at her.

"You're welcome to stay here as long as you are in town." Karen came up behind David and put her arm through his.

"Thank you." She told Karen.

"Men, they just don't think. I only wish I had been here sooner to offer it to you."

"Let's eat, so we can get out there and help some people." Jim came into the kitchen.

"I agree," Kara said as she picked up a plate.

Keeps opened his eyes when the lights kicked on. Something was going on, he could hear 25 talking.

"All of those cells, too," 25 told someone.

"Yes, ma'am," came another woman's voice.

Keeps could hear the other woman barking orders at whoever was in the other cell.

"Get up and follow me. You better clean every inch of you," he heard her telling someone.

The next two hours she had told ten people that. And after she had told them, he had heard water hitting the stone walls. The smell that hit him was of the filth being washed away.

His door opened and an elderly woman pulled a hose in along with a bar of soap and a towel. "You can wash if you want." She dropped the soap and kicked it towards him, then dropped the hose and pushed it with her foot so that he could reach it. She threw the towel at him, then turned and left.

His hands were chained to the wall, there was no way for him to strip and wash. He sat down and took his shoes and socks off.

"You might need this." 25 stood at the door holding a key. A guard stood behind her.

439

"Yeah, that might be nice," he told her.

"If he touches me, kill him," she told the guard as she walked towards him.

Keeps held his hands up as she unlocked the shackles from them. He didn't move till she was back at the door.

"You have ten minutes," she told him and pulled the door shut.

Keeps got up and stripped. He didn't care if the water was icy, just to be halfway clean would be great. He quickly washed then hosed down the entire cell. He still was in the towel when 25 opened the door.

"Feel better?" She asked him.

"Yes." He quickly pulled his pants and shirt on, then backed up to the wall and held out his hands.

The guard stood in the doorway again as she put the shackles back on his wrists, and then she closed his door.

Keeps heard another door shut then the lights went out. He sat down on the wet floor and leaned back against the wall.

By lunch they had treated over one hundred people. Kailia was exhausted; she hadn't got much sleep. She ate and laid her head on the table.

"Kailia." David tapped her shoulder.

"What?" She didn't lift her head.

"Why don't you go lie down on a cot in the back? You look exhausted," David told her.

"Yes, we can handle it, go lie down," Kara piped in.

Kailia lifted her head. "I hate to do that."

"Go." David pointed towards the back. "You won't do anybody any good if you work yourself to death."

"Alright, but don't let me sleep more than a couple of hours."

"Alright," Kara told her.

Kailia walked into the back room and lay down and closed her eyes.

"Kailia." Kara was shaking her arm. "It's time to get up."

Kailia opened her eyes. Kara was bent over her and David stood behind Kara. "How long was I out?" She asked Kara.

"Four hours," Kara smiled.

"What?" she sat up. "You were supposed to wake me after two."

"You were out of it, and I couldn't bear to wake you."

"I told her to let you sleep," David added.

"Is she awake?" Ruth came in the room.

"I'm up." Kailia got up off the cot. "Let's get back to work." She smiled.

The afternoon went by quickly and they were on their way back to David's just before dusk.

Karen met them at the door. "I hope you guys are hungry. I got a little crazy in the kitchen today." She smiled at them.

"It smells wonderful," Jim told her.

"It does smell good." Kyle smiled at her.

"Well, wash up and let's eat," Karen told them.

Soon they were all sitting around the table eating. Kailia got the feeling, the same one she always did when something just wasn't right. She talked and chatted with Kara while she scanned the room. She hoped she was feeling Handler, and not something else.

"You still look tired," Kara told her.

"I think I slept so good last night that my body wants more and the little nap I took this afternoon confirmed it."

"Little nap." Kyle looked at her. "You slept four hours."

"It sure didn't feel like four hours."

"It's the baby," Ruth told them. "I slept almost fifteen hours each night for a week when I was pregnant with Dema."

Dema, Kailia remembered David mentioning Dema last night. He had said something about her . . . Had she been taken from them? Was she one of the girls in the cells? How horrible for Ruth, for Omar. Well, maybe that explained him.

"I better be going." Ruth got up from the table.

"I think we all should turn in," Jim added. "We have one more day and the line never seems to end, so we need to get started early tomorrow to help as many as we can."

"I agree," Kara added.

"I won't argue with that." Kailia smiled and got up from the table.

They all left the table and went to their rooms.

Kailia went to the shower first. She needed to wake up; it was going to be a long night.

She walked back in the room in just her towel. Ruth had brought her bag today so she had her black suit and she would need it. She had no more than let her towel go, when she felt his presence.

"I know you're here." She pulled the robe on.

"Sorry." Handler's head appeared in the room as he removed his Wraith hood. "I didn't know you were going to drop your towel."

She smiled at him. "Sure." She walked over to him and put her arms around him and hugged him. "I am glad you're here."

"I have something for you." He told her once she let him go. He pulled a bag out from under his suit.

"What is it?" She asked as she opened it.

"Your own suit. I thought it might come in handy."

She smiled, "Nice." She put the bag on the bed and went and got her Bible. "I need to see where everyone is."

"I knew it was you using the satellite."

She turned on imaging, one in the kitchen, Kara, Jim and Kyle in their room, two in David's office. Three down in the bunker and eleven in the cells; she switched to the bug in David's office.

"Not now, I want to know you're going to hold up your end," 25 was talking.

"Not till Kara and the rest are out of the house. I am not going down in those filthy cells," David's voice was raised.

"I had them all cleaned, and the bedroom cleaned because I knew you would say that."

"I am not going down there."

"Then there is no deal, and Kailia will join them."

"No."

"Then I want you down there, now!"

"Fine, may Allah forgive me."

Kailia turned on the camera in the room between the cells and the bunker. David and Karen came in and the two guards were standing beside the bunker doors.

Karen said something to one of the guards and he went into the cells. David just stood there.

Kailia closed her eyes. *Now is the time, God, if this is Your will, then we need interference* . . . A shrill whistling sounded through the air, and the ground shook.

Kailia smiled and opened her eyes. Another sound and more shaking; the town was under fire.

Kailia looked back at the shield. Karen was shaken almost off her feet. She said something, and David headed towards the stairs.

"Great diversion," Handler said as Kailia put her suit on. "The switch to turn it on is in the neck."

"Kailia!" Kara was calling from the hall.

She pulled her robe over the suit and Handler put his hood back on.

"Kara," she said as she opened the door. Kyle, Jim and Kara stood at her door.

"Kailia." David came running up the hall as the ground shook so hard he almost fell. "We need to get them out of here now," David told her.

The ground shook and the house alarm started sounding.

"Get them to the bunker!" Karen came running up the hall. "I'll shut the alarm off!" She turned and went toward the front of the house.

"David, get them to your father's truck; wait there, we will bring the rest of them to you."

"Follow me," David told them.

"But what about the bunker?" Jim interjected.

"Come on, Jim," Kara told him, "she knows what she's talking about."

Kyle and Kara grabbed him by the arms and followed David.

Kailia followed after Karen. She was cursing the alarm panel as she tried to get it shut off, but the ground kept shaking and she kept hitting wrong numbers. Kailia never made a sound as she moved in behind her just as the ground stopped moving. Karen hit the last number and turned around right into the knife Kailia held.

Karen's eyes got large, "23." she gasped as she fell to the floor.

Kailia turned to find David standing there. "Why are you back?"

"I can help." He looked at Karen on the floor, blood soaking the rug. "They will be waiting for us downstairs," he told her.

"Alright." She pulled the robe over her head and turned on her suit. "You go first, I will be right behind you." All but her head and hands disappeared.

"Get your father out in the open."

"Ok." He looked at her one more time then turned and headed for the bunker. He stopped at the door. "Are you ready?" He looked behind him to find nothing.

"I'm right here." She touched his shoulder.

David walked out into the small room; the two guards were standing beside the cell doors. He walked to the bunker door and opened it.

"Is Karen in there?" He yelled toward the office door, but never entered.

The door opened and Shadar looked at his son, "No, is she not with you?"

"No." He backed into the room.

"Where are the Americans? Where is the girl?"

"What girl?" David looked at his father.

"Karen told me the American girl would be mine."

"What?" The anger in David's voice was clear. "You promised no more girls would be taken if I stayed."

Shadar pulled the gun from his holster on his side, "You are such a disappointment."

Shadar fell forward as the small hole appeared in his forehead. David turned to face the guards who were now at full attention. David watched as they both reached for their throats as the pain of the red that was running from their necks suddenly caught them off guard.

Kailia lifted her hood. "We need to get the girls out and destroy all the evidence." She looked at David, then turned to nothing. "He is here, too."

"We need to hurry," Handler told her.

David stood there looking at Kailia, then around him.

"It's ok, David." She touched his arm. "Let's get them out of here." She walked to the door of the cells.

"I don't know the code," He told her.

She had it open in no time. "You will have to command them to follow you, or they will not leave," she told him. "Get them out now, take them to the truck."

She opened the door to Keeps' cell. "Miss me?" She smiled at him.

"Here." Handler's hand appeared. He handed her a small canister.

Keeps held out the shackles and Kailia dropped one drop in each keyhole. In a matter of seconds, the lock froze and broke.

"We need to get 25 from upstairs and set some charges. There needs to be no evidence left."

445

"David has them loaded." Handler held 25 in his arms. He must have had the same thought.

"Put her there with Shadar. I need the charges from my room; I will meet you at the truck."

"I am not going anywhere till you go," Keeps told her.

"Here." Handler handed her four charges. She set one in the cell block and two in the small room by the bodies of Shadar and 25, then one in the stairs to David's office.

"I need the Bible from my room." she told them, "I will be right back."

Kailia sprinted through the house to her room. The Bible lay on her nightstand where it always lay. She picked it up and turned to find Saja standing right behind her holding a knife at her stomach.

"You are evil, and you will die."

Kailia felt the knife as it sliced into her.

"No!" She heard Keeps from the door. Saja turned to face Keeps. She fell without warning. Handler removed his hood from behind him.

Kailia stumbled forward; Keeps caught her before she could hit the ground. The sound of incoming rockets sounded and the ground shook so violently that Keeps fell forward, pitching Kailia onto the bed.

"Get out of here!" She yelled at Keeps.

"I will not leave you!" He got to his feet.

Pain ripped through her. Blood was flowing freely from the knife wound. Keeps pulled off his shirt and wrapped it around her. She closed her eyes and lay back on the bed; her head was starting to spin.

The verse Kara had quoted went through her head. *You need not be afraid of sudden disaster or the destruction that comes upon the wicked.* Kara had said it meant people were going to pay for their transgressions against God. Karen and Shadar had paid with their lives, and if it was now time for her to pay, then she was ready.

"Handler." she opened her eyes.

"Yes," he said.

"Get him out of here."

Keeps looked down at her. "I am not leaving without you," He went to pick her up.

"Keeps." She pulled him close to her. "Seth, I love you with my very soul, brother." She took hold of his shoulder and he fell out cold on her.

"Get . . . him . . . out." She closed her eyes. She felt something being placed in her hand. She opened her eyes long enough to see Handler pick Keeps up.

"He will hate me for this." He looked at her, then he left the room.

Kailia looked in her hand. He had placed a syringe in it. She stabbed it in her leg and pushed what was in into her system and closed her eyes.

Alright, God, I am ready, just take me. She saw the bright light from behind her eyelids.

Seven years later . . .

"Are you Carrie Braker?" One of the two men said when Carrie opened the door.

"Yes, and you must be Brandon." She smiled, her heart began to pound. "Todd didn't tell me you were Brandon Clearwater. Please come in." She held the door open for the two men to come in. They were both dressed alike in white T-shirts and jeans. The only real difference was one carried a shoulder satchel. They were both handsome. The other man looked just like Brandon with his dark skin, hair, and eyes. She looked closely from one to the other, and smiled.

Brandon couldn't help but notice the baby grand to his left as he entered the house. There were also several acoustics setting on stands beside it.

"Do you play?" He asked Carrie.

"Yes, I do," Carrie answered him.

"Beautiful piano." He couldn't help but walk over and look at it.

"Hi, I am Tim MacCarthy." Tim stuck out his hand to Carrie.

"Nice to meet you, Tim," she smiled.

"May I?" Brandon still stood looking at the piano.

"Sure, go ahead."

"He just can't help himself," Tim told her. "I think music is in his soul."

Brandon sat down on the bench and laid his hands on the keys. There was hand written sheet music in front of him. He played through the first stanzas. It was beautiful!

"Did you write this?" He asked Carrie.

"Yes." She walked over to the piano where Brandon sat. Tim followed her. "I have been working on it for years."

Brandon played through the entire piece.

Tim watched Brandon as he played. He had truly been given a gift. He looked at Carrie; she was quite pretty with her sandy blonde hair and blue eyes.

"It's beautiful! You have real talent," Brandon told Carrie.

"Thank you. I know this is going to sound really bad, but I started writing it after hearing your album 'Lindsey's Lullabies'; it just inspired me so much. The way you had the orchestra accenting not dominating, and the cellos and guitars and . . . well, I loved it."

"Thank you." He looked up at her. "That album got me through a rough spot in my life." He glanced at Tim. Brandon got up from the piano. "Sorry, I have a weakness for music."

"Music is no weakness." Carrie told him, "it is all of your life and soul wrapped up in a flowing rhythm."

Brandon smiled at her; she had passion. "It most certainly is."

"Please, come sit down." Carrie motioned towards the couch.

"Thank you," Brandon told her as he walked over and sat down. Tim put his satchel at the side of the couch and sat down beside Brandon.

"Now, what can I do for you? Todd said you were interested in my house." She sat down in the chair opposite Brandon.

"Well, my friend Tim here, has been planning to build for a couple of years and when Todd told me about your house I knew it was something like Tim was looking for."

Carrie looked over at Tim. His T-shirt had gapped at the neck and she could see the choker he wore. She looked up into his eyes; her heart felt like it might beat out of her chest.

"Mom, can I get on ... oh, I didn't know we had company."

Tim looked at the small boy who entered the room. He had sandy blonde hair and blue/green eyes. He looked at Carrie then back to the boy.

"I'm Colt." He stuck out his hand.

Brandon took his outstretched hand. "I'm Brandon; it's nice to meet you, Colt."

"You look an awful lot like Brandon Clearwater," Colt told him.

"That's because I am him." He smiled at the boy.

"Wow, I have never meet a celebrity before." He smiled, then turned to Tim. "Colt." He stuck out his hand to Tim.

"Tim," He took his hand.

"So what do you do, Tim?" Colt asked.

"I am a computer programmer." He smiled.

"Cool, me, too!" He turned to look at Carrie. "I am going to log on for awhile. I have some work I need to do."

"Ok," she told him.

Colt turned and went up the stairs and closed his door.

"How old is he?" Tim asked.

"Seven going on thirty." She smiled.

"Does he really do programming?" Tim asked her.

"He does just simple stuff right now, but give him a few years and ... well, he will put us all to shame."

"You and your husband must be so proud." Tim smiled.

"Never been married, but I am proud of him."

"So, tell us about your house." Brandon looked at Tim, then at Carrie.

"Well, it is fully integrated and clean. I have two wind mills which I am sure you saw, but I also have six solar cells, and ..."

A small beep in the background brought Carrie to her feet. "Could you excuse me for a moment?" She left the room without looking at either man.

Tim still was in shock. Could it possibly be true? He looked towards the stairs. No, he told himself he was just imagining it. Concentrate on the house.

"What is it, Lindsey?" Carrie said when the kitchen door closed behind her. A small slit opened on the bar and a computer monitor emerged.

"I have detected a Wraith." An avatar stood on the screen.

"Show me." The screen turned black and then the house and everything in the yard appeared in blue. The Wraith showed up as a green moving image.

"Is it close enough to break it?" Carrie asked.

"Not yet, but if it continues on it's current course it will be soon."

"Lindsey, scan the two men in the living room. I want bone structure. Then, construct a 3D image from the results you get."

"That will take five minutes."

"I also want the fusion broken and an image; beep me when both are complete."

Carrie left the kitchen. "Sorry, about that. Now, let's see, oh yes, I make enough energy here to supply all my needs and during windy months I make enough to supply part the town."

"Impressive." Brandon looked to Tim. "Is that something like you want?"

"Yes, but what about your water? I want to be self-reliant." Tim tried to keep his mind on the business at hand.

"There are two wells on my property, and one natural spring. I have several natural filters in place and irrigation set up."

"Tell me about the house. Is it fully integrated?"

"Yes, let me show you. Lindsey?"

Tim's heart jumped. Just a coincidence?

A large screen came from the ceiling. "Yes?" An avatar appeared.

"This is Lindsey, my home computer system."

A small beep went off and Carrie got up once again. "Please feel free to ask her anything. I will be right back, sorry."

"What systems do you run?" Tim asked as Carrie went into the kitchen.

"Show me," Carrie said. The screen appeared out of the countertop again.

"Here are the 3D images. The one on the right is proportioned right, but the one on the left is not." Carrie smiled at the image on the screen.

"Show me the Wraith." Another image appeared on the screen. She shook her head and laughed. "Thank you." She turned to leave.

"Any action?"

"None for now."

The screen slid back into the cabinet as she left the kitchen.

"I monitor every cell minute by minute to optimize potential use," Lindsey was saying from the screen.

"Do you include security?" Tim asked Lindsey as Carrie sat down.

"Yes, I monitor all perimeters, which includes the house, every structure, and the land."

"What other kind of security do you provide?" Tim looked at Carrie. It just couldn't be a coincidence. The boy looked just like him and Lindsey was the computer's name.

"Be specific, please," Lindsey told Tim.

"What kind of security are you talking about?" Carrie looked at Tim who was staring at her.

Brandon looked at Tim who was staring at Carrie. Something was up with him; he knew him well enough to know something was going through his head.

"Advanced ones, like face recognition," he never took his eyes from Carrie.

"I have two programs on that line; one is facial, and the other is bone," Lindsey replied.

"Wow." Brandon had heard of bone recognition, and now knew what was going on with Tim. "Is that about all you wanted to know, Tim?" Brandon stood up.

"You should have brought Clare to see the house." Tim's eyes never left Carrie's.

Carrie looked at Brandon. "Who's Clare?"

"My wife." He looked at Tim. What was he doing?

"How long have you been married?" She was still looking at Brandon.

"Just over two years," he told her.

"They're expecting their first in January," Tim added.

Ok, this was crazy, what was going on? Brandon looked at Tim who was still staring at Carrie.

"Lindsey," Tim said, "have you ran those security programs on us?"

"Yes," she answered.

Brandon's heart almost stopped. Carrie must know that Tim was not who he said he was.

Carrie and Tim stood up slowly their eyes locked.

"Lindsey, how close is our intruder?" Carrie asked.

"Twenty five feet and closing," she replied.

"Turn off his suit when he steps on the porch, if he hasn't revealed himself." Her eyes never left Tim's.

Tim looked towards the porch, then back to Carrie. He didn't know he was being followed.

Brandon sat back down. He didn't know what else to do. He felt completely helpless. He looked from Carrie to Tim. Had he messed up, and got them all killed? How was he supposed to know she was an agent?

"Ten feet and closing," Lindsey announced.

"Open the door, Lindsey."

Tim looked at Carrie. "What are you doing?"

"Trust me." She smiled at him.

Carrie walked out on to the porch. Tim walked to the doorway.

"I know you're here."

"One foot," Lindsey announced.

Carrie stepped onto the top step and looked at the bottom one. "Do I have to be coming out of the shower for you to show yourself?"

Handler lifted his hood as he stepped on the bottom step. "I didn't know you were going to drop your towel." He smiled at her. "I'm glad you're not dead." He was now on the top step with her.

"Inside first." She turned and walked past Tim.

"How long have you been following me?" Tim asked Handler as the door shut.

"Lindsey, initiate Cloak, and secure Colt."

Every window in the room turned blue.

"What is going on?" Brandon stood up. He looked at Tim, then Handler, then Carrie.

"Lindsey, change name reference to Vi, please."

Carrie closed her eyes for a moment and turned to Brandon. "I am so happy that you finally found someone. For years I have felt so guilty; wished I could have been the one. But I wasn't the one with the plan, although for years I thought I was."

Carrie saw the instant Brandon put it all together.

"Lindsey!" He grabbed her and pulled her into his arms. "I thought you were dead!"

"We all did," Handler spoke.

"Did you know it was me before she ran the scan?" Tim asked.

Brandon released her, but his eyes were glassy.

"I had my suspicions. You never could change as much as me." She walked over and touched the choker then placed her hand on his chest. "But then there was this, and your reaction to Colt. So I knew I was right."

Tim pulled her into his arms.

Brandon looked at Keeps holding Lindsey. It had taken him a long time to forgive him. He had blamed him for her death. Handler had been the one that told him about her being pregnant. His thoughts turned to his wife Clare. She was the one who had suggested he write the album for Lindsey. If it hadn't been for that album and Clare, he would have never forgiven him. Now standing looking at him holding her, he had peace.

Carrie pulled from his arms and walked over to Handler and put her arms around him.

"You remember the last words I said to you?" He held her tightly.

"Yes, did he?" She asked.

"With a passion." He let her go.

"I'm sorry." She looked up at him.

"How long have you been following me?" Tim asked him.

"Since the day you walked out," he told him.

The four of them sat down and Carrie listened as each of them took their turn telling their story.

"I thought you were dead," Keeps started. "The last thing I remember was taking off my shirt and placing it around your knife wound, then I woke in the back of a truck surrounded by people I didn't know and you weren't there. I wanted to kill him for leaving you."

"The minute the house blew." Handler looked at Carrie, then to Keeps. "I regretted leaving you, dead or not, and from the moment he awoke I knew there was only one thing I could do for him. So, I went back, but there was nothing left of the house but rubble. David and I dug around for two weeks in it. I figured if I brought your body back maybe it would give him some closure, but I couldn't find anything but your Bible. When I got back, King told me Keeps hadn't eaten or slept since I left, and I had been gone for three weeks."

"I worked on setting back up the network." Keeps picked up the story. "It was all I knew to do. Every time I tried to sleep I would relive leaving, so I chose not to sleep. I had no appetite, so I didn't eat. One night I returned to my room to find an old nasty bag on my bed. I will never forget pulling that big old Bible out of it." Tears streamed from his eyes. "It was half burnt, ripped and falling apart."

Brandon sat there listening; he had heard some of this, but not in as much detail as they were telling it now.

"When I opened the hidden compartment I found a blue dart." Tim looked at Handler, "I didn't even hesitate to use it."

"What's a blue dart?" Brandon asked.

"It is a small ring with what looks like a thorn on it. Each toxicity level has a color. Blue is deadly," Handler told Brandon, then turned back to Carrie. "He looked like death walking. I figured if he looked like it, he probably felt like it. So I took a red dart and painted it blue," he looked back at Brandon, "Red is . . ."

"Is like being hit by a Mack truck." Keeps finished his sentence. "I awoke three days later with him sitting beside me. He looked like crap; first time I can ever remember seeing him looking like that." Keeps smiled at him. "I was still mad at him, but I knew he had gone back for her and was trying to say he was sorry." Handler and Keeps looked at each other, then Keeps continued with the story.

"After a few days I got out your jump drive. The password for me was easy, but it took me a week to get up the power to watch the video. It took me a month to figure out Brandon's phrase for his block. I guess I would have never figured it out if I hadn't opened your guitar case."

"Some lawyer called and told me he had a will and he needed to see me. I had inherited some things," Brandon picked up the story. "I was in New York at the time, just played at the Garden. They showed up at my hotel March 17th, 7 pm; I will never forget that date. I opened the door and the first words out of his mouth were, 'Are you alone?' Tim introduced himself as John Newberry, Attorney at Law; said he had the last will and testament of one Lindsey Lorain Jacobs."

"I didn't know if I would be able to tell him or not, so I took Handler with me. I about lost my nerve in the elevator on the way up. But once he opened the door I knew he deserved the truth," Keeps talked again.

"I felt like my world had just ended. I couldn't believe it when he told me you were gone. At first I was just heartbroken, but then he proceeded to tell me about what had happened at Cherry Point and then that he was one of the last people to see you alive. I felt betrayed by both of you, then just angry at him. I wanted to kill him! For the first time in my life I wanted to kill someone."

"He handled telling Brandon so well, that we left Brandon's. I decided it was time to tell Keeps about the baby. I didn't think of it affecting him like it did." Handler spoke up. "But he went from finally coming around, to back in a state of depression, one like I have never seen. He worked about three months, but he was just there. He didn't talk, didn't eat, slept very little and then one day he left."

"I had suddenly gone from just thinking I had lost the woman I loved, to losing the woman I loved and a child I never knew about." Keeps looked at Carrie with tears streaming down his face.

456

"I followed him for over two months. Day after day he wandered through the streets picking fights and looking for death until I couldn't take it anymore. I didn't know anyone else, so I called Brandon." Handler looked at Brandon.

"I was still pissed, but when Handler told me about the baby, my heart broke for him. What if it had been my child? He had tried to help me and her." Brandon looked at Keeps again.

"We met in Nashville and picked Keeps up the next day," Handler added.

"I don't remember any of it. The only thing I remember was wanting to die," Keeps threw in.

"Thanks to the wonderful drugs Handler brought me, it only took a matter of days to get him eating. But it took an album to get us both on the road to recovery." Brandon smiled at Tim.

"I worked as a roadie for three years before Brandon talked me back into working with computers. I guess I am a computer geek to the core. I started Cloak and Dagger Security Programming the following year."

"The year I wrote the album, I sold New Beginnings to Todd, but I still call and check on him every year." He smiled. "And last year he told me of this house they had remodeled, and I told Tim."

Carrie got up and stood looking at all three of them. How could she ask for their forgiveness? How could she explain that it was only by the grace of God and an angel that she survived? Would they understand, when she really didn't understand it all herself? Did it matter?

"I need to ask that you let me talk without interrupting me, or I may not get out what I have to say." Tears ran down her cheeks.

"First." She turned to Brandon. "I love you, dearly. You have always and will always have part of my heart. I never meant to hurt you in any way, especially by breaking the promise I made to you."

Carrie turned to Handler. "To you I need to say thank you. I always thought Keeps had me covered, but it was you that came into the field and saved my butt. It was you who followed me in the field to watch over me. And it was you who was there for Keeps when I wasn't. Thank you."

Carrie turned to Keeps, tears rolled as she fell to her knees in front of him. She was now crying so hard that she was shaking visibly and was having trouble speaking. "And you . . . the Cloak . . . Cloak to my Dagger . . . the father . . . to my son . . . I beg . . . beg . . . your forgiveness." She closed her eyes and took a breath, "I have been praying . . . for years that you would find me . . . and now that you have . . . I pray that you will never leave me."

Tim wiped the tears from his eyes and reached over the side of the couch and pulled his satchel into his lap. He then reached inside it and pulled out an old rag which he carefully unfolded to revel the big old, worn Bible.

"Forgiveness is what we none deserve, but all receive." He handed her the Bible. "Marry me, Carrie."

EPILOGUE

Three years later

I WAS SO EXCITED about going to pick up my new/old car. Tim had gotten me one to replace my Sixty-Eight Camaro I had left in Nashville. This one, however was not black, but Candy Apple Red. It was sitting outside Carl's Custom Car Shop when we pulled up.

"Well," Tim asked me, "what do you think?"

"I will let you know after I take her for a spin." I smiled at him.

"That is so cool; do I get to drive it when I turn sixteen?" Colt asked from the backseat of the truck.

He was only ten now, but I could understand, who wouldn't want to drive it?

"We'll see," I told him while all the time saying *Not on your life* in my head!

"She is all ready to go." Carl handed me the keys. "I don't know half the things that are in that car, but I know it has a sound system and security system that can't be beat." He grinned.

I took the keys, clicked the locks, and opened the door. It put my other one to shame. Fully leather, heated and cooled seats, five speed manual transmission. It was sharp!

"I want to ride home with you," Colt told me.

"Too, too, Mommy." Lorain, our two year old, was poking me in the side.

"Have Dad get your carseat," I told her.

I didn't get to do all the Fast and Furious driving I would have liked to since the kids were with me, but I did get her up to eighty on a straight stretch. I also wanted to do a doughnut turning into the driveway, but did my best to keep myself under control as I turned in. As I got close to the house I could see a black Hummer sitting outside, one just like John used to pick me up in. I sure don't know why he picked John. He looked more like a Derek or Mac, but if Handler wanted his name to be John, then that's what we would call him.

"Vi?"

"Yes?" My car's computer link to the house worked perfectly.

"Is that John?"

"Yes," she replied.

John got out as I turned the engine off. "Sweet!" He walked up beside my car running his finger over the edge of the hood.

"Uncle John." Colt got out and gave him a hug. "Where have you been? I've missed you."

John hadn't been here in almost a year. Which made me wonder what was up, especially with him being in the Hummer. In all the time he had come, he had never come in it, so now I had to wonder was he here on business or pleasure.

"Look at you, Miss Lorain; I think you have grown a foot." John undid Lorain's car seat and pulled her out of the car just as Tim drove up.

"John," Tim said with a confused look on his face, "what's with the Hummer?"

"We need to talk." He gave a serious look. "In the office," he added.

I knew he meant away from the kids, or he would have just said *in the house*. Both were secure, but the office was off limits to the kids.

I took the kids to the kitchen for a snack as John and Tim went into the office. Vi's screen popped up out of the bar with a message written on it; *Come to the office as soon as you get them settled.*

"Colt, would you please watch after your sister for a little while for me?" I asked.

"Sure."

"And Colt, stay in the house," I added. I was now starting to worry. John being here on business was something I wasn't liking the idea of.

"I don't know about that," Tim was saying as I entered the office.

"Don't know about what?" I asked.

"King wants us to do some Intel work."

"She wants Tim, too; she still doesn't know about you," John looked at me.

"We don't do that stuff anymore, John, you know that."

"I know, but . . ." John paused.

"But what?" Tim asked.

"It's like the world has gone mad since you died, and you left." John looked at me then, Tim. "There are only three of us left, and the new guys aren't cutting it."

"Three of the original ten? Are you including Carrie and me?"

"Yes! The new agents don't stand a chance without you two. The new Intel and mission experts are anything but that. They are green and have no clue what is really going on. We need help if we are going to win the war on evil."

I don't think I had ever seen John so upset. He was really worried.

"John has a message, do I let it through?" Vi's computer voice spoke up.

"Let it through," I told her. John's phone immediately beeped.

"King wants to talk to you." He looked at Tim after he got off the phone.

I closed my eyes. *Lord what do we do?* I didn't like the thought of people dying over bad Intel, but did I hate it bad enough to start working for King again?

"When?" Tim asked.

"She's in the Hummer."

Tim stood to his feet. "She's here?"

What better way to hide her identity than to call her King, which you always assume is male? I had always been curious as to who it was.

"Yes, she insisted on coming."

"What was she thinking?" Tim walked around the table. He was quite upset, which I guess I hadn't expected.

"She hasn't been the same since she lost The Maker." John looked at me. "And now that all the team is gone but us two, she is taking it quite personally."

"She should." I found I was quite angry about the whole thing. "Who is it that she thinks she is? God? We weren't made to be altered at a person's whim; I don't care what the purpose was."

"Carrie." Tim tried to calm me. "You don't understand."

"What's to understand?" I was going to go give her a piece of my mind. I stood and headed for the door.

"Wait." John got to the door before I did and blocked it. "Don't judge her for what others have done."

What 'others' was he talking about? Wasn't she the one who gave the orders? "What do you mean others?"

"She was given this position, and not by choice. When the husband got the job, it was dropped in her lap. And the fact he doesn't even know about this job . . . well, it's just ridiculous."

"What are they going to do if one is single, leave it in the hands of the previous?" Tim looked at John.

"Stop right there, you are confusing me to no end," I butted in.

"Here." Tim got out of his office seat. "Read this. Vi, load file labeled Protected Custody out of my secure files."

"Verified voice recognition, file opening," Vi said.

I sat down at the computer and started looking through the file. It was started back in the late Fifties when spies were gaining momentum. It had changed with each new King. You could plainly see what was important to each of them. It wasn't until the late Sixties that they got involved with more than just the spy game. By the late Seventies they were seeking out enemies of the U.S. and wiping them out. By the Eighties, the game had really gotten serious and elite teams had been formed to eliminate threats to the world, not just the U.S. The Nineties are what got my attention most; the genetic alteration testing had begun. The two preceding Kings had stopped the genetic testing, but the ten of us were already being trained. They had also started working on not just the threats on countries, but on terror of every kind, drug trafficking and human trafficking. John and Tim were right, the current King had done her best with what she had, and we had been the most successful team ever recorded, but once the mole got in, everything had started failing. By the time I left, the team took a nose dive. The King had tried to gather new teams, but she wasn't qualified, and the major players she knew clearly had their own interests at heart instead of the good of the people. Each file was detailed and vague at the same time. There were small notes added in like thoughts, which each King had added. They all seemed to be a little overwhelmed with the job, but yet they each wanted to do their best and understood—well, sort of understood—the reason for their job.

One note in particular caught my attention:

> *I shall try to do my best, but in doing so, I must make it very clear that I understand that each person sees things differently. With each passing year things change, what once was considered wrong, now people accept. What I may see as a threat, the next person might not. To me, our great nation once stood on the Truth of God has become corrupt like the city of Sodom, and it will fall just like her. But I also see something that gives me hope, something I did not even see just a few days ago. I see an*

agency placed in the hands of one that still seeks God's council for every action. I pray that He will lead me as I make decisions that will affect the outcome of so many lives. I also want to be clear in this. He has put me here for a purpose and I will do my best to deliver His will because I know: My life is not my own!

"Bring her in, John." I looked up at Tim.
"Are you sure about this?" He asked.
"Never more sure of anything in my life."

Forty-Five minutes later . . .

"Mom, was that the President's wife with Uncle John?"
"Yes, Colt, it sure was."

Life happens—it is fast—paced and ever changing. Sex, drugs, alcohol are popular and out of control, but in the midst of all this there is a purpose. Whether we see it or not, things are happening for a reason. Just like "23", our lives can seem crazy and out of control, yet in control; our emotions can play havoc with our minds and hearts. But if we call out and seek the truth, we will find that the very One that made us has a purpose for us, and just because our lives have been wild or we have done crazy things does, not mean we were not being used and cannot be used in the future. Acts 9:1-31 tells of just such a man that killed and destroyed but was changed. Take a look and you will find we all can be used in this life for the purpose of the One who created us.

CPSIA information can be obtained at www.ICGtesting.com
Printed in the USA
LVOW110321190412

278257LV00002B/73/P